英語閱讀技巧完全攻略 2

Success With Reading

作者 Zachary Fillingham / Owain Mckimm / Judy Majewski

譯者 劉嘉珮／丁宥榆　審訂 Treva Adams / Helen Yeh

U0033933

全英文學習訓練英文思維及語感
可調整語速／播放／複誦模式訓練聽力

◀ 全文閱讀

◀ 單句閱讀色底
表示單字級等

◀ 單句閱讀

單句循環

語速設定

- 標示高中字彙、全民英檢、多益字級，
  掌握難度，立即理解文章
- 設定自動／循環／範圍播放，
  訓練聽力超有感
- 設定 7 段語速、複誦間距及次數，
  扎實訓練聽力
- 設定克漏字比率學習，提高理解力、
  詞彙量及文法
- 睡眠學習，複習文章幫助記憶

快速查詢字義
理解文章內容

課後閱讀測驗檢驗理解力

強力口說練習

錄下發音和原音比對辨識，精進口語能力。

單字分析掌握單字力

提供全書總單字量及單字表，掌握單字難易度，針對不熟單字加強學習。

目錄 Contents

簡介 Introduction 006
使用導覽 How Do I Use This Book? 010

UNIT 1 Reading Skills 閱讀技巧 012

1-1 Subject Matter 明辨主題 014

1. Incredible India 014
2. Braille 016
3. When Lightning Strikes 018
4. Inflation 020
5. How Many Stars Are There? 022

1-2 Main Idea 歸納要旨 024

6. Magicians 024
7. Running Marathons 026
8. Dangerous Dust 028
9. Watch Out for These Killer Creatures! 030
10. Lost in the Sahara Desert 032

1-3 Supporting Details 找出支持性細節 034

11. The Printing Press 034
12. Owls 036
13. Thomas Edison's Inventions 038
14. Exploring the World, One Couch at a Time 040
15. Jazz Music 042

1-4 Author's Purpose and Tone 明瞭作者目的和語氣 044

16. Comic-Con, the Greatest Convention on Earth 044
17. Tasmania 046
18. The World's Fastest Train 048
19. World War I 050
20. The Grand Canyon 052

1-5 Cause & Effect 理解因果關係 054

21. When Cats Met Humans 054
22. The Nile River 056
23. The Power of Positive Thinking 058
24. Orangutans 060
25. Can Jogging Change the World? 062

1-6	Clarifying Devices 釐清寫作技巧	064
26.	Norse Mythology	064
27.	Slipper Culture: A Practical Tradition	066
28.	Honey Badger	068
29.	Giacomo Puccini	070
30.	The Origin of Numbers	072

1-7	Making Inferences 進行推論	074
31.	Julius Caesar	074
32.	Dining Dos and Don'ts	076
33.	Fly Me to the Moon	078
34.	Old Wives' Tales	080
35.	Area 51	082

1-8	Problems and Solutions 問題與解決之道	084
36.	BASE Jumping	084
37.	Hannibal	086
38.	Colossal Squid	088
39.	United Kingdom, Disunited Europe	090
40.	Freedom Riders	092

1-9	Fact or Opinion 分辨事實與意見	094
41.	Glass	094
42.	The Bedouin	096
43.	Blockchain: A Revolutionary Technology	098
44.	Venus	100
45.	*Tyrannosaurus Rex*	102

1-10	Review Test 實力檢測	104
46.	The Grand Duchess Anastasia of Russia	104
47.	Platinum	106
48.	Green Houses	108
49.	Learning to Believe in Yourself	110
50.	Nightmares	112

目錄 Contents

UNIT 2 Word Study 字彙學習   114

2-1 Synonyms (Words With the Same Meaning) 同義字   116

51.	A Beloved Member of the Family	116
52.	The Andes Mountain Range	118
53.	Chanel	120
54.	The London Underground	122
55.	The Prepper Movement	124

2-2 Antonyms (Words With Opposite Meanings) 反義字   126

56.	Seeing Smart	126
57.	The Loch Ness Monster	128
58.	The Nobel Peace Prize	130
59.	The Crown Jewels	132
60.	Spelunking	134

2-3 Words in Context 依上下文猜測字義   136

61.	Insects	136
62.	Ernesto "Che" Guevara	138
63.	The Tweet That Started a Movement	140
64.	The Minotaur	142
65.	The Pencil	144

2-4 Review Test 實力檢測   146

66.	Douglas Bader	146
67.	The Yeti	148
68.	Morse Code	150
69.	The Sonnet	152
70.	What Is Your Carbon Footprint?	154

UNIT 3 Study Strategies 學習策略   156

3-1 Visual Material 影像圖表   158

71.	Map: The Dream of Flight	158
72.	Calendar: Linda's Business Trip	160
73.	Table: The Mile Run	162
74.	Bar Graph: Skyscrapers in the World	164
75.	Spreadsheet: Tracking the Inventory	166

3-2	Reference Sources 參考資料	168
76.	Table of Contents: Ichiro Suzuki	168
77.	Index: Purgatory	170
78.	Encyclopedia: Farming	172
79.	Dictionary: Lazarus of Bethany	174
80.	The Internet: The High Price of Beauty	176

UNIT 4 Final Reviews 綜合練習 178

4-1	Final Review (I) 綜合練習（I）	180
81.	A Humanitarian Crisis in Myanmar	180
82.	Are Sharks Really That Dangerous?	182
83.	Superstition	184
84.	Cleaning Up the Ocean Bit by Bit	186
85.	Tuscany	188
86.	Whaling	190
87.	"Bathing" in the Beauty of Nature	192
88.	Index: Lord Byron	194
89.	Line Graph: The Advertising War: Old Versus New	196
90.	How to Be Happy: Yale's Most Popular Course	198

4-2	Final Review (II) 綜合練習（II）	200
91.	*Mimosa Pudica*	200
92.	The Newbery Medal	202
93.	Trans Fats	204
94.	The Terrible Tragedy of Ireland's "Great Hunger"	206
95.	Lake Hillier, the Pink Lake in Australia	208
96.	Baobab Tree	210
97.	Table of Contents: Branding Your Company	212
98.	Attention Seeking on Social Media	214
99.	Calendar: A Busy Social Life	216
100.	Fighting on the Side of Japan: The Forgotten Story of Taiwanese Imperial Japan Servicemen	218

課文中譯	220
習題解答	261

簡介 Introduction

　　本套書共分四冊，目的在於培養閱讀能力與增進閱讀技巧。書中共有 100 篇文章，不僅網羅各類主題，還搭配大量閱讀測驗題，以訓練讀者記憶重點與理解內容的能力。

　　本書依不同主題劃分為四大單元。每單元主要介紹一種閱讀攻略。讀者不僅能透過本書文章增進閱讀能力，還能涉獵包羅萬象的知識，包括藝術與文學、動物、歷史、科學和運動等主題閱讀。

主要特色

• 包羅萬象的文章主題

　　本書內容涵蓋各類多元主題，幫助讀者充實知識，宛如一套生活知識小百科。囊括主題包括：

社會學		科學		其他主題	
	藝術與文學		動物／植物		體育
	歷史				
	地理與景點				
	文化		健康與人體		
	政治／經濟				
	語言傳播		網路或科技		神祕事件
	環境保育				
	人物		科學		
	食物				

• 全方位的閱讀攻略

　　本書以豐富的高效率閱讀攻略，幫助讀者輕鬆理解任何主題文章的內容。書中閱讀攻略包括：

1 閱讀技巧（Reading Skills）

幫助你練習瞭解整體內文的技巧。此單元涵蓋以下項目：

❶ 明辨主題（Subject Matter）

文章主題是文章中最概括的含意。瞭解文章的整體概念，可幫助你理解文中的細節內容。

❷ 歸納要旨（Main Idea）

文章要旨代表的是文章想傳達的大意，有可能是一種想法或事實。文章要旨通常會以主題論述的方式表達。

❸ 找出支持性細節（Supporting Details）

支持性細節是作者用來支持文章主題句的說明，例如事實、直喻、說明、敘述、比較、舉例等，或是任何能佐證主題的資訊。

❹ 作者目的和語氣（Author's Purpose and Tone）

作者寫作有其目的性，例如說明、陳述、宣導、安慰等。不論目的為何，在文章中皆有跡可循，有時可靠著作者傳達文章內容的「語氣」和「態度」，來判斷其寫作目的。

❺ 理解因果關係（Cause and Effect）

為了完全了解事件始末，重點就是要清楚事件的發生原因以及最後結果。事件發生的原因就稱為「**因**」（**cause**），最後結果就稱為「**果**」（**effect**）。because of（由於）和 as a result of（因而）等片語用於說明「**原因**」（**cause**），as a result（結果，不加 of）、resulting in（因此）和 so（所以）等片語則用來說明「**結果**」（**effect**）。

❻ 釐清寫作技巧（Clarifying Devices）

釐清寫作技巧包括瞭解字彙、片語的應用，以及分辨作者用來讓文章大意與支持性細節更加清楚、更引人入勝的寫作方式。有時候，最重要的釐清技巧就是要能分辨「文章類型」和「作者意圖」。

❼ 進行推論（Making Inferences）

「推論」意指運用你已知的資訊，來猜測未知的情況。作者通常會在文章中透露訊息，讓讀者能自行推論文意。

❽ 問題和解決之道（Problems and Solutions）

文章的開頭通常會先提出一項議題或問題，再以明確的解決方法作為總結。文章中間的陳述說明相當關鍵，因為通常包含了解決問題的過程。

❾ 分辨事實與意見（Fact or Opinion）

判斷某種說法是「**事實**」（**Fact**）或「**意見**」（**Opinion**），是很好的思考方式。「事實」可經由其他資訊來源來驗證。只要是事實，就有對錯之分。而「意見」是某人對某事物的感覺。因此，你可以不認同他人「意見」，卻無法否認「事實」。

2 字彙練習（Word Study）

能幫助你練習累積字彙量與理解文章新字彙的技巧。本單元涵蓋以下項目：

❶ 同義字（意義相同的用語）（Synonyms: Words With the Same Meaning）

英文的詞語十分豐富。事實上，許多看似不同的詞語，其實意義都相同。如果你想表達正在享用的冰淇淋很好吃，你可以輕鬆地運用 acceptable（可接受）、excellent（很棒）、nice（很不錯）、pleasing（令人心曠神怡）、super（超讚）或 amazing（好吃得不得了）等同義用語。

❷ 反義字（意義相反的用語）（Antonyms: Words With Opposite Meanings）

英文的字彙十分豐富，並有許多詞語的意義恰好相反。有些反義字表達出兩種可能性的其一意義，例如 dead（死亡）和 alive（活著）；也有其他不同變化的詞彙，例如 huge（龐大）、giant（巨大）、big（大）等詞，都是 small（小）的反義字。學會越多反義字，你的字彙量就越能有所增進，也能讓寫作內容更加生動有趣。

❸ 依上下文猜測字義（Words in Context）

如果不認得某字，再怎麼與生字大眼瞪小眼，也無法猜透它的意思。但是如果你瀏覽上下文，也許就能很快意會這詞彙的意思。詞彙的上下文能讓你理解其意義。

3 學習策略（Study Strategies）

　　幫助你理解文意，並運用文章中不同素材來蒐集資訊，培養查詢資料的基本能力。影像圖表和參考來源等資訊，不會直接呈現出文章的含意，而是以圖片、編號清單、依字母順序編列的清單，和其他方式來展示資訊。本單元涵蓋以下項目：

❶ 影像圖表（Visual Material）

　　表格、圖片、圖表和地圖，比文字更能呈現繁複的資訊，例如事物的關聯性與其模式風格。要理解這類的素材，必須先仔細閱讀標題、查看圖說，然後閱讀表格行列的表頭，以及圖表上的座標軸說明。瞭解影像圖表的版面陳列後，即可解讀所含的資訊。

❷ 參考來源（Reference Sources）

　　字典、百科全書和地圖冊等參考來源，能讓你的閱讀問題迎刃而解。圖示、表格與圖表，能幫助你在閱讀的時候，更快理解複雜的資訊。學會運用內文裡的不同參考來源，可大幅增進整體閱讀理解力。

4 綜合練習（Final Reviews）

　　以豐富的閱讀素材和推敲式問題，幫助你有效複習學過的內容。此單元目的在檢視你對本書所提供之學習資訊的吸收程度。為了檢測你理解內文的能力，請務必於研讀前述單元之後，完成最後的綜合練習單元。

• 最佳考試準備用書

　　本書適合初學者閱讀，亦為準備大學學測、指考、多益、托福及雅思等考試的最佳用書。

使用導覽 How Do I Use This Book?

Unit 1 Reading Skills

1-1 Subject Matter
1-2 Main Idea
1-3 Supporting Details
1-4 Author's Purpose and Tone
1-5 Cause and Effect
1-6 Clarifying Devices
1-7 Making Inferences
1-8 Problems and Solutions
1-9 Fact or Opinion

Unit 2 Word Study

2-1 Synonyms (Words With the Same Meaning)
2-2 Antonyms (Words With Opposite Meanings)
2-3 Words in Context
2-4 Review Test

全方位的閱讀攻略

每單元主要介紹一種閱讀攻略，幫助讀者更加輕鬆理解任何主題文章的內容。

包羅萬象的閱讀主題

內容涵蓋各類多元主題，包括藝術與文學、歷史、文化與科學，不僅能充實讀者的知識，亦可加強閱讀能力。

♠ Walter George (1858–1943)

Year	Name	Time	Place
1865	Richard Webster	4:36.5	England
1868	William Chinnery	4:29	England
1868	Walter Gibbs	4:28.8	England
1874	Walter Slade	4:26	England
1875	Walter Slade	4:24.5	London
1880	Walter George	4:23.2	London
1882	Walter George	4:21.4	London
1884	Walter George	4:18.4	Birmingham
1894	Fred Bacon	4:18.2	Edinburgh

source: http://www.infoplease.com/ipsa/A0112924.html

琳瑯滿目的彩色圖表

琳瑯滿目的彩色圖表，有助
於讀者學習使用圖表，幫助
快速理解文章內容，增加閱
讀趣味性。

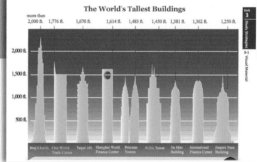

實用的主題式練習題

每篇文章後均附有五題選擇題，用以檢測
閱讀理解能力，並加強字彙認知力。讀者
可運用此類練習來有效評估自己的程度，
以作自我實力之檢測與提升。

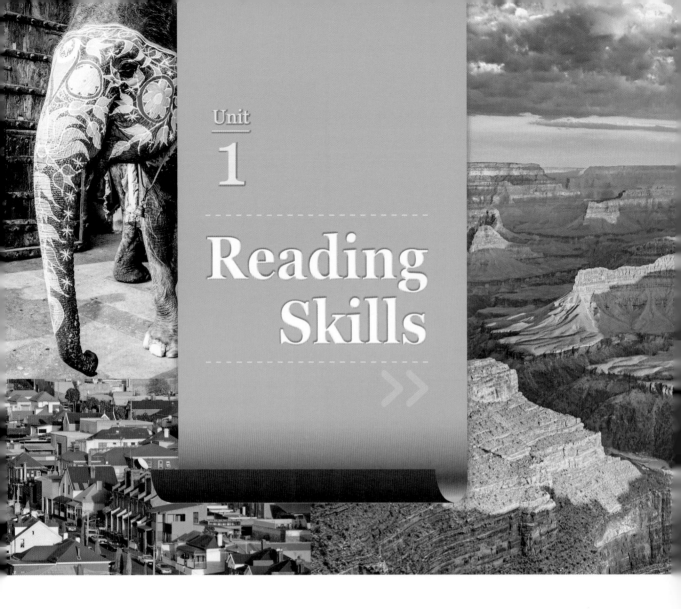

Unit

1

Reading Skills

1-1 Subject Matter

1-2 Main Idea

1-3 Supporting Details

1-4 Author's Purpose and Tone

1-5 Cause and Effect

1-6 Clarifying Devices

1-7 Making Inferences

1-8 Problems and Solutions

1-9 Fact or Opinion

1-10 Review Test

There is a wealth of information out there, and it is accessible to anyone. The key to unlocking it is your reading skills. These skills help us absorb the facts that are buried in every magazine or newspaper article. That's not all. They also help us organize these facts so that we better comprehend them.

Think of it this way: reading skills don't just help us understand **what** an author writes, but **why** he or she writes it as well. This is what makes reading skills so valuable in every area of life, from elementary school to the world of business.

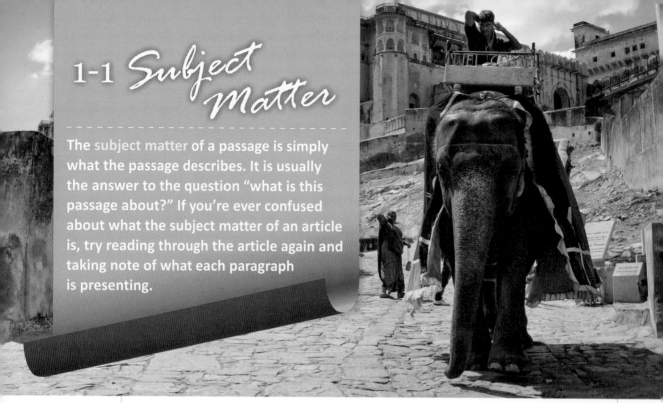

The subject matter of a passage is simply what the passage describes. It is usually the answer to the question "what is this passage about?" If you're ever confused about what the subject matter of an article is, try reading through the article again and taking note of what each paragraph is presenting.

1 | Incredible India

001

1   India is located in Asia between the Middle East and China. It has a long and fascinating history. India is also quickly becoming a wealthy country thanks to its rapidly developing economy.

2   Over 6,000 years ago, the people living in the Indus River basin built up a unique and thriving civilization. It transformed the entire area into a center of trade and religion and allowed for hundreds of years of wealth and prosperity.

3   Some say that this Indus civilization was just as vibrant as ancient Mesopotamia or Egypt. Culturally, it produced many of the world's important religions such as Hinduism, Buddhism, and Sikhism.

4   The golden age of the Indus civilization came to an end when the Aryans invaded in 1500 BC. This was first in a long line of foreign invasions that included the Persians, Greeks, Mongols, and eventually European merchant vessels and British colonialism.

5   In 1857, the people of India grew tired of foreign domination and rebelled against the British East India Company, a British monopoly that controlled most of India at the time. The rebellion ultimately failed.

« Indian woman

As a result, Great Britain absorbed India as a formal colony of the British Empire.

6 India would not remain a colony forever. During the first half of the 20th century, millions of Indians participated in a nationwide political movement led by Mahatma Gandhi. Gandhi organized peaceful demonstrations of civil disobedience that were aimed at resisting British rule. On August 15, 1947, India finally gained its independence, and on January 26, 1950, it became the Republic of India.   25

7 India has gone through many important economic changes and reforms. If you consider India's purchasing power, it is now the sixth largest economy in the world. It also has a youthful population that will continue to drive economic growth over the next decade.   30

« Amber Fort in Jaipur, Rajasthan, India

8 Yet India is also grappling with some big problems, such as poverty, illiteracy, and malnutrition. Like many other Asian countries,   35 there is a growing wealth gap between people who live in the countryside and those who live in the city. These are some of the problems that future governments will need to tackle.

⌄ Hinduism can be traced back to Iron Age India.

⌃ Gandhi (1869–1948)

Questions

_____ 1. Another good title for this passage might be _____.
   a. India: The Once and Future Power
   b. India: The Peaceful Country
   c. India: The Oldest Country on Earth
   d. India: The Economic Powerhouse

_____ 2. This passage focuses on a(n) _____.
   a. military   **b.** technology   **c.** civilization   **d.** economy

_____ 3. The final paragraph is mostly concerned with India's _____.
   a. history   **b.** problems   **c.** language   **d.** military

_____ 4. The fifth and sixth paragraphs are mainly about _____.
   a. the history of Britain in Asia
   b. the rise and fall of British colonialism in India
   c. life in India under the Mongols
   d. Mahatma Gandhi

_____ 5. The seventh paragraph focuses on India's _____.
   a. leaders   **b.** people   **c.** cuisine   **d.** economy

« the statue of
Louis Braille
(1809–1852) at
his birthplace
(cc by Kou07kou)

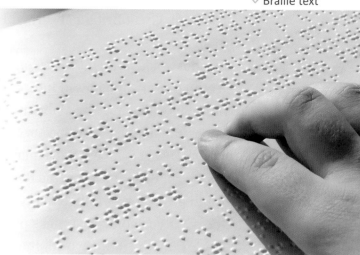

2 Braille

1   Just because people lose their sight doesn't mean that they can't read anymore. They just learn to read in a different way.

2   Blind people read by running their fingers over pages that have groups of tiny raised dots. These dots represent different letters, and they form an alphabet that's just like ours. This writing system is called braille.   5

3   Braille has a very interesting history. Its story begins around 1800, when a French soldier named Charles Barbier created a system of raised dots so that soldiers could read messages in the dark. Napoléon wanted his troops to be able to communicate in the dark 10 without giving away their positions. In the end, this so-called "night writing" system was too complicated for soldiers to learn. It had to be rejected by the military.

4   Years later, Charles Barbier met Louis Braille at the National Institute for the Blind in Paris. Louis Braille had been blind since 15 the age of four, and he immediately recognized both the potential importance of Barbier's system and its major flaw. Louis set to work on making it easier to use, and eventually the braille system was born.

5   In braille, each letter, or cell, is made up of a rectangle in which 20 there can be a combination of up to six raised dots or an absence of dots. The six dots

⌄ Braille alphabet cells

are arranged in a grid of two dots horizontally by three dots vertically. The dots are numbered 1, 2, and 3 from top to bottom on the left column and 4, 5, and 6 from top to bottom on the right column. There can be 64 different combinations. Braille has also evolved to accommodate differences in other languages. For example, Greek braille is different from Chinese braille. 25

⌄ Perkins NEXTGEN Brailler

6 Blind people can also write in braille. Most use a special typewriter, called the Perkins Brailler, which types braille onto paper. Nowadays, computer keyboards with braille symbols are also available. 30

7 It is amazing that a military technology from the Napoleonic Wars has grown into something that has improved the lives of countless blind people around the world. 35

Questions

_____ 1. Another good title for this passage might be _____.
  a. The Innovations of Napoléon
  b. Reading Without Sight
  c. A Cure for Blindness
  d. The Origin of the Perkins Brailler

_____ 2. The passage is mainly about a(n) _____.
  a. art
  b. soldier
  c. writing system
  d. institute for the blind

_____ 3. The third paragraph is mostly about one of the Napoleonic Wars' _____.
  a. victories
  b. inventions
  c. battles
  d. blind people

_____ 4. The fifth paragraph deals mainly with _____.
  a. the way braille sounds
  b. the way braille is written
  c. the origin of braille
  d. where the name braille came from

_____ 5. The second paragraph focuses on _____.
  a. what braille is
  b. where you will find braille
  c. who invented braille
  d. why braille is important

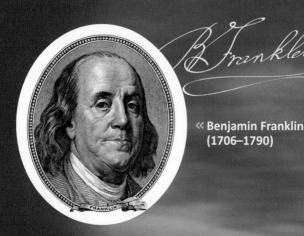

« Benjamin Franklin
(1706–1790)

3 When Lightning Strikes

1   Lightning is what we call those bright flashes in the clouds during a thunderstorm. Occasionally, a bolt of lightning will streak downward toward the ground. Thunder often accompanies lightning, creating a stunning natural display of light and sound.

2   Lightning has fascinated humans for thousands of years. The ancient Greeks believed that lightning bolts meant their god Zeus was angry. By 1752, our understanding had become a lot clearer and more scientific. That was the year that Benjamin Franklin used a key, a kite, and a raging thunderstorm to prove that lightning was, in fact, electricity.

⌄ cloud-to-ground lightning

3   Since then, scientists have discovered that lightning is actually a discharge of static electricity. This electricity builds up when water droplets in the clouds come into contact with each other. Eventually, the static charge reaches a point where it tries to escape to somewhere that is less charged, and this place may be the ground. The resulting shift in static charge is a flash of lightning.

4   Cloud-to-cloud lightning is the most common type, and it can sometimes be observed from great distances. Cloud-to-ground lightning is the second most common, and it is the biggest threat to human life and property. There are other types of lightning as well, such as ball lightning, positive lightning, and perhaps the weirdest one of all: ground-to-cloud lightning.

5   Lightning can reach temperatures of over 29,000°C, which is hotter than the sun. It can also strike the same place over and over again. Skyscrapers

5

10

15

20

25

>> Lightning hits a tree.

⌃ Lightning is a discharge of static electricity.

and other tall structures might get struck several times over the course of
a single storm. That's why it is never a good idea to stand under a tall tree
during a thunderstorm. A better option would be to stay in a car, because the   30
metal can protect you, or to lie flat on the ground in an open area.

6   Over the past two decades, around 36 people are killed by lightning each
year in the United States. Lightning is just as dangerous as other natural
disasters like tornadoes and hurricanes. While it's true that your chance of
being struck by lightning is very low, it's always better to be safe than sorry.   35

Questions

_____ 1. Another good title for this passage would be _____.
    a. Flashes in the Sky
    b. The Amazing Benjamin Franklin
    c. A Guide to Lightning Safety
    d. The Dangers of Lightning

_____ 2. The passage is mainly about a(n) _____.
    a. storm   **b.** invention
    c. thunder   **d.** natural phenomenon

_____ 3. The fifth paragraph is mostly concerned with lightning _____.
    a. safety   **b.** science
    c. color   **d.** frequency

_____ 4. The second paragraph centers on lightning's _____.
    a. risks   **b.** historical impact
    c. types   **d.** description

_____ 5. Which paragraph describes the modern scientific beliefs behind lightning?
    a. The first paragraph.   **b.** The second paragraph.
    c. The third paragraph.   **d.** The fourth paragraph.

4 Inflation

004

1   Jim took the $10 he had been saving carefully for months and buried it in his backyard. Forty years passed before he decided to dig it up and buy something nice. The only problem was that by 2018, his $10 wasn't even enough to buy an iPhone case for his grandson.

2   What happened? Everything became more expensive while Jim's   5 money maintained its original value. Jim forgot about inflation.

3   Inflation is when the cost of goods and services rises in an economy. It is generally seen as a negative economic force, because rising prices can eat away at a household's finances. Governments and central banks try their best to control inflation, and they do so   10 by trying to keep the inflation rate under three percent.

4   There are several economic factors that can cause inflation. The first is the expansion of a country's money supply. If there is more money being printed, the money's value goes down, and prices will go up as a result. Inflation can also be caused by demand for a   15 product exceeding the amount of available supply. Another trigger for inflation is an increase in the price of items or materials needed to produce a good or service. For example, since gasoline is needed to power tractors on farms, an increase in the price of gas will cause food prices to go up as well.   20

5   Inflation can sometimes spin out of control when a population loses all confidence in the value of its money. This is called "hyperinflation." While there are several different definitions, most

⌄ Due to the economic crisis and hyperinflation, the black-market exchange rate for one US dollar has reached 250,000 bolívars in Venezuela.

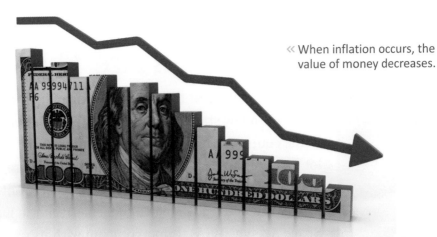

« When inflation occurs, the value of money decreases.

economists agree that hyperinflation occurs when a country's monthly inflation rate exceeds 50 percent. At a rate that high, money is losing half of its value every month.

25

6 There are many historical examples of hyperinflation wreaking havoc on a country's economy. In China in 1947, the highest yuan bill available was 10,000. By 1949, the government was issuing 500,000,000-yuan bills. Similar inflation crises took place in Germany during the 1920s, France during the French Revolution, and Argentina during the 1980s. The government of Zimbabwe has also been fighting a persistent hyperinflation crisis since 2008.

30

« A trigger for inflation is an increase in the price of gasoline.

Questions

_____ 1. Another good title for this passage might be _____.
    a. When Prices Go Up and Up   **b.** The History of Inflation
    c. Saving According to Jim   **d.** The Dangers of Hyperinflation

_____ 2. This passage is mostly about _____.
    a. an economic phenomenon   **b.** farming equipment
    c. economic history   **d.** money strategies

_____ 3. The final paragraph centers on hyperinflation's _____.
    a. dangers   **b.** effects
    c. definition   **d.** historical examples

_____ 4. The first paragraph is mostly about _____.
    a. inflation   **b.** an iPhone case
    c. a man saving his money   **d.** the price of gas

_____ 5. The fourth paragraph deals mainly with inflation's _____.
    a. definition   **b.** causes   **c.** history   **d.** benefits

5 | How Many Stars Are There?

⌃ stars in the night sky

1 If you look up at the night sky from a busy city street, you'll see a few stars shining brightly. Do the same thing in the countryside or from a mountaintop, and you'll see a lot more of them. Just how many stars are there in space? You could try counting them yourself if you want, but it's probably a better idea to ask the experts at the European Space Agency (ESA). It has come up with its own estimates on the number of stars in our universe.

2 According to the ESA, there could be as many as 10^{23} stars in the universe. However, this is only a rough estimate. Remember that Albert Einstein's Theory of Relativity states that time is not constant. Therefore, astronomers might be counting stars and galaxies that disappeared a long time ago.

3 This giant number includes stars that are much larger than our sun, and others that are much smaller. It takes into account the trillions of galaxies that are spread out across our universe. Some of these galaxies are considered to be dwarf galaxies because they have as few as 10 million stars. Others are giant galaxies because they have more than a trillion stars.

4 The ESA estimate also includes the Milky Way, which is our solar system's home galaxy. Our sun is actually a medium-sized star. It's a member of the white cloud of stars in the Milky Way that can sometimes be seen stretching across a moonless night sky. According to ESA astronomers, the Milky Way is made up of at least 100 billion stars.

5 Many stars have planets orbiting around them. In fact, some astronomers believe that there are as many planets as there are stars out there. Perhaps intelligent life exists on these planets, just waiting to be discovered. If that's the case, maybe there are a few alien astronomers who can give us a more accurate answer regarding the number of stars in the universe.

galaxy »

« Many stars have planets orbiting around them.

Questions

_____ 1. Another good title for this passage might be _____.
  a. Welcome to the Milky Way   **b.** A Star Is Born
  c. Counting the Uncountable   **d.** Europe's First Space Agency

_____ 2. This passage is mostly about _____.
  a. stars   **b.** galaxies   **c.** planets   **d.** Albert Einstein

_____ 3. The fourth paragraph is mostly concerned with _____.
  a. the ESA   **b.** our galaxy   **c.** the sun   **d.** dwarf galaxies

_____ 4. The first paragraph focuses on _____.
  a. destroying stars   **b.** counting stars
  c. mapping stars   **d.** understanding stars

_____ 5. The final paragraph is mostly about _____.
  a. the Milky Way   **b.** our solar system
  c. stars   **d.** life on other planets

1-2 *Main Idea*

>> magician

Authors write for a reason, and in any given passage the author is trying to communicate his or her point to you, the reader. The main idea or point of an article is not always obvious, so when reading, don't forget to ask yourself, "What point is the author trying to make?"

6 | Magicians

(006) **1**   Magicians are performers who create illusions and do magic tricks. Magicians appear to produce something from nothing—pulling a dove from an empty hat, for example—or they may make something disappear (such as a magician's assistant who vanishes from a cabinet). They can seemingly transform one thing into another, such as changing a lady into a tiger, or they can destroy something and then restore it to its original state (for example, cutting a person in half, and then that person showing up looking quite healthy).   5

2   Magicians have many other skills, including teleportation, escapology, levitation, penetration, and prediction. A magician often uses a combination of these skills with each trick.   10

3   Magicians do seem to have some kind of supernatural power. There is indeed something mysterious about them. Perhaps it is their energy, knowing smile, and perfectly timed gestures.   15

4 I often closely watch magicians doing their tricks in the hope of understanding their mysterious art. I focus on their long-fingered hands and their every movement. Maybe, if I watch closely enough, one day I will see the flash of a coin being tucked into the cuff of a jacket or a card slipped from one hand to another.   20

« A magician might pull doves from an empty hat.

5   Those who know the art of magic say that magicians are merely masters of deception. The secret of their art is actually simple: A magician distracts the audience by making people look at one place ²⁵ while he or she is secretly changing or moving an object elsewhere. When the audience's attention returns to the magician, the magic has already been done.

6   To be honest, many magicians are very good at what they do. However, I will continue trying to catch their deception. I just need ³⁰ to remember that when magicians are around, things are not always as they seem!

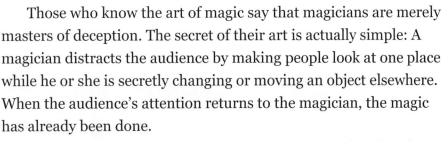

» levitation

Questions

_____ 1. What is the main point of the article?
    a. Magic shows should be against the law.
    b. Magicians use supernatural powers to perform tricks.
    c. Watching magicians perform requires a lot of concentration.
    d. Magicians perform tricks by skillfully deceiving the audience.

_____ 2. What is the main idea of the first paragraph?
    a. Magicians can perform medical miracles.
    b. Magicians do a lot of tricks with animals.
    c. Magicians are very dangerous people.
    d. Magicians appear to have amazing powers.

_____ 3. What is the main point discussed in the fourth paragraph?
    a. Magicians must have long fingers to perform magic tricks.
    b. Magic tricks are very complicated and require special powers.
    c. The author wants to figure out magic tricks by observing magicians closely.
    d. Magicians often use objects such as coins and cards to work their magic.

_____ 4. What is the fifth paragraph mainly about?
    a. Magic tricks work because magicians are able to divert people's attention.
    b. Magicians use magic to make the audience obey their commands.
    c. People who go to magic shows need to pay close attention to the magician.
    d. There are too many things to look at during a magic show.

_____ 5. What point does the author make in the final paragraph?
    a. Magicians should be more honest with the audience.
    b. Magicians are clever and good at misleading people.
    c. Some things—such as magic—are not meant to be understood.
    d. People should be careful around magicians.

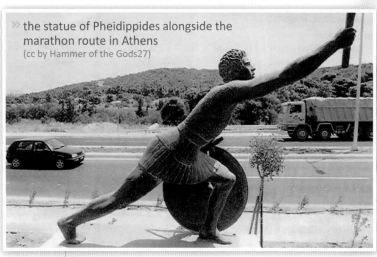

the statue of Pheidippides alongside the marathon route in Athens
(cc by Hammer of the Gods27)

7 | Running Marathons

1 A marathon is a running race that covers exactly 42.195 km. Other long races may be called marathons, but the term is used incorrectly if these races are longer or shorter than 42.195 km.

2 Many big cities now host marathons, which are very popular tourist attractions. Every year, thousands of people travel from all over the world to watch or compete in marathons in London, Berlin, and Boston. Around the world, more than 800 marathons are held annually, with many athletes competing in more than one marathon each year.

3 According to legend, a Greek soldier and messenger by the name of Pheidippides once raced from the town of Marathon to Athens, a distance of about 42 km. Pheidippides ran without stopping because he carried important news that the Greek army had defeated the Persians at the Battle of Marathon. When he arrived in Athens, Pheidippides exclaimed, "We have won." Then he dropped to the ground and died from exhaustion.

4 Thankfully, few modern marathon runners die from exhaustion. Today's runners prepare properly and drink enough water while they are competing.

5 In 1896, when the first modern Olympics were held in Athens, officials decided to recall the ancient glory of Greece by hosting a marathon.

⌃ Samuel Wanjiru (1986–2011) in 2007 (cc by Den Haag CPC 2007)

Since then, the Men's Marathon has traditionally been the last event of the Games, with the finish line inside the Olympic stadium. In the 2004 Summer Olympics, the traditional route from Marathon to Athens was used for the race, and it ended in Panathinaiko Stadium.

6   At the 2008 Summer Olympics in Beijing, the winner of the Men's Marathon was Samuel Wanjiru from Kenya, who set an Olympic record with a time of 2:06:32. At the 2012 London Olympics, Ethiopian runner Erba Tiki Galana won the gold medal in the Women's Marathon, finishing the race with a new Olympic record of 2:23:07.

30

Questions

_____ 1. What is the main idea of the article?
  a. Marathons are popular around the world and are an important part of the Olympics.
  b. Running a marathon requires courage, strength, and endurance.
  c. The Greeks invented the marathon, which is occasionally an Olympic event.
  d. The 2008 Olympics ended with a record-breaking time in the Men's Marathon.

_____ 2. What is the third paragraph mainly about?
  a. The first marathon was slightly shorter than the current length of 42.195 km.
  b. In ancient times, runners often collapsed and died after running marathons.
  c. Running a marathon in Greece can be especially difficult and dangerous.
  d. The first marathon was run by a Greek solider who was delivering news of a victory.

_____ 3. What is the main idea of the fifth paragraph?
  a. The 2004 Summer Olympics were held in Greece at the Panathinaiko Stadium.
  b. The marathon was added to the Olympics in 1896 to honor Greek history.
  c. The Summer Olympics were first held in Greece in 1896 and again in 2004.
  d. The Men's Marathon is the first event of the Olympics, with the finish line in the stadium.

_____ 4. What main point is discussed in the second paragraph?
  a. Marathons are popular events around the world.
  b. Only big cities can host marathons.
  c. Many runners compete in several races each year.
  d. Tourists are allowed to run in marathons.

_____ 5. What is the final paragraph mostly about?
  a. Men from Kenya generally run faster than women from Ethiopia.
  b. It takes two to three hours to run a marathon in China.
  c. A woman set a new marathon record in Beijing in 2008.
  d. Both men and women run marathons but not always at the same speed.

≪ Tiki Gelana (1987–) in 2012 Olympic Women's Marathon (cc by Tom Page)

8 Dangerous Dust

1   Some things just shouldn't be mixed together. Take sand and wind for example. Everyone enjoys the feeling of sand under their feet at the beach. And what's more relaxing than a nice breeze on a hot and humid day? But if you take enough sand, and enough wind, and put them together . . . Well, let's just say there's nothing relaxing about it.   5

2   We're talking about sandstorms, of course. Sandstorms are a type of weather phenomenon that occur when powerful winds blow across sand or dust. The winds pick up loose sand particles and carry them into the atmosphere, creating giant dust clouds. Sandstorms can   10 stretch for hundreds of kilometers, lasting anywhere from a few hours to several days.

3   Though beautiful, these dust clouds can be a real problem for anyone trapped inside of them. For one thing, they make it impossible to see anything. All someone can do is to find a safe spot and wait   15 for it to pass. Unsurprisingly, sandstorms also leave a thick layer of dust wherever they go. Sand will find its way into clothes, electronics, buildings, cars—really anything you can think of. And in the most extreme cases, sandstorms can be quite dangerous. In 2015, one powerful sandstorm killed eight people across two countries in   20 the Middle East. Hundreds of others ended up in the hospital for breathing problems.

⌃ Winds pick up loose sand particles and carry them into the atmosphere.

⌄ Sandstorms can make things difficult to see.

People in dry regions are most at risk of sandstorms.

4 Since sandstorms are powered by strong winds and sand, it's dry regions that are most at risk. The Middle East and North Africa frequently suffer sandstorms due to their large deserts, and so, too, does northern China with the Gobi Desert, and Australia with its dry central regions. 25

5 Sandstorms are expected to get worse in the future as a result of global warming. As Earth's climate heats up, some regions will become drier, increasing sand and dust. It's up to all of us to help fight global warming and keep sandstorms under control. After all, who wants to wear eye protection and a face mask to school every day? 30 35

Questions

_____ 1. What point does the author make in the final paragraph?
    a. We should fight global warming to reduce sandstorms.
    b. Global warming will bring sandstorms under control.
    c. Eye protection is important during a sandstorm.
    d. Earth's climate is slowly heating up.

_____ 2. What is the main idea of the article?
    a. Sandstorms are getting worse every year.
    b. Sandstorms leave a thick layer of dust wherever they go.
    c. Sandstorms can sometimes be deadly.
    d. Sandstorms are an interesting and threatening phenomenon.

sandstorm in Atacama Desert, Chile

_____ 3. What is the second paragraph mainly about?
    a. What a sandstorm is.   **b.** Where sandstorms occur.
    c. The dangers of sandstorms.   **d.** How to survive a sandstorm.

_____ 4. What is the main idea of the first paragraph?
    a. Everyone deserves a day at the beach.
    b. Some things shouldn't be mixed together.
    c. There's nothing relaxing about a sandstorm.
    d. A breeze can be relaxing on a hot day.

_____ 5. What is the main point of the third paragraph?
    a. There are some extremely large sandstorms.
    b. Sandstorms can be annoying and dangerous.
    c. You should find a place to hide when a sandstorm hits.
    d. Dust gets into everything during a sandstorm.

Watch Out for These Killer Creatures!

» hippopotamus

∧ People mistakenly think the shark is the deadliest beast.

∧ golden poison dart frog (cc by Wilfried Berns)

∧ When all the victims are counted, humans are the most dangerous creatures on Earth.

1 When asked to identify the world's most dangerous creature, some people might say the lion or the tiger. Others might guess that the shark is the deadliest beast. But they would all be wrong. There is another, more dangerous creature that has killed far more people than any of these animals.

2 The box jellyfish is among the deadliest creatures of the seas. Also known as a sea wasp, this animal has venom that can easily kill a human. In fact, about a hundred people around the world die every year from box jellyfish stings. Box jellyfish can sting you in shallow water and they can sting you on dry land. So be careful where you step next time you're walking on a beach!

3 Killer creatures can come in small packages, like the golden poison dart frog. Found in Colombia, these bright little creatures can fit on the palm of your hand. But if you actually held one, you'd be dead in a matter of minutes. Just one of these little frogs carries enough poison to kill up to 20 humans.

4 Then there's the hippopotamus, or "hippo" for short. Hippos are found in sub-Saharan Africa. Many view these giant plant-eaters as cute and passive, but in reality, they're very dangerous. Some researchers have called hippos the most aggressive animals on Earth. Even lions and crocodiles realize the danger and tend to avoid hippos in the wild. Hippo attacks are believed to result in around 500 deaths every year in Africa.

5 But none of these animals are the deadliest. That title belongs to none other than human beings. Through murder, violence, and war, we have killed more people than any other animal has. It is estimated that during the 20th century alone, up to 188 million people were killed in various wars. It's hard for any hippo, jellyfish, or dart frog to compete with that sad statistic.

5

10

15

20

25

30

^ **box jellyfish**
(cc by gautsch.)

Questions

_____ 1. Which sentence best states the main idea of the article?
  a. Too many people have been killed by humans over the years.
  b. There is a lot of disagreement over the world's deadliest creature.
  c. There are many deadly creatures, but humans are the deadliest.
  d. Hippos are one of the world's deadliest creatures.

_____ 2. What is the main idea of the first paragraph?
  a. Sharks are the deadliest creatures in the world.
  b. People are often surprised by which animal is the deadliest
    in the world.
  c. People believe that lions are the deadliest creature in the world.
  d. There are many different brutal animals in the world.

_____ 3. What point does the author make in the third paragraph?
  a. Golden poison dart frogs are very small and very deadly.
  b. Golden poison dart frogs are found in Colombia.
  c. Golden poison dart frogs can fit in the palm of your hand.
  d. Golden poison dart frogs have enough poison to kill 20 humans.

_____ 4. Which sentence best states the main idea of the fourth paragraph?
  a. Hippos are the deadliest creature in Africa.
  b. Hippos may be cute, but they're actually very dangerous.
  c. Lions and crocodiles tend to avoid hippos in the wild.
  d. Over 500 Africans die from hippo attacks every year.

_____ 5. What is the main point of the final paragraph?
  a. Humans tend to fight a lot of wars.
  b. Humans are considered an animal, too.
  c. The number of deaths from wars is a sad statistic.
  d. Humans are the deadliest creature in the world.

JELLYFISH

031

10 Lost in the Sahara Desert

1   The Sahara Desert in Northern Africa is the largest hot desert in the world. This fierce land stretches about 1,800 km from the north to the south and about 4,800 km from the east to the west. Temperatures can easily exceed 40°C in the daytime during summer and can fall to -10°C at night in winter. More than 8,000 years ago, the Sahara was a fertile land where farmers grew millet. As the annual rainfall in the area gradually decreased, it became a huge desert. Most areas of this desert average 10 cm of rain per year. The Sahara has one of the harshest climates in the world.

2   Gary Smith and a few of his adventurous friends decided to hike across the Sahara. Supporters in cars, who carried food and water for the group, accompanied them.

3   One day, Smith got separated from the rest of the group. He was soon lost in the desert and could not figure out which direction to go. Then a sandstorm covered the area. It was not a big storm, but when it was over, Smith was even more confused. In the unbearable heat, he quickly finished his water. He was forced to spend that night out in the open, and he almost froze to death.

4   The next day, he walked on aimlessly. His limbs ached, his lips were cracked and bleeding, and he had a terrible headache, but he would not stop. Smith was determined to survive. After the second night, he started to worry about dying. He realized that his friends might not find him in time. It was late on the third day that Smith collapsed.

5   When Smith awoke, he was in an air-conditioned vehicle with his friends. He had been found by a group of bedouins who were traveling in a caravan. The bedouins returned him to his group of friends. Smith was lucky to have survived.

⌄ Sahara Desert

Questions

sandstorm

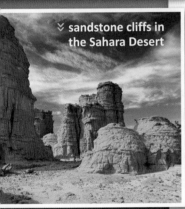
sandstone cliffs in the Sahara Desert

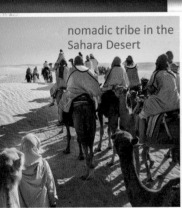
nomadic tribe in the Sahara Desert

_____ 1. What is the main idea of the first paragraph?
   a. The Sahara Desert is very large, dry, and has extreme temperatures.
   b. The Sahara Desert doesn't get much rain.
   c. The people of the Sahara Desert have always been farmers.
   d. No one has been able to measure the size of the Sahara Desert.

_____ 2. What is the main point of the third paragraph?
   a. Given the extreme heat, Smith drank his water too quickly.
   b. Sandstorms can cause groups to become separated.
   c. Smith got lost and barely survived the harsh conditions.
   d. Desert temperatures can quickly go from very hot to very cold.

_____ 3. What is the main idea of the fourth paragraph?
   a. Smith developed some type of disease and almost died.
   b. Smith started to despair and lost his will to live.
   c. Smith had to spend a second night out in the open.
   d. Smith's will to live kept him going, despite the hardships.

_____ 4. What is the main idea of the final paragraph?
   a. There should be more air-conditioning in the Sahara Desert.
   b. Bedouins are very kind people who always travel in groups.
   c. Smith would likely have died if he hadn't been found by the Bedouins.
   d. Smith's friends should have tried harder to find him.

_____ 5. What point is the author trying to communicate with this article?
   a. Surviving alone in a harsh environment like the Sahara Desert can be challenging.
   b. Heat stroke and confusion are the biggest dangers in the Sahara Desert.
   c. Smith should have stayed in one place instead of wandering around the desert.
   d. The Sahara Desert is fertile and should be used for farmland, not recreation.

Authors use details to support the main idea. These may come in the form of examples, descriptions, definitions, facts, and many more. Pay attention to the content of these details as they provide important information. If you don't read carefully, you might misunderstand the point the writer's trying to make.

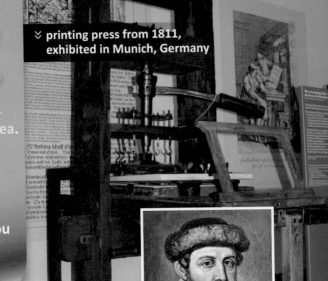

⌄ printing press from 1811, exhibited in Munich, Germany

» Johannes Gutenberg (c. 1395–1468)

11 The Printing Press

011

1 What do you think is mankind's most important invention? Is it the computer, the telephone, or the wheel? Many people say that it is the printing press, a machine that allows us to reproduce unlimited copies of books and documents.

2 Before the printing press, books were copied by hand. Ancient Roman book publishers sometimes sold as many as 5,000 copies of a book that had been copied by slaves. But copying a book was such a time-consuming and expensive activity that often only a few copies of each book were made. As a result, only a small fraction of the population had access to books and learned to read. 5 ... 10

3 While the printing press was invented in 1450 by Johannes Gutenberg, a goldsmith from Germany, printing had already been around for quite some time. Around 5,000 years ago in ancient Mesopotamia, carved stones serving as seals or stamps were used to make impressions in clay. Later in China, wooden blocks were carved with text, coated in ink and then pressed onto paper or cloth. Instead of using a page-sized block of carved wood, however, Gutenberg's printing press used small, metal blocks, each with just a single letter. To print a page, all the printer had to do was assemble the necessary letters and start the machine. Whereas wooden blocks would quickly become damaged, the metal letter 15 ... 20

⌃ movable metal type and composing stick descended from Gutenberg's press

blocks were durable, and if one was found to have a flaw, it could easily be replaced without affecting the entire page. What Gutenberg achieved with his printing press was the ability to mass-produce books 25 quickly, cheaply, and efficiently.

4 After 1450, thousands of copies of a popular book or newspaper could be printed rapidly and inexpensively. Books and newspapers with ideas and images from all over the world became widely available to the public. The impact of Gutenberg's machine is sometimes 30 compared to the impact of the Internet, as it has allowed millions of people to gain access to new and exciting knowledge. As knowledge fuels human intelligence, mankind's astounding technological and scientific progress over the last 500 years owes no small debt to Gutenberg's remarkable printing press. 35

Questions

_____ **1.** Which of the following is NOT true about the printing press?
   a. It was invented in the 15th century.
   b. It was the first form of printing.
   c. It made printing quick and efficient.
   d. It was invented by Johannes Gutenberg.

_____ **2.** The printing press allows people to _____.
   a. make as many copies of a book as they want
   b. create a book using less paper
   c. improve their handwriting skills
   d. copy a book without the author's permission

≪ Gutenberg press replica at the Featherbed Alley Printshop Museum in Bermuda
(cc by Aodhdubh)

≫ "Modern Book Printing" sculpture in Germany commemorating inventor Gutenberg
(cc by Lienhard Schulz)

_____ **3.** In ancient Rome, books were _____.
   a. printed using wooden blocks   **b.** carved into stone
   c. copied out by slaves   **d.** printed using Gutenberg's press

_____ **4.** Which of the following is true about Gutenberg's metal blocks?
   a. They were less durable than wooden blocks.
   b. They were not easily replaced.
   c. It caused big problems if one got damaged.
   d. Each one had only a single letter on it.

_____ **5.** The printing press has been compared to the Internet because _____.
   a. it has allowed people to acquire knowledge
   b. it was invented in Germany
   c. it has allowed people to communicate over long distances
   d. it can be used by anybody with little difficulty

12 | Owls

(012)

1　To say someone is "as wise as an owl" is a great way to compliment their intelligence, but it's a strange comparison when you think about it. After all, owls are not particularly smarter than other birds, and crows are widely acknowledged to be the smartest of all birds. Why then are owls so often associated with wisdom? Their excellent night vision and sharp hunting skills may be part of the reason, but the idea probably goes back as far as the ancient Greeks, whose goddess of wisdom, Athena, was often depicted holding an owl.

2　Indeed, owls have been a part of our legends and folklore for as long as humankind has recorded history. In some cultures, perhaps owing to their nighttime activity and screeching calls, owls are often associated with bad luck and misfortune. The ancient Romans, for example, thought the shriek of an owl meant that death was close at hand and even believed that witches would turn into owls in order to suck the blood from innocent babies.

3　Did you know, though, that not all owls are nocturnal? Generally speaking, owls with dark eyes hunt during the night, but those with orange eyes are crepuscular, meaning they hunt their prey during the twilight hours of dusk or just before dawn. Owls with yellow eyes hunt during the day.

4　In fact, an owl's eyes are perhaps one of its most remarkable features. They are so big compared to the owl's small skull that instead of being round like our eyes, they are shaped like long tubes. The eyes may also account for up to five percent of an owl's body weight, but because of the eyes' strange shape, an owl cannot roll its eyes like we can. Rather, to see from side to side, an owl must move its entire head, and these birds can manage a turn of as much as 135 degrees in either direction. This incredible vision allows owls to hunt scurrying insects, darting mice, and lightning-fast rabbits in the dark. They truly are remarkable creatures, whatever their reputation for intelligence.

5
10
15
20
25
30

⌃ *Minera* (statue of Athena holding an owl) (2nd century A.D., with 18th-century restorations) in the Louvre (cc by Janmad)

⌄ Owls with dark eyes hunt during the night.

Questions

1. Owls are thought of as wise because they were associated with _____.
   - **a.** the goddess Athena
   - **b.** witches
   - **c.** the ancient Romans
   - **d.** the nighttime

2. To the ancient Romans, the call of an owl meant _____.
   - **a.** a new beginning
   - **b.** bad weather
   - **c.** death
   - **d.** good luck

3. Which of the following statements is NOT true?
   - **a.** Owls with orange eyes are usually crepuscular.
   - **b.** An owl can turn its head only 135 degrees to the left and 135 degrees to the right.
   - **c.** Owls hunt mice, insects, and rabbits.
   - **d.** Owls are widely acknowledged to be the smartest of all birds.

4. What is mentioned as the reason that owls cannot roll their eyes?
   - **a.** They have small skulls.
   - **b.** Their eyes are shaped like long tubes.
   - **c.** Their eyes are too large and heavy.
   - **d.** They are not intelligent enough.

5. According to the article, owls are sometimes associated with misfortune because _____.
   - **a.** they are usually active at night and make scary noises
   - **b.** their eyes are big and spooky
   - **c.** the way they turn their heads looks unnatural
   - **d.** they kill cute creatures like mice

» The ancient Romans believed witches would turn into owls.

» Owls with orange eyes are crepuscular.

mouse

« Owls hunt mainly insects, mice and rabbits.

rabbit

insects

Thomas Edison (1847–1931) in 1915

13 (013)
Thomas Edison's Inventions

1   The lightbulb is one of the most important inventions of the last 200 years. It has allowed us to do things at night that would otherwise be inconceivable. Can you imagine lighting up a highway with candles or trying to drive your car using the dim glow of gas 5 lamps? Many people believe that the lightbulb was invented by Thomas Edison, but is that really the case?

2   Edison was born in 1847 in Milan, Ohio, USA. In school, Edison was often absentminded, and his teachers did not think he was an intellectual. In 1854, his family moved to Port Huron, Michigan, 10 where the young Edison sold candy and newspapers on trains from Port Huron to Detroit. These early sales experiences allowed Edison to cultivate his talents as a businessman and eventually led him to found 14 companies, including General Electric, which is still flourishing today. 15

3   Edison started his career as an inventor in Newark, New Jersey, and in 1878 he formed the Edison Electric Light

Thomas Edison's first successful lightbulb model

» Thomas Edison and his early record player, 1877–April 1878

Company. During his first public demonstration of his incandescent lightbulb on December 31, 1879, he said, "We will make electricity so cheap that only the rich will burn candles." Lightbulbs were not the only things Edison worked on. He also established the first industrial research laboratory in Menlo Park, New Jersey. There, Edison and his assistant, William J. Hammer, worked on the telephone, developed the electric railway, and patented the United States' first movie camera.

4   However, Edison did not invent many of the things he is said to have invented, but he did improve them so that they could be sold to the public. He did not invent the electric lightbulb, for example, which had been invented seven decades earlier. He did, however, develop a long-lasting, practical electric lightbulb and start the first company that made and sold them. The only major invention that Edison did invent was the record player. It was this invention in 1877 that made him renowned the world over as the Wizard of Menlo Park.

« Edison's Menlo Park laboratory, reconstructed at the Henry Ford Museum in Michigan (cc by Andrew Balet)

Questions

_____ 1. When he was at school, Edison's teachers thought he was _____.
   a. a genius   **b.** smart but lazy
   c. not very bright   **d.** a clown

_____ 2. Which of the following did Edison NOT work on?
   a. The electric railway.   **b.** The record player.
   c. The movie camera.   **d.** The steam engine.

_____ 3. Which of the following did Edison actually invent?
   a. The lightbulb.   **b.** The telephone.
   c. The movie camera.   **d.** The record player.

_____ 4. Edison discovered his talents as a businessman by _____.
   a. working as a salesman   **b.** studying business at university
   c. working with William J. Hammer **d.** founding General Electric

_____ 5. Which of the following statements is true?
   a. Most of Edison's inventions weren't useful.
   b. Edison made existing inventions more marketable.
   c. Edison was not well known in his day.
   d. None of Edison's companies exist anymore.

14 Exploring the World, One Couch at a Time

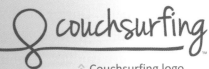

⌃ Couchsurfing logo

1   The term "couch surfing" has changed over the years. It used to refer to sleeping on the couches of friends and family and having no fixed address of one's own. People didn't couch surf for fun; they did it because they had nowhere else to go. But in the age of the Internet, the number of couches on offer has increased dramatically. Now, when people go couch surfing, they're   5 heading out to explore the world.

2   There's one website at the heart of the modern couch surfing movement: Couchsurfing.com. Think of it as Facebook-meets-Airbnb. Established back in 2003, the website is now one of the oldest social networks. It currently has over 15 million users.   10

3   Here's how the website works. If you have a couch, you can offer it to users who are visiting your city. If you're going on vacation, you can search for an available couch at your destination. People with available couches, also called "hosts," are not allowed to accept any money from their guests. In fact, the only fee on Couchsurfing.com is an annual charge meant to confirm a user's   15 identity.

4   You may be thinking: Don't people abuse this system? After all, who doesn't want to travel for free? Couchsurfing.com gets around this by focusing on a user's reputation. It's up to the hosts to pick who can sleep on their couch. They decide based on a variety of factors, including profile information,   20 pictures, and user reviews. But perhaps most important of all is whether or not you've offered a couch in the past. Couchsurfing.com is a close-knit community

⌃ Couch surfing lets you experience what it's like to live like a local.

⌃ People can make lifelong friends from couch surfing.

based on mutual exchange—if you give, you'll get. And safety is always an important concern for hosts and guests alike.

5   The couch surfing movement continues to change the way we view travel. 25 To a couch surfer, traveling doesn't need to be expensive. It also doesn't

need to involve being locked away in a hotel room. Instead, you can experience the lives and habits of locals, in their own homes. And 30 best of all, you can make some lifelong friends in the process.

« Couchsurfing.com, a close-knit community with over 15 million users

Questions

_____ 1. Which of the following statements about Couchsurfing.com is NOT true?
    a. The website has more than 15 million users.
    b. The website never asks for money from its users.
    c. The website is at the center of the couch surfing movement.
    d. The website was established back in 2003.

_____ 2. What did the term "couch surfing" mean before the Internet age?
    a. Staying in hotel rooms when you traveled.
    b. Shopping for the most comfortable couch.
    c. Heading out to explore the world.
    d. Sleeping on your friends' couch.

_____ 3. Which of the following is NOT something a host will consider when deciding whether to accept a guest?
    a. Their profile information.   b. Their pictures.
    c. Their gender.   d. Their reviews from other users.

_____ 4. How does Couchsurfing.com avoid people taking advantage of free lodging?
    a. It focuses on the reputation of its users.
    b. It charges its users a high annual fee.
    c. It only allows a select few people to join the website.
    d. It punishes users who never offer a couch.

_____ 5. Which of the following is true about modern couch surfing?
    a. It can be very expensive.   b. It's a great way to make friends.
    c. It's not very popular.   d. It's very frustrating.

trumpet

15
Jazz Music

>> Louis Armstrong (1901–1971) was a much-imitated innovator of early jazz.

JAZZ COMPOSER AND TRUMPETER

32

USA

LOUIS ARMSTRONG

1   To some, jazz sounds like a musical mess; to others, it's the most expressive and animated form of music around, a combination of styles and musical traditions that reflects the blended nature of the American society where it developed.

5

2   Jazz originated in the early 20th century in the United States, particularly in the cities of New Orleans and Chicago. The word "jazz" is thought to have begun as a West Coast slang word meaning "spirit" or "vigor." The first recorded usage of the word appears far away from the world of New Orleans music in the sports pages of a West Coast newspaper in 1912, where it was used to describe the unpredictable curve of a certain baseball player's pitch. Around 1915, however, "jazz" was first used to refer to the kind of restless, improvised music emerging in Chicago at the time.

10

15

3   A combination of spiritual music, blues, ragtime, and even military music, jazz owes a large part of its development to the elaborate funeral processions held by the African-American communities of New Orleans. Many of the early jazz musicians played at these processions, and as a result, the instruments of the marching band—like drums, trumpets, and trombones—became the basic instruments of jazz.

20

25

4   Though jazz's early influences are clear, jazz itself is very difficult to define. This is because one of the most important parts of jazz is improvisation. In jazz, a performer may change melodies, harmonies, or time signature at will. Whereas European classical music is sometimes seen as a composer's music, the performer's role being mainly to play

30

the music as the composer intended, jazz is often seen
as being under the control of the musicians themselves.
A jazz song is spontaneous; it develops naturally from 35
the performers' interactions with each other on stage.
It isn't planned or under the restrictions of strict rules.
This has allowed jazz to produce countless subgenres:
bebop, swing, cool jazz, acid jazz, free jazz, jazz-funk,
and jazz rap being only a few examples. 40

Questions

1. Where did jazz music originate?
   a. In Europe.   b. In the United States.
   c. At a funeral.   d. On a baseball field.

2. Which of the following is NOT mentioned as having an influence on
   jazz music?
   a. New Orleans funeral processions.
   b. Spiritual songs.
   c. European classical music.
   d. Blues music.

3. What is the reason given for jazz being difficult to define?
   a. An important part of jazz is improvisation.
   b. No one knows the origins of the word "jazz."
   c. Jazz originated a long time ago.
   d. Jazz has many different influences.

trombone

4. When the word "jazz" first appeared in print, it was describing
   _____.
   a. the music of Chicago
   b. the African-American community
   c. a famous composer
   d. a baseball player's pitch

5. Which of the following is NOT true about jazz?
   a. A jazz song develops from the performers' interactions
      with each other.
   b. The basic instruments of jazz are those of a marching band.
   c. Bebop and swing are subgenres of jazz.
   d. Jazz music has many strict rules and restrictions.

Every author has a goal in mind when he or she writes something. Sometimes the purpose is to entertain readers with a funny or sad story. Other times the goal is to inform readers about a topic that is important to the author. There is always a clue to help us discover the author's purpose, goal, and that is the tone of his or her writing.

⌃ official logo of Comic-Con
(cc by Gage Skidmore)

16 Comic-Con, the Greatest Convention on Earth

1   For most people, summer means swimming, picnics, camping, and maybe a hike in the mountains. But not me. When temperatures start to rise, I'm thinking about one thing and one thing only: Comic-Con.

2   San Diego Comic-Con is an annual, three-day comic and pop culture convention. For someone like myself who collects things, it's the greatest show on earth. There are booths selling anything you could imagine: comics, anime, card games, toys, and movie gear. You can also wait in line to get an autograph from your favorite artist, author, or movie star. And if you run out of money (which often happens), you can take in a celebrity discussion panel. As if that wasn't enough, Comic-Con is also when most of the year's hottest movie trailers are released.

5

10

≫ the San Diego Convention Center, location of the San Diego Comic-Con

3   Back when I started going to Comic-Con, it was still flying under the radar. I remember attending the eighth annual Comic-Con in 1978. It wasn't even very crowded, and everyone was an outsider or a hardcore fan like me.

4   Nowadays, Comic-Con is a very big deal! This year, over 135,000 people attended, enough to make it the largest comic and pop culture festival in the world. The convention pumps around $140 million into the local economy every year. And it's not just the hardcore fans coming anymore. Comic-Con is a mainstream event now, and you never know who you'll run into waiting in line. It could be your high school soccer coach, or even your own grandmother!

5   Some of my old Comic-Con friends don't like this new era. They complain about how the convention has "sold out" to the masses. They whine about it not being what it used to be. Well, I say: "the more, the merrier!" Comic-Con has always been about bringing people together to enjoy their shared hobbies. So, I hope to see you all at next year's Comic-Con!

« crowds packing the walkway outside the 2016 San Diego Comic-Con

« cosplayers at the 2013 San Diego Comic-Con
(cc by Heng Ung)

Questions

_____ **1.** What is the author's purpose in this passage?
    a. To describe an event.   **b.** To warn about danger.
    c. To offer a solution.   **d.** To state a problem.

_____ **2.** What is the author's tone in the first paragraph?
    a. Hopeful.   **b.** Tragic.   **c.** Serious.   **d.** Playful.

_____ **3.** What's the author's purpose in the third paragraph?
    a. To suggest a different course of action.
    b. To tell a personal story.
    c. To tell a joke.
    d. To offer a solution to a problem.

_____ **4.** What's the author's tone about his friends' opinions in the final paragraph?
    a. Critical.   **b.** Sad.   **c.** Objective.   **d.** Grim.

_____ **5.** What's the author's purpose in the fourth paragraph?
    a. To shock the reader.   **b.** To provide background details.
    c. To warn about danger.   **d.** To describe a problem.

17 | Tasmania

1   Tasmania is a large island located about 240 kilometers to the south of Australia.

2   It is 364 kilometers long from its northernmost point to its southernmost point, and about 306 kilometers long from west to east. Tasmania is also a state within Australia, and it includes the island of Tasmania and other surrounding islands.

3   What else is there to know about Tasmania? A whole bunch! The island got its distinctive name from the Dutch explorer Abel Tasman, who first discovered the island on November 24, 1642. As for life in Tasmania, well for one it certainly isn't very crowded. Only about 526,700 people call Tasmania their home as of 2018, and approximately 225,000 of them live in the capital city of Hobart.

4   The weather might be one reason why there are so few people living in Tasmania. Summer in Tasmania lasts from December to February, and winter lasts from June to August. However, Tasmania's weather can change very abruptly. One day you might be sipping mango juice in 40-degree heat, and a few short days later the weather is cold enough to freeze the juice in your glass.

5   Tasmania has earned the nickname the Natural State because it has so much uninhabited space. In total, about 45% of the island has been set aside for nature reserves. These reserves are home to several unique types of plants and animals, some of which can't be found anywhere else in the world. One such animal is the Tasmanian devil. This small, doglike creature is known for having a bad temper. Tasmania is also home to 11 of Australia's 211 native frog species, and three of them are restricted to the state: the Tasmanian tree frog, the Tasmanian froglet, and the moss froglet.

6   Tourists know a good thing when they see it, and they've been flooding into Tasmania in recent years. Where else in the world can you watch the Sydney to Hobart Yacht Race in the morning and get bitten by a wallaby in the afternoon?

⌄ Tasmanian froglet (cc by Tnarg 12345)

⌃ Tasmanian tree frog (cc by Tnarg 12345)

5

10

15

20

25

30

35

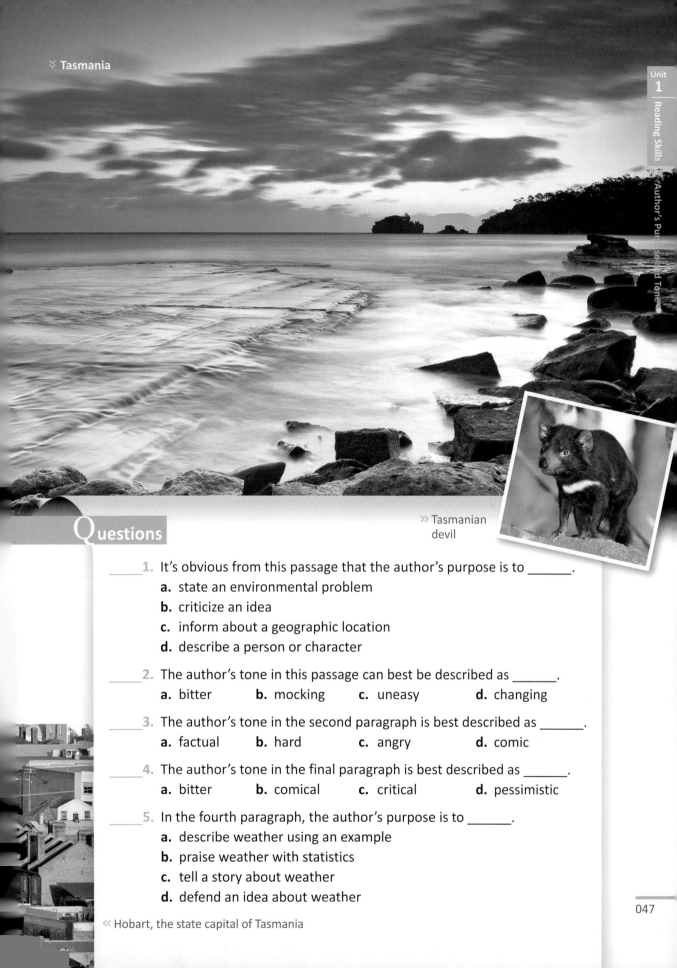

>> Tasmanian
devil

Questions

_____ 1. It's obvious from this passage that the author's purpose is to _____.
 a. state an environmental problem
 b. criticize an idea
 c. inform about a geographic location
 d. describe a person or character

_____ 2. The author's tone in this passage can best be described as _____.
 a. bitter **b.** mocking **c.** uneasy **d.** changing

_____ 3. The author's tone in the second paragraph is best described as _____.
 a. factual **b.** hard **c.** angry **d.** comic

_____ 4. The author's tone in the final paragraph is best described as _____.
 a. bitter **b.** comical **c.** critical **d.** pessimistic

_____ 5. In the fourth paragraph, the author's purpose is to _____.
 a. describe weather using an example
 b. praise weather with statistics
 c. tell a story about weather
 d. defend an idea about weather

« Hobart, the state capital of Tasmania

018 18 | The World's Fastest Train

1   Over the past few decades, train speeds have been steadily increasing. Many trains today can travel faster than helicopters, and some can even go faster than small airplanes. Countries have taken advantage of these technological advances and built high-speed railways in order to transport people and goods between major cities.   5

2   According to the International Union of Railways (UIC), a high-speed train is one that travels at a speed of over 200 kilometers per hour. Most high-speed trains travel at speeds ranging between 250 and 300 kilometers per hour. They were originally introduced to win back travelers who were switching over to airplanes. Nowadays,   10 high-speed train networks can be quite expensive to build, but once complete they can make a big contribution to a country's economic development. In fact, high-speed trains are thought to be more energy efficient and less damaging to the environment than using cars and highways to move people around.   15

3   The very first modern high-speed rail line was built in Japan in 1964, just in time for the Tokyo Olympics. It was called the Tōkaidō Shinkansen, and it linked Tokyo and Osaka. The train was capable of reaching speeds of over 256 kilometers per hour. Then in 1977, Europe got its very first high-speed train in Italy, connecting Rome

⌃ Tōkaidō Shinkansen

▽ Transrapid series 09 vehicle at the Emsland Test Facility, Germany

△ the fastest train of all, JR Central L0 series maglev train, on the Yamanashi test track (cc by Maryland GovPics)

and Florence. Since then, high-speed rail networks have continued to expand across Europe and Asia, though they are still not popular in North America.

4   It's almost like new high-speed train world records are made to be broken. In 1996, Japan's Shinkansen set a new speed record of 443 kilometers per hour. In 2003, the German Transrapid train left the Shinkansen in the dust, hitting speeds of over 500 kilometers per hour. Transrapid didn't have very long to enjoy its victory. In 2007, the French company TGV stole away the crown for fastest high-speed train when it achieved staggering speeds of 574.8 kilometers per hour. Yet the fastest train of all is the Japan Railways maglev train, which uses magnetic levitation to float above the rails. This train has hit speeds of up to 603 kilometers per hour.

△ the Taiwanese HSR, derived from Shinkansen

25

30

Questions

_____ 1. It's obvious from this passage that the author's purpose is to _____.
- **a.** inform about an invention
- **b.** state a problem
- **c.** offer a solution
- **d.** describe a person or character

_____ 2. In the final paragraph, the author's purpose is to _____.
- **a.** criticize an idea
- **b.** persuade the reader
- **c.** evaluate a problem
- **d.** describe a series of events

_____ 3. The tone in the final paragraph can best be described as _____.
- **a.** grim
- **b.** tragic
- **c.** playful
- **d.** cruel

_____ 4. The author's tone in this passage can best be described as _____.
- **a.** objective
- **b.** absurd
- **c.** arrogant
- **d.** ironic

_____ 5. The tone in the third paragraph is best described as _____.
- **a.** uneasy
- **b.** evasive
- **c.** loving
- **d.** formal

19 | World War I

▼ World War I

1   World War I broke out in 1914, and it was the first global war in human history. It had produced more than 40 million casualties by the time it ended in 1918; this included 21 million wounded and 20 million killed. Over 60 million European soldiers participated in the war.

2   The war resulted from changes in the balance of power in Europe. Germany became a unified country in 1871, and its expanding power began to threaten established European powers such as Great Britain, France, and Russia. When an assassination in Bosnia forced Russia to come to the assistance of one of its allies, the Central Powers (Germany and Austria-Hungary) declared war on the Entente Powers (France, Britain, and Russia) and World War I erupted.

3   Within weeks, most European countries had entered the war. Italy joined the Entente Powers' side in 1915, and then the United States joined in 1917. On the side of the Central Powers, the Ottoman Empire entered in 1914, followed by Bulgaria in 1915.

▼ Italian and Austro-Hungarian army in WWI

4   "World War I," "The Great War," "The War to End Wars"— no matter what name it goes by, it was a horrible conflict. At the start of the war, military tactics had not evolved to include new inventions like heavy artillery and the machine gun. The end result was trench

>> Bulgarian soldiers in a trench in World War I

∨ Russian troops in a trench in World War I (1917)

warfare, where both sides dug long trenches that were often only a few hundred meters apart. Soldiers spent months in the trenches, suffering from disease, rats, lice in their hair, and rotten food. They lived like this until their commanding officer announced that it was time to attack the enemy trench. Then they would climb out and charge into "no man's land," stepping on land mines and getting tangled up in barbed wire, all while being shot at by enemy machine guns.

Eventually, new inventions such as tanks and airplanes helped to break the stalemate of trench warfare, and World War I came to an end in 1918. Although the Entente Powers won the war, they lost the peace. It would only be 20 short years before the outbreak of World War II.

Questions

_____ 1. It's obvious from this passage that the author's purpose is to _____.
   a. describe a person or character   **b.** state a problem
   c. offer a solution   **d.** inform about a historical event

_____ 2. The author's tone in the second paragraph can best be described as _____.
   a. objective   **b.** joyous   **c.** playful   **d.** wondering

_____ 3. The author's purpose in the fourth paragraph is to _____.
   a. evaluate a problem   **b.** describe a situation
   c. criticize a person   **d.** persuade the reader

_____ 4. The author's tone in the fourth paragraph can best be described as _____.
   a. suspicious   **b.** cruel   **c.** grim   **d.** loving

_____ 5. The author's tone in the final paragraph can best be described as _____.
   a. critical   **b.** sensational   **c.** wondering   **d.** comic

20 The Grand Canyon

1 The Grand Canyon is one of the biggest and deepest canyons in the world. Its size, along with being easily accessible to visitors, has made it one of the most popular tourist attractions in the United States.

2 The Grand Canyon is well known for its beautiful and colorful landscape, and every year it draws about five million visitors, 17% of whom are from outside the United States. The canyon is the result of the Colorado River cutting a channel through massive rocks over a period of six million years. The canyon we see today is 446 kilometers long, between 6.4 and 29 kilometers wide, and about 1.86 kilometers deep.

3 The walls of the canyon record the many millions of years that it took the Colorado River to slowly gnaw its way through the rocks. To a geologist, these walls contain valuable details about the many different eras in our planet's history. To a tourist, they're just plain beautiful and make for an unforgettable photograph opportunity.

4 The first European to view the Grand Canyon was the Spaniard García López de Cárdenas in 1540. Back then, it was inhabited by Native American tribes that believed the canyon was a holy place. Nowadays, it's part of the Grand Canyon National Park, which is one of the oldest parks in the United States. The park covers 4,926 square kilometers, most of which is in the state of Arizona. Park headquarters can be found at the Grand Canyon Village, where most of the popular scenic viewpoints are also located.

⌄ bighorn ewe at the Grand Canyon

<< the Grand Canyon National Park

5   There are many activities that visitors to the canyon can enjoy,   25 including whitewater rafting and helicopter or airplane tours. Visitors who want to enjoy a more leisurely view of the canyon can take the Coconino Canyon Train. The park also completed the installation of a new glass walkway—the Grand Canyon Skywalk in 2007, which extends beyond the edge of the Grand Canyon.   30

6   One thing that no tourist should do at Grand Canyon National Park is approach or feed the wild animals. It's not only illegal but also dangerous because it can change an animal's habits and lead to attacks on humans.

Questions

1. It's obvious from this passage that the author's purpose is to _____.
   - **a.** tell a personal story
   - **b.** inform about a certain location
   - **c.** criticize an idea
   - **d.** evaluate a problem

2. The tone in the third paragraph can best be described as _____.
   - **a.** disapproving
   - **b.** tragic
   - **c.** cruel
   - **d.** admiring

3. The author's tone in the final paragraph can best be described as _____.
   - **a.** stern
   - **b.** cheerful
   - **c.** angry
   - **d.** gentle

4. In the final paragraph, the author's purpose is to _____.
   - **a.** anger the reader
   - **b.** entertain the reader
   - **c.** puzzle the reader
   - **d.** warn the reader

5. The author's tone in the fourth paragraph can best be described as _____.
   - **a.** angry
   - **b.** objective
   - **c.** comic
   - **d.** joyous

<< The Grand Canyon Skywalk at Eagle Point is a popular attraction at the Grand Canyon. (cc by Purple)

1-5 Cause and Effect

Everything happens for a reason. Are you tired today? Maybe you shouldn't have stayed up late last night. Hungry? Then you haven't eaten enough. Identifying causes and effects in a passage can help us organize information in a logical way, so we can better understand it.

21 | When Cats Met Humans

1 When people think of house cats, a couple of words come to mind: "cute," "cuddly," and "proud," to name a few. However, one word that doesn't usually come up is "obedient." Isn't that a bit strange given the fact humans have kept cats as pets for over 9,000 years?

2 Without any reliable historical records to go on, we can only guess at how humans and cats were originally brought together. Most historians believe that cats were one of the last animals to be tamed and kept as pets in early human settlements in the Middle East. They were tamed after other, more useful animals like cows, dogs, pigs, and sheep. After all, it's not like a house cat can pull a plow, produce delicious milk, or protect a settlement from bandits.

3 There are some other things that cats are very good at, like killing mice and other vermin. According to some researchers, this might be how cats and humans originally became friends. When early humans began farming for food, their grain stores were a big target for hungry mice. Wild cats weren't going to let their prey escape, so they followed the mice right into human villages. As time went on, cats got used to living near humans. Eventually, the wild cat of 9,000 years ago became the house cat of today.

>> Humans have kept cats as pets for over 9,000 years.

4 This explanation of how cats became domesticated is fascinating because it explains why house cats are still so independent. Unlike dogs, cats seem like they could ditch their human masters and 25 return to the wild at any moment. Their natural abilities haven't disappeared: their excellent night vision and hearing, their sense of smell, and their agility are all still there.

5 House cats are also still able to hunt for their own food. Some owners may even occasionally wake up to see little gifts from their 30 cat, like dead birds, rats, or squirrels. This sort of thing doesn't seem to bother us too much, since there are now more than 600 million cats living in homes around the world.

>> Cats are good at catching mice.

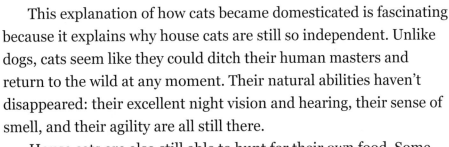

Questions

_____ 1. According to the article, which of the following caused cats and humans to come together?
   a. A religious belief that cats are magical.
   b. Cats' ability to produce delicious milk.
   c. Cats' natural abilities of night vision.
   d. Mice raiding early human grain stores.

_____ 2. Why were cats tamed after other animals such as dogs, pigs, and cows?
   a. Cats were not thought of as useful as the other animals.
   b. Cats weren't discovered until much later.
   c. Cats were considered to be very dangerous.
   d. Cats carried various diseases.

_____ 3. Since cats still have their natural abilities, they are able to _____.
   a. sleep   **b.** hunt   **c.** smell   **d.** exist

_____ 4. Cats lived with humans for a long time, so they _____.
   a. eventually became pets   **b.** spread diseases to humans
   c. learned to live with dogs   **d.** lost their night vision

_____ 5. Why can no one be certain about how cats became pets?
   a. The historical records are full of contradictions.
   b. The historical records have been lost.
   c. The historical records cannot be translated.
   d. There are no historical records.

22 | The Nile River

1   Measuring in at almost 6,853 kilometers in length, the Nile is the longest river in the world.

2   Most people associate the Nile with Egypt, but in fact, only about 22% of the river can be found there. Perhaps this association came from the ancient Egyptians. After all, one of the world's oldest civilizations began on the banks of the Nile. The ancient Egyptians relied heavily on water from the Nile for their food. Every year between June and September, the Nile would flood. The flood produced a thick layer of black silt that was ideal for growing crops. These annual floods carried on for thousands of years until 1970, when the Egyptian government completed the Aswan Dam.

3   The Nile also provided a valuable mode of transportation for trading with other civilizations, from Europe to Southwest Asia. It helped Egypt turn into a trading center that brought the entire ancient world together.

4   The Nile River has two major tributaries: the White Nile and the Blue Nile. The White Nile got its name from the white clay that flows in its waters. It starts at Lake Victoria in central Africa. The Blue Nile, on the other hand, starts at Lake Tana in Ethiopia, and it joins the White Nile near the Sudanese capital of Khartoum. The Blue Nile is very important for Egyptians because it accounts for 56% of the Nile water that flows northward through Egypt and into the Mediterranean Sea.

5   The Nile is still a fundamental part of life in Egypt. The river accounts for almost all of Egypt's drinking water. It also provides the water needed to grow food. But Egypt may be facing water shortages in the near future. Egypt's

the Nile River

5

10

15

20

25

population is projected to grow over the next few decades, which will increase the demand for Nile River water. Demand will also increase in the countries where the Nile's tributaries are located, including Ethiopia and Burundi. To remedy the problem, the Egyptian government is planning to renovate the Aswan Dam and increase its water efficiency. It's also encouraging people to move inland and away from the Nile in order to reduce crowding. 30 35

Questions

_____ 1. What was the cause that helped the Nile turn ancient Egypt into a global trading center?
   a. Nile water was a world famous trade good.
   b. Nile water grew the food needed to feed traders.
   c. The Nile provided a convenient means of transportation.
   d. The Nile helped the Egyptian navy conquer half the world.

_____ 2. Why do Egyptians consider the Blue Nile to be more important than the White Nile?
   a. The Blue Nile has better-tasting water.
   b. The Blue Nile has more water.
   c. The Blue Nile is closer to Egypt.
   d. The Blue Nile is a longer tributary.

_____ 3. Most people associate the Nile with Egypt because _____.
   a. it was an important part of ancient Egyptian life
   b. it starts in Egypt around the Mediterranean Sea
   c. all of the Nile's tributaries start in Egypt
   d. most of the Nile is located in Egypt

_____ 4. According to the article, why is the Nile still an important part of Egyptian life?
   a. Because it is a primary source of drinking water.
   b. Because it has military significance.
   c. Because it provides Egyptians with a place to swim.
   d. Because it produces all of Egypt's energy.

_____ 5. Concern about overpopulation on the banks of the Nile has produced which of the following effects?
   a. A new capital city is being built in the desert.
   b. The government wants people to move inland.
   c. Access to the Nile is now restricted.
   d. Egypt has given up on farming.

≪ Aswan Dam

≪ The Nile passes through Cairo, Egypt's capital city. (cc by Raduasandei and Arad)

23 | The Power of Positive Thinking

023

1   There is a glass on the table, filled up halfway with water. How would you describe the glass: half empty or half full? If your answer was "half full," then prepare yourself for an exciting life in which anything is possible. If you said "half empty" on the other hand, you might just be in for a life of failure and sorrow. It may sound crazy, but that's the mysterious power of positive thinking!

2   Experts believe that positive thinking has several important benefits. First off, it can make us feel happy about our life. If someone focuses on all of the good things that they have, he is much less likely to feel bad about his life. Compare that to someone who's always complaining and dwelling on the negative side of any situation. The positive thinker will generally be the happier of the two.

3   Positive thinking can also improve our health. Several studies have shown that human biology is linked with psychology. One study in particular revealed that wounds take longer to heal for people who are exposed to depressing situations in their job. It has also been proven that people who are highly stressed are more susceptible to catching a cold and the flu.

4   Some people even believe that positive thinking can affect the world around us. In the 2006 book *The Secret*, author Rhonda Byrne

describes a "law of attraction." This law is based on the notion that positive thinking attracts positive things, and negative thinking attracts negative things. Thus, if you think about a new sports car, you might just get one. But whatever you do, try not to think about being taken hostage at the bank!

5 Positive thinking may improve our minds, bodies, and even the universe around us, but how do we get started? According to Richard Wiseman, a former magician turned professor of psychology, the best way to change how we think is to change our behavior. He believes that if someone practices smiling every day, he or she will think happier thoughts.

« If someone practices smiling every day, he or she will think happier thoughts.

Questions

_____ 1. In the sentence "This law is based on the notion that positive thinking attracts positive things," what is the effect?
   a. The law.
   b. Positive things being attracted.
   c. Positive thinking.
   d. Being based on a principle.

_____ 2. According to the article, a person who always thinks about losing his or her job might _____.
   a. have a higher resistance to the flu
   b. attract negative energy from other people
   c. actually lose his or her job one day
   d. start to feel happier about his or her life

_____ 3. If people want to change the way they think, they should first change _____.
   a. their behavior
   b. their appearance
   c. their friends
   d. their job

_____ 4. According to the article, a person who has a very depressing job might _____.
   a. be the best kind of positive thinker
   b. suffer from health problems
   c. eat more than other people
   d. be breaking the law of attraction

_____ 5. According to the article, people who practice smiling every day will _____.
   a. be happy   b. be successful   c. be healthy   d. be tired

⌄ People highly stressed are more liable to catch colds.

⌃ young
orangutan

(024)

24
Orangutans

1   Orangutans are a species of ape native to the rain forests of Indonesia and Malaysia. They are large and intelligent, and their bodies are covered with a distinctive reddish-brown hair that helps them blend in with their surroundings. Orangutans are known for their long arms, which are about twice as long as their legs. Their arms came to be this long because of evolution. After all, the average orangutan spends around 90% of its time swinging in the trees.

2   Orangutans live for about 35 years in the wild and spend their first 10 years with their mothers. Some researchers believe that orangutans remain with their mothers so long because there are so many survival skills that they must learn before they can function on their own.

Female orangutans give birth once every eight years, which is the longest period between births of any mammal. Females can weigh up to 50 kilograms, and males sometimes weigh over 100 kilograms. Orangutans are the most solitary of the great apes, and males and females come together only to mate. Males have large throat sacs that they use to make loud mating calls to females. These calls can also serve to warn off any nearby males.

⌃ Orangutans are the least social of the great apes, but individuals do commonly interact.(Wikipedia)

3   Orangutans are very intelligent, and they are considered to be the smartest primate apart from humans. Adult orangutans are able to teach their young how to make tools and find food. Their learning abilities and problem-solving skills are even better than chimpanzees, which are the closet living relatives to humans.

4   Orangutans spend most of their time looking for food. While fruit makes up 65% of their diet, they will also eat leaves, shoots, seeds, bark, insects, and bird eggs. Sometimes, an adult orangutan will build a small nest high up in the trees for a place to sleep.

5

10

15

20

25

30

» Captive orangutans may use objects in creative ways.
(cc by Postdlf)

5   There are only about 78,500 orangutans left in the wild, and some believe that

35 orangutans could disappear within the next decade. The orangutan's habitat is being threatened by deforestation, mining, forest fires, poachers, farming, and the illegal trade

40 of wild animals. Orangutan populations are particularly threatened because of these animals' slow rate of reproduction. The fewer orangutans there are in the wild, the harder it will be to save this fascinating species.

Questions

_____ 1. Orangutans have been known to build nests in the trees because _____.
    a. they need a place to reproduce   **b.** they need a place to sleep
    c. they need a place to eat   **d.** they need a place to die

_____ 2. It's hard to see an orangutan in the jungle because _____.
    a. its hair blends into the surroundings
    b. it only moves around at night
    c. it spends a lot of its time underground
    d. it sleeps under leaves 65% of the time

_____ 3. The orangutan is currently under threat because _____.
    a. a disease is wiping orangutans out
    b. human activity is destroying orangutan habitats
    c. its primary source of food is disappearing
    d. there is no forest material for making nests

» Fruit is the most important part of orangutans' diet.

_____ 4. A young orangutan has much to learn before it can survive on its own, so _____.
    a. it always travels with other orangutans
    b. it hides for the first five years of its life
    c. it relies on its father to find food
    d. it remains with its mother for a long time

_____ 5. Orangutans spend most of their time in the trees, so _____.
    a. they get more sunlight than any other animal
    b. their arms have evolved to be quite long
    c. their diet has become 65% tree bark
    d. they have no use for hunting tools

25 Can Jogging Change the World?

1   There's a group of joggers who are determined to get our planet back into shape. Whenever they come across a plastic bottle or wrapper during a run, they stop to pick it up. Their aim is to clean up the environment and get a great workout in the process.

5 2   These people are called "ploggers." The term is a combination of "jogger" and the Swedish word "plocka upp," which means "pick up." The plogging movement began in Sweden when a concerned citizen named Erik Ahlström started a website called Plogga. The website sought out volunteers to participate in group plogs in and around Stockholm. Since then, plogging
10 has been spreading far and wide. There are now plogging clubs in Norway, Finland, Germany, and the United States. Social media has been key in the global growth of plogging. No matter where you're from, there's probably a Facebook group for
15 ploggers in your country.

>> a triumphant plogger

3   Plogging has proved popular for a variety of reasons. Most important of all is that it lets people feel like they're actually making a difference. It's easy to feel powerless in
20 the face of massive environmental issues like global warming. However, litter is a local issue, and it's one where we can all make a noticeable impact. Ploggers are proud of the amount of trash that they
25 remove from public parks and spaces. Try searching for "plogging" on social

>> Ploggers are proud of the amount of trash that they remove from public spaces.

media. You'll find triumphant pictures posted by ploggers around the world of their latest trash haul.

4   Plogging has fitness benefits as well. Bending over to pick up trash
30 works out muscles that you wouldn't otherwise use when jogging. Repeating these motions can turn jogging into a full-body workout. Plogging is also a good reason for inactive people to get outside and get moving. After all, who doesn't want to help clean up where
35 they live?

>> Plogging lets people feel like they're making a difference.

Questions

1. What is the effect of bending over to pick up trash while out on a jog?
   a. It can make you less tired.
   b. It works out different muscles.
   c. It helps reduce global warming.
   d. It makes you proud of where you live.

2. Why do people feel powerless in the face of global warming?
   a. It is such an old problem.
   b. It is such a dangerous problem.
   c. It is such a massive problem.
   d. It is such a depressing problem.

3. What caused plogging to spread around the world?
   a. Social media.
   b. Global warming.
   c. The environment.
   d. Norway.

4. What was the effect of Erik Ahlström starting the Plogga website?
   a. People stopped caring about the environment.
   b. Litter became the top environmental concern.
   c. The worldwide plogging movement was born.
   d. A Facebook group was created for plogging.

5. Why do ploggers often post pictures on social media?
   a. Because they want people to get in shape.
   b. Because they're proud of the amount of trash they've cleaned up.
   c. Because they earn money from the Plogga website.
   d. Because they want more followers from Sweden.

1-6 Clarifying Devices

Clarifying devices are important tools for any author. They can include the overall structure of an article and particular words that help to guide a reader along a certain path. Clarifying devices can often help answer the question "Is this article a timeline, biography, or narrative story?"

>> Ragnarok

(026)

26
Norse Mythology

1   Hundreds of years ago, a powerful race of tall, blonde Scandinavian warriors swept through northern Europe like wildfire. They were sometimes called Norsemen, Northmen, or Normans, but most people know them as Vikings. They raided and eventually settled down on the coasts of Europe during the ninth and 10th centuries. Their culture was rooted in a rich and fascinating mythology that attempted to make sense of the world around them.

2   Norse mythology contains nine worlds, and it is based around gods that are called the Aesir. Just like the Vikings themselves, these gods are proud and violent warriors. They live in a heaven-like realm called Asgard. According to the legends, the gods eat, drink, and fight one another while they wait for the approach of Ragnarok. The word Ragnarok means "doom of the gods." When Ragnarok arrives, the gods will be forced to do battle with giants, and several major gods will be destroyed. Ultimately, the world will be submerged in water so that new life can rise up from the destruction.

3   This legend is one of the reasons why Norse mythology is more interesting than the mythology of any other ancient culture.

5

10

15

⌄ Scandinavian warrior

20 The Norse gods knew that they were doomed, but they accepted their fate and tried to live an honorable life. In a sense, these gods are very similar to humans. They also frequently display other human character traits, such as jealousy, anger, lust, and greed. All Norse mythology deals with important issues that are still relevant to this day.

25 **4** Another interesting fact about Norse mythology is that it took hundreds of years for it finally to be written down. Up until then, it was passed down orally from generation to generation. This allowed the stories to grow and adapt alongside Scandinavian culture, capturing all of the bitterly cold,

30 constant migrations, and the Viking's warrior code.

5 If you ever find yourself bored and wanting to read about gods that are just like us humans, then you should pick up a copy of the *Prose Edda*. It's a good place to start your journey through

35 Scandinavian history!

>> title page of a manuscript of the *Prose Edda*

≪ Aesir

Questions

_____ 1. This article can best be described as _____.

    a. a timeline   **b.** a personal story

    c. a descriptive essay   **d.** a biography

_____ 2. In the final paragraph, the author captures the reader's attention by _____.

    a. offering advice   **b.** telling a personal story

    c. offering a biased opinion   **d.** warning the reader

_____ 3. The first sentence of the passage, "Hundreds of years ago . . . Scandinavian warriors swept through northern Europe like wildfire," is an example of a(n) _____.

    a. explanation   **b.** simile   **c.** opinion   **d.** statistic

_____ 4. In the first sentence of the third paragraph, "This legend is one of the reasons why Norse mythology . . .," the author captures the reader's attention by using a(n) _____.

    a. metaphor   **b.** personal story

    c. interesting fact   **d.** biased opinion

_____ 5. The final sentence of the third paragraph, "All Norse mythology deals with important issues . . ." is an example of a(n) _____.

    a. statistic   **b.** warning

    c. generalization   **d.** piece of advice

27 Slipper Culture: A Practical Tradition

1   The thought of wearing shoes inside your house probably disgusts you. Imagine all the dirt, garbage, and dog poop on the streets being brought into each room in your house as you walk around! 5
You certainly wouldn't wear shoes inside your friends' houses either. It would be rude to bring dirt and germs into their house. Surprisingly, taking shoes off inside a house is not a universal custom.

2   China, Taiwan, Korea, and Japan are **among** the countries where it is polite to take off shoes before stepping inside a home. The tradition of 10 removing shoes outside houses is over a thousand years old! This tradition seems to have started for different reasons. In Japan, floors in houses had *tatami* mats where people slept and ate. In order to keep these mats clean, people wore slippers inside but took them off before stepping onto the *tatami*. In Korea, houses were heated using *ondol*, or pipes filled with 15 hot water under the floor. Wearing slippers instead of shoes would allow people to feel the heat and stay warm. Both *tatami* and *ondol* are still used in Japanese and Korean houses today, helping the custom of removing shoes to continue.

3   Going shoeless inside is not only a practical way to keep your house 20 clean. The custom has also come to symbolize respect. In Korea and Japan, both students and teachers show their respect for their schools by taking off their shoes and wearing slippers. Students and teachers take their shoes

⌃ Japanese elementary school students taking out their slippers from a locker

⌃ In Korea, houses were heated with *ondol*.
(cc by 四葉亭四迷)

« Shoe cabinets inside a house could be a shoes-off sign. (cc by Bonsoni.com)

off at the school door and put on slippers. Then they carry their shoes to the special shelves outside their classroom. 25

4 So how can you tell if you need to take your shoes off before entering someone's house? You can look for clues. There might be shoes sitting outside the door of the house. Another sign would be a row of shoes or shoe cabinets inside the house. Lastly, your host will probably be ready 30 with a pair of slippers for you as they welcome you inside.

Questions

_____ 1. How does the author grab the reader's attention in the first paragraph?
    a. Statistics.   **b.** Personal Story.   **c.** Emotional Appeal.   **d.** Quotation.

_____ 2. Why does the author use **among** in the second paragraph?
    a. To show that there are more countries which follow the custom of removing shoes before entering a home.
    b. To explain that these countries started the custom of removing shoes before entering a home.
    c. To make it clear that only these countries follow the custom of removing shoes before entering a home.
    d. To tell readers that these countries are located near each other.

_____ 3. In the second paragraph, what does the author use to explain the origins of removing shoes inside?
    a. Humor.   **b.** Statistics.   **c.** Opinions.   **d.** Facts.

_____ 4. How is the information in this article presented?
    a. In chronological order.   **b.** By topic.
    c. In order of importance.   **d.** By country.

_____ 5. What type of information is given to readers in the last paragraph?
    a. Facts.   **b.** Personal story.   **c.** Biased opinion.   **d.** Advice.

» In Japan, people take off their slippers before stepping onto the *tatami*.

28
Honey Badger

>> honey badger eating

<< porcupine

1   What is the one animal you would want on your side in a fight? You probably picked a lion, a tiger, or a rhino, right? If so, you just overlooked one of the world's toughest mammals: the honey badger. Sure, it doesn't have a very dangerous-sounding name, but this animal lives for two things: fights and honey. 5

2   Honey badgers are sometimes called "ratels," and they can be found throughout Africa and southern Asia. They have a well-deserved reputation for being one of the most fearless animals in the world, and they are excellent predators. Stories are often told of honey badgers attacking animals much larger than themselves. Some of 10 these stories even describe honey badgers driving lions away from the big cats' prey and stealing a meal from the king of the jungle.

^ scorpion

<< tortoise

3   Honey badgers are very good at hunting snakes, and they can kill and eat a snake that is longer than their own body in less than 15 minutes. They also eat earthworms, scorpions, hares, porcupines, 15 tortoises, and even crocodiles, but of course, honey is one of their preferred foods. A honey badger can withstand hundreds of bee stings while scooping the honey out of a beehive. Sometimes, however, the honey badger **pays the ultimate price** for its meal. Honey badgers have been found stung to death next to a beehive. 20

<< Honey badgers eat mostly meat.

4   Honey badgers are about 67 to 107 centimeters in length and can weigh up to 16 kilograms. A female honey badger will have one cub at a time, and she spends about 14 months raising her cub. A cub depends on its mother for food and shelter. Since cubs can hinder their mother's hunting, they are generally left behind in the den, 25 where they may be attacked and gobbled up by other honey badgers. As disgusting as this is, it stands as yet another reason why honey badgers are the toughest and most ferocious animals in the world.

5   The world has begun to notice the honey badger's 30 impressive talent. In 2011, a popular YouTube video created an Internet sensation with the phrase "Honey badger don't care." Now honey badgers appear on T-shirts, cups, and mouse pads the world over.

honey badger

>> skeleton of a
honey badger

Questions

___ 1. In the first paragraph, the author tries to stimulate the reader's interest by _____.
   a. directly addressing the reader
   b. presenting some statistics
   c. stating one clear fact
   d. creating a metaphor

___ 2. In the final paragraph, quotation marks are used to show _____.
   a. a word being used in an unusual way
   b. a direct quote from an outside source
   c. a line of speech in the main story
   d. a complex term

>> hare

___ 3. In the final sentence of the fourth paragraph, "As disgusting as this is . . . honey badgers are the toughest and most ferocious animals in the world," the author captures the reader's attention using a _____.
   a. biased opinion   b. personal story
   c. metaphor   d. statistic

___ 4. This passage can best be described as a _____.
   a. timeline   b. biography
   c. descriptive essay   d. set of instructions

___ 5. In the third paragraph, **pay the ultimate price** is an example of a _____.
   a. metaphor   b. simile   c. myth   d. joke

069

29 Giacomo Puccini

≫ Giacomo Puccini (1858–1924), c. 1907

1 More than 150 years ago, on a bright and cold day in Tuscany, Albina Magi gave birth to a baby boy. When Michele Puccini, the boy's father, looked at his son for the first time, he felt very proud. Little did he know that this tiny newborn would one day become one of the most important composers in the history of Italian opera.

≫ original 1884 advertisement for *Le Villi*

2 Giacomo Puccini was born into a family that had produced musical directors for the local cathedral for over 100 years. The young Puccini was expected to continue the family tradition, but a **dark cloud** settled over his life when he was still an adolescent. Puccini's father died when the boy was just six years old. Fortunately, the local cathedral took responsibility for educating him and reserved the position of musical director for him when he was old enough.

3 The young Puccini wasn't sure he wanted to follow the path that had been laid out for him. In 1876, he saw a performance of Giuseppe Verdi's *Aida* and became convinced that his destiny was to write operas. After he graduated from school in 1883, he submitted his first completed composition to a local contest for one-act operas. The judges didn't like it at all, but Puccini's friends insisted and even paid some of their own money to organize a public showing. When Puccini's *Le Villi* was finally shown, most of the audience was amazed by its grace and dramatic power. This goes to show that you can't always rely on the opinion of "**experts**."

≫ cover of the libretto for *Tosca*

4 Puccini created a scandal in 1890 when he ran away with a married woman named Elvira Gemignani. Even though they had a confrontational relationship and fought often, the two of them were married in 1904 after Elvira's husband died.

≫ *La Bohème* poster

5   Puccini continued to work until he died from complications 35
arising from throat cancer in 1924. With masterpieces like *La
Bohème*, *Tosca*, and *Madama Butterfly*, Puccini established himself
as a legend of Italian opera. Some people even say that Puccini was
"the greatest composer of Italian opera after Verdi." Given the beauty 40
of all of Puccini's work, it's hard to argue against them.

∨ Geraldine Farrar
in *Madama
Butterfly*, 1907

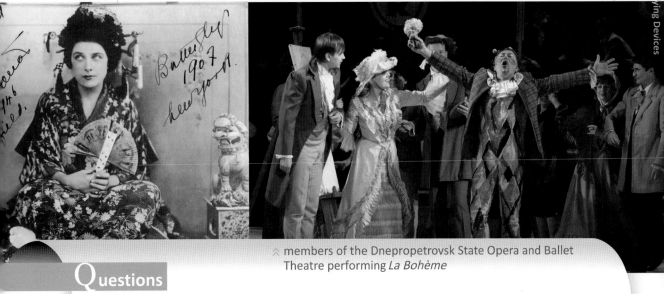

⌃ members of the Dnepropetrovsk State Opera and Ballet
Theatre performing *La Bohème*

Questions

_____ 1. This article can best be described as a(n) _____.
   a. descriptive essay   b. biography
   c. legend   d. ordered list

_____ 2. In the first paragraph, the author captures the reader's attention using
   a _____.
   a. statistic   b. argument   c. joke   d. narrative story

_____ 3. In the final sentence of the third paragraph, the word **experts** appears
   in quotation marks because _____.
   a. the author is quoting an expert opinion
   b. the author disagrees with the normal meaning
   c. the author is speaking directly to the reader
   d. the author is using a technical word

_____ 4. The basic pattern used to develop this passage is _____.
   a. chronological order   b. a personal narrative
   c. comparison and contrast   d. question and answer

_____ 5. In the second paragraph, the **dark cloud** that settles over Puccini's life
   is an example of a _____.
   a. legend   b. metaphor   c. statistic   d. exaggeration

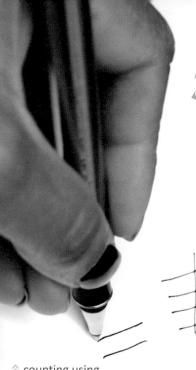

30 The Origin of Numbers

1   A number is defined as an abstract concept that is used for counting and measuring. As for when exactly humans started using these abstract concepts to count, no one is totally sure. It could be around 30000 BC, when our ancestors started making marks on cave walls probably in order to help them count. These are called "tally marks," and they were originally discovered in a cave in South Africa.

2   Tally marks could only go so far. After all, it's impossible for a tally mark to represent large numbers. If early humans had to count to 10,000, they would have to cover their cave in marks. For 100,000, the cave walls would end up looking **black as night** in no time!

3   The solution came around 3400 BC, when the early Mesopotamians invented the first numerical system that could handle large numbers. Mesopotamia is considered to be the earliest human civilization and it is often called the Cradle of Civilization. It was located in an area that is now part of modern-day Iraq. Ancient Mesopotamians farmed and lived in towns and cities. They knew how to make things out of

5

10

15

20

⌃ counting using tally marks

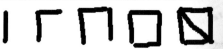

⌃ cultures using Chinese characters tally by forming a character that consists of five strokes

⌃ tally marks used in France, Spain, and South America

⌃ tally marks used in most of Europe, Australia, and North America; typically clustered in groups of five

≫ Mesopotamia is called the Cradle of Civilization.

copper, gold, wood, stone, and bricks. The Mesopotamians needed a way   25
to measure land, canals, buildings, defensive walls, and the seasons, so
they invented a sophisticated counting system based on the number 60.

4　　The first people to invent a counting system based on the number 10,
like the one we use today, were the ancient Egyptians. The Egyptians were
great builders, and they started to use a base-10 number system sometime   30
around 3100 BC.

5　　The Egyptians were the most advanced of all ancient civilizations,
but they always used positive numbers, and they had no concept of zero.
It wasn't until 500 BC in India when zero was first used. The Mayans
in South America also developed the concept of zero for their counting   35
system. By the seventh
century, the concept of zero
had reached Cambodia, and
later spread to China and the
Islamic world.   40

》 numerical system

Questions

_____ 1. This article can best be described as a _____.
    a. timeline   **b.** biography   **c.** narrative story   **d.** ordered list

_____ 2. The second paragraph is developed by the author _____.
    a. giving a personal opinion on ancient Egypt
    b. arguing the importance of numbers
    c. asking and answering questions
    d. describing the concept of tally marks

_____ 3. The first sentence of the fifth paragraph is an example of a _____.
    a. joke   **b.** biased opinion **c.** statistic   **d.** myth

_____ 4. In the final sentence of the second paragraph, **black as night** is an example
    of a _____.
    a. metaphor   **b.** exaggeration   **c.** simile   **d.** fact

_____ 5. In the first paragraph, the author helps develop the concept of numbers by
    _____.
    a. arguing the importance of numbers
    b. listing the civilizations that used numbers
    c. describing the earliest counting method
    d. comparing two different number systems

Often sentences don't have just one simple meaning. The information they give suggests possibilities, opinions, and consequences that are not directly stated on the page. Making inferences means taking a step back from the text and deciding what the words might mean in a wider context.

≫ Gaius Julius Caesar
(100 BC–44 BC)

31 Julius Caesar

031 **1**   During the period of history when Rome was the strongest power in the Western world, Gaius Julius Caesar emerged as an important leader and powerful politician. Caesar was also a great   5 general, and he was instrumental in changing the Roman Republic into the Roman Empire.

⌄ Gaius Julius Caesar changed the Roman Republic into the Roman Empire.

2   Julius Caesar lived from 100 BC to 44 BC. His early life was extremely eventful. When he was just 16 years old, he became the head of his family after his father died. At the age   10 of 17, he became the Flamen Dialis, the high priest of Jupiter. The holder of this position had to not only be a noble himself but also be married to a noble, so he broke off his engagement to a common girl and married the daughter of an important politician. When he was 25, he was captured by pirates but managed to negotiate his way out   15 of trouble and eventually tracked them down and executed them all.

3   In 59 BC, Caesar was elected as consul of Rome, an office similar to that of president. However, the Senate, the most important council of the government in ancient Rome, wanted to limit Caesar's power. Caesar knew that he needed strong political allies, so he   20 made an unofficial partnership with a wealthy and powerful general named Pompey and another well-connected politician named

Crassus. With the help of these two, Caesar managed to
secure substantial power, and after his term as consul,
he became governor of Gaul (present day France and   25
Belgium). Over the next 15 years, Caesar expanded his
power, invading new lands for Rome, and eventually defeated his former
ally Pompey in battle to become the state's absolute ruler.

4   The Senate was dissatisfied with the fact the Caesar was ruling Rome
without them, so in 44 BC, Caesar was lured to a temple and killed by   30
a group of senators who stabbed him 23 times. Those
senators hoped to restore the Republic. However,
Caesar's assassination led to a Roman civil war. As a
result, Rome became a permanent dictatorship and
remained so for centuries.   35

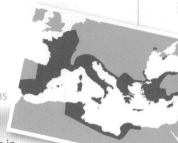

Questions

» the extent of the Roman Republic in
40 BC after Caesar's conquests

____ 1. Which of the following can be inferred from the second paragraph?
   a. Even at a young age, Caesar wanted to gain power.
   b. Caesar was not very good with words.
   c. Caesar came from a common family.
   d. It was Caesar's dream to become a pirate.

____ 2. What is most likely the reason that Caesar chose Pompey and Crassus as allies?
   a. They pressured Caesar into choosing them.
   b. They were friends of Caesar's from childhood.
   c. They could influence the Senate.
   d. The people of Rome voted for them.

____ 3. Which of the following can be inferred from the third paragraph?
   a. Caesar thought invading new lands was not important.
   b. Becoming governor of Gaul was Caesar's ultimate ambition.
   c. The Senate trusted Caesar with a lot of power.
   d. Pompey and Caesar became great enemies.

____ 4. How do you think the senators felt about the civil war that started after Caesar's
   death?
   a. Relieved.   **b.** Frustrated.   **c.** Indifferent.   **d.** Joyful.

____ 5. By doing which of the following could Caesar most likely have avoided being killed?
   a. Allowing the Senate to govern Rome.
   b. Avoiding going to temples.
   c. Having a bigger army.
   d. Being more popular with the common people.

32 Dining Dos and Don'ts

^ table setting following the "outside-in" rule

[1] "Napkin on lap, knife and fork."

[2] My father used to say that before meals to remind my brother and me to prepare ourselves for eating. This meant putting our napkins on our laps, holding our forks in our left hands and our knives in our right. Dad didn't know it, but he had taught us the "continental" style of dining. In the "American" style, the fork is held in the right hand and the knife in the left. We were Americans, but manners are manners.

[3] Ours were informal meals, but many rules of behavior govern even family dinners. When leaving the table temporarily, one should leave one's knife and fork crossed on one's plate. When finished eating, one should place them parallel at the top of the plate with their handles on the right edge of it. As for the napkin, it should be left on your chair if you're coming back to the table. When you've finished, place it to the left of your place setting.

[4] The place setting is made easier by the "outside-in" rule. This means one should use the utensils farthest from one's plate first, working inward as the meal progresses. Consider forks, which are on the left side of one's place setting. The salad fork is to the left of the dinner fork, which is to the left of the dessert fork. Just keep moving to the right with each course and you'll be fine.

[5] But when do you start eating? At informal meals, wait until everyone has been served. If there is a host, however,

5

10

15

20

25

>> pause

>> ready for a second plate

>> finished

>> excellent

>> don't like

^ location of cutlery in different situations

>> Bringing manners back into dining makes it a more social and special activity.

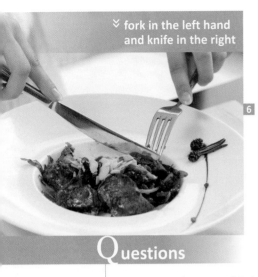

❯ fork in the left hand and knife in the right

you may eat whenever he or she asks you to. Pass dishes to the right, and always ask your fellow diners to pass you whatever you need. It is rude to reach across the table.

6   Obviously, most people don't follow all of these rules, and sadly many people follow almost none of them. Bringing manners back into dining makes it a more social and special activity, as it was for earlier generations. So thanks, Dad; I still start each meal the way you said to.

30

35

Questions

_____ 1. What would the author of this article probably say about table manners?
   a. People worry too much about them.
   b. They're only important on formal occasions.
   c. More people should observe them.
   d. They remind him of his father.

_____ 2. What can be inferred from the second paragraph?
   a. Table manners vary from country to country.
   b. No one knows about table manners anymore.
   c. The author's family is very strange.
   d. You should always hold a fork in your left hand.

_____ 3. Which of the following does the author suggest in the final paragraph?
   a. Rules about dining are becoming popular these days.
   b. He misses his childhood very much.
   c. People today have no respect for anything.
   d. Old people have better table manners than young people.

_____ 4. Which of these would be a mistake at a Western dinner?
   a. Placing your napkin on your chair when you go to the toilet.
   b. Accepting a dish of vegetables from the person on your left.
   c. Using your dessert fork to eat the first course of the meal.
   d. Putting your knife and fork on your plate after you finish eating.

_____ 5. What can be inferred from the fifth paragraph?
   a. You should always wait for your host to start eating before you do.
   b. It's polite to wait for your friends to be served before you eat anything.
   c. Reaching across the table is all right if you're the host of the meal.
   d. You should start eating immediately when your food is served.

^ lift-off SpaceX rocket

33 Fly Me to the Moon

^ Dennis Tito (1940–) *(left)* in the Soyuz 2 Taxi Flight, April 2001

1   Space travel used to be an impossible dream, reserved only for highly trained astronauts in expensive government programs. But that all changed on April 28, 2001. On that day, an American businessman named Dennis Tito became the first tourist to visit space. His trip marked the birth of a new era of space tourism.

2   Six other tourists followed Dennis Tito into space over the next few years. They included South Africa's Mark Shuttleworth and Canada's Guy Laliberté. Like Tito, these tourists rode on a Russian Soyuz rocket and visited the International Space Station (ISS). Their tickets didn't come cheap, costing anywhere from US$20–40 million for a week or two among the stars. But it must have been worth it: one tourist named Charles Simonyi enjoyed it enough to go twice.

3   This early stage of space tourism didn't last very long. In 2009, Russia suspended the tourist flights due to a lack of available seats. Space on Russia's Soyuz rockets was needed for American astronauts after NASA stopped its own space shuttle flights.

4   The year 2009 wasn't the end of space tourism, though. Quite the contrary, it set the stage for bigger and better things. Several companies are now working on their own private spaceships. There's SpaceX, which is owned by Elon Musk. In 2018, the company's Falcon Heavy rocket launched a Tesla car into space during a test flight. Amazon founder Jeff Bezos has also launched a space tourism company called Blue Origin. Its New Shepard ship intends to carry passengers to the edge of space and let them experience weightlessness.

>> White Knight Two and SpaceShipTwo
(middle), 2010 (cc by Jeff Foust)

5   The advance of private space tourism hasn't always gone smoothly. Virgin Galactic was leading the space tourism race until its SpaceShipTwo test vehicle crashed in 2014, killing the co-pilot. The SpaceShipTwo crash serves as a tragic reminder of the high stakes in space travel. But we humans will never get anywhere if we don't take risks. And with a little hard work and luck, we all might just reach the stars someday.

25

30

⌃ the Soyuz MS-01 spacecraft docked to the International Space Station, 2016

Questions

⌄ Charles Simonyi (1948–) *(center)* at the bottom of the Soyuz launch pad before the launch of the Soyuz TMA-14, March 26, 2009

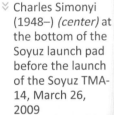

_____ **1.** What can we infer from the second paragraph?
   a. Early space tourists tended to be from one country.
   b. Early space tourists tended to be very wealthy.
   c. Early space tourists tended to be risk-takers.
   d. Early space tourists tended to be young.

_____ **2.** What can we infer from the third paragraph?
   a. Russia and the United States have cooperated in space.
   b. Russia's space program was smaller than the United States'.
   c. Tourists were welcomed by the United States space program.
   d. The United States was investing heavily in space technology.

_____ **3.** What can we infer about Elon Musk in the fourth paragraph?
   a. He may be the CEO of the Tesla car company.
   b. He has run out of money.
   c. He is scared of flying.
   d. He works at Blue Origin.

_____ **4.** What does the author probably think about space tourism?
   a. It's a big waste of money.
   b. It should only be allowed by government space programs.
   c. It's an important step in humanity's development.
   d. It should be slowed down and carefully researched.

_____ **5.** What probably happened after the SpaceShipTwo crash in the final paragraph?
   a. The United States government banned space tourism.
   b. Virgin Galactic lost ground against its competitors.
   c. People around the world lost interest in space travel.
   d. Most companies gave up their plans for space tourism.

Unit **1**

Reading Skills

1-7

Making Inferences

079

34 Old Wives' Tales

1   Old wives' tales are pieces of advice that are supposed to solve common medical or domestic problems. They are usually passed down orally from one generation to the next, and there are only a few cases where they have been written down. Some solutions found in old wives' tales   5 are true, although most have been disproved by science.

"Eating candy before bedtime gives you nightmares" is a common old wives' tale.

2   Often, old wives' tales take the form of warnings and were a way to discourage poor or undesirable behavior in one's children. For example, "Eating candy before bedtime gives you nightmares" is a common   10 old wives' tale that was probably thought up to stop children from eating too many unhealthy snacks. Similarly, "White spots on your fingernails means you've been lying" is a plain attempt at tricking naughty children into telling   15 the truth, while the motives behind "Watching too much TV makes your eyes turn square" are fairly obvious.

3   Other old wives' tales attempt to give advice about how to avoid or cure illnesses.   20 "If you go outside with wet hair, you'll catch a cold" is an old wives' tale that's still commonly heard to this day. However, colds are not caused by cold weather, wet hair, and chills. Instead, they are caused by viruses.   25

4   "Feed a cold, starve a fever" means that you should eat plenty of food when you have a cold, but not eat when you have a fever. This piece of wisdom probably comes from the fact that people with a fever usually lose their appetite anyway.   30 Medical science has found that the body stops eating as much when you have a

"Feed a cold, starve a fever" means that you should eat plenty of food when you have a cold, but not eat when you have a fever.

« "If you go outside with wet hair, you'll catch a cold" is an old wives' tale.

fever because a lack of food stimulates your immune system to fight bacterial infections, while eating a little more stimulates your immune system to combat viruses, like colds. 35

5 There are literally hundreds of other old wives' tales. Some sound ridiculous and others are more sensible, but they all represent a time when superstition and folklore were commonplace and unchallenged. While there may be truth in a few of them, if you hear one, it's best not to take it too seriously. 40

Questions

_____ 1. Which of the following can be inferred from the first paragraph?
   a. Old wives' tales are passed on only by mothers, not by fathers.
   b. Old wives' tales can be found in many medical books.
   c. People who passed down old wives' tales couldn't write.
   d. If you hear an old wives' tale, it's not likely to be true.

_____ 2. From the information in the second and third paragraphs, which of the following would likely be a reason for telling an old wives' tale?
   a. To stop your child performing a bad habit.
   b. To give a friend advice on his or her relationship.
   c. To find a missing object.
   d. To get a baby to fall asleep.

_____ 3. By reading the fourth paragraph, what can we infer about how some old wives' tales originated?
   a. People thought they were rules given by God.
   b. They were thought up to advertise certain products.
   c. They were interpretations of natural phenomenon.
   d. They were parts of popular songs.

_____ 4. Which of the following can we infer from the third paragraph?
   a. A cold is the most common virus.
   b. Some old wives' tales are still believed by many people.
   c. Only rainy countries have old wives' tales.
   d. Old wives' tales are more reliable than doctors' advice.

_____ 5. What would be the author's advice to someone citing an old wives' tale about a medical problem?
   a. If you heard it from your mother, it's probably true.
   b. If it sounds like sensible advice, I'd follow it.
   c. Don't listen to it. Go see a doctor.
   d. If it's something that many people believe, follow it.

35 | Area 51

>> Area 51 border

1   In the middle of the Nevada desert, tucked between a former nuclear test site and an Air Force base, is a remote piece of land known as Area 51. The US government has never officially recognized the existence of Area 51, and until recently, it did not appear on maps of the region. It is not possible to walk or drive into the site, and for many decades, planes could not fly overhead. Given the mystery surrounding Area 51, it is not surprising that rumors and stories about it—the strangest involving aliens and spaceships—have flourished over the years.

ⵢ Area 51
warning signs

2   Some details are known about Area 51. The base was built in the mid-1950s and contains a mix of buildings, landing strips, and parking ramps. During the Cold War, the US government built and tested experimental aircraft there, including the U2 spy plane and the F-117 fighter jet. The testing of military aircraft and weapons continues today, along with the site's status as a top-secret base.

3   Rumors about alien visitors and spaceships at Area 51 are understandable. Some of the new planes tested here have had unusual shapes, lights, and flight patterns. Stories about frozen aliens in a large underground complex there are related to rumors about a spaceship crashing in Roswell, New Mexico, in 1947; and the existence of underground facilities at Area 51 has since been confirmed. The strangest rumors—involving secret treaties between the US government and aliens that supposedly allowed the aliens to kidnap local citizens and grind them up for food—are a little **harder to explain**.

4   Curiosity about Area 51 is unlikely to fade anytime soon. The base has been featured in numerous movies, books, and TV shows, as well as on websites. Although former employees have recently been allowed to talk about some of the aircraft they tested, people who have theories are still insisting that alien spacecraft were worked on there. No solid evidence of these spaceships has ever been presented, however. In the meantime, visitors continue to flock to the Nevada desert from around the globe in the hope of seeing something out of this world.

Questions

_____ 1. Why did the unusual test planes most likely cause rumors about spaceships?
   a. People thought a science fiction movie was being filmed at the base.
   b. Odd shapes and lights are known to attract aliens and spaceships.
   c. The test planes may have looked like spaceships to some people.
   d. People may have seen strange-looking creatures inside the planes.

_____ 2. When the author states that some rumors are **harder to explain**, he or she
   likely believes _____.
   a. these rumors are more believable than the others
   b. these rumors are more difficult to clear up
   c. these rumors should be translated into English
   d. these rumors are top secret for a good reason

_____ 3. Which statement best expresses the author's attitude toward Area 51?
   a. Rumors about aliens and spaceships are understandable, but probably not true.
   b. Rumors about aliens and spaceships are likely true because the base is top secret.
   c. Stories about spy planes and spaceships are equally suspicious.
   d. The US government should be honest and put an end to the rumors.

_____ 4. Why is Area 51 most likely not shown on official maps of the region?
   a. Because Area 51 is not a city or town.
   b. Because the government doesn't want aliens to find the base.
   c. Because most of the structures are underground.
   d. Because top-secret aircrafts are tested there.

_____ 5. What can be inferred from the final paragraph of this passage?
   a. People around the world are fascinated with stories about aliens and spaceships.
   b. So much has been written about Area 51 that it is no longer a top-secret military base.
   c. The US government once forced employees to work on spaceships at Area 51.
   d. Visitors to the Nevada desert are likely to end up on TV or in the movies.

⌄ The town Rachel, near Area 51, enjoys celebrity among aviation enthusiasts and UFO hunters.

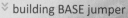
≫ building BASE jumper

Articles often begin by stating a problem and conclude by presenting a solution to the reader. All of the information in between is important, because it usually relates to how a problem is solved. Remember to ask yourself, "Is what I'm reading a problem, or a solution?"

36 | BASE Jumping

036

≫ parachute

1 BASE jumping is an extreme sport that involves jumping off of tall structures while wearing a parachute. It has become popular with people who are always looking for new and exciting things to do. Because BASE jumping is very dangerous, it is sometimes considered a stunt or daredevil activity, rather than a sport.

2 BASE is an acronym that stands for buildings, antennas, spans (bridges), and earth (cliffs). These are the four types of terrain that BASE jumpers will use as a starting point for their jumps. If a BASE jumper performs a jump off each of the four categories, they can apply for a BASE number. A BASE number qualifies them as a recognized BASE jumper.

3 Carl Boenish got the sport started in 1978 when he filmed four of his friends jumping from El Capitan in California. In 1984, he jumped off of the Troll Wall, a mountain in Norway. Unfortunately, tragedy struck only two days later when Carl was killed attempting a second jump from the same spot.

4 The death of the sport's inventor is proof of how dangerous this sport can be. While it's true that BASE jumping has become safer thanks to improvements in the equipment, many experienced veterans and newcomers to the sport are still injured or killed every

5

10

15

20

year. There are no reliable statistics on the number of people hurt while BASE jumping, but it is often thought to be more dangerous than skydiving. 25

5   Because so many people have died, BASE jumping has not gained widespread acceptance. In fact, the sport is considered to be illegal in most countries. If someone wants to make a jump, that person needs to get permission to use both the starting place and the landing area. Some places, like the Troll Wall in Norway, have 30 banned BASE jumping because it is considered to be too dangerous.

6   BASE jumping is an extremely dangerous sport. It can result in you being injured or even killed. If you're looking for a thrill, just remember to think before you leap!

Questions

_____ 1. What is the problem that keeps BASE jumping from becoming very popular?
- **a.** It's too hard to learn.
- **b.** The equipment is too expensive.
- **c.** It's too dangerous.
- **d.** It's too boring.

_____ 2. How have many countries solved the problem of people BASE jumping?
- **a.** They distributed safety equipment.
- **b.** They educated the public on BASE jumping.
- **c.** They made BASE jumping illegal.
- **d.** They reduced the height of BASE jumping spots.

⌃ BASE jumper jumping off a big cliff

_____ 3. How has BASE jumping tried to solve the problems it faces as a sport?
- **a.** With better safety equipment.
- **b.** With media campaigns to convince the public.
- **c.** With new stunts and tricks.
- **d.** With colorful jumping uniforms.

_____ 4. What is the problem faced by someone who wants to BASE jump from a skyscraper?
- **a.** Most skyscrapers don't have roof access.
- **b.** Skyscrapers aren't considered to be a proper jump point.
- **c.** The person would need to get permission first.
- **d.** The conditions at the top of skyscrapers is too windy.

⌃ BASE jumping

_____ 5. What problem did the inventor of BASE jumping face?
- **a.** He ran out of money.
- **b.** He became too old for the sport.
- **c.** He had records that were all broken.
- **d.** He was killed by the sport.

37 | Hannibal

037

1   Hannibal was a Carthaginian general and tactician who lived from 247 BC to 183 BC. He is credited as being one of the greatest military commanders the world has ever known.

2   Hannibal lived during a time when the Roman Republic ruled over most of the Mediterranean region. He wanted to attack Rome, but he didn't have enough ships to cross the sea and to approach the city from the south, which is where the Romans would be expecting an attack. So instead, Hannibal led a massive army of troops and war elephants from Spain, over the Pyrenees Mountains, through the Alps, and finally down into northern Italy, where he caught the Romans off guard.

Hannibal
(247–183 BC)
(cc by Jastrow)

3   In northern Italy, Hannibal conquered local tribes and defeated the famed Roman army in several battles. He didn't have enough equipment to lay siege to the city of Rome itself, so he engaged in small battles in order to build up his resources. He managed to remain in northern Italy like this for 10 years, until the Romans assaulted his home city, and he was forced to return.

4   Hannibal returned to Carthage and faced the Romans in the Battle of Zama in 202 BC, but his forces were overwhelmed. The battle resulted in Rome winning the 17-year-long Second Punic War, and Carthage never recovered its former status as a powerful empire. As for Hannibal, he went into politics and pushed for reforms, but when his reforms angered members of the Carthaginian aristocracy and Rome, he had to escape into exile. During his exile, he served as a military advisor

5

10

15

20

25

ancient ruins of Carthage in Tunisia

to Antiochus III of Syria, who was fighting a war against Rome. Once again, Rome was eventually victorious and Hannibal was forced to flee. 30

5   Even long after his death, Hannibal's name alone inspired fear in the Roman Republic. Great leaders like Napoléon Bonaparte and the Duke of Wellington were keen students of his methods. Even now, people will still use the famous phrase 35 "Hannibal is at the gates" when a country is faced with the possibility of a crushing defeat.

Questions

_____ 1. What was the problem that Hannibal faced when he first considered attacking Rome?
   a. His troops were poorly trained and ineffective.
   b. He didn't have enough ships for a direct attack.
   c. He didn't have enough war elephants.
   d. His maps were out of date and useless.

_____ 2. How did Hannibal go about solving the problem of attacking Rome?
   a. He took a different route over the mountains.
   b. He purchased 200 new ships.
   c. He waited for the Roman army to come to him.
   d. He snuck into Rome on transport ships.

_____ 3. How did the Romans solve the problem of Hannibal's lengthy military campaign in northern Italy?
   a. They attacked Hannibal directly in the north.
   b. They kidnapped Hannibal's family.
   c. They got Antiochus III to attack Hannibal.
   d. They attacked Hannibal's home city.

_____ 4. When he was in northern Italy, how did Hannibal gather resources for an attack on Rome?
   a. He imported supplies from Carthage.
   b. He attacked small armies and took their supplies.
   c. He ordered his troops to eat Roman horses.
   d. He planted his own crops and stored wheat.

_____ 5. After the war, why did the Carthaginian aristocracy see Hannibal as a problem?
   a. Hannibal continued to attack Roman troops.
   b. Hannibal spoke out against rich people.
   c. Hannibal pushed for bold political reforms.
   d. Hannibal was often drunk and violent.

38 Colossal Squid (038)

1 Scandinavian sailors have whispered about giant, squid-like sea monsters called kraken for centuries. Some stories describe a kraken bumping the side of a ship and knocking a few unlucky sailors overboard. In others, the kraken wraps its giant tentacles around the entire ship and pulls it under the waves. 5

2 While this might sound a little bit like the plot from a scary movie, what if krakens actually do exist? Maybe it's just hard to prove they do because they are exceptionally rare. After all, is a kraken any stranger than a whale or any other massive creature that lives in the sea? 10

3 It's possible that these legendary sea monsters are actually colossal squids. The colossal squid, sometimes called an Antarctic squid, is the largest known squid species. These animals are thought to live in the Antarctic Ocean, but keen observers have spotted them off the coasts of South America, South Africa, and New Zealand. 15

4 It's hard for us to know a lot about colossal squids because they live in the depths of the ocean. However, we can learn a thing or two about them by studying other animals that aren't so mysterious. For example, we know that sperm whales hunt colossal squid because people have come across sperm whales with cuts and bruises all over their bodies. These injuries are caused 20 by the sharp hooks on a colossal squid's tentacles. Some scientists even believe that it's possible for a colossal squid to come away victorious from a fight with a sperm whale.

5 Scientists have also come up with a few ways to study colossal squid in their natural environment. In 2004, researchers from Japan lowered a dead 25 squid on a giant hook 900 meters into the Pacific Ocean. A colossal squid took the bait, and they were able to capture it on film. Unfortunately, the squid eventually got away, losing one of its tentacles in the process. Judging by the length of the tentacle the scientists recovered, they estimated that an adult colossal squid is about 14 meters long. That's almost twice the length 30 of a bus, and it might be just big enough to take out a wooden ship.

« colossal squid on display in the Museum of New Zealand Te Papa Tongarewa (cc by Y23)

⌃ The colossal squid is the largest known squid species. (cc by Benjamindancer)

Questions

_____ 1. What is the problem that might be making it hard to prove that krakens exist?
   a. They are too dangerous for scientists to study.
   b. They have already been extinct for a long time.
   c. They are incredibly rare and hard to find.
   d. They are not a priority, and no one will fund research.

_____ 2. Why are colossal squids so hard to study?
   a. They live at extreme depths.   b. They are very dangerous.
   c. They have unique biology.   d. They die in the sunlight.

_____ 3. Scientists have tried to solve this problem by _____.
   a. studying how global climate changes affect the squid
   b. studying other animals that come into contact with squids
   c. studying dinosaurs to find a link with modern squids
   d. studying regular-sized squids and estimating

_____ 4. How did scientists solve the problem of not knowing what a colossal squid looks like in its natural habitat?
   a. They studied some of the squid's closest relatives.
   b. They used advanced radar to scan for colossal squids.
   c. They lowered a giant hook into the ocean with bait.
   d. They used a miniature submarine to explore extreme depths.

_____ 5. How did Japanese scientists determine the size of an adult colossal squid?
   a. They measured a regular squid and estimated.
   b. They measured a colossal squid in a sperm whale's stomach.
   c. They measured the tentacle from a colossal squid.
   d. They measured a baby colossal squid and estimated.

⌃ tentacle

Brexit

» Brexit marked the first time a country had ever decided to leave the EU.

39 | United Kingdom, Disunited Europe

1   On June 23, 2016, 51.9 percent of the United Kingdom's voters chose to exit the European Union. The decision, nicknamed Brexit, marked the first time a country had ever decided to leave the Brussels-based EU. That departure hasn't even happened yet, but it is already proving difficult for
5   both sides.

2   Among the main reasons for the victory of the leave movement was immigration. The United Kingdom was unhappy with Europe's open-door policy, which forced the state to accept more immigrants than it wanted. Other problems included the free movement of EU citizens between
10   member countries and the union's plans for expansion. Finally, there was the estimated 350 million pounds (NT$14 billion) the UK was paying for EU membership every week. Leave voters saw their win as a return to British independence.

3   A lot of people disagreed. Remain voters won in Scotland and London,
15   reflecting both the national and urban/rural divisions of the UK. Prime Minister David Cameron, a remain supporter, resigned immediately after the vote. The British pound dropped to its lowest value since 1985. Even former US president Barack Obama got involved, warning of possible trade difficulties if voters chose to leave. None of that mattered, however, and the
20   Brexit became a reality.

Birmingham's Bin Brexit in Brum march for a People's Vote on leaving the EU to coincide with the Conservative Party conference being held in the city, September 30, 2018 (cc by Ilovetheeu)

4 But how can such a thing be made to happen? More than two years and countless meetings later, no one seems to be sure. For Cameron's successor, Theresa May, the challenge is to create a separation that will satisfy everyone. Most UK politicians favor a hard Brexit, giving the EU no say in Britain's
25 legal or trade decisions. Others, however, agree with the EU's desire for a soft Brexit, with more cooperation between the two sides. With the Brexit scheduled to happen in March, 2019, time is running out for a deal. Some fear this will lead to a crash Brexit, in which the divorce will be complete and immediate.

5 Recent events make it clear that neither British nor EU leaders want to
30 back down regarding the terms of the Brexit. All the rest of us can do for now, therefore, is to watch and wait.

Questions

⌃ Theresa May, UK prime minister, arriving for a meeting with European Union leaders in Brussels, June 28, 2018

_____ 1. How did the United Kingdom solve the problem of public unhappiness with its membership in the European Union?
  a. By forcing its prime minister to resign.
  b. By allowing its citizens to vote on the issue.
  c. By immediately leaving the European Union.
  d. By asking Barack Obama for his opinion.

_____ 2. Which of the following people would most likely see the United Kingdom's decision to leave the European Union as a problem?
  a. An English farmer.   b. A Scottish voter.
  c. A UK politician.   d. An immigrant living in Germany.

_____ 3. Which of the following was NOT one of the problems that led to the success of the "leave" movement?
  a. Too many people from other EU countries coming to the United Kingdom.
  b. The extremely high cost of EU membership.
  c. The EU's plans to admit new member countries.
  d. The unpopularity of prime minister David Cameron.

_____ 4. What is one problem that might exist between the UK and the EU after the Brexit actually happens?
  a. The movement of people between the UK and the EU.
  b. Deciding where the borders of the UK and the EU are.
  c. Choosing a new prime minister for the UK.
  d. The fact that the EU's headquarters are in Brussels.

_____ 5. How are the UK and the EU trying to solve the problems created by the Brexit vote?
  a. With another vote.   b. With a war.
  c. With meetings.   d. By watching and waiting.

40 | Freedom Riders

1   The African-American Civil Rights movement was the struggle from 1955 to 1968 to achieve equal rights for black people in the United States. It involved the hard work of thousands of personnel all over the country, and all with one goal in mind: equality for everyone.

2   The Freedom Riders were one segment of this massive struggle. These were people of all ages and different backgrounds who wanted to challenge the racial segregation laws that existed in the southern United States. At the time, all buses, trains, and airplanes in the south had separate facilities for white and black people. However, the US Supreme Court had ruled that it was illegal to have separate facilities on any bus that crossed state lines. So the Freedom Riders would fill a bus with mixed races in a northern state and get off in the south, in defiance of the local laws.

3   This might sound like a minor protest now, but it was a huge deal at the time. When the original 13 Freedom Riders went on their first bus ride into the south, they were beaten several times. No matter how bad it got, they never fought back. They firmly believed in the concept of nonviolent resistance.

4   Things got particularly bad when their bus pulled into Anniston, Alabama, on May 14, 1961. There was such a huge mob waiting for them that the bus driver decided not to stop. However, someone

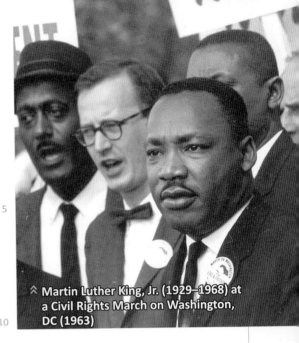

⌃ Martin Luther King, Jr. (1929–1968) at a Civil Rights March on Washington, DC (1963)

⌃ Robert F. Kennedy (1925–1968) speaking to a Civil Rights crowd in 1963

≫ Freedom Rider Jim Zwerg (1939–) in 1961 after being beaten

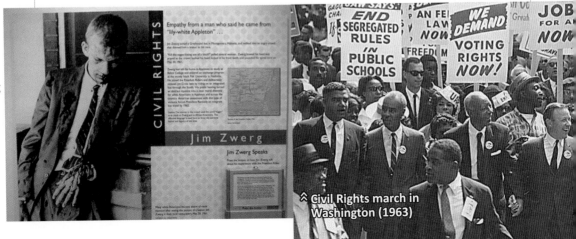

⌃ Civil Rights march in Washington (1963)

managed to slash the bus's tires, so they didn't get very far. When the bus finally stopped, someone in the mob smashed a window and threw a firebomb into the bus. The Freedom Riders rushed out and were beaten with bats as they stepped off the bus. According to witnesses, the only thing that stopped the Freedom Riders from being executed that day was an undercover agent who shot into the air to clear the mob. 30

As more and more Freedom Riders headed south, President Kennedy became alarmed at the violence. He struck a deal with southern governments that they could arrest the Freedom Riders as long as they kept them safe. Still, the Riders kept coming, until eventually the segregation laws were changed. 35

>> Some freedom riders were jailed in the Mississippi State Penitentiary.

Questions

_____ 1. According to the Freedom Riders, what was the problem with laws in the south?
    a. They were too vague.   **b.** They weren't strict enough.
    c. They weren't fair to everyone.   **d.** They were too old.

_____ 2. How did the Freedom Riders go about solving the problem?
    a. They campaigned to elect a new president.
    b. They challenged the laws with their actions.
    c. They organized a huge march in Washington.
    d. They organized a protest in Anniston, Alabama.

_____ 3. Who saw the equal treatment of white and black people as a problem?
    a. The bus drivers.   **b.** People in the north.
    c. People in the south.   **d.** Government agents.

_____ 4. How did President Kennedy solve the problem of increasing violence?
    a. He ordered the army to stop the Freedom Riders.
    b. He made a deal to provide protection for the Freedom Riders.
    c. He passed a law giving the Freedom Riders what they wanted.
    d. He made a memorable speech to the nation.

_____ 5. According to a Freedom Rider, what's the best way to respond when faced with violence?
    a. Fight back.   **b.** Not fight back.
    c. Shout.   **d.** Spit.

1-9 *Fact or Opinion*

Everyone has opinions; it's something that cannot be avoided. What we can avoid is absorbing someone else's opinions without thinking them through. So when you read a sentence, ask yourself, "Would everyone agree with this?" If the answer is "yes," then you're probably dealing with a fact.

41 | Glass

(041)

1   Glass is used to make everything from windows and bottles, to spacecraft tiles, radiation shields, fiber optic communication cables, and even certain types of fabric. Since glass is absolutely everywhere in our lives, people tend to take this indispensable material for granted.

2   Glass is neither a solid nor a liquid. It is something in between, and this gives it unique properties. Glass is made from sand. First, the sand is exposed to extremely high temperatures until it melts. Then the red-hot sand can be poured and molded into almost any shape before it cools. Adding certain chemicals when the glass is still hot can change its basic properties. For example, the **Gorilla Glass** that is used to make smartphones and laptops is so strong because it was processed with a potassium salt bath at a temperature of 400 degrees Celsius.

3   The melting point of glass ranges between 500 degrees and 1,650 degrees Celsius, depending on the type. Different types of glass can also weigh anywhere from two to eight times as much as water. This wide range of properties has helped to make glass the most useful material in the world.

4   Humans are thought to have used naturally occurring glass for tens of thousands of years. However, it was in Egypt and Mesopotamia around 3500 BC that humans started making glass beads on their

❯ Quartz sand (silica) is the main raw material in commercial glass production.

5

10

15

20

own. Around 3,250 years later, the Romans developed new ways to produce inexpensive glass that could be used to make windows and other household items. These techniques eventually spread to Scandinavia and China.

5 Glass isn't just practical, but it's beautiful as well. In fact, glass 25 has been used to create some of the best art in the history of human civilization. In the late 20th century, people began to appreciate both ancient glass objects and modern glass art. The world's largest collection of glass art can be found at the Corning Museum of Glass, in Corning, New York. It has over 200,000 glass objects in its 30 collection. Sometimes, it's a whole building that's a work of art. The wonderful Crystal Cathedral in Los Angeles is one such example. It makes extensive use of glass to create a stunning impression.

Questions

⌄ the Crystal Cathedral

⌄ historic glass displayed in the Corning Museum of Glass (cc by Chris Dlugosz)

_____ 1. The sentence "Glass is made from sand," in the second paragraph is a statement of _____.
   a. fact   **b.** opinion

_____ 2. Which of the following is a fact?
   a. Glass is the most beautiful kind of art.
   b. Humans couldn't survive without glass.
   c. Humans have made glass for thousands of years.
   d. The Crystal Cathedral is a beautiful building.

_____ 3. Which of the following statements about **Gorilla Glass** is a fact?
   a. It is processed in a potassium salt bath.
   b. It is the best type of smartphone glass.
   c. It is too heavy.
   d. It reflects too much light.

_____ 4. Which of the following is an opinion?
   a. The Crystal Cathedral is made of glass.
   b. Glassmaking spread from Rome to Scandinavia.
   c. People shouldn't take glass for granted.
   d. Glass can occur naturally.

_____ 5. Which of the following statements about glass is an opinion?
   a. It is beautiful.   **b.** It can range in its melting point.
   c. It can range in its weight.   **d.** It can protect against radiation.

095

42 | The Bedouin

1   Living in the largest, hottest desert in the world is a little crazy. However, the bedouin people have been living in the Sahara for centuries, and many of them still follow the same ancient traditions as their ancestors.

2   The name "bedouin" is derived from the Arabic word *bedu*, meaning   5
"inhabitant of the desert." It is a generic name for the various tribes of nomadic people who dwell in the desert, tending their herds of goats and camels, leading caravans through the vast sea of dunes, and trading in the desert towns and villages that they pass through. They often travel, set up tents for a brief period of time,   10 and then move on, following their herds. What an interesting lifestyle!

3   The bedouin pay little attention to the laws of nations but have strong individual codes of honor. Bedouin systems of justice are based on these honor codes. According to   15 such codes, punishments are usually swift and harsh. For example, the ordeal by fire is a famous bedouin ritual to determine whether someone is lying. It is voluntary, and involves the accused person licking a burning hot metal object. If they end up with a burnt tongue after three licks, then they were lying. This is a cruel   20 practice that should be ended.

4   The bedouin do not respect national borders. They tend to cross from one

↟ bedouin shepherd in Syrian Desert

bedouin man

country to another at will. The governments of these countries tolerate the bedouin coming and going, but their wandering is not officially condoned.

Over the past hundred years, many bedouin have shifted from their traditional nomadic way of life to seminomadism. A few have even decided to settle down in cities throughout the Middle East. Their desire for a better life as well as some government policies in Egypt, Israel, and other countries, have combined to convince some bedouin to become normal citizens. Of course, this means they must give up their existence as stateless nomadic herders. Many governments are trying to help the bedouin settle in their countries by providing them with housing, schools, hospitals, and health care.

Questions

___ 1. The sentence "Living in the largest, hottest desert . . . is a little crazy" in the first paragraph is an example of a(n) _____.
   a. fact   **b.** opinion

___ 2. Which of the following is an opinion?
   a. The bedouin have been provided housing.
   b. The bedouin do not respect state borders.
   c. The bedouin tend herds of goats and camels.
   d. The bedouin lifestyle is very interesting.

___ 3. Which of the following statements about bedouin traditions is an opinion?
   a. The bedouin ignore national borders.
   b. The ordeal by fire is a cruel practice.
   c. The ordeal by fire is a voluntary ritual.
   d. Bedouin justice is based on a code of honor.

___ 4. Which of the following statements is a fact?
   a. The bedouin live in the Sahara desert.
   b. Egypt should convince more bedouin to settle.
   c. The bedouin lifestyle is harsh and unnecessary.
   d. The most interesting part of the bedouin life is the wandering.

⌃ bedouin tents in the Sahara desert

___ 5. The sentence "The name 'bedouin' is derived from the Arabic word *bedu*, . . ." is an example of a(n) _____.
   a. opinion   **b.** fact

43

⌃ Through blockchain technology, information is saved in a "block" connected to the blocks that came before and after it.

⌃ Blockchain can be used to record financial transactions and to store data and cryptocurrency.

Blockchain:
A Revolutionary Technology

1   If you spend any time using technology, you probably have a long list of passwords. Remembering usernames and complicated passwords is one of the most annoying aspects of the technological age. You might have also heard news reports about hackers who steal passwords and financial information. Companies spend millions of dollars keeping information safe and away from hackers. 5
A solution was invented in 2008 by someone using the name Satoshi Nakamoto.

2   Blockchain technology is making the Internet more secure through a creative solution. Rather than keeping important information in a single database, the information is spread across a network of computers. Because all the computers record the information, it doesn't matter if one computer is hacked. The 10
information is saved in a "block" that is connected to the blocks that came before and after it. A chain of information blocks is created, which gives the process the name "blockchain."

3   Because blockchain can be used on different types of transactions, it is sure to become part of our everyday lives. Blockchain can be used to record financial 15
transactions, agreements, and contracts, and to store data and cryptocurrency. Satoshi Nakamoto created blockchain to keep records of people buying and selling with Bitcoin, a cryptocurrency. Technology companies are already using blockchain. Microsoft and IBM are using blockchains to help companies keep track of their supply chain. For example, food companies quickly track food 20
that has made people ill. They can also save money by using the data from the blockchain to prevent food waste. Blockchains can be public, for transactions between two people, or private, for transactions between two companies.

4   The *Harvard Business Review* called blockchain a "quiet revolution."
As more companies use blockchain, businesses will increase efficiency as they 25
buy and sell. Information and records will be secure from hackers. Companies like banks may become less important as people can buy and sell directly using blockchain to record the transaction. With so many ways it can be used, blockchain might become a part of everyday life in the same way the Internet is.

⌄ blockchain workflow

1 A wants to send money to B

2 The transaction is represented online as a block

3 The block is broadcasted to every party in the network

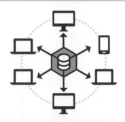

4 The network approves the transaction

5 The block is added to the existing blockchain in a transparent and unalterable way

6 The transaction is complete

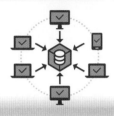

Questions

_____ 1. Which of the following sentences is an opinion about blockchain?
  a. Blockchain can be used on different types of transactions.
  b. Blockchain was invented in 2008.
  c. Blockchain can be used to prevent food waste.
  d. Blockchain is sure to become part of our everyday life.

_____ 2. Which of the following sentences is a fact about blockchain?
  a. Blockchain is a creative solution.
  b. Blockchain spreads information across a network of computers.
  c. Blockchain will become as important as the Internet.
  d. Blockchain might take the place of banks.

_____ 3. The sentence "Microsoft and IBM are using blockchains to help companies keep track of their supply chain" is an example of a(n) _____.
  a. fact   b. opinion

_____ 4. The sentence "Remembering usernames and complicated passwords is one of the most annoying aspects of the technological age" is an example of a(n) _____.
  a. fact   b. opinion

_____ 5. Which of the following is an opinion that the author of this article would most likely have about blockchain technology?
  a. Blockchain will probably be replaced by better technology.
  b. Blockchain is too complicated for average people to understand.
  c. Blockchain will make our lives easier.
  d. Blockchain has spread since its invention in 2008.

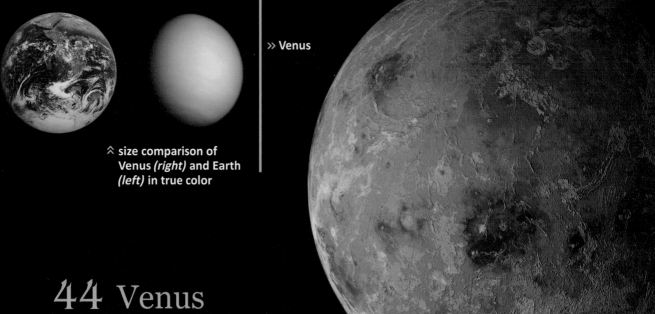

» Venus

⌄ size comparison of Venus *(right)* and Earth *(left)* in true color

44 Venus

 (044)

1   Venus was the Roman goddess of love and beauty, and her name was bestowed upon the bright planet whose orbit is between Mercury and Earth. The planet Venus looks beautiful and serene, but when you get down to the planet's surface, it's a deadly wasteland.

2   Apart from Earth's moon, Venus is the brightest object in the night sky. It looks a little bit like a beige marble. In ancient times, Venus was also known as the morning star or the evening star because it was only visible at dawn or dusk. For centuries, it has fascinated astronomers who could not see through the planet's veil of thick clouds. Venus is sometimes called Earth's sister planet because its size, mass, bulk, and gravity are all similar to Earth.

3   It takes Venus 225 Earth days to move around the sun. But a day on Venus, which is the time it takes for the planet to make one full rotation, lasts an incredible 243 Earth days. That means a day lasts longer than a year on Venus.

4   The surface of Venus is extremely harsh. The planet's dry atmosphere is primarily made up of CO_2, and air pressure on the

5

10

15

» Venus is always brighter than the brightest stars outside our solar system, as can be seen here over the Pacific Ocean. (cc by Brocken Inaglory)

surface is over 90 times higher than on Earth. The temperature on
Venus can reach as high as 471 degrees Celsius. This intense heat is the
result of the dense CO2 atmosphere, which traps gas and heat on the   20
surface and creates a powerful global warming effect.

5 The Russians have landed several probes on Venus in order to find
out more about the planet. None of their probes survived for more than
50 minutes. The planet's heat and atmospheric pressure is just too
severe. The Americans have also attempted to learn more about Venus.   25
They sent Pioneer Venus 1 and Magellan into orbit around the planet.
These unmanned spacecraft were able to map the surface using radar.
They produced detailed images of enormous plateaus, huge volcanoes,
long lava flows, deep canyons, and the craters that were formed by
meteorite impacts on Venus. These are the most beautiful images taken   30
of a planet in the history of human space exploration.

⌃ cloud structure in the Venusian atmosphere, revealed by Pioneer Venus Orbiter

Questions

_____ 1. The sentence "These are the most beautiful images
taken of a planet in the history . . ." in the final
paragraph is an example of a(n) _____.
   a. fact   b. opinion

_____ 2. Which of the following is an opinion?
   a. Venus orbits between Mercury and Earth.
   b. Venus looks like a beige marble.
   c. A year lasts 225 Earth days on Venus.
   d. Air pressure on Venus is over 90 times higher than on Earth.

_____ 3. The sentence "The planet's dry atmosphere is primarily made up of
CO_2 . . ." in the fourth paragraph is an example of a(n) _____.
   a. fact   b. opinion

_____ 4. Which of the following statements about Venus is a fact?
   a. It looks beautiful and serene.
   b. It was named after a Roman goddess.
   c. It should be named after a Greek goddess.
   d. It is the most mysterious of all planets.

_____ 5. Which of the following statements about a volcano on Venus is based
on opinion?
   a. The volcano is 550 meters high.
   b. The volcano is composed of carbon.
   c. The volcano looks like it's about to erupt.
   d. The volcano has not erupted for exactly 2,000 years.

The *T. rex* got its name from the Greek words meaning "tyrant lizard king."

45 (045)
Tyrannosaurus Rex

1   Over 65 million years ago, when dinosaurs ruled the planet and mammals were just small, rodent-like creatures, the undisputed king of the dinosaurs was the *Tyrannosaurus rex*, or *T. rex*. The *T. rex* got its name from the Greek words meaning "tyrant 5 lizard king." This is a fitting name because most evidence suggests that the *T. rex* was at the very top of the food chain.

2   Fossils from the United States have shown that the *T. rex* lived in forests. It had a body that was built to hunt: two powerful legs for chasing down its prey and a jaw lined with razor-sharp teeth 10 that could bite through meat, bone, and the toughest scales. Because of its powerful short neck and well-developed jaw muscles, the force of a *T. rex* bite is thought to be the strongest of any known creature, living or extinct. It could be used to gobble up 230 kilograms of meat and bone in just one swallow. 15

3   The *Tyrannosaurus rex* was about 12 meters long, 4.6 to 6 meters tall, and it weighed up to 7.5 tons. Its skull was enormous at 1.5 meters long, and even its eyeballs were 7.6 centimeters in diameter. The *T. rex* was obviously the coolest predator ever to have existed, but

⌃ probable *tyrannosaurus* footprint from New Mexico (cc by Rufous-crowned Sparrow)

≫ scale chart for various specimens of *Tyrannosaurus rex*

10 m

3 m

Specimen #
- FMNH PR2081 ("Sue")
- AMNH 5027
- BHI 3033 ("Stan")
- BMRP 2002.4.1 ("Jane")

Tyrannosaurus rex

strangely, it actually isn't the largest meat-eating dinosaur we know of. That record belongs to the *spinosaurus*, which was substantially larger than the *Tyrannosaurus rex*.

4 How fast could the *T. rex* move? Some experts say that it could reach speeds of up to 24 kilometers per hour, while others say that it could only manage speeds of about 17 kilometers per hour. Whatever the case, the *T. rex* was probably fast enough to be feared by other dinosaurs. Just the thought of trying to escape and hearing a roar and the ground thump behind you is enough to give someone nightmares!

5 Some experts believe that the *T. rex* was a hunter and a scavenger, while others suggest that it was just a scavenger, but one look at its appearance should be enough to know that the *T. rex* was probably the most dangerous hunter that ever lived.

Questions

1. The statement ". . . the *T. rex* was probably the most dangerous hunter that ever lived" is an example of a(n) _____.
   a. fact   **b.** opinion

2. Which of the following is a fact?
   a. The *T. rex* was the coolest predator ever.
   b. The *T. rex* could swallow 230 kilograms at a time.
   c. The *T. rex* has a scary-sounding name.
   d. The *T. rex* probably had a terrifying roar.

3. Which of the following statements about the *T. rex* is an opinion?
   a. It had eyeballs that were 7.6 centimeters wide.
   b. It could manage speeds from 17 to 24 kilometers per hour.
   c. It was not the largest meat-eating dinosaur ever.
   d. It had arms that looked like tiny sticks.

4. The sentence "The *T. rex* got its name from the Greek words meaning 'tyrant lizard king'" is an example of a(n) _____.
   a. fact   **b.** opinion

5. Which of the following would be an opinion that the author of this article would most likely have?
   a. A *T. rex* could beat a *spinosaurus* in a fight.
   b. Some believe the *T. rex* was not only a hunter but also a scavenger.
   c. A *T. rex* could weigh up to 7.5 tons.
   d. A *spinosaurus* is larger than a *T. rex*.

⌃ The forelimbs might have been used to help *T. rex* rise from a resting pose, as seen here. (Wikipedia)

⌃ the *tyrannosaurus* at the Field Museum of Natural History in Chicago

(046)

46
The Grand Duchess Anastasia of Russia

≫ Grand Duchess Anastasia in 1904

^ Grand Duchess Anastasia (1901–1918), c. 1910

1   Anastasia, the youngest daughter of the Russian royal family, was mischievous, intelligent, and lovable when she was a child. She was born on June 18, 1901, one of five children, and held the title Grand Duchess, as did her three sisters.   5

2   She was a kind and loving girl and helped her mother visit and comfort wounded soldiers during World War I. However, being part of the Russian royal family during that time turned out to be disastrous. In February 1917, revolution broke out in Russia. Anastasia's father,   10 Tsar Nicholas II, gave up the throne, and he and his family were placed under house arrest. This was not the end of their troubles. In October, the Communists started a second revolution in order to overthrow the temporary government that had replaced the Tsar.   15 Anastasia and her family were moved to safety by the government, but the Communists eventually gained complete control of Russia, and the royal family was moved to what was to be their final destination, a house of special purpose in Yekaterinburg.   20

^ *(from left to right)* the Grand Duchesses Maria, Tatiana, Anastasia, and Olga, 1914

3   In the early morning of July 17, 1918, Tsar Nicholas II and his family—wife, four daughters, and a son—were executed by the Russian secret police.

4   Due to the fact that the location of her grave was largely unknown

during the decades of Communist rule, Anastasia's possible survival became one 25
of the best-known mysteries of the 20th century. Some people thought that she
might have escaped the execution, helped secretly by one of the guards.

5   Several women came forward and claimed to be her, hoping to become the
heir to the tremendous wealth that the real Anastasia would have been entitled
to. The most famous of these was Anna Anderson, who 30
declared that she had faked her death among the bodies of
the royal family members and had escaped with the help of a
guard. Anna Anderson died in 1984, and DNA tests performed
on her remains showed that she was not related to the royal
family. Finally, in 2008, forensic investigations revealed that 35
Anastasia was indeed killed with her family, and thus the
rumors of her survival finally ended.

» The movie *Anastasia*
was named after the Grand
Duchess Anastasia.

Questions

____ **1.** What is the main point discussed in the second paragraph?
  a. Tsar Nicholas II gave up his throne and was replaced by a temporary government.
  b. There were two revolutions in Russia in 1917, one in February and one in October.
  c. During the revolutions, the royal family experienced many troubles.
  d. Anastasia was a kind girl who helped comfort wounded soldiers.

____ **2.** The final paragraph focuses on _____.
  a. the myth of Anastasia's survival   **b.** Anastasia's personality
  c. Anastasia's descendants   **d.** films about Anastasia

____ **3.** The author's purpose in this article is to _____.
  a. state a problem   **b.** criticize
  c. inform   **d.** entertain

____ **4.** Which of the following is an opinion?
  a. Anastasia had three sisters and one brother.
  b. Anastasia was part of the Russian royal family.
  c. Anastasia was a kind and loving girl.
  d. Anna Anderson was not the real Anastasia.

____ **5.** The myth of Anastasia's survival started because

  _____.
  a. a secret letter was found revealing the secret
  b. people thought it would make a good movie
     plot
  c. anti-Communist governments spread the rumor
  d. no one knew where her body was buried

⌃ Nicholas II, Emperor of Russia,
and his family, c. 1913

47 | Platinum

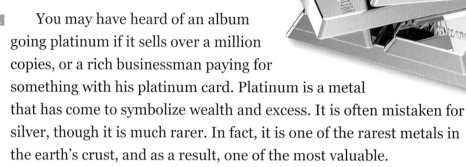
>> platinum ingots

1   You may have heard of an album going platinum if it sells over a million copies, or a rich businessman paying for something with his platinum card. Platinum is a metal that has come to symbolize wealth and excess. It is often mistaken for 5 silver, though it is much rarer. In fact, it is one of the rarest metals in the earth's crust, and as a result, one of the most valuable.

≪ platinum ore
(cc by Alchemist-hp)

2   Platinum is no ordinary metal. It is resistant to damage from weather and even from many types of acids, keeping its beautiful silvery shine under almost any conditions. These unique properties 10 have made it important in the production of laboratory equipment as well as, more obviously, jewelry. Most limited-edition watches are made from platinum, as they do not become dull or dirty as gold does.

≪ platinum card

3   Owning some platinum jewelry is one of the best status symbols on the planet. Gold is about 30 times more common than platinum, 15 and so during periods of economic stability and growth, platinum's price remains almost twice the price of gold. Its scarcity prompted King Louis XV of France to declare that platinum was the only metal fit for a king, and Queen Elizabeth II of England's mother wore a crown whose frame was made of platinum. 20

4   Despite its luxurious appearance, platinum is primarily used in a far less glamorous field. Around 45% of all platinum mined is not used to make expensive jewelry but is, rather, used in the motor industry as an essential part of a vehicle's exhaust system. Platinum converts the harmful gasses that come out of a vehicle's engine into safer gases, 25 thus reducing the pollution that's emitted.

>> Platinum is often mistaken for silver.

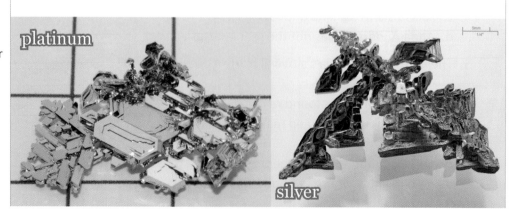
platinum

silver

≫ Platinum can dissolve only in hot aqua regia. (cc by Alexander C. Wimmer)

5 In the past, platinum mostly came from mines in South America, where the native tribes had been using it for centuries. Today, about 80% of the world's platinum comes from South Africa. However, if we really want a steady supply of platinum, we have to be prepared to travel for it, as the most abundant supply of platinum is found not on Earth, but on the moon. 35

30

⋏ A common use of platinum is for catalytic converters in automobiles. (cc by Stahlkocher)

Questions

_____ 1. Which of the following statements is true?
    a. Platinum is the same color as gold.
    b. Platinum is rarer than gold.
    c. Platinum is mostly used to make jewelry.
    d. Most of the world's platinum comes from the moon.

_____ 2. According to the article, what problem does platinum solve for watchmakers?
    a. They need a metal that doesn't discolor.
    b. They need a cheap metal to produce many watches.
    c. They need a metal that resembles silver.
    d. They need a metal that's resistant to acid.

_____ 3. In the first sentence, the writer creates understanding by _____.
    a. appealing to the reader's sense of humor   **b.** making a comparison
    c. using clear and vivid adjectives   **d.** referring to something familiar

_____ 4. What's the main idea expressed in the third paragraph?
    a. Platinum is a rare metal.
    b. Platinum is a luxury item.
    c. Platinum is almost twice as expensive as gold.
    d. Queen Elizabeth II's mother wore a crown containing platinum.

_____ 5. From the information in the article, which of the following do you think is most likely to happen?
    a. Platinum will cease to be useful to us.
    b. Abundant platinum supplies will be discovered in China.
    c. A platinum mine will be set up on the moon.
    d. Gold will replace platinum in vehicle exhaust systems.

48 Green Houses

1 Saving the environment is a hot topic right now, and most companies are thinking of ways to "go green," that is, they want to reduce pollution and save electricity. In the construction industry, this trend is also becoming popular not only for large buildings but also for people's homes. People are keen to know how they can make their homes more sustainable and hopefully save some money on utility bills in the process.

⌄ green houses with solar panels and a wind turbine

2 So how do you reduce energy use in your home, and how do you make your home eco-friendly? The answer might be to build a "green" house. Green houses look similar to the houses we live in today, with a few noticeable differences. They have solar panels installed on the roofs or have a system of converting wind power into electricity to generate their own power. During the daytime, when the house is not occupied, power is generated and stored in batteries for later use at night. This energy is completely free, and if there's any excess power it can be sold back to an electricity grid at a profit. Imagine getting paid by a power company instead of paying them! Most importantly, solar and wind power are pure, clean forms of energy which will not cause damage to the environment.

3 Another way that green houses stay eco-friendly is by cutting their energy consumption as much as possible. One of the main reasons we use so much power in our homes is to heat or cool them. Green houses are specially designed to keep the temperature inside stable without using any power, preserving the heat in winter and keeping it out in summer. 30

4 Finally, green houses are built largely from recycled materials, including recycled plastic, paper, and rubber. This way, they can ease the burden on the environment for raw materials. You can paint your next house whatever color you like, but if you want to save money and help the environment, just make sure it's green through and through! 35

Questions

_____ 1. The second paragraph mostly focuses on _____.
    a. the damage that fossil fuels can cause
    b. how a solar panel works
    c. how a green house creates and uses power
    d. eco-friendly ways to keep you house warm

_____ 2. Which of the following is NOT a benefit of having a green house?
    a. You can save money.   b. It's better for the environment.
    c. You can earn money.   d. Your house will be safer.

_____ 3. Which problem is solved by the special design of green houses?
    a. Heating and cooling the house.   b. Keeping the house clean.
    c. Creating clean energy.   d. The high cost of electricity bills.

_____ 4. The writer ends the article with _____.
    a. a broad statement   b. a moving story
    c. a statistical survey   d. a play on words

_____ 5. What can be inferred from the final paragraph?
    a. Most of the materials we recycle go to building green houses.
    b. The environment is under pressure from the need for raw materials.
    c. Painting your house green will save you money.
    d. If you live in a green house, you don't have to recycle.

» Green houses often have solar panels installed on the roof.

49 Learning to Believe in Yourself

>> goal setting

1   Becoming an outgoing and confident person is like climbing a mountain. If you develop good habits, you start to feel better about yourself, and the summit seems within reach. But minor setbacks can easily lead to more difficulties. And before you know it, you're at the base of the mountain again, and the summit is nowhere in sight.   5

2   How do you keep climbing? It begins with positive behavior and habits. The most important of all is to avoid comparing yourself to others all the time. Now, this is easier said than done, because there's always someone to compare yourself to. It might be a character on your favorite television show, or a friend on your social media feed. But as   10 the popular phrase goes, "You do you." Don't worry about what they're doing; just be yourself.

3   The second most important step is to set objectives for yourself. Maybe you want to learn a new language, take up jogging, or get good grades in your class. The goal itself doesn't matter.   15 What matters is that it's *your* goal. And when you achieve it, you'll feel good about yourself. Try starting out with small aims and get more ambitious as you go along.

« Avoid comparing yourself to others.

» Believing in yourself is the first secret to success.

4   Next, surround yourself with positive people. Good energy can improve your life in a lot of ways. If there are people around you who are being mean 20 or negative, it can make you anxious and frustrated. Think of your friends, classmates, or just people in your life, and ask yourself: Is this person a positive influence? If not, maybe you should distance yourself from them.

5   Now you know the basic habits needed to build self-confidence. But here's some valuable advice to keep in mind along the way: don't be hard on 25 yourself. Don't hesitate to give yourself a pat on the back when you succeed. And even more importantly, don't beat yourself up when you fail. After all, we're only human. Accepting this fact is the key to truly accepting yourself.

≫ accepting and believing in yourself

⌃ Surround yourself with positive people.

Questions

_____ 1. According to the article, which of the following is a good habit for building self-confidence?
   a. Compare yourself to others.   **b.** Set goals for yourself.
   c. Be hard on yourself.   **d.** Always listen to advice.

_____ 2. Which of the following statements from this article is a fact?
   a. "We're only human."
   b. "The goal doesn't matter."
   c. "Being confident is like climbing a mountain."
   d. "Most important is to avoid comparing yourself to others."

_____ 3. What is the most likely profession of the person who wrote this article?
   a. A police officer.   **b.** A lawyer.
   c. A scientist.   **d.** A school counselor.

_____ 4. How is the information in this article mostly presented?
   a. In alphabetical order.   **b.** In order of importance.
   c. In random order.   **d.** In historical order.

_____ 5. What is the author's tone in this article?
   a. Playful.   **b.** Sad.   **c.** Serious.   **d.** Critical.

50 | Nightmares

1   Many of us have woken up in the night, covered in cold sweat and feeling a deep sense of fear. Terrible images flash through your head as you recall the horrifying things you've just experienced. This is often followed a few moments later by a sigh of relief, though. It was all just a bad dream.

2   Nightmares are vivid dreams that tear you out of a deep sleep and leave you with a strong negative emotion. In the past, people thought that nightmares were caused by an evil spirit called a mare, which tormented sleepers with bad dreams—hence the name "nightmare." Now, however, we know that nightmares can be caused by both psychological and chemical factors.

3   Stress and worry are two of the most common causes of nightmares. Adults may have dreams in which they are unable to escape from danger or are falling from a great height. These kinds of nightmares are usually connected to strong doubts or fears they have at work or in their personal lives. Repeated nightmares can also come after experiencing something particularly scary or upsetting, such as being attacked or witnessing a violent event. People will often relive these events night after night during their sleep, and it can sometimes take professional help to rid them of these bad dreams.

5

10

15

20

⌃ evil spirit

⌄ Getting professional help can help you get rid of bad dreams.

⌃ Nightmares are vivid dreams that leave you with a strong negative emotion.

4 Another reason for nightmares, and one that's easier to avoid, is eating late-night snacks. Eating food late at night means your brain will be more active when you sleep, and so you are more likely to have vivid, realistic, 25 and often frightening dreams. Additionally, taking certain types of drugs, especially ones that affect chemicals in the brain such as those that combat depression, are likely to lead to nightmares.

≪ Repeated nightmares can come after scary experiences.

5 If your sleep is often disturbed by the same nightmare, there's a simple technique that you can perform to stop it. You should try to 30 think up an alternate, happy ending to your nightmare and rehearse it in your mind while you're awake. Think about it again just before you go to sleep, and your mind should replace the frightening ending with the happy one you've rehearsed. Sweet dreams!

Questions

≫ late-night snack

_____ 1. Which of the following is presented as a solution to certain kinds of nightmares?
   a. Eating a late-night snack.
   b. Taking antidepression drugs.
   c. Rehearing an alternate, happy ending.
   d. Falling from a great height.

_____ 2. How would you describe the author's tone in the first paragraph?
   a. Distressed and then relieved.   **b.** Depressed and then anxious.
   c. Serious and then nervous.   **d.** Comic and then tragic.

_____ 3. What is the main idea of the third paragraph?
   a. If you have nightmares, you may need professional help.
   b. Being unable to escape from danger is a common nightmare.
   c. People have nightmares all the time.
   d. Stress and worry cause nightmares.

_____ 4. Which of the following is NOT true about nightmares?
   a. Nightmares often come from experiencing something upsetting.
   b. Nightmares leave you with a strong negative emotion.
   c. Nightmares result from both psychological and chemical reasons.
   d. People used to think nightmares were caused by the moon.

_____ 5. Most of the article is focused on _____.
   a. how to treat nightmares
   b. the causes of nightmares
   c. examples of common nightmares
   d. how the word "nightmare" originated

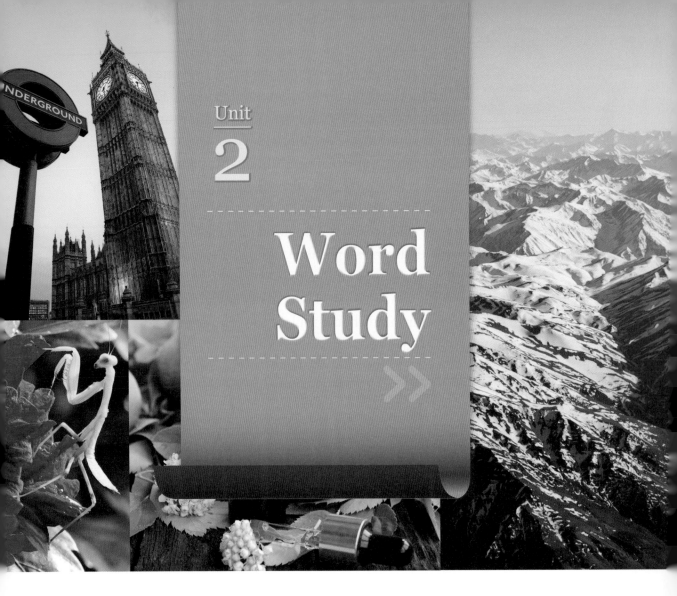

Unit
2

Word Study

2-1   Synonyms (Words With the Same Meaning)

2-2   Antonyms (Words With Opposite Meanings)

2-3   Words in Context

2-4   Review Test

It's difficult to develop good reading skills if you don't know what any of the words in a sentence mean. English can be particularly challenging, as it is a language with more than 400,000 words just waiting to be memorized. Luckily, there are also a few word skills that will help you work out the meaning of an unknown word. This section will help teach you these skills. Once you have reached the end of it, unfamiliar words won't seem so scary anymore. In fact, you might begin to look forward to coming across them!

2-1 *Synonyms*

English has the largest vocabulary of any language, with many words sharing a similar meaning. If you come across a difficult word while reading, try thinking of a simpler word that could take its place. Being able to think of different words that mean the same thing is an important skill for improving your reading comprehension.

⌄ Pets are often viewed as family members.

51 A Beloved Member of the Family

(051)

⌃ Some hotels welcome pets.

⌄ luxurious clothing for dogs

1   When **browsing** social media, we see people proudly sharing pictures of their pets. When walking down the street, it's common to see strollers with dogs or cats instead of babies. Although pets were once a **luxury** in many Asian cultures, an expanding middle class means more people can now afford to   5 have pets. Countries where pet ownership is on the rise include Japan, South Korea, Taiwan, India, Singapore, and Indonesia.

2   For young working adults and older people whose children are grown up, pets are often viewed as members of the family. These owners are happy to spend money to **pamper** their   10 pets. Pet lovers and businesses that produce pet products make up the "pet economy." In China, the amount of money spent on these products is expected to increase 21 percent per year. In Asia overall, the rate is eight percent per year.

3   Now, the pet industry includes a wide range of pet products, from   15 practical yet luxurious clothing for dogs to fancy cat trees for kitties. You can buy booties and a raincoat to protect your dog from **inclement** weather. And don't forget about expensive leashes and collars, of course.

« Pet lovers prefer high-quality pet food to keep their pets healthy.

Grooming, bathing, and nail clipping are available at pet spas, which even provide massages for sore muscles. 20

4 Pet lovers want their cats and dogs to be healthy and safe. They prefer high-quality pet food, with ingredients that meet the same standards as food for humans. In fact, the monthly price for some gourmet pet food is the same as that for human food! Of course, besides nutritious meals, all pets need to see a 25 veterinarian periodically to stay healthy as well.

5 When owners go on vacation, their cats or dogs can stay in a pet hotel. Even better, some hotels welcome pets. The Four Seasons, a five-star hotel chain throughout Asia, even offers a menu especially for pets.

6 The expansion of the pet economy shows that many owners are **enthusiastic** 30 about spending money to keep their pets clean, healthy, and happy. After all, they are part of the family.

Questions

_____ 1. "When **browsing** social media, we see people proudly sharing pictures of their pets." Which of the following has the same meaning as **browsing** in the sentence above?
   a. Writing a comment.   **b.** Studying carefully.
   c. Taking a photo.   **d.** Looking through.

_____ 2. "Although pets were once a **luxury** in many Asian cultures, an expanding middle class means more people can now afford to have pets." Which of the following has the same meaning as **luxury** in the sentence above?
   a. Necessary action.   **b.** Something expensive.
   c. Against traditions.   **d.** Risky choice.

_____ 3. "These owners are happy to spend money to **pamper** their pets." Which of the following has the same meaning as **pamper** in the sentence above?
   a. Own.   **b.** Feed.   **c.** Spoil.   **d.** Ignore.

_____ 4. "You can buy booties and a raincoat to protect your dog from **inclement** weather." Which of the following has the same meaning as **inclement** in the sentence above?
   a. Stormy.   **b.** Scorching.   **c.** Dangerous.   **d.** Unpredictable.

_____ 5. "The expansion of the pet economy shows that many owners are **enthusiastic** about spending money to keep their pets clean, healthy, and happy." Which of the following has the same meaning as **enthusiastic** in the sentence above?
   a. Excited.   **b.** Practicing.   **c.** Considering.   **d.** Unsure.

>> the Andes
mountain range

52 The Andes Mountain Range

1   Look at a map of South America, and you'll see a long, curving **spine** of mountains running down the entire western coast of the continent. This enormous stretch of volcanic **peaks** and lofty ridges runs from north to south through a total of seven countries and covers a distance of over 7,000 km, passing through the equator and ending near the icy waters of the Southern Ocean.

2   The Andes has an average height of 4,000 meters above sea level, and its highest **peak**, Aconcagua, reaches an altitude of 6,962 m. This makes the Andes the highest mountain range outside Asia. The Himalayas are, of course, the highest mountain range in the world; however, due to the fact that the Andes pass through the equator, the summit of Mount Chimborazo in Ecuador is the point on the earth's surface that is farthest from the earth's core.

⌄ ancient Incan city in the Andes

3   The Andes is an area of stunning diversity in landscape, climate, wildlife, and plants. The northern part of the Andes is humid, hot, and rainy—**conditions** perfect for rainforests. Indeed, the Amazon rain forest borders much of the northern Andes, and the mighty Amazon River even begins its life as a small trickle of water emerging from a cliff face high up in the

5

10

15

20

Aconcagua in Argentina is the highest peak in the Andes.
(cc by Daniel Peppes Gauer)

mountains. The central region is milder, while the southern Andes are cold and largely uninhabited. The climate in the Andes can be so unpredictable that the local residents say they often experience "four seasons in one day." 25

4 Despite its **changeable** climate, one of the most important civilizations of the last thousand years—the Incan civilization—developed in the Andes. The Incans carved terraces into the steep slopes of the mountains to grow crops such as potatoes and corn. In 1532, the Spanish **conquered** the Incans. The name Andes is thought by some to come from the Spanish word *andén*, which means "platform." 30

5 The Spanish built a colonial city in Quito, which now attracts thousands of tourists every year. From the city, tourists can take day trips to go hiking, climbing, river rafting, and exploring, all while enjoying the majestic beauty of the Andes.

Quito is packed with historical monuments and architectural treasures.

historic colonial buildings in Quito

Questions

_____ 1. Which of the following words has the same meaning as **spine** in the first sentence of the article?
   a. Backbone.   **b.** Height.   **c.** Country.   **d.** Distance.

_____ 2. "The northern part of the Andes is humid, hot, and rainy—**conditions** perfect for rain forests." Another word for **conditions** is _____.
   a. positions   **b.** ranges   **c.** circumstances   **d.** backgrounds

_____ 3. "Despite its **changeable** climate, one of the most important civilizations of the last thousand years—the Incan civilization—developed in the Andes." Which of the following words could replace **changeable** in the sentence above?
   a. Fixed.   **b.** Irregular.   **c.** Attractive.   **d.** Comfortable.

_____ 4. Which of the following words is closest in meaning to **peak** in the first sentence of the second paragraph?
   a. Center.   **b.** Summit.   **c.** Area.   **d.** Volcano.

_____ 5. "In 1532, the Spanish **conquered** the Incans . . ." Which of the following words has the same meaning as **conquer**?
   a. Construct.   **b.** Grow.   **c.** Represent.   **d.** Defeat.

≙ **Chanel boutique**

≈ Chanel No. 5 perfume

(053) 53 | Chanel

In 1909, Gabrielle Bonheur "Coco" Chanel **founded** the House of Chanel, a Parisian fashion house. Born on August 19, 1883, Chanel was one of the most respected designers of the 20th century, and she made a long-lasting impact on the fashion industry. She **transformed** high-style fashion by replacing traditional uncomfortable and restrictive clothing with a new casual and elegant style, allowing women to feel comfortable in their clothes as well as retain a high sense of fashion.

Coco Chanel originally made decorated hats that were worn by fashion-conscious French women. In 1913, though, she introduced a range of comfortable women's sportswear that allowed for freedom of movement, and her **tasteful** clothing became widely known in France for its simplicity. Some years later, her legendary perfume, Chanel No. 5, was launched, and it has since become one of the most famous **fragrances** of all time, worn by just about every female megastar of the past 60 years. Marilyn Monroe even said that all she wore to bed was a few drops of Chanel No. 5.

Chanel's status as a fashion **legend** was even more firmly established when she released the "little black dress," a sexy dress made of thin black silk that caused a stir in fashion circles and is imitated to this day.

« Coco Chanel (1883–1971)
(cc by chariserin)

4 When World War II began, Chanel retired, closing her dressmaking business so that her company only continued to sell accessories and jewelry. Her relationship with a Nazi officer during the war resulted 30 in her exile to Switzerland and her years of decreasing popularity. In 1954 she came back to France, started selling clothing again, and soon rose to the upper ranks of fashion marketing and design.

5 Coco Chanel died on January 10, 1971, at the age of 87. During her life, she led a fashion revolution that still inspires 35 many of today's greatest fashion designers. When German-born designer Karl Lagerfeld was appointed artistic director for the House of Chanel in 1983, a new, modern, and more adventurous style was introduced, and once again, Chanel was at the head of fashion. 40

⌃ *Coco Before Chanel* movie poster

⌵ Chanel handbag (cc by Liu Wen Cheng)

Questions

_____ 1. "In 1909, Gabrielle Bonheur 'Coco' Chanel **founded** the House of Chanel, a Parisian fashion house." A synonym for the word **found** is _____.
   a. design   **b.** sell   **c.** establish   **d.** cause

_____ 2. "Chanel's status as a fashion **legend** was even more firmly established when she released the 'little black dress,' . . ." The word **legend** in the sentence above could be replaced by which of the following words?
   a. Myth.   **b.** Marvel.   **c.** Tale.   **d.** History.

_____ 3. ". . . her **tasteful** clothing became widely known in France for its simplicity." A synonym for the word **tasteful** in this sentence is _____.
   a. famous   **b.** delicious   **c.** comfortable   **d.** stylish

_____ 4. "She **transformed** high-style fashion by replacing traditional uncomfortable and restrictive clothing with a new casual and elegant style, . . ." Another word for **transform** is _____.
   a. influence   **b.** change   **c.** create   **d.** destroy

_____ 5. "Some years later, her legendary perfume, Chanel No. 5, was launched, and it has since become one of the most famous **fragrances** of all time." The word **fragrances** in this sentence could be replaced by _____.
   a. scents   **b.** garments   **c.** accessories   **d.** designs

54 The London Underground

1 The London Underground, opened on January 10, 1863, was the world's first subway system, and it remains one of the world's largest underground rail networks. Also known as the Underground and the Tube, it serves 270 stations and has about 402 kilometers of **track**, making it the world's fourth-longest subway system by route length.

2 The Tube carries about 1.35 billion **commuters** a year, with up to five million passengers using the system every weekday. One of the things that makes the Tube so convenient is its clear and easy-to-follow map. The Tube map, designed in 1931, was a **unique** creation and has influenced almost every urban rail map since then. The stations represented on the map are not necessarily in the positions that they would be on a geographical map of the city. This would make the map too tangled and difficult to read. Instead, the emphasis is on having the stations arranged in the proper order, with the connecting stations lined up correctly. In addition, the system's 11 lines are color-coded to make it even easier for passengers to comprehend the map.

3 As many **frustrated** Londoners would surely confirm, though, the Underground is also famous for its delays. It is estimated that the average commuter loses around three days per year as a result of late trains. Another

≪ The London Underground serves 270 stations and has about 402 kilometers of track.

≪ London Underground sign, first used in 1908. Now this logo is used by other London transportation systems.

big problem of the Underground is overcrowding, especially during the morning 25 and evening rush hours. While many stations have been rebuilt in an attempt to combat this problem, congestion is still common, and trains often have to skip a station and carry on to the nearest uncrowded one. A lack of air-conditioning on some of the trains can also make journeys uncomfortably hot in summer, with temperatures in some of the deep tunnels reaching 30 34.5°C or even higher.

4 Despite these flaws, the London Underground is one of the world's safest and most convenient ways to travel. Accidents are incredibly **rare**, with only one fatal accident per 300 million journeys. As anyone who 35 has been to London will tell you, exploring that great city without the Tube would be unthinkable.

⌃ London underground train

Questions

_____ 1. "The Tube map, designed in 1931, was a **unique** creation and has influenced almost every urban rail map since then." Which of the following words could replace **unique** in the sentence above?
a. Well-known. **b.** Constant. **c.** One-of-a-kind. **d.** Simple.

_____ 2. "As many **frustrated** Londoners would surely confirm, though, the Underground is also famous for its delays." Which of the following words has the same meaning as **frustrated**?
a. Late. **b.** Carefree. **c.** Uncomfortable. **d.** Annoyed.

_____ 3. "The Tube carries about 1.35 billion **commuters** a year, with up to five million passengers using the system every weekday." Another word for **commuter** is _____.
a. traveler **b.** train **c.** carriage **d.** resident

_____ 4. "Accidents are incredibly **rare**, with only one fatal accident per 300 million journeys." Which of the following words is closest in meaning to **rare**?
a. Dense. **b.** Risky. **c.** Uncommon. **d.** Painful.

_____ 5. "Also known as the Underground and the Tube, it serves 270 stations and has about 402 kilometers of **track**, . . ." The word **track** can have several meanings. In which of the following sentences does it have the same meaning as in the sentence above?
a. The hunters were able to track the prey with dogs.
b. The coal trains run along this railroad track.
c. It was more a dirt track than a road.
d. I jog around the track every morning for one hour.

>> **Extreme preppers believe the end of the world is coming.**

55
The Prepper Movement 🎧055

1   Have you ever wondered what you'd do if disaster struck? Where would you get your food? How would you survive without running water and electricity? If you've ever **pondered** these questions before,
5   then you might have what it takes to be a prepper.

2   Preppers, or survivalists as they're sometimes called, are people who are preparing for the worst. Some of them seem like panicked and crazy individuals who are convinced the world is going to end. But those are just the extreme preppers.
10   Most of them are simply preparing for more **likely** events like forest fires, earthquakes, or economic collapse. Some are simply

⌃ a copy of *Survival Under Atomic Attack*, a Civil Defense publication issued in 1950

⌃ Preppers' principles include storing a year's supply of essentials.

« bread aisle with empty racks as residents shopped and prepared for Hurricane Irma, September 2017

worried about a loved one passing away and leaving their family finances in trouble.

3 Preppers like to live by five major **principles**: keep a year's supply of essentials such as food and water; be independent; be self-sufficient; be hardworking; and don't be wasteful. For the most part, these rules are good advice for anyone who's worried about the future. Public **criticism** tends to focus on the more extreme preppers. They are the ones who store guns and train their children to use deadly weapons. It's like they're preparing for a war without knowing who they'll be fighting against.

4 It's understandable that survivalism breeds such extreme behavior, given its origins. The prepper movement grew out of the Cold War years, when people lived in daily fear of being wiped out by a nuclear bomb. Government broadcasts advised people on how to survive a nuclear attack, and millions of them caught the survivalist **bug**. Since then, events like Y2K, 9/11, and H1N1 have caused interest in survivalism to grow. It just goes to show that the human desire to survive is one that will never really go away.

>> A ready-to-go preparedness kit is a common item for preppers.

Questions

_____ 1. "If you've ever **pondered** these questions before, then you might have what it takes to be a prepper." Which of the following words could replace **pondered** in the sentence above?
   a. Forgot.   **b.** Discovered.   **c.** Confused.   **d.** Considered.

_____ 2. Which of the following words could replace **likely** in the second paragraph?
   a. Probable.   **b.** Enjoyable.   **c.** Serious.   **d.** Surprising.

_____ 3. Which of the following words could replace **principles** in the third paragraph?
   a. Leaders.   **b.** Beliefs.   **c.** Weaknesses.   **d.** Experiences.

_____ 4. What does the word **criticism** in the third paragraph mean?
   a. Knowledge.   **b.** Encouragement.
   c. Disagreement.   **d.** Fury.

_____ 5. "Government broadcasts advised people on how to survive a nuclear attack, and millions of them caught the survivalist **bug**." Which of the following words has the same meaning as **bug** in the sentence above?
   a. Organization.   **b.** Disaster.
   c. Tool.   **d.** Virus.

↟ smart contact lens

56 | Seeing Smart

(056)

2-2 Antonyms

For every good, there's a bad, and every night will eventually give way to day. English is full of words that have opposite meanings, and authors often use these opposite concepts to make their writing more interesting. So when you learn a new word, take a second to think about what its opposite is.

1   Smart contact lenses? Yes indeed! The race is on to develop and sell technology that can be placed directly onto a human eye. It sounds like science fiction, 5 but in fact, it's already being done, at least in laboratories.

2   In 2014, Google announced that it was developing a special contact lens for diabetics. This "smart" lens would monitor blood sugar levels by **constantly** measuring the amount of sugar in one's tears. This information would be sent to the wearer's smartphone, and 10 possibly to his or her doctor as well. The result? Diabetics would be able to keep track of their blood sugar without the need for actual blood tests.

3   Unfortunately, the sugar in a person's tears is not an accurate indication of that person's blood sugar level. 15

↟ Colormax contact lenses can cure color blindness.

≫ concept of smart contact lens

↟ Smart contact lenses for augmented reality purposes are being developed.

Experts **dismissed** the Google contact lens as an impossible idea. Work continues, but there's been no word on the project for some time.

[4]   Others, however, have been more successful with this type of technology. Colormax contact lenses are able to cure color blindness, and are already available. Researchers have also developed contact lenses that can instantly 20 focus the eyes, thus helping people with vision problems.

[5]   How is such a thing possible? Tiny, **extremely** thin microchips are placed in the middle layers of contact lenses. This keeps them away from the surface of the eye, so there is no danger to the wearer—we hope! The chips store information which can then be sent to an outside device or saved in the lenses 25 themselves. This is the very **cutting edge** of research and development.

[6]   Medical applications may be the most **obvious** use for smart contact lenses, but there are others. Night vision lenses are in the works. Sony has patented a lens that can record video of anything a person sees. It is powered and operated by blinks of the eye, if you can believe that. Not to be outdone, Samsung has 30 been developing lenses for game-playing purposes. It seems clear that smart contact lenses will continue to evolve and become more accessible in the future.

Questions

_____ 1. Which of the following means the opposite of **constantly** as it is used in the second paragraph?

    a. Always.   **b.** Never.   **c.** Correctly.   **d.** Incorrectly.

_____ 2. Which of the following means the opposite of **dismissed** as it is used in the third paragraph?

    a. Forgot about.   **b.** Looked forward to.

    c. Praised enthusiastically.   **d.** Laughed at.

_____ 3. Which of the following is the opposite of **extremely** as the word is used in the fifth paragraph?

    a. Slightly.   **b.** Very.   **c.** Noticeably.   **d.** Uncomfortably.

_____ 4. Which of the following ideas is NOT on the **cutting edge** as the phrase is used in the fifth paragraph?

    a. Taking pictures with a telephone.

    b. Sending people to other planets.

    c. Measuring blood sugar with a contact lens.

    d. Creating robots that have human senses.

_____ 5. Which of the following means the opposite of **obvious** in the sixth paragraph?

    a. Difficult.   **b.** Important.   **c.** Strange.   **d.** Secondary.

the legendary Loch Ness monster

∧ Loch Ness (cc by Sam Fentress)

57 The Loch Ness Monster

(057) **1** In the middle of Scotland, far from any of the big cities, lies the mysterious Loch Ness. While it is not the largest lake in Scotland, it is the deepest body of water in the United Kingdom, and it contains more freshwater than all of the lakes in England and Wales combined. Loch Ness is 230 meters deep in some places. However, its **impressive** depth is not why Loch Ness is famous. It's famous because of its **legendary** inhabitant: the Loch Ness monster, which is also known as Nessie.

∨ Most people describe the Loch Ness monster as a strange animal with a long neck and a small head. (cc by Michael Hicks)

2 People have been claiming the existence of a strange creature in Loch Ness for hundreds of years. The first report came in 1933, when a British man and his wife claimed to have witnessed a **monstrous** animal moving slowly across the road toward the loch. There have been many other sightings since then. Most of them describe a strange animal with a long neck and a small head, somewhat similar to the plesiosaur, a dinosaur from the early Jurassic period. Over the years, people have called this strange creature a "monster fish," "sea serpent," and "dragon." Eventually, they settled on "Loch Ness monster." Most people claim to have caught a glimpse of the monster somewhere in the dark water, though there are a few

5

10

15

20

» reconstruction of Nessie as a plesiosaur outside Museum of Nessie (cc by StaraBlazkova)

who swear they saw it on land near the loch. Several people have taken photographs of the creature, but their pictures always seem to end up **blurred**. Many of these photos have been proven to be hoaxes.   25

3   Although several attempts have been made to prove that the Loch Ness monster exists, the results have always been inconclusive. Most scientists agree that the existence of such a creature in the loch is unlikely, and they regard the sightings as a mix of hoaxes and wishful thinking. Nevertheless, this does not **discourage** people to come and   30 see for themselves. Thousands of tourists flock to Loch Ness every year hoping to be lucky enough to spot the monster. Real or not, the home of the   35 Loch Ness monster has become one of the United Kingdom's most celebrated tourist destinations.   40

⌃ *Cryptoclidus* model used in the Channel Five TV program "Loch Ness Monster: The Ultimate Experiment"

Questions

_____ 1. Which of the following means the opposite of **impressive** as it is used in the first-paragraph sentence "However, its **impressive** depth is not . . ."?
 a. Unimportant. **b.** Influential. **c.** Statistical. **d.** Imposing.

_____ 2. Which of the following means the opposite of **legendary** in the first paragraph?
 a. Lofty.   **b.** Intense.   **c.** Unknown.   **d.** Respectable.

_____ 3. Which of the following is an example of something that most people would NOT think is something that is **monstrous**, as the word is used in the second paragraph?
 a. A dragon.   **b.** A dinosaur. **c.** A teddy bear. **d.** A giant spider.

_____ 4. Which of the following means the opposite of the word **blurred** as it is used in the second-paragraph sentence ". . . but their pictures always seem to end up **blurred**"?
 a. Complicated. **b.** Clear.   **c.** Expensive.   **d.** Tragic.

_____ 5. Which of the following means the opposite of **discourage** in the final paragraph?
 a. Anger.   **b.** Sadden.   **c.** Delete.   **d.** Support.

58 | The Nobel Peace Prize

058

1   Of the six Nobel Prize categories, the most well-known is **undoubtedly** the Nobel Peace Prize. The Nobel Prizes for peace, physics, chemistry, literature, and medicine were first given out by the estate of Swedish scientist Alfred Nobel in 1901. In 1969, a prize for economics was added. According to Alfred Nobel's will, the peace prize should be awarded to the individual who has done "the best work for **fraternity** between nations, the disbanding or reduction of standing armies, and the promotion of peace congresses." Every year, Nobel Peace Prize winners must travel to Oslo in Norway to receive their award. The ceremony for the other five prizes takes place in Stockholm, Sweden, instead. In the **presence** of the King of Norway, the Nobel Peace Prize winner receives a diploma, a medal, and a document confirming the prize amount.

⌃ Alfred Nobel (1833–1896)

2   The Nobel Peace Prize winner is selected by a committee of five people after reviewing the cases of thousands of applicants. The careful screening of applicants is one of the reasons why the peace prize is so glorious in the eyes of the public.

Nobel Peace Prize Winners

⌄ Martin Luther King, Jr. (1929–1968)

⌄ Nelson Mandela (1918–2013)

⌃ Mother Teresa (1910–1997)

⌃ the Dalai Lama (1935–)

3 Some past recipients of the prize include Albert Schweitzer, Dr. Martin Luther King, Jr., Mother Teresa, Mikhail Gorbachev, Nelson Mandela, the Dalai Lama, Bishop Desmond Tutu, and former US President Jimmy Carter.   25 Past Nobel Peace Prize winners were usually selected for their bravery and dedication to the promotion of peace or for their tireless efforts working on humanitarian issues. Many past recipients are people who struggled to establish democracy in their countries.

4 There have been some intense controversies in   30 the past, both in terms of nominations and people who were overlooked. One such example is the awarding of the peace prize to US President Obama in 2009. At the time of the award, he had just started his term in office. Many people wondered how much   35 he could have done for world peace in just one year.

5 Regardless of a few **controversial** recipients, the Nobel Peace Prize remains a powerful global symbol of people coming together to accomplish something **positive**.   40

⌃ Obama's peace prize was controversial and was called a "stunning surprise" by *The New York Times*. (cc by Pete Souza)

Questions

_____ 1. Which of the following means the opposite of **undoubtedly** in the first paragraph?
   a. Rapidly.   **b.** Questionably.   **c.** Interestingly.   **d.** Consequentially.

_____ 2. Which of the following means the opposite of **fraternity** as it is used in the first-paragraph phrase ". . . the best work for **fraternity** between nations"?
   a. Origin.   **b.** Confusion.   **c.** Hatred.   **d.** Change.

_____ 3. Which of the following means the opposite of the word **presence** as it is used in the first-paragraph sentence "In the **presence** of the King of Norway, . . ."?
   a. Absence.   **b.** Sense.   **c.** Present.   **d.** Innocence.

_____ 4. According to the final-paragraph, someone or something that is **controversial** is NOT _____.
   a. questionable   **b.** arguable   **c.** disputable   **d.** safe

_____ 5. Which of the following means the opposite of **positive** in the final-paragraph phrase "a powerful global symbol of people coming together to accomplish something **positive**"?
   a. Neutral.   **b.** Negative.   **c.** Explosive.   **d.** Original.

(059)

59 The Crown Jewels

1 "Crown jewels" is a term used to describe the jewelry that belongs to a country's royal family. These **valuable** treasures are usually passed down from one generation to the next. They serve as a powerful symbol of the royal family's right to rule over a country. While there are royal families with crown jewels all around the world, one of the most famous collections belongs to the British royal family.

2 The British Crown Jewels have been stored in the Tower of London since 1303. The collection includes crowns, scepters, orbs, swords, and other priceless artifacts. The British Crown Jewels are considered to be the most valuable collection of jewels in the world. They are also among the world's largest collections of jewels. The oldest piece in the collection is a golden spoon that dates back to the 13th century.

3 Many people find the crown to be the most **fascinating** piece of the British Crown Jewels collection. The Imperial State Crown was made in 1838. Many of its gems are of **ancient** origin. It has around 2,800 diamonds (including the 317-carat Cullinan II diamond), more than 270 pearls, 17 sapphires, 11 emeralds, and 5 rubies.

« King George VI (1895–1952) is holding the Scepter with the Cross, which contains the 530-carat Cullinan I diamond.

It has been used in the coronation of every British monarch since Queen   30
Victoria, who herself was crowned with the lighter State Crown.

4   The Scepter with the Cross, made in 1661, is another important
artifact in the collection. Its **central** feature is the Cullinan diamond,
also known as the Great Star of Africa, which is the largest gem-quality
diamond in the world. The Scepter with the Dove, also made in 1661,   35
symbolizes the Holy Ghost. During the coronation, the monarch holds
the Scepter with the Cross in his or her right hand and the Scepter with
the Dove in the left.

5   The Sovereign's Orb, also made in 1661,
is a religious symbol that indicates the   40
monarch's status as supreme governor of the
Church of England.

6   The crown jewels were stolen by Thomas
Blood in 1671, but he was caught, and they
were returned **unharmed**. Since then, there   45
have been many other attempts to steal them,
but none have been successful.

⌃ the orb as part of the crown
jewels of Poland (cc by Gryffindor)

Questions

⌃ Imperial
State
Crown

_____ 1. Which of the following means the opposite of **valuable** in the sentence
"These **valuable** treasures are usually passed down . . ."?
   a. Rare.   **b.** Immense.   **c.** Cheap.   **d.** Brilliant.

_____ 2. Which of the following means the opposite of the word **fascinating** as it is
used in the third-paragraph sentence "Many people find the crown to be
the most **fascinating** piece . . ."?
   a. Worrying.   **b.** Annoying.   **c.** Painful.   **d.** Boring.

_____ 3. Which of the following means the opposite of **ancient** as it is used in the
third-paragraph sentence "Many of its gems are of **ancient** origin"?
   a. Recent.   **b.** Eastern.   **c.** Amazing.   **d.** Divine.

_____ 4. Which of the following means the opposite of **central** as it is used in the
fourth-paragraph sentence "Its **central** feature is the Cullinan diamond, . . ."?
   a. Minor.   **b.** Durable.   **c.** Stormy.   **d.** Suitable.

_____ 5. Which of the following means the opposite of **unharmed** as it is used in the
final-paragraph sentence ". . . but he was caught and they were returned
unharmed"?
   a. Tame.   **b.** Harassed.   **c.** Damaged.   **d.** Steep.

60 | Spelunking 060

1 Spelunking, or caving, is an exciting and dangerous recreational sport that involves exploring caves around the world. If this sounds like a fun adventure, keep in mind that spelunkers crawl through mud and dirt, climb **steep** rock faces, squeeze through narrow openings between rocks, and even swim through tunnels of pitch-black water. That doesn't sound like a **casual** sport! In fact, most outsiders regard spelunking as an extreme sport that can be quite risky at times.

2 There are many cave systems that are still unexplored, and spelunkers strive to be the first to set foot in them. This could mean trouble, because they are exploring an area that has never been seen before. There can be sudden drops and even flash flooding if the cave is near water. If a spelunker gets injured, gets lost, or loses contact with the surface, his or her life might be in danger.

3 Proper equipment can be the difference between a spelunking adventure and a **tragedy**. Having enough light is important, because losing the ability to see what's around them can put the spelunkers in a vulnerable situation. Cavers should always wear a hard hat with a light mounted on it, and they should have extra batteries on hand. **Sturdy** clothing and footwear, ropes, first-aid kits, food, ladders, and other emergency equipment are all also very important.

4 Air quality can be a problem when exploring caves. Some caves are air-locked, and they have high levels of carbon dioxide. Without expensive detection equipment, it can be difficult to know if the air in the cave is bad. Usually, the first sign that a cave has foul air is the spelunker beginning to feel **fatigued**, anxious, hot, or clumsy. To help protect against this and other dangers, spelunkers are advised to always explore in groups.

⌃ spelunker
(cc by Dave Bunnell)

5 Spelunking first became a recreational sport in the early 20th century. The term "spelunking" was coined by Clay Perry in the 1940s, and since then it has become popular around the world. There are caving organizations for the administration and oversight of caving activities in many countries, the oldest being the French National Speleological Society, founded in 1895.

Questions

_____1. Which of the following is the closest to the opposite of **steep** as it is used in the first-paragraph sentence ". . . crawl through mud and dirt, climb **steep** rock faces, . . ."?
   a. Gentle.   **b.** Dangerous.   **c.** Bold.   **d.** Rocky.

_____2. Which of the following means the opposite of **casual** as it is used in the third-paragraph sentence "That doesn't sound like a **casual** sport"?
   a. Accessible.   **b.** Intense.   **c.** Light.   **d.** Ancient.

_____3. Which of the following means the opposite of **tragedy** as it is used in the third-paragraph sentence "Proper equipment can be the difference between a spelunking adventure and **tragedy**"?
   a. Breath.   **b.** Chapter.   **c.** Blessing.   **d.** Disaster.

_____4. Which of the following means the opposite of **sturdy** as it is used in the third-paragraph sentence "**Sturdy** clothing and footwear . . . are all also very important"?
   a. Intelligent.   **b.** Weak.   **c.** Plastic.   **d.** Tight.

_____5. Which of the following means the opposite of **fatigued** as it is used in the fourth-paragraph sentence "Usually, the first sign that a cave has foul air is the spelunker beginning to feel **fatigued**, . . ."?
   a. Energetic.   **b.** Apologetic.   **c.** Annoyed.   **d.** Confused.

« Stephens Gap, a vertical cave in Alabama (cc by Ky MacPherson)

When you come across an unfamiliar word, and you're not quite sure what it means, remember to take a close look at the words around it. Other words in a sentence can give you valuable clues. For example, consider the sentence "Jim was cold, wet, and miserable." Could miserable mean something good? Probably not.

⌃ entomologist

61 Insects

(061)

1   Insects are something that we come across every day, and most people see them as a big annoyance. However, these annoying little creatures are actually quite remarkable and an **essential** part of our ecosystem.

2   All insects have six legs, and unlike us, they don't have any bones.   5
An insect's body is divided into three distinct yet connected parts.
On the outside, there is an exoskeleton that acts like a suit of armor, helping to provide **rigidity**. While many species of insect can fly, there are still many that can't.

3   We know all this because of the hard work of entomologists,   10
which is the name of someone who studies insects.
Entomologists **have their work cut out for them** because there are more species of insects on Earth than all other types of living creatures combined. According to some sources, there are around one million known species of insects, and probably around 30 million species that have yet to be discovered.

⌃ insects

Entomologists **estimate** that insects make up 95% of all   20
animal life-forms on our planet.

⌃ stick insect

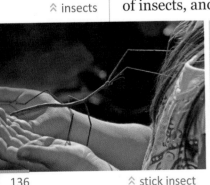

≪ mymaridae   ≫ insects

4 Insect size can range from the tiny mymaridae, which is about 0.139 millimeters long, to the stick insect, which can sometimes be over 55
25 centimeters in length. While no one is sure which insect is the heaviest in the world, the giant weta is definitely a competitor for the title, weighing in at around 70 grams.

5 Some insects are **pests**, such as mosquitoes, lice, bedbugs, flies, termites, locusts, and weevils. These insects can transmit disease,
30 damage structures, or destroy crops. Nevertheless, many insects are beneficial to the environment. They can loosen the soil, pollinate flowers and other plants, or produce useful substances such as honey, wax, and silk. Some insects feed on dead animals and fallen trees. Insects are often food for other
35 types of animals. Therefore, it can sometimes be dangerous to use insecticides to control pests. These chemicals don't just damage the environment, but also kill lots of insects that aren't doing us any harm.

≫ giant weta

⌃ insecticide

Questions

_____ 1. Which of the following is closest in meaning to the word **essential** in the first-paragraph sentence ". . . little creatures are . . . an **essential** part of our ecosystem"?
   a. Annoying.   **b.** Awake.   **c.** Obvious.   **d.** Necessary.

_____ 2. Which of the following words is closest in meaning to **rigidity** in the second-paragraph sentence ". . . there is an exoskeleton . . . helping to provide **rigidity**"?
   a. Stiffness.   **b.** Suspicion. **c.** Cooperation. **d.** Distribution.

_____ 3. Which of the following words is closest in meaning to **estimate** in the third-paragraph sentence "Entomologists **estimate** that insects make up 95% of all animal life-forms . . ."?
   a. Disturb.   **b.** Guess.   **c.** Illustrate.   **d.** Lack.

_____ 4. What does **have their work cut out for them** mean in the third-paragraph sentence "Entomologists **have their work cut out for them** . . ."?
   a. They don't have any work to do.   **b.** They have a hard time finding jobs.
   c. They have a lot of work to do.   **d.** There are not many entomologists.

_____ 5. Which of the following is closest in meaning to the word **pest** in the final-paragraph sentence "Some insects are **pests**, such as mosquitoes, lie, bedbugs, . . ."?
   a. Something that is very small.   **b.** Something that is troublesome.
   c. Something that can fly.   **d.** Something that has an exoskeleton.

62 Ernesto “Che” Guevara

062

22-year-old Ernesto Guevara in 1951

Ernesto Guevara (1928–1967) in his trademark olive-green military fatigues and beret

1 Ernesto Guevara was born in Argentina in 1928. During his boyhood, he was a big reader, a lover of poetry, a skilled chess player, and an excellent athlete. In 1948, he entered the University of Buenos Aires to study medicine. After completing his studies, he traveled through South America, helping the sick in some of that continent’s poorest nations. The trip **exposed** him to poverty and suffering on a daily basis, and he eventually vowed to do something about it.

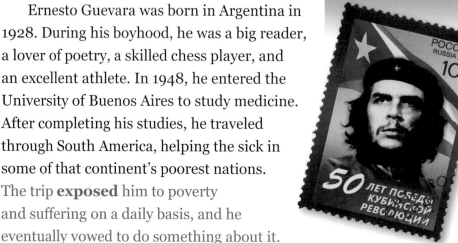

2 His first stop as a **revolutionary** was Guatemala. He went there in 1953 because he wanted to assist in Guatemalan President Jacobo Arbenz’s ambitious program of land **reform**. This is where Ernesto got his nickname “Che,” which means “hey,” because he used the casual term often in his speech. Che’s time in Guatemala was cut short when President Arbenz was overthrown by the American government in 1954. Che briefly took up the fight, but was soon forced to flee to Mexico.

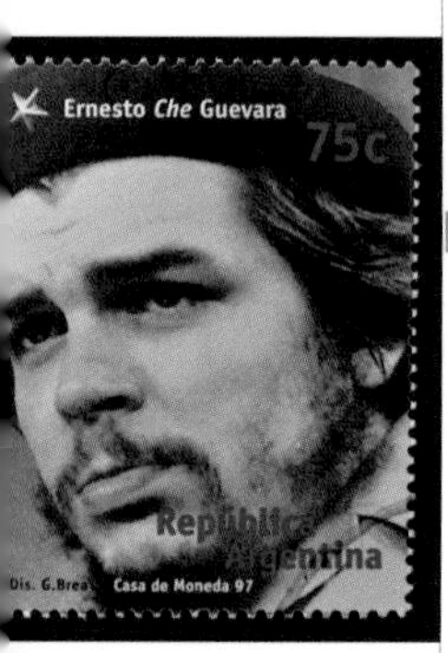

Ernesto Guevara in 1997

3 In 1956, Che joined a rebel group under the command of Fidel Castro. The group aimed to take down the government of Cuba and replace it with a communist government. At this point, Che gave up his profession as a physician and became a guerilla leader. In 1959, they managed to defeat the Cuban government and seize power.

4 After the communist victory in Cuba, Che was not **content**. He felt that there was still work to be done, and that he was a soldier, not a statesman. In 1965, Che

monument of Ernesto Guevara in La Higuera, Bolivia (cc by ConyJaro)

Ministry of Interior building, adorned with a steel sculpture of Ernesto Guevara, in Havana, Cuba

Guevara left Cuba to promote communist revolution elsewhere. Two years later, he was captured in Bolivia and **executed** by the Bolivian army.

Over 40 years after his death, Che remains a complex figure. He wrote several books, poems, and gave many memorable speeches over the course of his lifetime. Some people regard him as a romantic hero with the guts to sacrifice everything to help poor people. Others say that he was a traitor who helped destructive communist dictatorships come to power. Whichever you believe to be true, we are reminded of Che's life constantly on T-shirts, hats, posters, tattoos, and even bumper stickers.

Questions

_____ 1. Which of the following is closest in meaning to the word **exposed** in the first-paragraph sentence "The trip **exposed** him to poverty and suffering . . ."?
a. Showed.　　**b.** Massaged.　　**c.** Sacrificed.　　**d.** Stopped.

_____ 2. In the second paragraph, what does a **revolutionary** in the sentence "His first stop as a **revolutionary** was Guatemala" refer to?
a. Someone who works for the government.
b. Someone who fights in the army.
c. Someone who fights to change the government.
d. Someone who does not believe in fighting.

_____ 3. Which of the following is closest in meaning to the word **reform** in the second-paragraph sentence ". . . he wanted to assist in Guatemalan President Jacobo Arbenz's ambitious program of land **reform**"?
a. Satisfaction.　**b.** Improvement.　**c.** Intensity.　　**d.** Entertainment.

_____ 4. Which of the following is closest in meaning to the word **content** in the fourth-paragraph sentence "After the communist victory in Cuba, Che was not **content**"?
a. Angry.　　**b.** Satisfied.　　**c.** Lazy.　　**d.** Confused.

_____ 5. What does **execute** mean in the fourth-paragraph sentence "Two years later, he was captured in Bolivia and **executed** by the Bolivian army"?
a. To question someone.　　　**b.** To tickle someone.
c. To kill someone.　　　　　**d.** To release someone.

63 The Tweet That Started a Movement

1   You walk into your classroom and realize that you forgot to do your homework! Your friend says "Me too!" In that moment, you probably feel relief that you aren't the only one. The phrase "Me too" lets someone know that others feel the same way. In 2017, a tweet asked people to share if they had experienced the **ordeal** of sexual 5 abuse or sexual harassment, which is the receiving of inappropriate sexual comments or actions. This single tweet started the #MeToo movement.

2   #MeToo started in the United States, but **it** quickly spread around the world. In October 2017, The *New York Times* published an article 10 in which women told their personal stories of being sexually harassed or assaulted by a well-known Hollywood producer. If the women rejected his advances, their careers would be affected. Several days later, actress Alyssa Milano wrote the first #MeToo tweet. The phrase "Me too" was first used in 2006 by Tarana Burke in her organization 15 which supports victims of sexual crimes. Within nine days, the #MeToo tweet had been shared 2.3 million times in 85 countries.

3   As #MeToo spread around the world, it moved beyond the entertainment industry. Within a year, *Time* magazine had published a list of 140 famous men who had been **accused** 20 of sexual harassment or abuse while at work. It included politicians, heads of companies, reporters, authors, doctors,

⌄ Women's March protesters in front of the City Hall, San Francisco, January 20, 2018

» actress Alyssa Milano (1972–), the person who wrote the first #MeToo tweet

entertainers, and professors. In some countries, #MeToo was **adapted** to fit the language; #BalanceTonPorc (French meaning "**expose** your pig"), and #quellavoltache (Italian meaning "that time when"). Even in countries where the culture blamed abuse and harassment on the victim, women shared their stories. The #MeToo movement showed that many people around the world disagree with that mindset.

⌄ Women's March protesters, Philadelphia, January 20, 2018 (cc by Rob Kall)

4 It hasn't been easy for society to hear women share their experiences. Some people have said that #MeToo has gone too far, and that it is too easy to make accusations without proof. What is evident is that #MeToo has shown that people who have been harassed or assaulted at their job or school will no longer stay silent.

25

30

35

Questions

_____ **1.** Which of the following is closest in meaning to the word **ordeal** in the first-paragraph sentence ". . . they had experienced the **ordeal** of sexual abuse or sexual harassment . . ."?

    a. Unique situation.   **b.** Unpleasant experience.

    c. Difficult lesson.   **d.** Positive attitude.

_____ **2.** "Within a year, *Time* magazine had published a list of 140 famous men who had been **accused** of sexual harassment or abuse while at work." Which phrase could be used to replace **accused**?

    a. Said that another person has done something wrong.

    b. Stated that another person has not broken any rules.

    c. Stopped someone from committing a crime.

    d. Admitted that they are guilty of a crime.

_____ **3.** Which of the following is closest in meaning to the word **adapted** in the third-paragraph sentence "In some countries, #MeToo was **adapted** to fit the language . . ."?

    a. Adjusted.   **b.** Matched.   **c.** Written.   **d.** Learned.

_____ **4.** Which of the following is closest in meaning to the word **expose** in the third-paragraph sentence ". . . **expose** your pig . . ."?

    a. Save.   **b.** Cover.   **c.** Believe.   **d.** Reveal.

_____ **5.** "#MeToo started in the United States, but **it** quickly spread around the world." What does **it** mean in the sentence?

    a. The abuse.   **b.** The *New York Times*.

    c. The #MeToo movement.   **d.** A Hollywood producer.

64 The Minotaur

1 According to an ancient Greek legend, the Minotaur was a beast with a man's body and the head of a bull. It was kept in the Labyrinth, a twisting maze under the city of Knossos, which was the center of the Minoan civilization on the island of Crete.

2 Where did this creature come from? It all started when King Minos began to **quarrel** with his brothers over who had the right to rule Crete. In order to gain an advantage over them, King Minos asked the god Poseidon to give him a sign that he approved of his **reign**. He asked for a snow-white bull to sacrifice in honor of Poseidon. But when the bull arrived, King Minos decided that it was too delightful to sacrifice, so he kept it instead. When Poseidon learned of this insult, he devised a **scheme** to get revenge. Since King Minos was so fond of the bull, Poseidon made the king's wife fall passionately in love with the animal. The child that resulted from their union was a monster called the Minotaur.

3 With every passing year, the Minotaur became more and more savage. It slaughtered many people and caused terror and destruction on Crete. King Minos eventually ordered the architect Daedalus to build a massive maze,

5

10

15

20

⌃ Minotaur bust in the National Archaeological Museum of Athens

≫ *Theseus and the Minotaur in the Labyrinth*, 1861, tile design by Edward Burne-Jones (1833–1898)

≫ bronze statue of the Minotaur

or labyrinth, to trap the creature. Puzzled by the twisting maze, the Minotaur found that it could not escape. 25

Every nine years, seven girls and seven boys from Athens were dropped in the labyrinth to be **devoured** by the Minotaur. These sacrifices were a **tribute** to the gods. One day, the hero Theseus 30 volunteered to travel to Crete disguised as one of the victims and slay the Minotaur. With the help of Ariadne, King Minos's daughter, Theseus used a ball of string to avoid getting lost in the maze. When he came across the Minotaur, he drove his sword 35 through it and rescued all the Minotaur's prisoners. Theseus's skill and bravery helped him become one of the great heroes of Greek mythology.

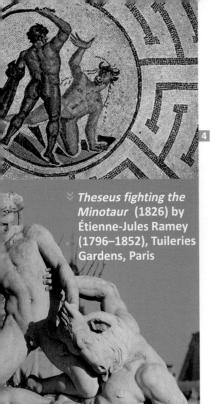

˅ *Theseus fighting the Minotaur* (1826) by Étienne-Jules Ramey (1796–1852), Tuileries Gardens, Paris

Questions

_____ 1. Which of the following is closest in meaning to the word **quarrel** in the second-paragraph sentence ". . . King Minos began to **quarrel** with his brothers . . ."?
   a. Surrender.   **b.** Argue.   **c.** Sink.   **d.** Inform.

_____ 2. What does **reign** mean in the second-paragraph sentence ". . . King Minos asked the god Poseidon to give him a sign that he approved of his **reign**"?
   a. A period of royal rule.   **b.** A hairstyle.
   c. A type of horse.   **d.** A kind of weather.

_____ 3. Which of the following is closest in meaning to the word **scheme** in the sentence ". . . he devised a **scheme** to get revenge"?
   a. Hand.   **b.** Wisdom.   **c.** Paper.   **d.** Plot.

_____ 4. What does **devour** mean in the fourth-paragraph sentence ". . . seven girls and seven boys . . . were dropped in the labyrinth to be **devoured** by the Minotaur"?
   a. To play.   **b.** To think.   **c.** To forgive.   **d.** To eat.

_____ 5. Which of the following is closest in meaning to the word **tribute** in the fourth-paragraph sentence "These sacrifices were a **tribute** to the gods"?
   a. Flag.   **b.** Picture.   **c.** Gift.   **d.** Idea.

» Early pencil cores were made of lead. (cc by Rob Lavinsky)

⌄ Most pencil cores are made of graphite nowadays.

« colored pencils

(065)

65
The Pencil

1   When most of us think about technology, we think of computers, smartphones, or 3D televisions. But technology can come in many different forms, and sometimes we can take past technological advances for granted. Take the pencil for example. This was once considered to be a **revolutionary** device that allowed us to record   5
our ideas quickly and cleanly. How revolutionary was it? Well, it has been almost 460 years since the graphite pencil was first invented, and it can still be found in classrooms around the world.

2   The earliest pencils were invented by the Romans, who used lead tubes to make markings on papyrus, an early form of paper. Even the   10
name "pencil" comes from the Latin word *penicillus*, which means "little tail." Although pencils do not contain the chemical element lead nowadays, many people still **refer to** the graphite in modern pencils as "lead."

3   The story of the modern pencil began in 1564, when a large   15
deposit of pure graphite was discovered in England. People found that it was perfect for marking sheep, and later it began to be used on paper. At first, the graphite was wrapped in string or sheep skin, and it quickly became popular with artists throughout Europe. The Italians further modified the graphite by **enclosing** it in wood. They   20
glued two wooden halves together around the graphite stick. This exceptional method is still in use today.

4 Nowadays, there are many different types of pencils. They're all graded according to their hardness on a scale that ranges from 9H (very hard) to 9B (very soft). Some pencils have replaced the black graphite with colored graphite. Pencils are undoubtedly popular. How widespread are they? Over 14 billion pencils are **manufactured** around the world every year. As for the wood required to make all these pencils, a good-sized tree will produce around 300,000 pencils.

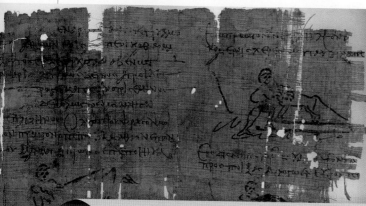

5 What about the answer to that **eternal** question of how long of a line could one pencil draw? The experts have even figured that out. The answer is around 113 kilometers.

25

30

35

« papyrus

Questions

F
H
2H
3H
4H
5H
6H
7H
8H
9H
9B
8B
7B
6B
5B
4B
3B
2B
B
HB

_____ **1.** Which of the following is closest in meaning to the word **revolutionary** in the first-paragraph sentence "This was once considered to be a **revolutionary** device . . ."?
 a. Silly. **b.** Unpopular. **c.** Innovative. **d.** Ancient.

_____ **2.** Which of the following is closest in meaning to the word **refer to** in the second-paragraph sentence ". . . many people still **refer to** the graphite in modern pencils as 'lead'"?
 a. Call. **b.** Assemble. **c.** Consult. **d.** Remember.

_____ **3.** Which of the following is closest in meaning to the word **enclose** in the third-paragraph sentence "The Italians further modified the graphite by **enclosing** it in wood"?
 a. Lock. **b.** Anger. **c.** Weep. **d.** Surround.

_____ **4.** Which of the following is closest in meaning to the word **manufacture** in the fourth-paragraph sentence "Over 14 billion pencils are **manufactured** around the world every year"?
 a. To close. **b.** To destroy. **c.** To make. **d.** To invent.

_____ **5.** What does the word **eternal** mean in the final-paragraph sentence "What about the answer to that **eternal** question . . ."?
 a. Something that lasts forever. **b.** Something that has ended.
 c. Something that is sad. **d.** Something that is frustrating.

« pencil grading chart

145

Douglas Bader (1910–1982)

⌄ Douglas Bader was an aviator during World War II.

066

66 | Douglas Bader

⌄ slow roll

1   Douglas Bader was one of the most famous British fighter pilots in World War II, not only because he was an excellent pilot but more so because he had no legs.

2   In 1928, at the age of 18, Bader joined the Royal Air Force (RAF) and soon became known as a natural pilot and an effective leader. After two years he was commissioned as an officer. Never one to follow the rules, Bader ignored his squadron commander's orders not to perform tricks under an altitude of 2,000 ft, and in 1931, while he was performing slow rolls at a very low altitude, his left wing hit the ground, and he crashed his airplane. Incredibly, he was not killed, but both of his legs had to be **amputated**, one above the knee and the other below.

3   Despite his terrible injury, Bader was unwilling to quit the RAF, and after recovering from his operation, he retook flight training and passed all the flight tests. The RAF, however, did not accept him back, and he was retired on medical grounds. Then in 1939, World War II broke out. Bader once again approached the RAF, requesting

5

10

15

20

⌄ Colditz Castle in 1945. Bader was a prisoner here for nearly three years.

that they take him back. In need of **experienced** pilots to fight in the war, the RAF allowed him to fly again.

4
     During World War II, he became an **ace** pilot, shooting down 22
25 German aircraft before his airplane was shot down in France. He was captured by the Germans and **imprisoned** for the rest of the war. His flying abilities, however, had earned him great respect among his captors, and they even allowed a new artificial leg to be dropped by a British bomber to replace the one damaged in the crash. With his tin
30 legs, Bader attempted again and again to escape, seeing it as his duty to **defy** his captors and return home at all costs.

5
     After the war, Bader became a campaigner for the rights of disabled people and dedicated the rest of his life to helping them. He was knighted for his work in 1976 and died of a heart attack
35 on September 5, 1982.

>> Douglas Bader House in Fairford is now the headquarters for the RAF Charitable Trust. (cc by Jonathan Billinger)

Questions

_____ 1. **Amputated** in the second paragraph most likely means "_____."
   a. locked in   **b.** massaged   **c.** cut off   **d.** tied up

_____ 2. Which of the following words is closest in meaning to **ace** in the first sentence of the fourth paragraph?
   a. First-class.   **b.** Fair.   **c.** Poor.   **d.** Arrogant.

_____ 3. "With his tin legs, Bader attempted again and again to escape, seeing it as his duty to **defy** his captors and return home at all costs." The context of this sentence suggests that **defy** means "_____."
   a. work with   **b.** rebel against
   c. give advice to   **d.** learn from

_____ 4. "He was captured by the Germans and **imprisoned** for the rest of the war." Which of the following words has the opposite meaning of **imprisoned**?
   a. Tortured.   **b.** Interviewed.   **c.** Freed.   **d.** Scolded.

_____ 5. "In need of **experienced** pilots to fight in the war, the RAF allowed him to fly again." Which of the following words could replace **experienced** in the above sentence?
   a. Patient.   **b.** Smart.   **c.** Fast.   **d.** Skilled.

67 The Yeti 🎧067

» yeti

1   Few mysteries have captured our imaginations like that of the yeti—a humanlike creature believed to inhabit the Himalayan Mountains of Nepal and China. The yeti has been part of
5 Himalayan legends for hundreds of years. Ever since the 19th century, when Westerners first began to tackle the area's towering mountains, reports of strange footprints and lone dark **figures** in the snow have returned home with them. Do these
10 creatures really exist, or are they simply the product of a climber's fatigue, bad weather, and a **vivid** imagination?

2   The name "yeti" means "rocky-place bear" in the Tibetan language, and the fact that the locals themselves freely compare the
15 yeti to a bear may give some clue to its true identity. Many experts suggest that the tracks of large bears, after being exposed to the weather for a time, often **appear** humanlike. In addition, the commonly heard description of the yeti, a tall creature covered with long dark hair, could just as easily be a description of a bear.

« purported yeti
scalp at Khumjung
monastery
(cc by Nuno Nogueira)

⌃ yeti scalp and Dr. Biswamoy
Biswas (zoologist, 1923–
1994) during the 1954 Daily
Mail Snowman Expedition

⌃ **Himalayan Mountains**

3 In 1986, one climber managed to take a photograph of a yeti. He saw it standing in the snow about 500 feet away, not moving or making any noise. What's more, under **analysis**, his photographs seemed to be genuine. Many took this as a sign that the yeti truly existed, but the following year when people returned to the area where the photos were taken, they found that the yeti was actually a large dark rock which, in the wind and snow, appeared to be a living creature.

20

25

4 Though most evidence of the Yeti has been explained away by science, a discovery in 2003 suggested that the idea of the yeti may not be as **far-fetched** as was once thought. On the island of Flores in Indonesia, the remains of an early human species that survived until as recently as 12,000 years ago were found. The fact that this early species existed alongside modern humans could give some credit to the existence of an early human species surviving in the high mountains of the Himalayas, as yet undiscovered by modern man.

30

35

≪ illustration of a yeti (cc by Philippe Semeria)

Questions

_____ 1. **Far-fetched** in the final paragraph most likely means "_____."
  a. easy to prove
  b. difficult to find
  c. easy to describe
  d. difficult to believe

_____ 2. "What's more, under **analysis**, his photographs seemed to be genuine." Which of the following words could replace **analysis** in the sentence above?
  a. Examination.
  b. Questioning.
  c. Description.
  d. Production.

_____ 3. ". . . are they simply the product of a climber's fatigue, bad weather, and a **vivid** imagination?" Which of the following words has the opposite meaning of **vivid**?
  a. Bright. **b.** Slow. **c.** Dull. **d.** Rich.

_____ 4. Which of the following words has a similar meaning to **appear** as it is used in the second paragraph?
  a. Exist. **b.** Seem. **c.** Emerge. **d.** Possess.

_____ 5. ". . . reports of strange footprints and lone dark **figures** in the snow have returned home with them." The word **figure** in this context means "_____."
  a. number **b.** shape **c.** picture **d.** model

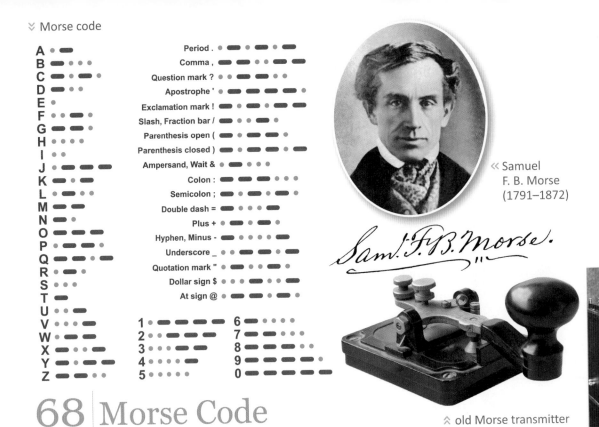

«Samuel
F. B. Morse
(1791–1872)

⌃ old Morse transmitter

68 | Morse Code

⌄ *Portrait of Mrs. Morse and Two Children* by Samuel F. B. Morse, 1824

(068) **1** Morse code is a **means** of communication that uses short and long elements, called dots and dashes, to send a message. These sequences of dots and dashes represent the letters, numbers, and punctuation marks of a given message. As messages can be sent and received using anything that can produce long and short pulses— radio waves, a flashlight, a drum—the system is highly flexible and practical even in conditions difficult for communication.

2 The system was originally created by Samuel F. B. Morse for use with his newly invented electric telegraph. Morse was originally a painter, but while working on a painting in Washington, he received a letter by horse messenger saying that his wife was dying. He rushed to his home in New Haven but was too late. His wife had already been buried. Morse knew that had the letter arrived faster, he would have been able to be at his wife's side before she **passed**. He therefore became obsessed with the problem of rapid long-distance communication.

3 In 1836, Morse produced the first telegraph set. The system sent pulses of electricity along wires to an electromagnet at the receiving end of the system.

5

10

15

20

When the electromagnet received a current, it engaged a mechanism that pushed a metal pen onto a piece of paper tape, marking the tape with a series of dots and **dashes**.

4   Originally, operators would read the message on the paper tape and then translate it into words. However, the operators soon   25
learned to translate the message directly by simply listening to the clicking sounds the machine made as it pushed the pen in and out of position, making the paper tape **unnecessary**. Nowadays experienced Morse code operators can easily translate up to 30 words per minute.   30

5   Although telegraphs are no longer used, Morse code remains an important form of communication for professional and amateur radio operators. The most famous group of letters used even today is SOS, the internationally recognized **distress** call, and is comprised of three dots   35
("S"), three dashes ("O"), and three dots ("S"), which would look like ". . . - - - . . ." on a paper tape.

« sending Morse code using telegraph

» birthplace of Samuel F. B. Morse, Charlestown, MA (cc by BPL)

Questions

_____1. "Morse code is a **means** of communication that uses short and long elements, called dots and dashes, to send a message." Which of the following words could replace **means** in the sentence above?
a. Condition.   **b.** Way.   **c.** Sense.   **d.** Income.

_____2. In the context of the second paragraph, what does the word **passed** mean?
a. Died.   **b.** Succeeded.   **c.** Agreed.   **d.** Overtook.

_____3. The word **dash** is used many times in the passage. What does it mean in the context of this article?
a. To hurry.   **b.** A small amount.   **c.** To smash.   **d.** A line.

_____4. "The most famous group of letters used even today is SOS, the internationally recognized **distress** call . . ." Which of the following words has the opposite meaning of **distress**?
a. Question.   **b.** Sorrow.   **c.** Safety.   **d.** Harm.

_____5. "However, the operators soon learned to translate the message directly . . . , making the paper tape **unnecessary**." Which of the following words could NOT replace **unnecessary** in the sentence above?
a. Unneeded. **b.** Pointless.   **c.** Essential.   **d.** Redundant.

151

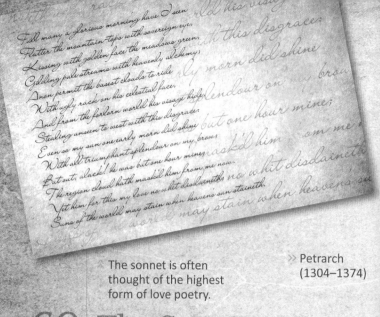

The sonnet is often thought of the highest form of love poetry.

>> Petrarch
(1304–1374)

69 The Sonnet

[1] Invented in Italy during the 13th century and developed by the Italian poet Petrarch, the sonnet is often thought of as the highest form of love poetry. Shakespeare's series of 154 sonnets exploring the themes of beauty, love, and mortality established him as a **master** sonneteer. It caused such an impact that his name is now used alongside Petrarch's to describe the two main forms of the sonnet.

[2] Whether Petrarchan or Shakespearean, all sonnets are 14 lines long and contain an essential element called the volta, or turn. In a sonnet, a poet commonly explores two **contrasting** ideas; the volta marks the place in the poem where the switch between the two ideas takes place. In a Petrarchan sonnet, for example, the volta almost always occurs in the ninth line; in other forms, the position of the volta is more flexible.

[3] Due to the abundance of rhyming words in Italian, the **rhyme scheme** of the Petrarchan sonnet is quite intense and requires many words that share the same rhyme. A Petrarchan sonnet, however, never ends in a pair of rhyming lines, meaning that the two contrasting ideas almost never come to a resolution. Instead, they stand opposed to each other, emphasizing the tension or struggle between them.

5

10

15

20

>> statue of Petrarch in the Uffizi Palace, in Florence

SHAKE-SPEARES

SONNETS

Neuer before Imprinted.

_____

_____

AT LONDON
By G. Eld for T. T. and are
to be folde by William Afpley.
1609.

⌃ title page of
Shakespeare's
Sonnets (1609)

4   Shakespeare, writing in English (which has far fewer
rhyming words than Italian), preferred to use a different rhyme
scheme and also to end his sonnets with a pair of rhymed lines.
This kind of ending allows writers to resolve the contrasting
ideas in their sonnets or even refute them dramatically in the
form of a last-minute twist, giving Shakespearean sonnets an
element of theater **lacking** in Petrarch's sonnets.

5   For some modern poets, the sonnet is old-fashioned, while
the strict rhyme scheme discourages those who prefer to write in free
verse. That being said, many modern poets have tried experimenting
with the form, adapting it to the world of modern poetry. One
particularly interesting adaptation is the word sonnet, a 14-line poem
in which each line contains only one word. It's
extraordinary that even after 700 years, the
sonnet continues to find ways of inspiring new
generations of poets.

25

30

35

40

⌃ William Shakespeare
(1564–1616)

Questions

_____1. "Shakespeare's series of 154 sonnets . . . established
him as a **master** sonneteer." The word **master** in
the sentence above refers to _____.
a. a person who builds masts for ships
b. a person who demands obedience
c. a person who is very skillful at doing something
d. a person who is in charge of everything

_____2. "In a sonnet, a poet commonly explores two **contrasting** ideas; . . ."
A word with a similar meaning to **contrasting** is _____.
a. conflicting   b. rhyming   c. puzzling   d. similar

_____3. The phrase **rhyme scheme** is used many times in this passage. In the
context of this article, what is the meaning of the word **scheme**?
a. Proposal.   b. Plot.   c. Sketch.   d. Arrangement.

_____4. A word with the opposite meaning of **lacking** in the fourth paragraph
is _____.
a. rare   b. present   c. possible   d. absent

_____5. "It's **extraordinary** that even after 700 years, the sonnet continues to
find ways of inspiring new generations of poets." **Extraordinary** in the
sentence above could be replaced by _____.
a. unlikely   b. remarkable   c. shameful   d. clear

70 | What Is Your Carbon Footprint?

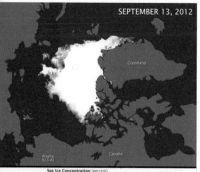

SEPTEMBER 13, 2012

Sea Ice Concentration (percent)

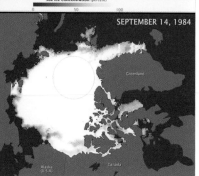

SEPTEMBER 14, 1984

⌃ The maps compare the Arctic ice minimum extents from 2012 *(top)* and 1984 *(bottom)*. (Wikipedia)

1 The term "carbon footprint" is often defined as the annual amount of carbon dioxide produced by a country, organization, or person via energy **consumed** and the waste created. Carbon dioxide and other greenhouse gases may warm the planet enough to melt the polar ice caps completely, so reducing our carbon footprint is certainly an important **goal**. 5

2 The three largest producers of carbon dioxide are China, the United States, and India. However, no matter what country you live in, if you have a typical modern lifestyle, you probably have a large carbon footprint. 10 For most countries in the developed world, the largest source of pollution is driving. US households have a carbon footprint of 48 tons of CO_2 per year—five times larger than the global average. While much of this comes 15 from indirect sources (fuel burned to produce goods far away from the customer), US households could reduce their direct carbon footprint by a huge factor by simply changing the kind of car the household uses. Housing comes a close second, with heating, lighting, and household waste contributing no small amount to a 20 family's carbon footprint.

≫ Carbon footprint is the annual amount of carbon dioxide produced by a country, organization, or person.

3 So, what can you do to **shrink** your carbon footprint? Making simple changes in your lifestyle can make a substantial difference to the amount of your carbon output. Adjusting your heating by just two degrees—higher in summer and lower in winter—can reduce 25 your annual carbon footprint by about a ton. Indeed, heating and cooling your house is one of the major contributors to your carbon footprint. By properly protecting your house against the weather, you could not only make a dent in the amount of pollution you produce, but you could also reduce your heating **expenses** by 24%. 30

4 Those who want to go even further and **eradicate** their carbon footprints altogether may need to do a little more, like install solar panels, religiously recycle, and completely change the way they get from place to place. Maybe in the future, we'll all be green-minded enough to make our personal carbon footprints completely 35 disappear.

⌃ Adjusting heating by two degrees higher in summer and lower in winter can reduce your carbon footprint.

⌄ Installing solar panels is a way to reduce one's carbon footprint.

Questions

_____ 1. "So, what can you do to **shrink** your carbon footprint?" Which of the following words is the opposite of **shrink**?
   a. Enlarge.   **b.** Vanish.   **c.** Lose.   **d.** Feed.

_____ 2. "Carbon dioxide and other greenhouse gases may warm the planet enough to melt the polar ice caps completely, so reducing our carbon footprint is certainly an important **goal**." Another word for **goal** in the sentence above is _____.
   a. score   **b.** net   **c.** aim   **d.** shot

_____ 3. As used in the final paragraph, the word **eradicate** means to _____ something.
   a. shorten   **b.** encourage   **c.** prevent   **d.** eliminate

_____ 4. In the context of the first paragraph, the word **consume** is closest in meaning to _____.
   a. eat   **b.** use   **c.** drink   **d.** buy

_____ 5. "By properly protecting your house against the weather, you could not only make a dent in the amount of pollution you produce, but you could also reduce your heating **expenses** by 24%." Which of the following words could replace the **expenses** in the sentence above?
   a. Costs.   **b.** Damages.   **c.** Calculations. **d.** Repairs.

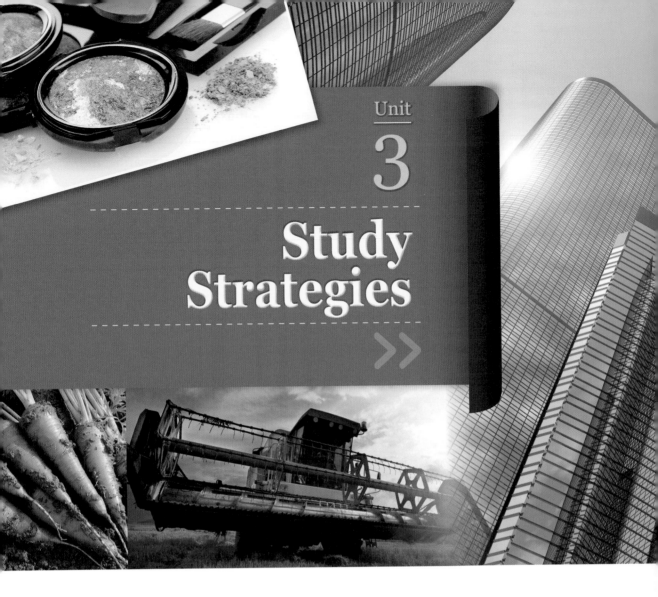

Unit 3

Study Strategies

>>

3-1   Visual Material

3-2   Reference Sources

In this unit, we are going to introduce two important tools for any English learner. The first one is different kinds of visual material. These are the pictures and other graphical data that allow us to visualize the information we read. Visualizing data can improve a student's reading experience and help him or her remember important facts during a test.

The second tool is reference sources. These are the various resources that we can turn to when we need to learn some specific information. By the end of this unit, you'll be able to find information and interpret it with greater efficiency.

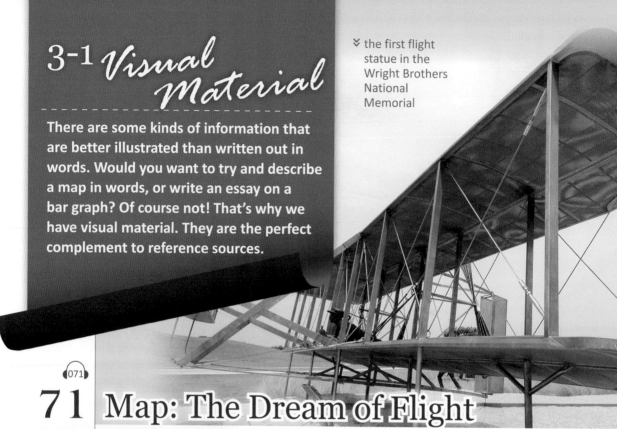

3-1 Visual Material

There are some kinds of information that are better illustrated than written out in words. Would you want to try and describe a map in words, or write an essay on a bar graph? Of course not! That's why we have visual material. They are the perfect complement to reference sources.

≫ the first flight statue in the Wright Brothers National Memorial

(071)

71 Map: The Dream of Flight

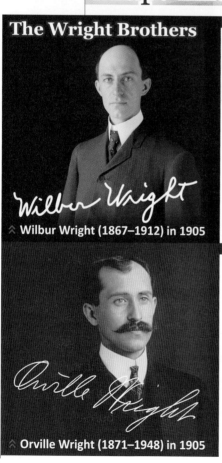

The Wright Brothers

≫ Wilbur Wright (1867–1912) in 1905

≫ Orville Wright (1871–1948) in 1905

[1] Mankind has dreamed of flying for thousands of years. Back in the 15th century, Leonardo da Vinci drew up plans for helicopters and gliders in Renaissance Italy. His designs never created a working model, though. That would come hundreds of years later, when the Wright brothers made a series of successful flights in the United States. They went on to invent the first controllable fixed-wing aircraft, one of the most important discoveries of the modern age.

[2] A flight museum is one of the landmarks that appear on the following map. Maps are illustrations that are meant to represent actual places, and each map uses different symbols to represent different points of interest and landmarks. There are many different types of maps, ranging from climate maps to topographic maps that display altitude. Tourist maps and street maps are also popular. Use the map on the next page to answer the following questions.

5

10

15

20

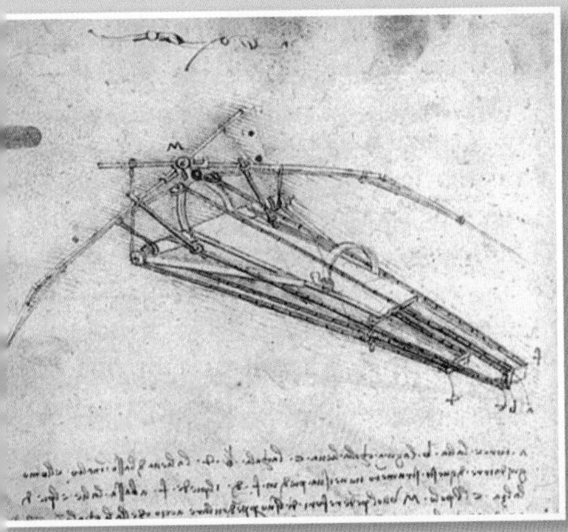

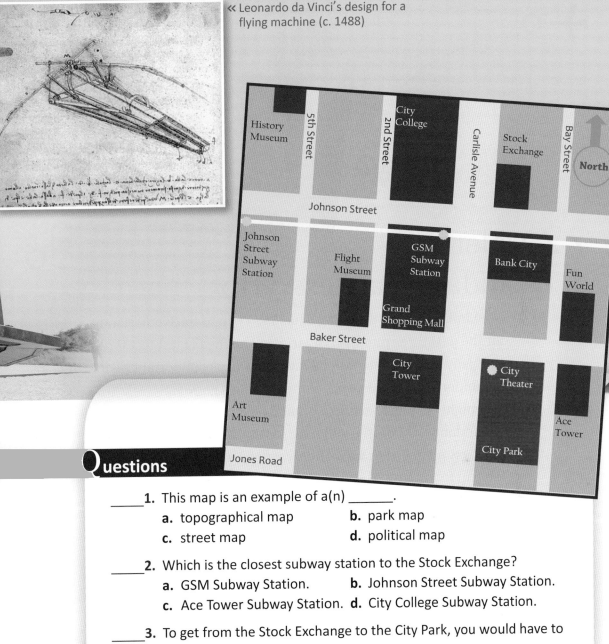

« Leonardo da Vinci's design for a flying machine (c. 1488)

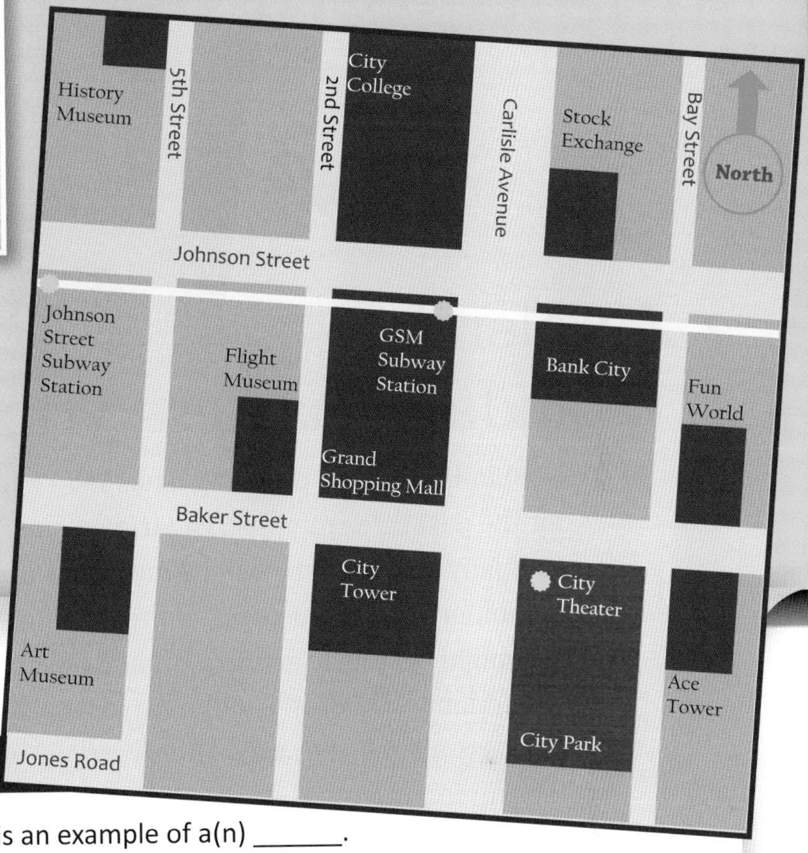

Questions

_____ **1.** This map is an example of a(n) ______.

a. topographical map **b.** park map
c. street map **d.** political map

_____ **2.** Which is the closest subway station to the Stock Exchange?

a. GSM Subway Station. **b.** Johnson Street Subway Station.
c. Ace Tower Subway Station. **d.** City College Subway Station.

_____ **3.** To get from the Stock Exchange to the City Park, you would have to travel ______.

a. north **b.** south **c.** east **d.** west

_____ **4.** To get to the Art Museum from the City Theater, you would have to travel ______.

a. north **b.** south **c.** east **d.** west

_____ **5.** Where is the Flight Museum?

a. The corner of Baker Street and Carlisle Avenue.
b. The corner of Fifth Street and Johnson Street.
c. The corner of Baker Street and Second Street.
d. The corner of Bay Street and Johnson Street.

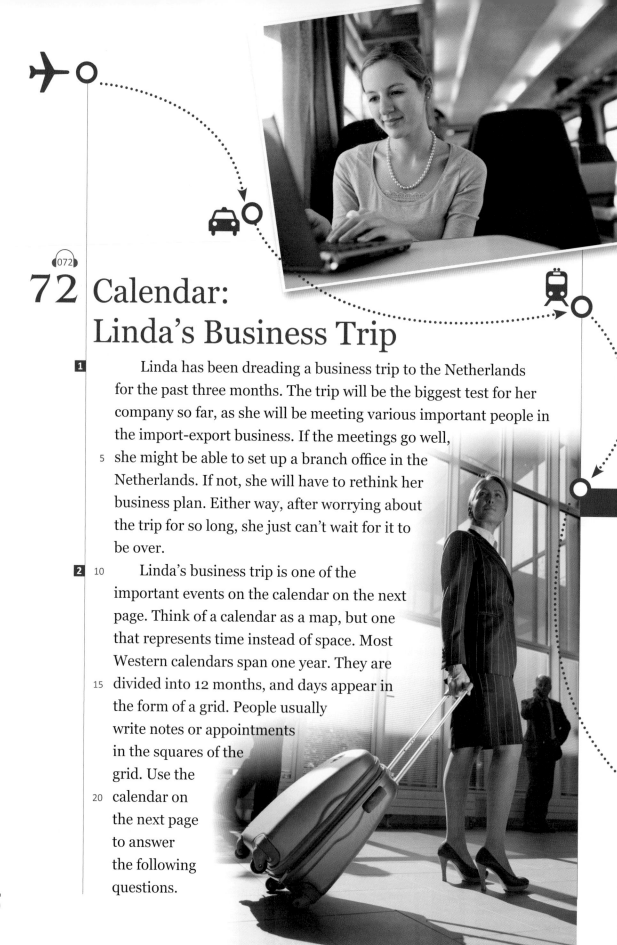

72 Calendar: Linda's Business Trip

1   Linda has been dreading a business trip to the Netherlands for the past three months. The trip will be the biggest test for her company so far, as she will be meeting various important people in the import-export business. If the meetings go well,
5 she might be able to set up a branch office in the Netherlands. If not, she will have to rethink her business plan. Either way, after worrying about the trip for so long, she just can't wait for it to be over.

2 10   Linda's business trip is one of the important events on the calendar on the next page. Think of a calendar as a map, but one that represents time instead of space. Most Western calendars span one year. They are
15 divided into 12 months, and days appear in the form of a grid. People usually write notes or appointments in the squares of the grid. Use the
20 calendar on the next page to answer the following questions.

March

Sunday	Monday	Tuesday	Wednesday	Thursday	Friday	Saturday
			1 Breakfast meeting with Bob at 9 a.m.	2	3 Lunch with the company directors	4
5 Fly to Amsterdam	6 Meeting with DaanWinkel at 11:00 at the Dutch head office	7 Check production at the factory. Dinner with the executives	8 Tour the factory at 2 p.m.	9 Strategy meeting with the managers at 10 a.m.	10 Meeting with the sales team at 9 a.m.	11 Fly home at 11 a.m.
12 Tennis with John	13 Back to the office. Report to Bob	14	15 Order Jane's birthday cake. Finalize the guest list for the party	16	17	18 Jane's birthday party at 6 p.m.
19	20	21	22	23	24	25

Questions

_____ **1.** On what day will Linda fly to Amsterdam?
- **a.** March 1.
- **b.** March 5.
- **c.** March 11.
- **d.** March 13.

_____ **2.** When does Linda plan to take a tour of the factory?
- **a.** March 10.
- **b.** March 12.
- **c.** March 1.
- **d.** March 8.

_____ **3.** How many days will Linda spend in Amsterdam?
- **a.** About three days.
- **b.** About 10 days.
- **c.** About six days.
- **d.** About four days.

_____ **4.** On what day of the week does Jane's birthday party fall?
- **a.** Monday.
- **b.** Tuesday.
- **c.** Friday.
- **d.** Saturday.

_____ **5.** What does Linda plan to do on March 12?
- **a.** Fly to Amsterdam.
- **b.** Celebrate Jane's birthday.
- **c.** Play tennis with John.
- **d.** Have lunch with the company directors.

« The mile run is a middle-distance foot race.

» Hicham El Guerrouj (1974–) in 2010
(cc by Sebastien)

73 Table: The Mile Run

(073)

1   The mile run is a one-mile race that has been popular in England for hundreds of years. Its distance is equal to around 1,600 meters, and the current world-record holder is Morocco's Hicham
5 El Guerrouj with a time of 3:43.13. In fact, the mile run is so old and storied that the English Parliament established the race's official distance all the way back in 1593. People around the world are still doing mile runs, even
10 though most of us have switched to the metric system.

2   Old mile-run records appear in the table pictured on the following page. Tables
15 are very useful tools because they can present large amounts of data in an accessible manner. They can also group different types of statistical information together,
20 convert one kind of information into another, or make comparisons between two different information sets. Use the table on the next page to answer the following questions.

⌃ stopwatch

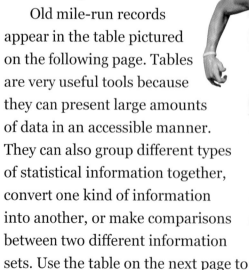

Year	Name	Time	Place
1865	Richard Webster	4:36.5	England
1868	William Chinnery	4:29	England
1868	Walter Gibbs	4:28.8	England
1874	Walter Slade	4:26	England
1875	Walter Slade	4:24.5	London
1880	Walter George	4:23.2	London
1882	Walter George	4:21.4	London
1884	Walter George	4:18.4	Birmingham
1894	Fred Bacon	4:18.2	Edinburgh

⌃ Walter George (1858–1943)

(Source: http://www.infoplease.com/ipsa/A0112924.html)

Questions

_____ 1. How many times did Walter Slade hold the record for best time?
   a. Once.   **b.** Twice.   **c.** Three times.   **d.** Six times.

_____ 2. According to the table, who was the last person to hold the record?
   a. Walter George.   **b.** Fred Bacon.
   c. William Chinnery.   **d.** Richard Webster.

_____ 3. In which place was the record broken the most times?
   a. England.   **b.** London.   **c.** Birmingham.   **d.** Edinburgh.

_____ 4. What was William Chinnery's record time?
   a. 4:26.   **b.** 4:18.4.   **c.** 4:36.5.   **d.** 4:29.

_____ 5. According to the table, where did the last record occur?
   a. England.   **b.** London.   **c.** Birmingham.   **d.** Edinburgh.

163

74 Bar Graph: Skyscrapers in the World

1   One World Trade Center (1 WTC), formerly known as the Freedom Tower, is the main building for the new World Trade Center in New York City. The tower was built to replace the twin towers that had been destroyed in a terrorist attack on September 11, 2001. It was completed in 2014 and is one of the tallest in the world. 5

≫ Taipei 101 (cc by Alton Thompson)

≪ One World Trade Center (cc by Joe Mabel)

2   The 1 WTC is one of several skyscrapers that appear on a bar graph of the world's largest towers on the following page. A bar graph is a graph in which information, usually in the form of statistics, is represented by vertical or horizontal bars. A bar graph offers basic, statistical information and allows you to evaluate a series of values, making for easy comparisons. Since the bars represent number values, the longest bar is the largest number, and the shortest bar is the smallest number. Use the bar graph on the next page to answer the following questions. 10 15 20

≫ Shanghai World Finance Center

≫ **Manhattan skyline with the One World Trade Center under construction (2012)** (cc by Joe Mabel)

The World's Tallest Buildings

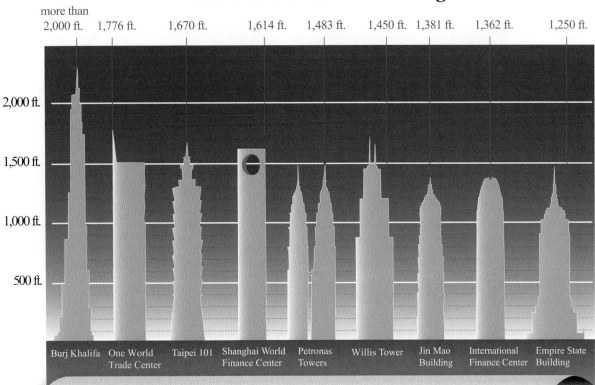

| more than 2,000 ft. | 1,776 ft. | 1,670 ft. | 1,614 ft. | 1,483 ft. | 1,450 ft. | 1,381 ft. | 1,362 ft. | 1,250 ft. |

| Burj Khalifa | One World Trade Center | Taipei 101 | Shanghai World Finance Center | Petronas Towers | Willis Tower | Jin Mao Building | International Finance Center | Empire State Building |

Questions

_____ 1. According to the graph, which is the tallest building?
   a. Taipei 101.
   b. One World Trade Center.
   c. Shanghai World Finance Center.
   d. Burj Khalifa.

_____ 2. According to the graph, which of the following buildings is taller than Taipei 101?
   a. One World Trade Center.
   b. Willis Tower.
   c. Empire State Building.
   d. Jin Mao Building.

_____ 3. According to the graph, which is the shortest building?
   a. Taipei 101.
   b. Shanghai World Finance Center.
   c. Petronas Towers.
   d. Empire State Building.

_____ 4. According to the graph, which of the following buildings is shorter than the Jin Mao tower?
   a. Willis Tower.
   b. Petronas Towers.
   c. International Finance Center.
   d. Taipei 101.

_____ 5. According to the graph, which of the following buildings is taller than the Shanghai World Finance Center?
   a. Jin Mao Tower.
   b. Willis Tower.
   c. Taipei 101.
   d. Petronas Towers.

⌃ Burj Khalifa

75 Spreadsheet: Tracking the Inventory

1   Tracking and updating inventory can be one of the hardest tasks for a small business owner. In the day-to-day bustle of work, people forget to update their records. But proper inventory records can lead to more intelligent ordering, which in turn leads to more profits. After all, no business owner wants to see a bunch of pointless products   5 rotting on their store shelves.

2   Inventory records are often kept in spreadsheets, and an example of a music store inventory is pictured on the following page. Spreadsheets are a great way to arrange data in tabular form, with rows and columns of information. Unlike a table, which might just be   10 a page or two long, spreadsheets can seemingly go on forever. They are databases that can be filled with huge amounts of information, especially statistical values. Use the spreadsheet on the next page to answer the following questions.

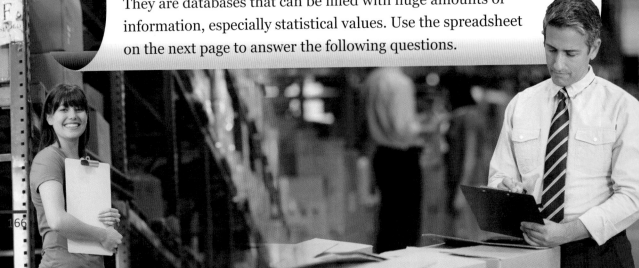

Questions

Artist	Album	Cost Price ($)	Stock (CDs)	Sale Price ($)	Sales (CDs)
Joe Goodman	*Love Is...*	12.50	110	19.50	100
Blue	*The Time Is Now*	11.95	300	21.95	86
Calypso Dude	*Yo-yo*	12.60	250	20.95	245
Crazy Kevin	*What?*	12.10	150	19.95	150

_____ **1.** Which is the cheapest album in terms of sale price that the store offers?

    a. *Yo-yo.*   **b.** *What?*   **c.** *Love Is . . .*   **d.** *The Time Is Now.*

_____ **2.** Which album does the store have the most copies of?

    a. *Yo-yo.*   **b.** *What?*   **c.** *Love Is . . .*   **d.** *The Time Is Now.*

_____ **3.** Which was the store's most successful album?

    a. *Yo-yo.*   **b.** *What?*   **c.** *Love Is . . .*   **d.** *The Time Is Now.*

_____ **4.** Which was the store's least successful album?

    a. *Yo-yo.*   **b.** *What?*   **c.** *Love Is . . .*   **d.** *The Time Is Now.*

_____ **5.** Which artist produced the album *Love Is . . .*?

    a. Joe Goodman.   **b.** Blue.   **c.** Calypso Dude.   **d.** Crazy Kevin.

3-2 Reference Sources

Any truly interesting or informative piece of writing has to have some information in it, and some of the best information can be found in reference sources . Whether it's a dictionary, encyclopedia, or the Internet, each type of reference material has advantages and disadvantages, so get to know them a bit better.

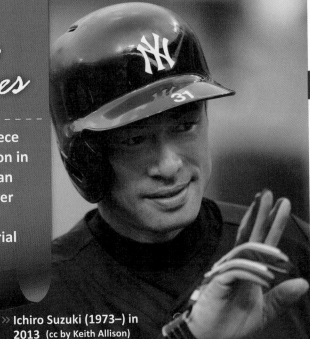

>> Ichiro Suzuki (1973–) in 2013 (cc by Keith Allison)

76 Table of Contents: Ichiro Suzuki

(076)

1   Ichiro Suzuki is one of the most famous Japanese baseball players of all time. He joined Major League Baseball's Seattle Mariners in 2001, and quickly established himself as one of the stars of the league. In fact, he played so well that some people think he should be voted into the Hall of Fame after he retires, even though he was already 27   5 years old by the time he arrived in the United States.

2   Ichiro Suzuki is featured in a chapter in the table of contents on the next page. A table of contents is always at the start of a book or magazine. It contains a lot of information that can be useful to the reader, including what sections, categories, and chapters are   10 within the publication. It also lists the page numbers of the chapters, so you can find what you're looking for very easily. Use the table of contents on the next page to answer the following questions.

≫ Ichiro Suzuki (2009)

≫ Suzuki meeting President Barack Obama (2009)

Questions

_____ **1.** On what page would you find the chapter on Ichiro Suzuki?
　　 a. 12. 　　 **b.** 14. 　　 **c.** 44. 　　 **d.** 46.

_____ **2.** What category does the chapter "Animal Proverbs" belong in?
　　 a. Geography. 　 **b.** Language. 　 **c.** Business. 　 **d.** People.

_____ **3.** What category does the chapter "Steve Jobs" belong in?
　　 a. Language. 　 **b.** Business. 　 **c.** Technology. 　 **d.** People.

_____ **4.** On what page would you find the chapter on *Twilight*?
　　 a. 48. 　　 **b.** 44. 　　 **c.** 38. 　　 **d.** 20.

_____ **5.** If you were interested in technology, which of the following chapters
　　 could you refer to?
　　 a. The Large Hadron Collider. 　 **b.** Ichiro Suzuki.
　　 c. EQ. 　　　　　　　　　　　 **d.** Fair Trade Businesses.

Contents

037

009

Week 1

Day 1
History
1. The Civil Rights Movement in the United States 10

Day 2
Psychology
2. EQ 12

Day 3
Language
3. Animal Proverbs 14

Day 4
Business
4. Who Stole My Money? 16

Day 5
People
5. Steve Jobs 18

Day 6
Arts & Literature
6. *Twilight* 20

Week 3

Day 1
Animals
13. Animal Rights, Yesterday and Today 38

Day 2
Geography
14. K2 40

Day 3
Language
15. Class and Accent 42

Day 4
People
16. Ichiro Suzuki 44

Day 5
Technology
17. The Large Hadron Collider 46

Day 6
Business
18. Fair Trade Businesses 48

77 Index: Purgatory

1 Purgatory is a part of the Catholic religion. It is a place that can be found somewhere between Heaven and Hell. According to Catholicism, good people go to Heaven and bad people are sent to Hell. People who are neither good nor bad go to Purgatory, where they get a chance to purify themselves.

2 Purgatory is one of the words that appears in the following index. An index is often found at the end of a book, and the information in an index is always presented in alphabetical order. Think of an index as being somewhat similar to a table of contents but with more specific topics. Also, topics in an index often provide several different pages where the topic can be found in the book. In this case, if you wanted to learn more about Purgatory, you would flip to page 330. Use the pictured index on the next page to answer the following questions.

>> depiction of
Purgatory
representing
the boundary
between
heaven
(above) and
hell *(below)*

Proteus, 326
Pryderi, 243, 326
Psalms, Book of, 9
Psyche, 88–89
psychoanalysis, 139
psychology, myth and, 326–329
psychosocial function, 361
psychosociology, myth and, 329
Ptah, 329
Pu Ngoe Nga Ngoe, 329
Pueblo myth and ritual, 329
puer aeternus, 105, 252, 253, 266, 270, 382
Puhvel, Jaan, 79, 798, 199
Pulque, 69
Puranas, 54, 184, 329–330
Pure Land Buddhism, 15, 57, 158, 290, 330
Purgatory, 330
Purity and Danger, 106
Purusha, 330
Pwyll, 243, 330
Pygmalion, 5, 331
pyramid texts, 79, 331
Pyramus, 331
Pyrrha, 99, 331

Questions

_____ 1. What page would help if you wanted to learn more about Ptah?
   a. 331 **b.** 90 **c.** 84 **d.** 329

_____ 2. What page would help if you wanted to learn more about Purusha?
   a. 106 **b.** 330 **c.** 350 **d.** 230

_____ 3. This book is likely to have the most information about which of the following topics?
   a. Pulque. **b.** Pygamalion. **c.** *Puer aeternus.* **d.** Proteus.

_____ 4. What pages would help if you wanted to learn more about pyramid texts?
   a. 79 and 331. **b.** 326 and 327. **c.** 243 and 326. **d.** 99 and 331.

_____ 5. How is information within an index ordered?
   a. By the date it occurred. **b.** By alphabetical order.
   c. By importance. **d.** By the country it occurred in.

78 | Encyclopedia: Farming

1   Farming is an extremely complex and important subject, as
humans have been farming for thousands of years. Early innovations
in farming seem rather simple now, like the need to rotate crops
to preserve soil quality. That's because farming has become a huge
international business, with most of our grains, meat, and dairy   5
products being controlled by large multinational companies operating
massive and complex factory farms.

2   Farming is featured in the encyclopedia that's pictured on
the next page. Encyclopedias are books that are jam-packed with
facts and data. The information in encyclopedias is arranged in   10
alphabetical order. Topics can include people, places, historical events,
inventions, and almost anything else you can think of. The reason why
encyclopedias are such valuable reference sources has to do with how
the information is presented. Encyclopedia entries aren't meant to
be overly complicated in order to allow readers to learn a lot in a few   15
minutes. Use the encyclopedia entry on the next page to answer the
following questions.

Questions

_____ 1. Which of the following statements about encyclopedias is NOT true?
   a. They include entries on famous people.
   b. They are helpful reference sources.
   c. They take a lot of time to explain simple subjects.
   d. Topics are usually arranged in alphabetical order.

_____ 2. In which paragraph in this encyclopedia entry would you likely find information about **tractors**?
   a. Origins of Farming.
   b. New Methods and Outlooks.
   c. Agricultural Revolutions.
   d. Dairy Farming.

_____ 3. Which of the following does this encyclopedia NOT cover in its entry on farming?
   a. The origins of farming.
   b. New inventions in farming.
   c. Modern farming.
   d. Banned farming techniques.

_____ 4. Which of the following is most likely the theme of this encyclopedia?
   a. Industry.   b. Religion.   c. Politics.   d. Plant life.

_____ 5. In which paragraph can we find information about when people first discovered how to scatter seeds?
   a. Dairy Farming.
   b. Origins of Farming.
   c. Agricultural Revolutions.
   d. New Methods and Outlooks.

(Source: The Kingfisher Children's Encyclopedia)

FARMING

Farming is the business of growing crops and raising livestock on the land to produce food, drink, textiles, and other products.

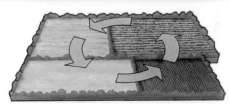

▲ In the early 1700s, English politician Charles Townshend created a four-field crop rotation system, which meant that a field did not have to be left fallow (empty) each year.

Items such as food, leather, cotton, and rubber come from farms. Farming is the world's biggest employer, taking up more than half of the working population.

▲ Rows of green crops growing in the middle of a barren, sandy desert are evidence of the enormous achievements in farming and irrigation techniques.

ORIGINS OF FARMING

Archaeological evidence shows that farming began around 11,000 B.C., when Stone Age people began to herd wild animals. Later, in 7000 B.C., people learned that scattered seeds would grow and multiply, providing food for themselves and their animals. The first crops were probably wheat and barley, cultivated with simple hoes and sticks.

AGRICULTURAL REVOLUTIONS

Dramatic developments in farming have occurred since then. Irrigation of crops in Mesopotamia in 4000 B.C. and the ox-drawn plow, invented in about 3000 B.C., made it possible to work difficult soils.

From the A.D. 1400s, the potato, tomato, turkey, chili, and corn were brought from America to Europe and Asia. New machinery, such as Jethro Tull's seed drill (1700), Eli Whitney's cotton gin (1793), and steam-powered tractors (mid-1800s) made farming less labor-intensive.

NEW METHODS AND OUTLOOKS

Since the 1970s, a "green revolution" based on artificially improved crops and fertilizers has increased food production in poorer nations. In developed countries, new machines and the rearing of livestock on mechanized farms have increased production.

DAIRY FARMING

Milk is produced on dairy farms from cattle, although goats, buffalo (bison), and sheep may also be kept for milk. On modern dairy farms, cattle are milked by machine.

79 | Dictionary: Lazarus of Bethany

>> Lazarus

(079)

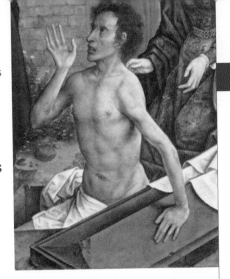

1   Lazarus, or Lazarus of Bethany, is a famous figure in the Christian Bible. He was a follower of Jesus, and when he fell ill one day, his sisters sent for Jesus to come and
5 help. By the time Jesus arrived, Lazarus had been dead for four days. However, Jesus proceeded to his grave and said a prayer. Lazarus then emerged, perfectly healthy. Many Christians believe that this was a miracle and proof that Jesus was a divine being.

2 10   Lazarus is one of the words that appears on the following dictionary page. A dictionary is a book that lists words along with their meanings, often in alphabetical order. Dictionaries often supply other information in addition to a word's definition, such as the word's part of speech and the language it originally came from. Some dictionaries also provide a sample
15 of the word being used in a sentence. Use the dictionary excerpt on the next page to answer the following questions.

⌄ resurrection of Lazarus from San Giorgio church

_____**1.** What part of speech is **layout**?

    a. A noun.   **b.** An adjective. **c.** A verb.   **d.** A preposition.

_____**2.** Which of the following is the correct definition for **layette**?

    a. A female movie star.   **b.** Clothes for a new baby.

    c. A type of African dog.   **d.** A bump in the road.

_____**3.** Which of the following words would appear before **layette**?

    a. Land.   **b.** Maple.   **c.** Never.   **d.** Lead.

_____**4.** Which of the following words would appear after **layout**?

    a. Lap.   **b.** Can.   **c.** Eagle.   **d.** Mop.

_____**5.** According to the article, which of the following is NOT something that dictionaries provide?

    a. A word's definition.   **b.** A word's part of speech.

    c. A synonym of the word.   **d.** An example sentence.

(Source: Macmillan English Dictionary)

L

one another

layette /leɪˈet/ noun [C] a set of all the things that you need for a new baby, especially clothes

layman /ˈleɪmən/ (plural **laymen** /ˈleɪmən/) noun [C] **1** someone who is not trained to a high or professional standard in a particular subject: **the layman** (=all laymen as a group) *a medical dictionary for the layman* ◆ **in layman's terms** (=in words that someone who is not an expert can understand) *What does that mean in layman's terms?* **2** someone who is a member of a Christian church but not officially employed by it as a priest, MINISTER etc

ˈlay-ˌoff noun [C] **1** a situation in which an employer ends a worker's employment, especially temporarily, because there is not enough work for them **2** a period of time when you are not working or performing an activity such as a sport, usually because you are ill or injured: *Owens is back in action today after a three-month injury lay-off.*

layout /ˈleɪaʊt/ noun [C] ★★ the way in which the different parts of something are arranged: *The user gradually becomes familiar with the layout of the keyboard.* **a.** the way in which the words and pictures on a page are arranged: *the layout of a business letter* ◆ **page layout** *a two-column page layout* **b.** the way in which something such as a room, building, or city is arranged: *The layout of your house and garden can deter crime.*

layperson /ˈleɪˌpɜː(r)s(ə)n/ (plural **laypersons** or **laypeople** /ˈleɪˌpiːp(ə)l/) noun [C] used instead of LAYMAN or LAY-WOMAN when you want to say that the person could be a man or a woman: **the layperson** (=all laypersons as a group) *How would you explain to the layperson how gene therapy works?*

ˌlay ˈreader noun [C] a member of some Christian churches who is not a priest but who is allowed to be in charge of some religious services or some parts of them

laywoman /ˈleɪˌwʊmən/ (plural **laywomen** /ˈleɪˌwɪmɪn/) noun [C] **1** a woman who is not trained to a high or professional standard in a particular subject **2** a woman who is a member of a Christian church but not officially employed by it as a priest, MINISTER etc

80 The Internet: The High Price of Beauty

1   If you were to ask someone, "Do you want to be beautiful?" not many would reply, "No." The fact is, most of us like to look good, and the big companies know it. A 2018 study found that the average American woman spends around $3,756 every year on beauty products. That adds up to around $225,360 over the course of their 5 entire lifetime. No wonder there are so many health and beauty websites on the Internet, like the one pictured on the next page.

2   The Internet is a very powerful tool for buying and selling products. But how do you take advantage of it? After finding an online shop using a search engine, take a look at the top of the page. 10 Usually, you will see several different categories. Clicking on these categories will sort the products being listed. If you want something in particular, find the magnifying glass icon on the webpage. That's the search bar; it's where you can type in the name of a specific product. Sometimes you can even ask a direct question, like "how 15 much is shipping?"

3   Use the pictured makeup website on the next page to answer the following questions.

« beauty products

Log In / Sign Up

DREAMSTORE

SEARCH   🔍   0 ITEMS 🛒

| brands | skin care | makeup | hair care | bath & body | naturals | men | beautyfix | specials | blog |

Face Makeup / All Products

FACE MAKEUP

REFINE BY

FACE MAKEUP

- ☐ Foundation
- ☐ Face Primer
- ☐ Face Concealer
- ☐ BB & CC Creams
- ☐ Setting Spray & Powder
- ☐ Blush
- ☐ Makeup Remover
- ☐ Face Highlighters & Contouring
- ☐ Face Bronzer
- ☐ Mattifier

View All

SORT BY   Best Sellers ⌄

Aphrodite's Tone
Liquid Foundation SPF 10

Artemis's Shade
Mineral Shading Powder

Hebe's Blush
Dreamy Bi-color Blush

Questions

_____ **1.** What is the theme of this webpage?
     a. Fitness equipment.   **b.** Makeup products.
     c. Art supplies.   **d.** Antique furniture.

_____ **2.** Which of the following items would NOT be found on this webpage?
     a. Hiking boots.   **b.** Color-guard shampoo.
     c. Eye shadow.   **d.** Beauty masks.

_____ **3.** Which of the following is NOT one of the categories on the webpage?
     a. Men.   **b.** Bath & body.
     c. Makeup.   **d.** Wellness.

_____ **4.** Which category should a user click if they were looking for lipsticks?
     a. Hair care.   **b.** Skin care.
     c. Makeup.   **d.** Naturals.

_____ **5.** According to the picture, what is the user currently shopping for?
     a. Vitamins.   **b.** Cosmetics.
     c. Bath salts.   **d.** Body wash.

Unit

4

Final Reviews

>>

4-1　Final Review (I)

4-2　Final Review (II)

During the course of this book, you will have intensively studied various reading and word skills, as well as practiced some important study strategies. Now it's time to put those skills to the test. In previous units, only one type of skill was tested after each article. You'll now be faced with the task of employing several different skills to the same article. Take this as an opportunity to consolidate your learning, put your new skills to the test, and find out your strengths and weaknesses. If you find yourself having trouble repeatedly with a particular strategy, go back and review the relevant section and try again. Practice makes perfect!

81

081

A Humanitarian Crisis in Myanmar

1   Genocide is one of the most serious crimes a government can be accused of committing. The word "genocide," which means the deliberate killing of a racial, political, or cultural group, was created in 1944 to describe the Holocaust. When a government or group kills innocent people because these people form part of an ethnic or religious group, it is considered genocide.

2   Both the United Nations and the International Criminal Court believe that the government of Myanmar is committing genocide against Rohingya people. The Rohingya are an ethnic group with their own language and culture. While nearly 88 percent of Myanmar is Buddhist, the Rohingya are Muslim. Although the Rohingya have lived in Myanmar since the 19th century, the government has never recognized them as citizens or as an official ethnic group. Most of Myanmar's 1 to 1.3 million Rohingya live in Rakhine State. The government places restrictions on where they can live and travel, go to school or work, and the number of children they are allowed to have.

3   Shockingly, the genocide against the Rohingya has occurred under the democratically elected government led by Aung San Suu Kyi. She won the Nobel Peace Prize during her 20 years as a political prisoner and many years as a champion of democracy.

4   A year after Aung San Suu Kyi became the state counselor (prime minister), the genocide began. The Rohingya who escaped to the neighboring country of Bangladesh said that their villages had been attacked. Going from house to house, the Burmese soldiers and Buddhist militiamen from nearby villages killed people, burned down

5

10

15

20

25

⌃ child survivors of the Holocaust after the liberation of Auschwitz concentration camp by the Red Army, January 1945

⌃ Rakhine State in Myanmar (cc by TUBS)

⌄ Rohingya refugees building makeshift tents, taking shelter in Balukhali refugee camp, September 25, 2017

houses, and raped women and girls. Since the first attacks in 2016, around 900,000 Rohingya have left their homes. Over 43,000 people are missing and likely dead.

5   Reporters and human rights groups are bringing international attention
30 to the crisis. They have urged Aung San Suu Kyi to speak against the violence. Although she is not the leader of Myanmar's military, she has influence. Instead, she claimed the Rohingya were terrorists who burned their own houses to gain sympathy. Despite her reaction, the international community is continuing to work for the protection of the Rohingya.

Questions

⌃ Aung San Suu Kyi (1945–) in 2013
(cc by Claude TRUONG-NGOC)

_____ 1. What is the main point of the article?
    a. The Rohingya are a minority ethnic group that has lived in Myanmar for almost 200 years.
    b. The international community believes that genocide first occurred during the Holocaust.
    c. International organizations believe that Myanmar is committing genocide against the Rohingya.
    d. Even democratic countries like Myanmar can commit genocide.

_____ 2. Which of the following statements is NOT true?
    a. The genocide against the Rohingya started after Aung San Suu Kyi became the prime minister.
    b. International organizations haven't done anything to help the Rohingya.
    c. The word "genocide" was created to describe the Holocaust.
    d. Over 800,000 Rohingya have had to leave their homes.

_____ 3. What can be inferred from Aung San Suu Kyi's response to the violence against the Rohingya?
    a. She will not ask the military to stop attacking the Rohingya.
    b. She has full control over the military's actions.
    c. She will begin to work with the international community.
    d. She agrees that genocide is being committed in Myanmar.

_____ 4. Which of the following statements about the genocide is an opinion?
    a. It is shocking that it has occurred under a democratic government.
    b. Around 900,000 Rohingya have been forced to leave their homes.
    c. Myanmar does not consider the Rohingya to be citizens.
    d. The international community is bringing attention to the crisis.

_____ 5. In the second paragraph, how does the author describe the life of the Rohingya in Myanmar?
    a. By telling a story.   b. By giving an example.
    c. By presenting statistics and facts.   d. By using chronological order.

82 | Are Sharks Really That Dangerous?

>> great white shark

1   Many people think of sharks as evil, man-eating monsters that hunt innocent swimmers down to attack and devour them. This image is far from the truth, however, and has largely been constructed by Hollywood movie producers who use this false impression to add an element of fear and danger to their movies.   5

⌄ tiger shark
(cc by OpenCage. info)

2   In fact, many shark species are not predators at all, but are scavengers who feed on already dead prey. Some, like the huge whale shark, have no teeth and are harmless to everything except tiny organisms called plankton. Out of over 470 shark species, only four have been involved in a significant number of fatal attacks on   10 humans: the great white shark, oceanic whitetip shark, tiger shark, and bull shark. These four huge, powerful species are capable of inflicting serious injuries on their victims. However, these species usually avoid contact with humans as we are not a part of their natural diet. In most cases of shark attacks,   15 the shark mistakes a human for a marine mammal. After taking a bite, it usually realizes its mistake and releases the person. The average number of fatal shark attacks per year is about six, and if you compare this to the amount of sharks killed each year by humans—over a hundred million—it's the sharks who should be   20 scared of us, not the other way around.

>> the teeth of the tiger shark, showing the serrated edges

3   Around 400 people die annually from snakebites in Sri Lanka alone, and about 40,000 Americans die each year in car accidents.

⌃ whale shark

Experts even say that you are far more likely to die from a bee sting than a shark attack. 25

4 So what does this mean? Like all dangerous animals, sharks must be respected, but in fact, they are nothing like the killing machines that they are made out to be in the movies. Sharks are amazing creatures. They've been around for almost 450 million years, possess excellent problem-solving skills, and even have the ability to sense an 30 organism's electromagnetic field. It's time we looked past the image of sharks as sea monsters and started to look at them with the wonder they deserve.

« oceanic whitetip shark

>> bull shark

Questions

_____ 1. Which of the following statements best summarizes the article?
   a. Sharks add an element of danger to a movie.
   b. Sharks are not as dangerous as many people think.
   c. More people die in car accidents than are killed by sharks.
   d. Sharks are extraordinary hunters.

_____ 2. The third paragraph is structured as a series of _____.
   a. statistics   **b.** questions and answers
   c. guesses   **d.** vivid images

_____ 3. In the final paragraph, the author's tone is one of _____.
   a. bitterness   **b.** pity   **c.** confusion   **d.** awe

_____ 4. How many people are killed by sharks each year?
   a. About 400.   **b.** About 40,000.
   c. About six.   **d.** About a 100,000.

_____ 5. Who or what is cited in the article as the primary cause of our current negative impression of sharks?
   a. The shark's problem-solving skills.
   b. Hollywood movie producers.
   c. The great white shark.
   d. The annual number of fatal shark attacks.

83
Superstition

» Friday the 13th is considered an unlucky day in Western superstitions.

1 Did you know that breaking a mirror will give you seven years of bad luck, or that cutting your nails on
5 a Sunday is just asking for trouble? And don't even think about opening that umbrella indoors; terrible things will happen if you
10 do!

2 Superstitions are powerful, often absurd beliefs that control the way we behave. You may dismiss superstition as something for old ladies or the overly naive, but have you ever worn a pair of lucky socks to an exam or kept a lucky
15 coin in your pocket during a sports game in the hope that it would help you win? Maybe you're more superstitious than you thought. While superstitions themselves may be weird, the reasons why they exist are, in fact, fairly simple.

3 Think of that time you wore those pink spotted socks to school and
20 happened to do well in a test. It could have been just chance, but the second and third time? Surely that was more than just blind luck. Not necessarily. Human beings often make links between things that are completely unconnected. When, by chance, wearing those socks and a good test score happened together again, that link became stronger.
25 And what about those times that you wore those ridiculous socks and nothing happened? Well, you've probably forgotten those occasions. We tend to selectively remember things that confirm what we want to be true, and forget the things that don't.

⌃ Hanging a horseshoe over the door is said to bring good fortune.

« blue Turkish eyes, sold as lucky charms to protect from bad things

30 **4**   In an experiment by the psychologist B. F. Skinner, pigeons were put in a cage along with a machine that regularly delivered food. The pigeons began associating the delivery of the food with whatever action they'd been doing when the food was delivered.

35 Skinner observed pigeons turning in circles, swaying their heads from side to side, or repeatedly going to a particular corner of the cage in the hope that food would appear as a result. They had linked their action with the delivery of food, when in fact the food would come no matter what

40 they did. Sound familiar? Humans may be the smartest of all creatures, but when it comes to superstition, we're just pigeons hoping to be fed.

ᐱ B. F. Skinner (1904–1990) (cc by Silly rabbit)

Questions

ᐯ Skinner observed pigeons turning in circles in the hope that food would appear.

_____1. Based on the article, which of the following do you think the author would recommend as an effective way to get a good test score?
   a. Wearing your lucky socks.   **b.** Breaking a mirror.
   c. Swaying your head from side to side.   **d.** Studying hard.

_____2. The first paragraph gives examples of _____.
   a. common superstitions   **b.** expert advice
   c. psychological experiments   **d.** lucky items

_____3. The purpose of the final paragraph is to _____.
   a. analyze the differences between humans and pigeons
   b. make fun of people who hold superstitious beliefs
   c. provide outside information that supports the author's claims
   d. inform the reader of a new development in the field of psychology

_____4. What can be inferred from the second paragraph?
   a. Having a lucky coin can make you better at sports.
   b. Logical people may still be guilty of superstitious behavior.
   c. Old ladies are statistically the most superstitious people.
   d. Everything we do is controlled by superstition.

_____5. Which of the following sentences represents the main idea of the third paragraph?
   a. Related things usually have a cause and effect relationship.
   b. Superstitious beliefs are not really true.
   c. Superstitious beliefs are a product of human psychology.
   d. We sometimes forget things that don't confirm our beliefs.

⌄ Plastic waste threatens sea life.

plastic on the ocean surface

84 Cleaning Up the Ocean Bit by Bit

(084) **1**   The Great Pacific Garbage Patch is an area of ocean littered with an **astonishing** amount of plastic. Located between Hawaii and California, it covers 1.6 million square kilometers, over twice the area of France. The 79,000 tons of plastic there threatens sea life as it breaks down and is **consumed**. Moreover, once it enters the food chain, the plastic could also impact on human health. Fortunately, a potential answer to the problem is already underway. The story of that solution and the young man who invented it is no less than amazing. 5

2   On September 8, 2018, a system named the Ocean Cleanup headed to the Great Pacific Garbage Patch. On the surface, **the system** resembles a huge pipeline in a gigantic "U" shape. Underneath the 600-meter-long pipeline-like structure, which keeps the whole device floating, is a huge three-meter-deep skirt. The solid skirt collects plastic as the Ocean Cleanup device is pushed along the sea. In addition to ocean currents, the system is moved by the wind and waves. As a slow moving device, it poses essentially no risk to sea life. 10 15

≫ Great Pacific Garbage Patch

GREAT PACIFIC GARBAGE PATCH

GARBAGE CONCENTRATION
Kilograms per square kilometers

0.01 0.1 1 10 100 200 miles

99% OF EVERYTHING IS PLASTIC

1.6 MILLION KM² 994.193 MILLION MILES

1.8 TRILLION PIECES OF PLASTIC

79,000 TONS OF GARBAGE

San Francisco

Hawaii

Mexico

Since it does not use a net design to trap the plastic, fish do not get caught in it. Instead, they swim either under or around the device.

3   The Ocean Cleanup system is the idea of a Dutchman named Boyan Slat. Now 24, Slat got the idea for his invention after scuba diving in Greece. Just 16 [20] at the time, he was shocked by the amount of plastic in the sea. He wondered why no one seemed to be dealing with such a major issue. Slat discovered tackling the problem using traditional methods would take an enormous amount of time and money. After spending a year thinking about possibilities, he **came up with** the idea for the Ocean Cleanup system at the age of 18. Thanks to his [25] brilliant solution, 50 percent of the Great Pacific Garbage Patch could be cleaned up in just five years. Slat is thinking even bigger than **that**, though. He aims to clean up 90 percent of the plastic in the world's oceans by 2040.

>> Boyan Slat
(1994–)
in 2018
(cc by DWDD)

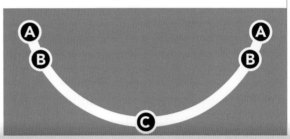

⌃ illustration of the Ocean Cleanup floating barrier *(top view)* (A: Navigation pod/B: Satellite pod/C: Camera pod) (cc by Weegaweek)

Questions

_____1. Which of the following words has the opposite meaning of **astonishing** in the first sentence of the article?
  a. Interesting.   **b.** Predictable.   **c.** Incredible.   **d.** Solid.

_____2. Which of the following words could replace **consumed** in the third sentence of the first paragraph?
  a. Broken.   **b.** Destroyed.   **c.** Eaten.   **d.** Melted.

_____3. What does **the system** in the second paragraph refer to?
  a. The Ocean Cleanup.   **b.** The Great Pacific Garbage Patch.
  c. Ocean currents.   **d.** Sea life.

_____4. In the last paragraph, the author states, "Slat is thinking even bigger than **that**, though." What does **that** mean?
  a. Getting rid of all the plastic in the world's oceans.
  b. Saving the sea life in the ocean.
  c. Cleaning up half of the Great Pacific Garbage Patch.
  d. Working on the Ocean Cleanup project.

_____5. In the sixth sentence of the last paragraph, what does **came up with** mean?
  a. Rejected.   **b.** Heard of.   **c.** Read about.   **d.** Developed.

Tuscany is famous for its breathtaking scenery.

85 | Tuscany (085)

≪ Florence

1   Located on the west coast of Italy, Tuscany is a beautiful region famous for its **breathtaking** scenery and its unrivaled artistic history.

2   Tuscany's most important industry is tourism. Every year, millions of people visit the aptly named Cities of Art: 5 Florence, Lucca, Pisa (home of the famous leaning tower), Siena, and San Gimignano. These cities are where some of history's greatest artists, among them Leonardo da Vinci and Michelangelo, were born or produced some of their best works. Of these cities, Florence is the most spectacular, and   10 its remarkable architecture and **extensive** collection of art **draws** over 10 million tourists every year. If you visit Tuscany, Florence is a must-see, but try to avoid the hot, crowded summer months when the ratio of tourists to locals can reach as high as 14:1. Indeed, many Florentines leave the city in summer, preferring to escape to quiet   15 villas in the beautiful Tuscan countryside.

≫ Lucca

3   Many say that to visit the Tuscan countryside is to visit **paradise**. Come evening, the rolling hills covered in vineyards and olive groves are washed in the gentle orange glow of the Tuscan sunset. Wine flows like water, and tables are piled high   20 with food known the world over for being unimaginably delicious.

4   Even if you're not usually partial to a glass of red wine, you should make an exception when you visit   25

≫ Pisa

« vineyards in Tuscany

Tuscany, as it is sure to change your mind. The region is famous for its **high-quality** wines made by master winemakers using traditions that have been passed down from generation to generation for centuries. Chianti, Brunello di Montalcino, and Vino Nobile di Montepulciano are some of the finest red wines in the world, though some of the best 30 examples will cost you a lot of money, Brunello di Montalcino being widely known as one of Italy's most expensive wines. Perhaps the best way to sample these wines and learn how they're made is to attend a wine-making course offered by one of the region's many vineyards.

5 Whether you're going to learn about the area's cuisine, 35 marvel at its fine art, or explore its extraordinary countryside, Tuscany is one destination that will never disappoint.

˅ Chianti Classico premium wine (cc by Arnaud 25)

⌃ Brunello di Montalcino is one of the world's most expensive wines.

Questions

_____ 1. The word **breathtaking** in the first paragraph is closest in meaning to _____.
   a. amazing   **b.** well-known   **c.** strange   **d.** tiring

_____ 2. "Many say that to visit the Tuscan countryside is to visit **paradise**." Which of the following could replace **paradise** in the sentence above?
   a. Hell.   **b.** Home.   **c.** Heaven.   **d.** Space.

_____ 3. "Of these cities, Florence is the most spectacular, and its remarkable architecture and extensive collection of art **draws** over 10 million tourists every year." The word **draw** can have several meanings. Which of the following is the meaning used in the sentence above?
   a. To take out.   **b.** To attract.   **c.** To sketch.   **d.** To perform equally well.

_____ 4. "The region is famous for its **high-quality** wines made by master winemakers . . ." Which of the following words could NOT replace **high-quality** in the sentence above?
   a. Excellent.   **b.** Low-class.   **c.** Luxury.   **d.** First-rate.

_____ 5. Which of the following words has the opposite meaning to **extensive** as it is used in the second paragraph?
   a. Famous.   **b.** Ancient.   **c.** Interesting.   **d.** Limited.

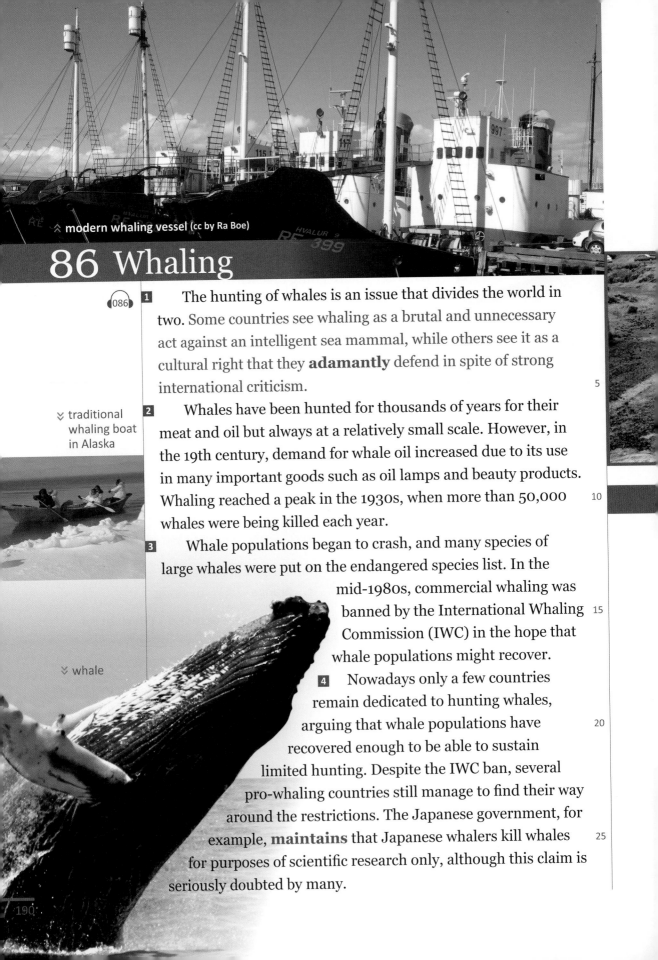

modern whaling vessel (cc by Ra Boe)

86 Whaling

(086)

1   The hunting of whales is an issue that divides the world in two. Some countries see whaling as a brutal and unnecessary act against an intelligent sea mammal, while others see it as a cultural right that they **adamantly** defend in spite of strong international criticism.   5

≫ traditional whaling boat in Alaska

2   Whales have been hunted for thousands of years for their meat and oil but always at a relatively small scale. However, in the 19th century, demand for whale oil increased due to its use in many important goods such as oil lamps and beauty products. Whaling reached a peak in the 1930s, when more than 50,000   10 whales were being killed each year.

3   Whale populations began to crash, and many species of large whales were put on the endangered species list. In the mid-1980s, commercial whaling was banned by the International Whaling   15 Commission (IWC) in the hope that whale populations might recover.

≫ whale

4   Nowadays only a few countries remain dedicated to hunting whales, arguing that whale populations have   20 recovered enough to be able to sustain limited hunting. Despite the IWC ban, several pro-whaling countries still manage to find their way around the restrictions. The Japanese government, for example, **maintains** that Japanese whalers kill whales   25 for purposes of scientific research only, although this claim is seriously doubted by many.

5 Whales are big, powerful animals, and so killing one can take a long time, resulting in a great deal of pain and suffering for the animal. This is seen as a cruel and unacceptable practice to those who are anti-whaling. The 30 argument is a **delicate** one, however, as many of the pro-whaling countries, such as Norway and Iceland, have whaling traditions that go back centuries. For them, whaling is a part of their national identity as well as an important source of income and food for many of their citizens.

6 In 2010, a compromise was suggested that would allow the pro-whaling 35 nations to hunt a limited number of whales under **strictly** controlled supervision, with whaling in the Southern Ocean banned completely. However, this plan was opposed by more than 200 scientists and experts. For now, the future of whaling remains 40 **uncertain**.

« killed pilot whales

» dominoes made from whale bones
(cc by Hannes Grobe)

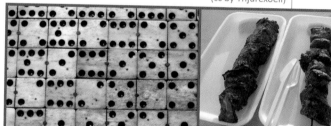

⌄ whale meat
(cc by Thjurexoell)

Questions

_____ 1. "Some countries see whaling as a brutal and unnecessary act against an intelligent sea mammal, while others see it as a cultural right that they **adamantly** defend in spite of strong international criticism." Another word for **adamantly** is _____.
   a. weakly   **b.** stubbornly   **c.** slowly   **d.** silently

_____ 2. Which of the following has the same meaning as **maintain** as it is used in the fourth paragraph?
   a. Continue.   **b.** Sustain.   **c.** Insist.   **d.** Support.

_____ 3. In the context of the fifth paragraph, a **delicate** argument is one that _____.
   a. has no evidence to support it   **b.** needs to be treated sensitively
   c. is impossible to disagree with   **d.** has gone on for a long time

_____ 4. "In 2010, a compromise was suggested that would allow the pro-whaling nations to hunt a limited number of whales under **strictly** controlled supervision, . . ." Which of the following words could replace **strictly** in the sentence above?
   a. Loosely.   **b.** Awkwardly.   **c.** Cruelly.   **d.** Firmly.

_____ 5. "For now, the future of whaling remains **uncertain**." Which of the following is the opposite of **uncertain**?
   a. Definite.   **b.** Vague.   **c.** Optimistic.   **d.** Prosperous.

87 | "Bathing" in the Beauty of Nature

1   When is a bath not a bath? The answer to that unusual question is, "When it's a forest bath." Forest bathing has nothing to do with getting naked or wet. Rather, it involves more of an imaginative type of bath—a "bathing in" of nature with your senses. Yet it doesn't mean doing a difficult hike in the woods, getting sweaty from exercise. This is a peaceful, more meditative exercise, and it's said to have numerous health benefits.

2   You may have never heard of this interesting form of health treatment, but it's not new. The Japanese have known of the advantages of forest bathing and been practicing it since the 1980s. Studies by the Japanese government around that time showed a strong link between forest baths and good health. The list of conditions that forest bathing is believed to be beneficial for is indeed impressive. It includes increasing the immune system, reducing the risk of heart disease, and lowering blood-sugar levels. Also, spending quality time in the forest has been linked to having lower blood pressure and fewer chemicals that cause stress. So impressed was the government that they made it part of the national health program. The Japanese Ministry of Agriculture, Forestry and Fisheries named the activity *shinrin-yoku*. Roughly translated, that means "forest bathing."

3   The exact reasons why forest bathing appears beneficial to one's health are a matter of debate. It could be simply that spending time in a less polluted, more relaxing environment with friends is the key factor. On the other hand, some researchers speculate the benefits have something to do with chemicals released by trees. Under this theory, the substance may have the power to increase the immune system's effectiveness.

4   Whatever the cause of the health benefits of forest baths, they are now catching on outside of Japan. The trend has recently become popular in the UK and the United States, for example. Given the positive research supporting the effects of forest bathing, it's likely the trend will continue to spread.

⌄ forest bathing

« Forest bath has become a trend.

⌃ Forest bathing is a meditative exercise.

Questions

_____ 1. What is this article mainly about?
   a. The reason hiking in forests is such a popular activity.
   b. Modern Japanese fitness trends.
   c. The health benefits of being in nature.
   d. The stressful characteristics of Japanese society.

_____ 2. Which of the following is NOT mentioned as a possible benefit of forest bathing?
   a. A reduction in blood pressure.
   b. A higher level of energy.
   c. Lower levels of stress.
   d. Reduced levels of sugar in the blood.

_____ 3. Which of the following sentences is an opinion about forest baths?
   a. The Japanese have known about forest baths since the 1980s.
   b. Americans and the British are becoming interested in forest baths.
   c. Forest baths are peaceful and meditative.
   d. In Japan, forest baths are part of the health plan.

_____ 4. According to some researchers, what causes forest baths to help the immune system?
   a. A chemical released by trees.
   b. A reaction in the brain.
   c. A peaceful sensation of relaxation.
   d. A slowing down of the flow of blood.

_____ 5. What can be concluded by the author's comments in the last sentence?
   a. The author believes more research is needed to support forest bathing.
   b. The author thinks more people in other countries will enjoy forest baths.
   c. The author doesn't know how long the trend of forest bathing will last.
   d. The author is positive that forest baths have a good impact on health.

88 | Index: Lord Byron

[088]

1   Described by one of his lovers as "mad, bad, and dangerous to know," Lord Byron is known as one of England's greatest poets, whose personality caused as much of a sensation as his poetry.   5

2   A series of shocking affairs and huge debts caused Byron to leave England in 1816, and he spent the rest of his life in a self-imposed exile in Europe. While fighting for the Greeks in their war of independence against the Turks, Byron   10 contracted a fever and died at the young age of 36, cementing his legend as a tragic, romantic hero.

3   Many biographies of Byron have been written over the years. To find information about a   15 specific part of Byron's life quickly, take a look at the index on the next page. An index is ordered alphabetically, with people entered according to their surnames. After each entry you'll find the page numbers on   20 which the topic is mentioned. William Scott, for example, is mentioned on page 376. Use the   25 pictured index on the next page to answer the following questions.

⌃ Lord Byron
(1788–1824)

≫ Lord Byron monument in Athens, Greece

≪ *Lord Byron in Albanian dress* (c. 1835) by Thomas Phillips (1770–1845)

^ Byron's Cave in Portovenere, Italy, is named in Byron's honor, because he meditated there and drew inspiration from the place for his literary works. (cc by Andrea)

Questions

_____ 1. On which pages would you find information about Byron's visit to Seville in Spain?
  a. 581 and 589.   **b.** 493–94.
  c. 191–94.   **d.** 594 and 638.

_____ 2. If you wanted to read about Byron's affair with Marianna Segati, you would turn to pages _____.
  a. 548-50 and 557
  b. 548, 549, 550, and 582
  c. 559, 569, 578, and 582
  d. 581 and 589

_____ 3. Which of the following people is mentioned most in the book?
  a. Robert Schumann.
  b. John Sheffield.
  c. Sir Walter Scott.
  d. Mary Godwin Shelley.

_____ 4. An account of Byron's relationship with Sir Walter Scott can be found on page _____.
  a. 219   **b.** 463
  c. 376   **d.** 634

_____ 5. Byron's letters to Alexander Scott are mentioned on page 634. Where else are they mentioned?
  a. 638 and 639.   **b.** 680 and 683.
  c. 759 and 761.   **d.** 559 and 569.

Schumann, Robert, 759, 761
Scott, Alexander, 594, 638; Byron's letters to, 634, 638, 639
Scott, Sir Walter, 219, 309, 313, 416; Byron's relationship with, 463
Scott, William, 376
Seaham, 432, 538, 444, 445, 446, 447
Segati, Marianna, 559, 569, 578, 582; Byron's affair with, 548–50, 557; Byron's break with, 581, 589
Segati, Signor, 548, 549, 550, 582
Self-Control (Brunton), 303
separation laws, 493–94
Seville, Spain, 191–94
Seward, Anna, 309
Sharpe, Richard "Conversation," 405
Sheffield, John, 166
Sheldrake, Mr., 43
Shelley, Clara, 598
Shelley, Elena Adelaide, 668
Shelley, Harriet Westbrook, 522
Shelley, Mary Godwin, 504, 514, 515, 517, 518, 528, 553, 592, 679, 680, 683, 686, 693, 694, 697, 699

SAVING YELLO

FREE download!

Save Yello from his out-of-bowl terror!

89 Line Graph: The Advertising War: Old Versus New

1   A war is currently raging between old and new in the world of advertising. On one side, there are the traditional formats like

5   television, radio, newspapers, and magazines. On the other side, there are the newer, digital mediums like websites, apps, and social media. Over the past

10   five years, companies have been

MORE HOPS, MORE Taste, MORE CHARACTER

HOP HOUSE 13 LAGER

⌃ billboard, a traditional format of advertisement (cc by Albert Bridge)

spending less to advertise on traditional formats. Meanwhile, digital ad sales have blown up.

2   The following pictured line graph shows traditional and digital ad spending growth in the United States from 2013 to 2018. The y-axis on

15   the left side shows the percentage of ad-spending growth. The x-axis on the bottom represents time. This kind of line chart can be very useful for comparing relative performance over a period of time. For example, the chart shows us how digital has been outperforming traditional ad spending by a wide margin. It also reveals that ad spending for

20   traditional formats actually decreased for some years.

Ad Spending Growth in the United States

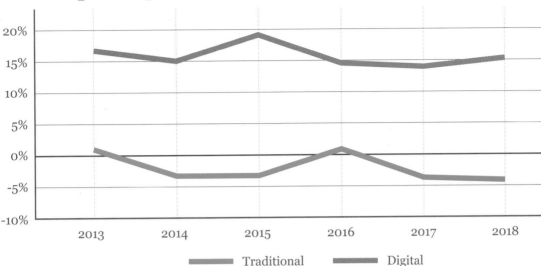

Legend: Traditional — Digital

Questions

_____ 1. What were the best years for ad spending growth in traditional formats?
   a. 2018 and 2015.   **b.** 2013 and 2016.
   c. 2013 and 2014.   **d.** 2015 and 2016.

_____ 2. What was the worst year for ad spending growth in digital formats?
   a. 2017   **b.** 2015   **c.** 2016   **d.** 2013

_____ 3. How much did ad spending grow in digital formats in 2015?
   a. 10%   **b.** 1%   **c.** 2%   **d.** 19%

_____ 4. In what years did ad spending in digital formats grow more than 16% but less than 20%?
   a. 2014 and 2018.   **b.** 2013 and 2015.
   c. 2016 and 2017.   **d.** 2015 and 2018.

_____ 5. What happened with digital ad spending growth between the years 2014 and 2016?
   a. It went down and then up.   **b.** It went down and stayed down.
   c. It went up and then down.   **d.** It stayed the same.

« the number of web ads collected in half an hour
(cc by Daniel Oines)

90 | How to Be Happy: Yale's Most Popular Course

1   Right now, you might be working to get into your dream college or that perfect job. But what if you were accepted to your dream college or got the ideal job and realized that it didn't make you happy? For many people, the pressure to

⌃ Yale University coat of arms

5 succeed in work or school **dominates** their lives. But even if they do well, they might not enjoy their lives. This was the case for students at Yale University, one of the highest-ranked universities in the United States.

2   As pupils at a top university, Yale students knew how to do well in

10 school. But Dr. Laurie Santos, a psychology professor at Yale, wanted her students to **prioritize** their mental well-being over their grades. She saw that students were stressed out and not enjoying their college life. Her **observations** matched the report that half the students at Yale had received mental health care services in 2013. Dr. Santos created a

15 course called Psychology and the Good Life. Twenty-five percent of the undergraduate students at Yale enrolled, making it the largest class in Yale's history.

Home ❯ Personal Development

The Science of Well-Being

About this course: "The Science of Well-Being" taught by Professor Laurie Santos overviews what psychological science says about happiness. The purpose of the course is to not only learn what psychological research says about what makes us happy but also to put those strategies into practice. The first part of the course reveals misconceptions we have about happiness and the annoying features of the mind that lead us to think the way we do. The next part of the course focuses on activities that have been proven to increase happiness along with strategies to build better habits. The last part of the course gives learners time, tips, and social support to work on the final assignment which asks learners to apply one wellness activity aka "Rewirement" into their lives for four weeks.

⌃ Show less

Created by: Yale University

Taught by: Laurie Santos, Professor
Psychology

« The Science of Well-Being, an online course taught by Dr. Laurie Santos (Source: https://www.coursera.org/learn/the-science-of-well-being)

⌄ Yale University

Yale University

3   Through Psychology and the Good Life, Dr. Santos taught students to change their habits and their **outlook** on what creates happiness. Dr. Santos's lessons used positive psychology and behavioral psychology. As students learned about what actually makes a happy and meaningful life, Dr. Santos's assignments challenged students to change their behavior. Her assignments included getting seven hours of sleep for at least three nights in one week, writing letters to show appreciation, getting exercise, and doing nice things for friends or strangers.

20

25

4   Because so many students enrolled in the course, it would be difficult for Yale to offer it again. But Yale decided to offer an online **version** called The

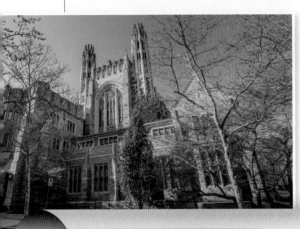

Science of Well-Being. In two months, 91,000 people around the world had enrolled. The comments from the online students and Yale students were similar: Dr. Santos has helped them focus on the important aspects of life and improve their mental health.

30

« Sterling Law Building, Yale University

Questions

_____1. "For many people, the pressure to succeed in work or school **dominates** their lives." Which word could replace **dominates**?
   a. Controls.   **b.** Expects.   **c.** Follows.   **d.** Experiences.

_____2. Which of the following means the opposite of **prioritize** in the second paragraph?
   a. Focus on.   **b.** Believe.   **c.** Write down.   **d.** Ignore.

_____3. What does **observations** in the second paragraph refer to?
   a. Dr. Santos thought mental well-being was important.
   b. Students in Yale were not happy.
   c. Dr. Santos's course was extremely popular.
   d. Students had healthy habits.

_____4. What is the meaning of **outlook** in the third paragraph?
   a. Appearance.   **b.** Manners.   **c.** Attitude.   **d.** Goals.

_____5. ". . . Yale decided to offer an online **version** called The Science of Well Being." What word could replace **version**?
   a. Schedule.   **b.** Form.   **c.** Brand.   **d.** Group.

91 | Mimosa Pudica (091)

≫ *Mimosa pudica* seeds

≪ *Mimosa pudica*

1   We've all heard of shy people before, but what about a shy plant? As crazy as it may sound, one actually exists. It's called the *Mimosa pudica*, from the Latin word meaning "sensitive plant." It's also known as the touch-me-not.

2   The *Mimosa pudica* is native to South and Central America. It is   5
a creeping annual or perennial herb, which means that it slowly expands across any surface it is attached to. However, the *Mimosa pudica*'s real claim to fame is its strange reaction to being touched. If someone touches the leaves of the *Mimosa pudica*, the leaves immediately fold up. This gives   10
people the impression that the *Mimosa pudica* is more of an animal than a plant.

3   The *Mimosa pudica*'s reaction is the result of a chemical that is released whenever the plant is touched. The chemical makes water within the plant move toward the stem, and   15
the plant's leaves fold inward as a result. Some scientists believe that this strange reaction is actually meant to be a form of defense against plant-eating animals.

4   It's not movement that makes the *Mimosa pudica* the most incredible plant in the world. Its leaves can also be   20
ground up and used to treat several diseases. In Indian traditional medicine, the *Mimosa pudica* is used to treat

≫ *Mimosa pudica* flower

swollen glands, and it is used to ease body pain and kidney disease in the Democratic Republic of the Congo. In fact, wherever the *Mimosa pudica* is found growing, there is usually a native culture that uses the plant to cure some kind of disease. 25

5 If you're fascinated by the idea of a moving plant, you don't need to worry; the *Mimosa pudica* is not a threatened species. In fact, it's the total opposite. The *Mimosa pudica* is listed in the global database of invasive species. An invasive 30 species is one that has been moved to a new habitat and is destroying the local species. Even though the *Mimosa pudica* originated in the Americas, it has spread to Africa, South Asia, the Pacific Islands, and Australia. In many of these countries, it is viewed 35 as a big problem.

« *Mimosa pudica* with leaves closed

Questions

_____ 1. The *Mimosa pudica*'s leaves fold inward when _____.
  a. it blooms   **b.** it rains   **c.** it is touched   **d.** it is sunny

_____ 2. Which of the following is an opinion?
  a. A chemical causes the *Mimosa pudica*'s leaves to move.
  b. The *Mimosa pudica* is considered to be an invasive species.
  c. The *Mimosa pudica* is the most incredible plant in the world.
  d. Body pain can be treated using the *Mimosa pudica*.

_____ 3. This passage is mostly about a plant that is _____.
  a. endangered   **b.** rare
  c. dangerous   **d.** unique

_____ 4. This article can best be described as a _____.
  a. personal story   **b.** descriptive essay
  c. timeline   **d.** biography

_____ 5. According to this article, what is the problem with *Mimosa pudica*?
  a. It is going to disappear soon.
  b. It is extremely poisonous.
  c. It smells terrible.
  d. It is destroying other species.

» sprouted *Mimosa pudica*

201

« the
Newbery Medal

» the 2013 guide
to the Newbery
and Caldecott
awards

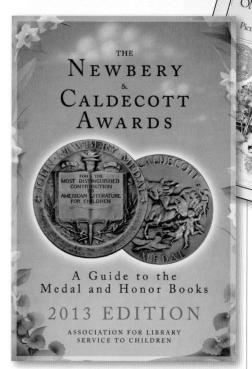

92 | The Newbery Medal

⌃ John Newbery
(1713–1767)

1   Reading a book can open the door to a wonderful new world of magic and discovery, which is why people all around the world love to read. There are many notable prizes that are awarded to the creative minds behind the books we enjoy. One such prize is for the best new work of children's fiction. It's called the Newbery Medal, and it has a long and fascinating history.

2   The award got started back in 1921, when Frederic Melcher suggested that the American Library Association give out an annual award for the best new children's book. Everyone agreed that it was a great idea, and they eventually decided to name the award after John Newbery, an 18th-century English publisher who had worked tirelessly to promote children's literature. The original goal of the Newbery Medal was to encourage creativity and establish children's literature as an art form on the same level as poetry, novels, and theater.

3   Since the Newbery Medal is an American Library Association award, it makes sense that the recipient has to be a citizen or resident of the United States. The winning book is selected by a committee that varies from year to year, but it usually has around 15 members. The process of picking a winner takes an entire year. First, there is a round of nominations where committee members pick the eligible books. Then, committee members read and reread the books throughout the year until a vote is eventually held to determine the winner. Sometimes the committee will

Newbery Medal award books

designate honor books, which are books that might not have won the award, but are still considered to be very impressive.

4   Next time you're at the bookstore, you might want to walk past the shelf with this year's Nobel Prize winner and proceed strait to the children's   30 section. As the Newbery Medal teaches us, children's literature is serious business.

Questions

_____1. The author's tone in the first paragraph can best be described as _____.
    a. skeptical   **b.** enthusiastic   **c.** formal   **d.** frustrated

_____2. The Newbery Medal was established to fix which of the following problems?
    a. Not enough children's books were being written.
    b. Children's books were considered too expensive.
    c. Children's books were not considered to be serious art.
    d. Too many people could not understand children's books.

_____3. Which of the following statements is an opinion?
    a. It makes sense that the Newbery goes to a US citizen.
    b. The Newbery Award was established back in 1921.
    c. Runners-up for the Newbery Award are sometimes called honor books.
    d. The Newbery committee usually has around 15 members.

_____4. Another good title for this passage might be _____.
    a. A History of the Nobel Prize
    b. Kids Literature and the Not Nobel Prize
    c. How to Write a Kids' Book in Three Days
    d. The Life of John Newbery

_____5. This article can best be described as a _____.
    a. descriptive essay   **b.** timeline   **c.** biography   **d.** personal story

≫ Trans fats are a popular ingredient in processed foods like fast food.

≫ Milk and meat from cows contains naturally occurring trans fats in small quantities.

93 Trans Fats 🎧093

≫ Paul Sabatier (1854–1941)

≫ Crisco was an early trans-fat product. (cc by Charles Sporn)

1 The story of trans fat is an interesting one, because it involves a discovery that started out as a miracle and ended up being deadly.

2 Trans fats are the result of an industrial process that thickens vegetable oils in order to make them more solid. They are also called "partially hydrogenated oils." Trans fats occur naturally in small amounts in many kinds of meat. However, they are also a popular ingredient in several processed foods, like canned soup, fast food, and frozen dinners.

3 The process of hydrogenating oils was first discovered in the 1890s by Paul Sabatier. The discovery enabled the production of margarine, which is still frequently used as a substitute for butter. An early trans-fat product was Crisco, which first went on sale in 1920. Crisco was a lard replacement that was used in baking bread, pies, cookies, and cakes. Up until the 1950s, trans fats were seen as a wonderful invention because they were cheaper than animal-based alternatives and most people agreed that they tasted better. The situation began to change in the 1960s.

4 From 1960 onward, scientific studies began to be published indicating that trans fats were bad for our health. At first, no one paid much attention to them, especially not the food corporations that were making lots of money from the sale of trans-fat products. It wasn't until the 1990s that the spotlight really fell on the health risks associated with trans

5

10

15

20

25

fats. Studies found that trans fats increase bad cholesterol levels while lowering good cholesterol, leading to an increased risk of heart disease, stroke, and diabetes. Most studies concluded that trans fats greatly contribute to the high rate of Americans who die each year from heart disease—about 630,000.

5 Given the risk, it's probably a good idea to keep an eye out for trans fats in your favorite foods. The American Heart Association recommends limiting your trans-fat intake to less than 1% of your daily calories. Luckily, most countries have now passed laws requiring food companies to clearly label the amount of trans fat in their products.

30

35

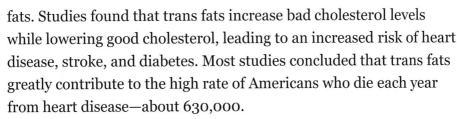

Questions

What Every Restaurant and Food Service Establishment Needs to Know About Trans Fat

⌃ poster from New York City's Board of Health encouraging consumers to limit trans-fat consumption

_____1. In the fourth paragraph, when the author mentions that the spotlight really fell on trans fats, that is an example of a _____.
  a. metaphor   **b.** joke
  c. statistic   **d.** comparison

_____2. Which of the following is a solution that governments have come up with in response to the problem of trans fats?
  a. Banning trans fats from all products.
  b. Fining companies that use trans fats.
  c. Putting a tax on products with trans fats.
  d. Clearly labeling products with trans fats.

_____3. The author's tone in this article can best be described as _____.
  a. angry   **b.** comical
  c. formal   **d.** playful

_____4. This passage is mostly about a(n) _____.
  a. ingredient   **b.** machine
  c. corporation   **d.** brand

_____5. What caused people to start paying attention to the amount of trans fats in their foods?
  a. A spike in heart disease around the world.
  b. A popular movie about trans-fat production.
  c. A series of negative scientific studies.
  d. An education campaign by food companies.

The Terrible Tragedy of Ireland's "Great Hunger"

⌃ potato plant stricken by Phytophthora (*Phytophthora infestans*)

1 The story of the Great Famine in Ireland is one of terrible starvation. It is also a true tale of how a government can make an awfully bad situation even worse. The Irish potato famine began in 1845 and lasted until 1852. For the Irish then, potatoes were an **essential** 5 food. Because people relied on potatoes so much, the effects of the famine were horrible. About one million people died from starvation and other related causes.

2 It was a fungus that led to a **massive** failure of potato crops. Half of the potato crops died in the first year. Initially, the problem was not 10 seen as particularly unusual because crop problems were nothing new. However, continually, for the next several years, the fungus continued to destroy potato crops.

⌃ victims of the Great Famine (*Illustrated London News*, 1849)

3 Historians often note that the British government's actions, or rather lack of action, contributed to the disaster. While some actions 15 were taken, many observers believe leaders did not do enough. Some taxes were reduced to make other food less expensive. As well, the government introduced work projects like road construction, so men could earn wages. **The measure**, however, has been criticized. The physically demanding work worsened the health of some men already 20 weakened by hunger. **This fact** most likely quickened the deaths of such unfortunate workers.

4 Perhaps the worst government mistake, historians suggest, is that Britain continued **exporting** food from Ireland during the famine. In fact, it appears exports of some food increased at that time. Crops 25

⌃ *An Irish Peasant Family Discovering the Blight of Their Store* (c. 1847) by Daniel MacDonald (1821–1853)

⌃ the Famine Memorial in Dublin, Ireland (cc by William Murphy)

such as peas and beans, and livestock such as rabbits and fish continued to be shipped out of Ireland. This all happened while thousands upon thousands of Irish men and women starved to death.

5   Also known as the Great Hunger, the Great Famine left its mark on Ireland and other parts of the world. It was one of the worst cases of famines of all   30 time. It led to Irish people relocating to the "New World"—North America. Indeed, one cannot truly understand Ireland and the Irish without knowing about this terrible time in the country's history.

« a food riot in an attempt to break into a bakery in Dungarvan, Ireland, during the Great Famine (*The Pictorial Times*, 1846)

Questions

_____**1.** In the first paragraph, the author wrote "For the Irish then, potatoes were an **essential** food." What does the word **essential** mean?
   a. Abundant.   **b.** Healthy.   **c.** Common.   **d.** Necessary.

_____**2.** The opposite of **massive** in the second-paragraph sentence "It was a fungus that led to a **massive** failure of potato crops" is _____.
   a. huge   **b.** difficult   **c.** tiny   **d.** historical

_____**3.** In the third paragraph, the author wrote "**The measure** . . . has been criticized." What does **the measure** refer to?
   a. Reducing taxes on food.   **b.** Taking little action.
   c. Hurting the health of Irishmen.   **d.** Paying men to build roads.

_____**4.** What does the author mean by **this fact** in the third-paragraph sentence "**This fact** most likely quickened the deaths of such unfortunate workers"?
   a. The health of the men was harmed by working hard.
   b. The wages paid to men were not enough to buy healthy food.
   c. The men were not really lucky to do the work.
   d. The deaths of some men happened quickly.

_____**5.** The opposite of **exporting** in the fourth-paragraph sentence ". . . Britain continued **exporting** food from Ireland during the famine" is _____.
   a. reporting   **b.** deporting   **c.** importing   **d.** affecting

95 Lake Hillier, the Pink Lake in Australia

095

1 There is a lake on an island in Western Australia. It's about 600 meters in length and 250 meters wide. It is called Lake Hillier, and it would be like any other lake if not for the fact that this lake is pink.

2 Lake Hillier is famous for its bright pink water. The first written record of Lake Hillier was made in 1802. That's when a British explorer named Matthew Flinders **stumbled across** the lake on his way to Sydney. Can you imagine how shocked he must have been to discover a giant body of water the color of bubble gum? 5

3 **Going for a dip** in Lake Hillier won't do you any harm, though the water might taste a bit gross. If you were to open your eyes while underwater, you'd see nothing but a thick veil of pink. It would almost be like swimming in a massive tub of stomach medicine. Another amazing thing about the water in Lake Hillier is that it maintains its pink color no matter where it goes. You can fill a container with it, and when you get home, it will be just as pink as when you found it. 15

4 Scientists haven't decided on what causes Lake Hillier's **trademark** color. Some believe that it's the result of a combination of low concentrations of certain nutrients, bacteria, and algae in the water. Others believe that it's caused by a **reaction** between sea salt 20

⌃ Matthew Flinders (1774–1814)

⌄ Lake Hillier is famous for its bright pink water.

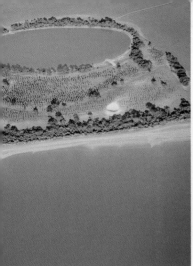

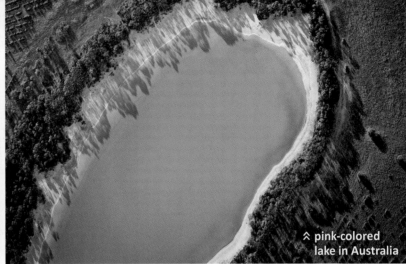

≫ pink-colored lake in Australia

≫ Australia has many pink lakes.

and red halophilic bacteria on the lake's shores. Perhaps we will never know for sure what gives Lake Hillier its **peculiar** color, and maybe it's better that way. Maybe Lake Hillier should remain an unsolved mystery for future generations to puzzle over.

25

5   If you want to see Lake Hillier for yourself without flying all the way to Australia, try looking for it on Google Maps or other satellite mapping software. It's hard to miss!

Questions

_____1. In the second paragraph, what does it mean that Matthew Flinders **stumbled across** Lake Hillier?
   a. He was searching for the lake.   **b.** He found the lake by accident.
   c. He was searching in a plane.   **d.** He was the last person to see the lake.

_____2. Which of the following words has the same meaning as **reaction** in the fourth-paragraph sentence ". . . it's caused by a **reaction** between sea salt . . ."?
   a. Response.   **b.** Decline.   **c.** Discovery.   **d.** Recovery.

_____3. In the third-paragraph sentence "**Going for a dip** in Lake Hiller . . .," what does **going for a dip** mean?
   a. Going for a swim.   **b.** Drawing a map.
   c. Testing the water.   **d.** Drinking the water.

_____4. In the fourth-paragraph phrase "what gives Lake Hillier its **peculiar** color," the word **peculiar** means _____.
   a. rare   **b.** shocking   **c.** small   **d.** strange

_____5. In the fourth-paragraph phrase "what causes Lake Hillier's **trademark** color," what does **trademark** mean?
   a. Business plan.   **b.** Money.
   c. Special feature.   **d.** Drawback.

⌄ Baobab trees in Madagascar. The baobab is the national tree of Madagascar.

96 Baobab Tree

(096) **1**   There is a type of tree that grows in Madagascar, and it goes by many names. Some people call it a baobab tree, while others use baob, bottle tree, or monkey bread tree. Scientists call it the *Adansonia*.

⌄ Baobab trees can reach heights of 30 meters.

2   Regardless of what you call it, the baobab is a very **interesting** tree. It has a very thick trunk that is used to store water and a relatively small canopy of leaves at the top. In fact, this canopy is so small that some people think it looks like the roots of a normal tree. This observation eventually produced yet another nickname: the upside-down tree. This characteristic is also the source of several local **legends** about the baobab tree. Some say that God flipped the tree because it kept walking away, and others say it was the Devil itself.

3   It's not just the tree's shape that's impressive, but its scale as well. They can grow to be 30 meters in height, with a trunk that's up to 10 meters in **diameter**. The tree also produces a fruit that's very rich in vitamins and nutrients.

4   Six out of nine baobab species can be found only on Madagascar, which is an island off the coast of Africa. Madagascar is famous for its numerous **unique** plant and animal species, but many of the island's natural habitats are currently under

5

10

15

20

25

⌃ The fruit of the baobab is about 18 cm long.

threat. Much of the local population lives on less than $2 a day, and they rely heavily on cutting down trees to make a living. This has resulted in about 80–90% of Madagascar's rain forest being destroyed. The government has responded to the crisis by establishing national parks and encouraging ecotourists to come and visit Madagascar. Only time will tell if this will be enough to save the **majestic** baobab tree.

30

35

« A baobab's trunk can be up to 10 meters in diameter.

∧ African baobab
(cc by Muhammad Mahdi Karim)

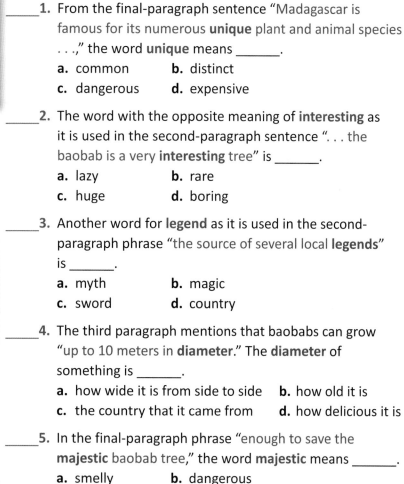

Questions

_____ **1.** From the final-paragraph sentence "Madagascar is famous for its numerous **unique** plant and animal species . . .," the word **unique** means _____.
  a. common   **b.** distinct
  c. dangerous   **d.** expensive

_____ **2.** The word with the opposite meaning of **interesting** as it is used in the second-paragraph sentence ". . . the baobab is a very **interesting** tree" is _____.
  a. lazy   **b.** rare
  c. huge   **d.** boring

_____ **3.** Another word for **legend** as it is used in the second-paragraph phrase "the source of several local **legends**" is _____.
  a. myth   **b.** magic
  c. sword   **d.** country

_____ **4.** The third paragraph mentions that baobabs can grow "up to 10 meters in **diameter**." The **diameter** of something is _____.
  a. how wide it is from side to side   **b.** how old it is
  c. the country that it came from   **d.** how delicious it is

_____ **5.** In the final-paragraph phrase "enough to save the **majestic** baobab tree," the word **majestic** means _____.
  a. smelly   **b.** dangerous
  c. grand   **d.** new

« The baobab tree can provide shelter for animal and human inhabitants.

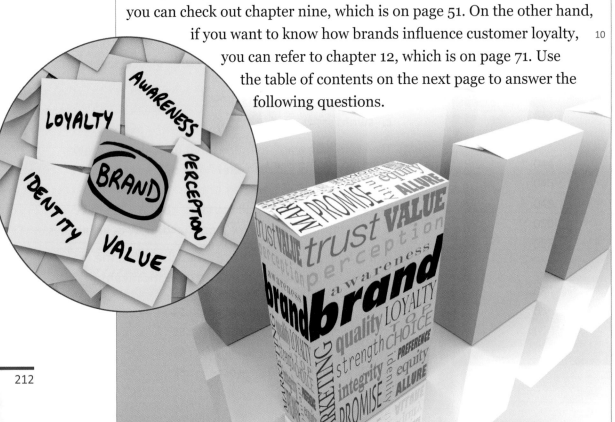

97 Table of Contents: Branding Your Company

1   Branding, or building your company's brand, has become an important aspect of international commerce. Luckily, there are many books and other reference sources available for businesspeople who want to discover the secrets of good branding.

2   The picture on the next page is of a table of contents from one of these books. It reveals that the contents of this book have to do with the various aspects of branding practices in the world of business. For example, if you want to read about how brands impact price elasticity, you can check out chapter nine, which is on page 51. On the other hand, if you want to know how brands influence customer loyalty, you can refer to chapter 12, which is on page 71. Use the table of contents on the next page to answer the following questions.

5

10

Part II	Sources of Business Value	21
4:	Strong Brands Command Market Share	23
5:	Strong Brands Create Barriers to Entry for Competitors	29
6:	Strong Brands Can Launch Successful Extensions	32
7:	Strong, Well-Defined Brands Find It Easier to Enter New Markets	39
8:	Strong Brands Can Attract and Retain Talent	45
9:	Strong Brands Have Lower Price Elasticity	51
10:	Strong Brands Can Command a Premium	60
11:	Strong Brands Can Deal With Market Disruption	66
12:	Strong Brands Have More Loyalty	71
13:	Strong Brands Are a Store of Trust	79
14:	Strong Brands Can Stimulate Innovation	85

Questions

_____ 1. What is Part II of the book called?
   a. Strong Brands Can Deal With Market Disruption.
   b. Strong Brands Are a Store of Trust.
   c. Sources of Business Value.
   d. Strong Brands Can Launch Successful Extensions.

_____ 2. Which of the following chapters comes before **Strong Brands Can Attract and Retain Talent?**
   a. Strong Brands Can Stimulate Innovation.
   b. Strong Brands Have More Loyalty.
   c. Strong Brands Can Deal With Market Disruption.
   d. Strong Brands Create Barriers of Entry for Competitors.

_____ 3. What page does the chapter **Strong Brands Can Command a Premium** start on?
   a. 66   b. 60   c. 85   d. 21

_____ 4. If you want to know how brands influence business competitors, you could turn to _____.
   a. page 29   b. page 45   c. page 79   d. page 85

_____ 5. If you want to learn how brands impact human resources, you could check _____.
   a. chapter 6   b. chapter 7   c. chapter 8   d. chapter 9

98 Attention Seeking on Social Media

≽ social media

1   Getting "likes" and comments on social media posts can be a great feeling. Knowing that your friends enjoyed reading your posts or looking at your photos is one of the reasons social media is so popular. But what if you feel like social media is negatively influencing your mood and using too much of your time? For some   5 social media users, getting likes and comments is taking over their lives. Psychology experts believe that people are becoming addicted to social media and using it in unhealthy ways.

2   Most social media users post about the fun or exciting events in their lives. They spend a lot of time trying to create perfect pictures   10 to impress their followers. Rather than focusing on real friendships, they rely on comments and likes to feel good about themselves. This connects to the other negative effect of social media, which is the belief that everyone else has a better life than you do. People share photos at cafés, but they probably don't share pictures of themselves   15 at home studying. Looking at social media might make you feel like you're the only one who isn't constantly having fun. Social media doesn't show what a person's life is truly like.

3   Social media can also popularize dangerous behavior. An alarming trend involves people taking photos in unsafe locations   20 or dangerous social media challenges to impress friends. In recent years, people have fallen over waterfalls and off bridges while trying to take photos of themselves. Others sneak onto the roofs

≽ Psychology experts believe that people are becoming addicted to social media.

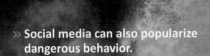
» Social media can also popularize
dangerous behavior.

of skyscrapers and stand on the edges to take photos. Social media
challenges have included eating a spoonful of cinnamon, which can   25
cause choking, and challenges with ice that can freeze the skin.

4   Too much use of social media can harm self-esteem and
relationships, and even encourage dangerous behavior. The easiest
way to avoid this addiction is to limit the time you spend on social
media. When you are with your friends and family, put away your   30
phone. Focusing on life outside of likes and comments will protect your
relationships and mental health.

Questions

⌃ The easiest way to avoid social media addiction is to limit the time you spend on it.

_____1. What is the focus of the second paragraph?
  a. The influence of social media on behavior.
  b. Unrealistic images on social media.
  c. How to take the best photos to post on social media.
  d. The problem of food pictures on social media.

_____2. Based on the article, which of the following is NOT true about social media?
  a. It encourages dangerous behaviors for the sake of taking impressive photos.
  b. It can become addicting for some users.
  c. It can encourage people to appreciate their lives.
  d. It doesn't tell the whole picture of someone's life.

_____3. What is the author's purpose in the fourth paragraph?
  a. To tell a story.   **b.** To criticize a person.
  c. To describe a situation.   **d.** To persuade the reader.

_____4. What is the effect of relying on social media to feel good about yourself?
  a. Getting likes and comments.   **b.** Using social media in an unhealthy way.
  c. Having many online friends.   **d.** Creating a realistic image of yourself.

_____5. Which of the following can be inferred from the third paragraph?
  a. Social media challenges are not influential enough to become a trend.
  b. Impressing friend on social media is important.
  c. Popular social media challenges are not necessarily safe.
  d. All social media challenges are dangerous and can cause injury.

99
Calendar : A Busy Social Life

1   Many of my friends are workaholics. They work from dawn until dusk every single day of the week, including weekends. They never have time to go out and have fun or enjoy their hobbies. Worst of all, they never have time to hang out with me! Let me tell you, the workaholic lifestyle is not for me. Sure, I work hard. You've got to pay the bills, right? But I'm a work-   5 to-live, not live-to-work kind of guy. You know what they say: all work and no play makes Jack a dull boy. That's why I try to have an active social life, including hanging out with friends on a regular basis, attending events, joining clubs, and taking classes. You name it, I'll try it. Having so many social commitments does need a lot of organization, though. That's   10 why I keep a calendar. Check out my fun-packed schedule for the next two weeks!

Mon.	Tue.	Wed.	Thu.	Fri.	Sat.	Sun.
27 18:00 Kickboxing Class	28 19:00 Beers with Andy	29 12:30 Lunch w/ Matt 19:00 Game Night w/ Simon	30 19:00 Spanish Class	31 18:00 Beers w/ Colleagues	1 Feb. 12:00 Picasso Exhibition 19:30 Dinner w/ Fiona 20:00 Dino's Birthday Party	2 09:00 Trip w/ Hiking Club 18:30 Movie Night w/ Friends
3 18:00 Kickboxing Class 20:00 KTV w/ Uni Friends	4 19:00 Game Night w/ Simon	5 20:00 U2 Concert	6 19:00 Spanish Class 21:00 Jenny's Farewell Party	7 20:00 Movie w/ Fiona	8 10:00 Brunch w/ Pete 13:00 Museum w/ Joe 23:00 clubbing w/ Friends	9 09:00 Trip w/ Hiking Club 18:30 Movie Night w/ Friends

Questions

_____ 1. What does Jack have scheduled for the 31st?
   a. A movie with his girlfriend, Fiona.   **b.** A trip with his hiking club.
   c. Beers with his colleagues.   **d.** Dino's birthday party.

_____ 2. What is probably the reason that has Jack rescheduled his regular Wednesday game night with Simon to Tuesday on the fourth?
   a. Because he has a date with Fiona.
   b. Because he has to go to a friend's party.
   c. Because he's going clubbing with friends.
   d. Because he has concert tickets.

_____ 3. At what time is Jack meeting Pete on Saturday, the eighth?
   a. 10:00 a.m.   **b.** 10:00 p.m.   **c.** 11:00 a.m.   **d.** 11:00 p.m.

_____ 4. What does Jack do every Sunday morning?
   a. Watch movies with his friends.   **b.** Go hiking.
   c. Visit a museum.   **d.** Attend Spanish class.

_____ 5. When does Jack have kickboxing class?
   a. Only on Monday, the 27th.   **b.** On Thursday afternoons.
   c. On Mondays at 6:00 p.m.   **d.** On Sundays at 6.30 p.m.

100 Fighting on the Side of Japan: The Forgotten Story of Taiwanese Imperial Japan Servicemen

1   When people think about World War II, the **major players** in that conflict typically come to mind. These include, of course, Germany, Japan, the United States, and Great Britain, among a handful of other nations. Taiwan's role during that time is not widely known, especially outside Japan and the ROC. However, it is quite interesting 5 from a historical and cultural viewpoint. Perhaps most interesting is a **category** of people known as Taiwanese Imperial Japan Servicemen.

2   The category of Taiwanese Imperial Japan Servicemen includes soldiers and those whose jobs were **unrelated** to battle. More specifically, it involved a wide range of positions, from cooks and 10 laborers to translators and pilots. In total, there were about 207,000 people from Taiwan who served in the Japanese military in this way. Initially, the inclusion of Taiwanese into the Japanese military was done through voluntary recruitment. That is, people were not forced to join. A strong motivation to volunteer as a Taiwanese Imperial 15 Japan Serviceman was the expectation of a better life. Generally, the volunteers were treated better by their imperial masters than other Taiwanese were. This included extra food for themselves and their families. As more and more Japanese were killed, the need for

⌄ drafted Taiwanese soldiers during World War II

⌄ Taiwanese students drafted as soldiers during World War II

20 replacements grew increasingly stronger. Finally, in 1945, Taiwanese were forced into the Japanese Army and Navy through conscription.

3 Taiwanese Imperial Japan Servicemen came from a variety of different backgrounds. Thousands
25 of **them** were aboriginals of Taiwan, whom the Japanese called *Takasago*. Others included Lee Teng-hui, who in 1988 became the first Taiwan president freely elected by the people. Lee's brother, Lee Teng-chin also served as a Taiwanese
30 Imperial Japan Serviceman in the Japanese Navy. He was killed during a battle in the Philippines. That makes him one of 30,304 Taiwanese people who died while being part of the Japanese military during World War II. Though now largely
35 forgotten, the era of Taiwanese Imperial Japan Servicemen remains a **fascinating** chapter in Taiwan's history.

≫ Lee Teng-hui (1923–) wearing kendo protector as a junior high school student in Taiwan under Japanese rule

≫ Lee Teng-hui, one of the Taiwanese Imperial Japan Servicemen

Questions

_____1. Which of the following, according to the first paragraph, is NOT a **major player** of World War II?
   a. Taiwan.   **b.** Germany.   **c.** The United States.   **d.** Japan.

_____2. Which word could replace **category** in the first-paragraph sentence ". . . most interesting is a **category** of people . . ."?
   a. Country.   **b.** Soldier.   **c.** Organization.   **d.** Group.

_____3. In the second-paragraph phrase "whose jobs were **unrelated** to battle," what does the word **unrelated** mean?
   a. Unnecessary.   **b.** Unconnected.
   c. Unfortunate.   **d.** Unable.

_____4. In the third-paragraph sentence "Thousands of **them** were aboriginals of Taiwan," what does **them** refer to?
   a. The Japanese Army.   **b.** Lee Teng-hui and his brother.
   c. Aboriginals living in Taiwan.   **d.** Taiwanese Imperial Japan servicemen.

_____5. The opposite of **fascinating** in the third-paragraph sentence ". . . the era of Taiwanese Imperial Japan Servicemen remains a **fascinating** chapter in Taiwan's history" is _____.
   a. difficult   **b.** unusual   **c.** boring   **d.** appealing

TRANSLATION

文章的字裡行間充滿許多唾手可得的知識，而涉獵關鍵就在於閱讀技巧。閱讀技巧能幫助我們吸收報章雜誌所透露的事實資訊，還能協助我們加以歸納整理，以便能更有效地理解資訊內容。

這樣想吧：閱讀技巧不只讓我們了解作者所寫的內容，也讓我們了解其撰寫原因。這就是為何不論是從小學、乃至於到商務職場等各個人生階段中，閱讀技巧都如此舉足輕重的原因。

1-1 明辨主題

文章的主題就是所謂的大意，通常能讓我們了解文章內容的大方向。如果你對某文章的主題感到不解，請試著再讀一遍，並且針對每段內文重點做筆記。

1. 不可思議的印度　P. 014

印度位於中東與中國之間的亞洲地帶，擁有悠久迷人的歷史。也因其迅速發展的經濟狀態，印度竄升為豐饒國家。

超過六千年前，印度河盆地的居民孕育出欣欣向榮的獨特文明。此文明讓該地區搖身一變，成為貿易與宗教中樞，並且享盡幾百年來的富庶安逸生活。

有人說，印度河文明的榮景可媲美古美索不達米亞或古埃及。以文化的角度而言，印度河文明是許多世界重要宗教的發源地，如印度教、佛教與錫克教。

不過，當亞利安人於西元前 1500 年入侵印度河流域後，印度河文明的「黃金時代」隨即告終。之後亦發生多次外族入侵事件，包括波斯人、希臘人、蒙古人，最後是歐洲商船與英國的殖民統治。

1857 年，印度人民開始厭倦外族統治，奮而起身反抗當時獨佔印度的英國東印度公司。然而抗爭行動最終失敗，大不列顛也因此正式將印度納入大英帝國殖民地的版圖。

但是印度不甘永遠淪為殖民地。20 世紀上半葉，上百萬名印度人參與甘地所帶領的全國政治運動。甘地組織了公民不服從的和平抗爭運動，表達反抗英國統治的訴求。1947 年 8 月 15 日，印度終於獨立，並於 1950 年 1 月 26 日正式更名為印度共和國。

印度歷經許多重要的經濟變遷與改革。如果你對印度的購買力有疑慮，印度現在可謂全球規模第六大的經濟體。且年輕的人口結構，亦能於未來十年持續推動印度的經濟成長率。

然而，印度尚有貧窮、文盲與營養不良等棘手問題待處理。與其他亞洲國家一樣，城鄉之間的人民貧富差距日益懸殊，這都是政府將來需要好好正視的問題。

2. 布雷點字法　P. 016

失明的人並不代表失去閱讀的能力，只要學習不同的閱讀方式即可。

視障者可藉由指腹觸摸頁面上多組微小凸點的方式來閱讀。這些凸點代表不同的字母，構成像我們一般人所用的字母表。這種書寫系統即稱為「布雷點字法」。

布雷點字法的歷史淵源十分有趣。大約西元1800 年時，法國士官巴比爾創造了點字系統，讓士兵即使在暗夜裡也能讀取訊息。這是因為拿破崙希望軍隊能在行跡不敗露的前提下，於黑暗環境之中通訊。但是這種「夜書」系統過於複雜而難以上手，因此不得不遭到軍方拒用。

多年後，巴比爾在巴黎的國立啟明學校認識了布雷。布雷四歲的時候即失明，他當下體認到巴比爾系統的重要潛力與其主要缺點。他開始著手簡化該系統，布雷點字系統就此而生。

在布雷點字法裡，每個布雷點字「字母」（或稱點字格）均由一個至多可填滿六凸點的長方形所組成（並以各點為凸點與否做變化）。此六凸點長方形的排列方式為每列兩點，每行三點。左行凸點由上到下的編號分別為 1、2、3，右行凸點由上到下的編號分別為 4、5、6，共有 64 種不同組合。

布雷點字法亦因應不同語言而有所調整。舉例而言，希臘文點字法就與中文點字法不盡相同。

視障者同樣能透過布雷點字法來書寫文字。多數視障者使用一種特殊的「柏金斯點字機」（Perkins Brailler），此打字機能將布雷點字打在紙張上。現在市面上也有配備布雷點字符號的電腦鍵盤。

布雷點字法由拿破崙戰爭使用的軍事技術所演化而來，竟然改善了全球無數視障者的生活，著實令人驚奇。

3. 細說閃電 　P. 018

「閃電」就是暴風雨時，雲層中所出現的銀白色閃光。有時候，一道雷霆閃電就這麼從天而降擊中地面。打雷通常會伴隨閃電現象，形成令人目瞪口呆的自然聲光美景。

幾千年以來，人類即對閃電著迷不已。古希臘人深信，閃電代表天神宙斯發怒。西元 1752 年，人們對於閃電原理有了更清晰且更科學的了解。因為就在這一年，富蘭克林透過一支鑰匙、一面風箏，以及一場狂風暴雨，證明了閃電實際上是一種電學現象。

至此之後，科學家發現閃電其實是靜電的放電現象。當雲層中的小水滴互相摩擦碰撞，就會累積靜電。當靜電累積至某種程度，就會試著往低電量的地表移動。而靜電位移的結果，即為我們所看到的閃電。

雲間閃電是最常見的類型，有時從遠方就可觀察得到。雲地閃電是第二種常見的類型，對人類生命財產的威脅最鉅。還有球狀閃電、正極閃電等其他閃電類型，以及最詭異的「地對雲閃電」。

閃電的溫度可高達攝氏 29,000 度以上，甚至超越太陽的熱度。閃電亦可能不斷襲擊同一個地點。光是一場暴風雨，高樓大廈與其他高聳建築結構就可能被閃電襲擊數次。這就是為何在雷電交加的風雨中，絕對不能站在大樹下的原因。最好的方式是待在車內，因為金屬能保護人身安全，或是到空曠區域平躺於地面。

近 20 年來，美國每年大約有 36 人因閃電雷擊而亡。閃電與龍捲風和颶風等天災一樣危險。雖然遭到雷擊的機率極小，但我們寧願防患未然，也不要終生遺憾。

4. 通貨膨脹 　P. 020

吉姆拿出他辛苦攢了數月並埋在後院的十元美金。經過了 40 年，他決定讓這筆錢重見天日，拿來買些好東西。但問題是，到了 2018 年，他的十元美金連幫孫子買個 iPhone 手機殼都不夠。

這到底是怎麼一回事呢？原因就在於物價越演越烈，而吉姆的錢卻仍維持原價值，他忘了考量通貨膨脹此因素。

當經濟體中的商品和服務價格攀升，就會產生「通貨膨脹」的問題。通膨通常是一種負面的經濟力量，因為物價上漲會為家庭生計帶來壓力。政府與中央銀行會盡量將通膨率維持在 3% 以下，藉此盡力控制通膨現象。

若干經濟因素會導致通膨問題，例如某國貨幣供應量大幅增加。印鈔數量過多時，貨幣價值就會下跌，物價因而上漲。當某商品供不應求，也可能產生通膨問題。另一個引發通貨膨脹的原因，就是商品或服務的零件或原料成本增加。舉例而言，由於農場牽引機需以石油驅動，因此油價上漲也會導致食物價格攀升。

當人民對其貨幣價值喪失信心時，有時會產生失控的通貨膨脹現象。這就是所謂的「惡性通貨膨脹」。雖然此名詞有多種不同定義，但多數經濟學家均認同，當某國每月通膨率超過 50% 的時候，就會出現惡性通貨膨脹問題。因為在通膨率如此高的情況下，貨幣每個月都在減少一半的價值。

惡性通貨膨脹大肆摧毀一國經濟的例子，歷史上比比皆是。1947 年，中國面額最大的紙鈔是 1 萬元。到了 1949 年，政府甚至發行了面額 5 億的紙鈔。1920 年代的德國、法國大革命期間的法國，以及 1980 年代期間的阿根廷，也遭遇過類似的通膨危機。而辛巴威政府自 2008 年以來，即一直在力抗不見起色的惡性通膨危機。

5. 天上到底有多少星星？ P.022

如果你站在喧囂的市區裡仰望夜空，能看到的閃爍星星應該寥寥無幾。但如果是在郊區或山上，則可看到滿天星斗的景象。外太空到底有多少星星呢？你可以試著細數，不過，詢問歐洲太空總署（ESA）的專家們可能比較快。歐洲太空總署已經自行估算得出宇宙繁星的數目。

根據 ESA 的數據，宇宙中的恆星可能有 10^{23} 顆之多。然而這只是粗估值罷了。還記得愛因斯坦的相對論提及：「時間並非絕對恆久不變」。因此，天文學家所計算的恆星與星系，可能早已消失殆盡。

此龐大數目含括體積大於太陽和更加渺小的恆星，也有將散佈於宇宙的數兆星系納入考量。有些星系屬於「矮星系」，因為系內僅有 1 千萬顆恆星。另有星系內超過 1 兆顆恆星的「巨星系」。

ESA 的估算數據包括我們太陽系所處的銀河系。我們的太陽是中等大小的恆星，並為銀河內白色雲狀星群的一員。有時抬頭仰望沒有月光的夜空，還可看見銀河橫跨空中。根據 ESA 天文學家的說法，銀河至少由 1 千億顆恆星構成。

許多恆星周圍都有以其公轉的行星軌道。事實上，某些天文學家相信，行星數量與恆星一樣繁多。或許有高等生物居住於此類行星，等待我們的發掘。倘若真是如此，也許外星天文學家能更精確地告訴我們，宇宙中究竟有多少恆星。

1-2 歸納要旨

作者撰文有其原因，並以各段落文字向讀者傳達訊息。文章的大意或主旨不一定顯而易見，所以閱讀的時候，別忘了在心中提問「作者到底想要表達什麼重點？」

6. 魔術師的奧妙 P.024

魔術師是創造錯覺與變出神奇把戲的表演者。他們可以無中生有，例如從空蕩的帽子裡秀出一隻鴿子；或者讓人憑空消失，像是從魔術箱內人間蒸發的助手。魔術師似乎也具備移形換物的能力，例如將美女變成老虎；或是破壞某物後，再施展還原大法，比如將某人一切為二，最後那人竟完好如初地站在大家面前。

魔術師還有許多其他技法，包括瞬間位移、逃脫術、人體漂浮、穿越術以及預言術。他們通常會在表演各種魔術的時候，穿插運用不同技法。

魔術師似乎具備某種超能力，亦散發一種神祕氣息。或許這是因為他們的磁場、會意的微笑，以及完美配合的手勢動作所致。

魔術師表演魔術時，我常會仔細觀察，希望藉此了解神祕的箇中藝術。我會專心凝視他們修長的雙手與各種動作。也許，只要觀察得夠仔細，就能看出錢幣其實是塞進外套袖口，或撲克牌其實是被快速換至另一手的短暫破綻。

熟稔魔術竅門的人說，魔術師僅是善用障眼法的大師罷了。他們的祕訣其實很簡單：魔術師能讓觀眾分心，在觀眾將注意力放在別處時，趁機巧妙變換或移動某物至他處。當觀眾回神後，魔術師早已完成「魔術」伎倆。

老實說，許多魔術師確實手法精湛，但我仍會繼續試著破解他們的障眼法。我僅須記住一件事：只要有魔術師在的地方，眼見就不一定為憑！

7. 馬拉松賽跑 P.026

馬拉松是一項明確規定距離為 42.195 公里的路跑比賽。或許也有其他長途路跑賽稱為「馬拉松」，但倘若其路跑距離並非 42.195 公里，即誤用了此名詞。

現今許多大城市皆舉辦馬拉松活動，使其成為十分熱門的觀光景點。每年均有來自世界各地的上千名旅客前往倫敦、柏林和波士頓觀賽，或參加馬拉松比賽。全世界每年舉辦的馬拉松賽事超過八百場，許多選手每年參加不止一場。

傳說從前一位名為費迪皮迪茲的希臘士兵兼信差,從馬拉松鎮跑到42公里外遠的雅典。由於費迪皮迪茲身負傳達希臘軍隊在馬拉松之役戰勝波斯人的重要捷報,因此他馬不停蹄地奔跑。費迪皮迪茲在抵達雅典後,大喊「我們贏了!」,旋即因體力透支而倒地不起。

幸好現代馬拉松路跑賽選手鮮少因體力無法負荷而不支倒地。現在的選手都會於賽前充分準備,參賽時亦會補充足夠的水分。

1896年,雅典舉辦第一場現代奧運會,當時大會決定以舉辦馬拉松賽的方式,重現古希臘的榮耀。自此之後,奧運的傳統即以男子馬拉松閉幕,並將終點線設於奧運體育場內。2004年的夏季奧運路跑賽即採用馬拉松鎮往雅典方向的傳統路線,而終點就是帕那辛納克體育場。

2008年夏季舉辦的北京奧運,男子馬拉松賽的冠軍是來自肯亞的塞謬·瓦吉魯,他創下2小時06分32秒的奧運紀錄。2012年的倫敦奧運,來自衣索匹亞的蒂基·格拉娜贏得女子馬拉松賽金牌,她以2小時23分07秒的成績刷新奧運紀錄。

8. 危險粉塵　P. 028

有些事物就是不應同時出現,風和沙就是最好的例子。每個人漫步海灘時,都喜歡砂粒在腳底下的感覺;天氣炎熱潮濕時,最愜意的感受莫過於微風的吹拂。但如果足量的風和沙同時出現,根本談不上「愜意」二字。

沒錯,我們指的就是沙塵暴。沙塵暴是一種天氣現象:強風颳過沙漠時,就會產生沙塵暴。風捲起鬆散的沙塵粒子,夾帶至大氣中,即形成巨大的塵雲。沙塵暴的範圍可延伸數百公里,維持幾小時到幾天的時間都有可能。

塵雲雖然看似壯麗,卻會對風暴內的受困者造成很大的問題。例如,極差的能見度讓受困者只能先在安全遮蔽處等候沙塵暴結束。無庸置疑,沙塵暴凡走過必留下厚厚一層沙塵痕跡。舉凡衣物、電子產品、建物、汽車等任何想像得到的物品,均無一倖免。沙塵暴甚至可能造成極危險的情況。2015年,一場橫掃中東地區的強大沙塵暴,造成兩國共八人罹難。上百人因呼吸問題送醫。

由於沙塵暴的主要成因來自強風與沙塵,因此乾燥地區形成沙塵暴的風險最高。中東和北美地區便因廣袤的沙漠區而飽受沙塵暴之苦;中國北部的戈壁沙漠與乾燥的澳洲中部亦不遑多讓。

全球暖化將使沙塵暴的威力越演越烈。隨著地球氣溫升高,某些地區會變得更加乾燥,產生更多的沙塵。抵禦全球暖化與避免沙塵暴失控,人人有責。畢竟,誰想天天佩戴護目鏡與口罩上學呢?

9. 當心殺手級生物!　P. 030

被問及何謂世上最危險的生物,不少人可能都會回答獅子或老虎。有些則會猜想鯊魚才是最致命的野獸。其實不然,還有比上述動物奪走更多人命的危險生物。

箱型水母名列最致命的海洋生物。擁有「海蜂」別稱的箱型水母,毒液可讓人類迅速死亡。事實上,每年世界各地均有大約一百人受到箱型水母螫刺而死亡。箱型水母可能出沒於淺水區或是陸地,螫刺人類。因此漫步海灘時,請當心腳下!

有些殺手級生物體積嬌小,例如金色箭毒蛙。棲息於哥倫比亞的鮮豔箭毒蛙只有巴掌大。倘若真的手捧一隻箭毒蛙,不到幾分鐘就會命喪黃泉。因為箭毒蛙的小小身軀,居然容納了足以毒死20人的毒液。

接下來是棲息於撒哈拉沙漠以南非洲地區的河馬。很多人覺得這些草食性的龐然大物十分可愛慵懶,但其實河馬是相當危險的生物。部分研究人員稱河馬為「地表最具侵略性的動物」。連獅子和鱷魚都曉得其危險,因而對野生河馬退避三舍。據說非洲每年發生將近500起遭到河馬攻擊的死亡事件。

但是,上述動物都還不是最致命的生物。人類才是當之無愧的殺手級生物。謀殺、暴力與戰爭所殘殺的人數，超越任何動物的致死率。光是 20 世紀，就有高達 1 億 8 千 8 百萬人死於各種戰事。無論是河馬、水母或是箭毒蛙，均難以匹敵如此令人哀傷的統計數據。

10. 撒哈拉沙漠迷途記 P.032

北非的撒哈拉沙漠是全世界面積最大的炎熱荒漠。這片廣闊沙地南北距離約 1,800 公里，東西距離約 4,800 公里。夏季白天氣溫可輕易達到攝氏 40 度，冬季夜間則可降至攝氏零下 10 度。超過八千年前，撒哈拉原為農夫種植小米的肥沃田地。隨著降雨量逐年遞減，撒哈拉最終成為偌大的沙漠。多數撒哈拉地區的平均年降雨量為 10 公分，擁有世上最嚴峻的氣候條件。

蓋瑞・史密斯與幾名充滿冒險精神的朋友，決定徒步橫越撒哈拉沙漠。開車隨行的支援團隊，則幫忙運送食物和飲用水。

某天，史密斯不慎與隊友走散。沒多久就在沙漠裡迷失了方向，完全摸不著頭緒該往何處前進。隨後來了一場沙塵暴，雖然規模不大，但等到沙塵退去，卻讓史密斯更加迷惘。在令人難以忍受的酷熱氣候下，他很快就喝光了隨身的飲用水，並且被迫露宿於沙漠之中，差一點凍死。

隔天，史密斯漫無目的地走著，四肢痠痛、嘴唇龜裂出血，頭也疼得受不了。但史密斯仍勇往直前，因為他擁有強大的求生意志。度過第二晚之後，他開始憂心自己是否會命喪沙漠，因為隊友們可能無法及時搜救他。到了第三天晚上，史密斯終於撐不下去而不省人事。

當史密斯醒來的時候，發現自己躺在開著冷氣的車內，還有隊友的陪伴。原來，是一支貝都因人隊伍營救了他，將他送回隊友身邊。史密斯能夠存活下來，真是非常幸運的一件事。

1-3 找出支持性細節

作者會以細節來佐證主旨，文章中的細節包含舉例、敘述、定義說明、事實等其他眾多資訊。一定要特別留意這類細節內容，因為它們通常會透露重要訊息。如果沒有仔細注意這些細節，就會誤解作者想傳達的重點。

11. 印刷機的起源 P.034

你覺得人類最重要的發明是什麼？是電腦、電話、還是汽車？很多人會說是「印刷機」。因為印刷機能讓我們無限複製各種書籍文件。

在印刷機問世之前，書籍以手工抄寫的方式複製。古羅馬時代的出版商有時可售出高達五千冊書籍，完全由奴隸抄錄。由於複印一本書實在太費時且成本高昂，所以每本書複製的數量不多。因此，僅有少數族群得以讀書識字。

雖然印刷機是由德國金匠古騰堡於 1450 年所發明，但印刷概念其實早已行之有年。大約在五千年前的古美索不達米亞，就懂得用雕刻的石塊做為封章或印章，蓋印於黏土上。不久後，中國人開始在木塊刻上文字，塗上墨汁，壓印於紙張或布面。不過，有別於一頁大小的印刷木塊，會刻上所有內容，古騰堡的印刷技術使用小型金屬塊，且每塊僅刻上一個字母。如需印刷一頁內容，印刷工人僅需排列所需字母，再啟動印刷機即可。況且，木塊很容易毀損，活字金屬塊較為耐用，如果發現某金屬塊有瑕疵，也容易替換而不會影響整頁的印刷。古騰堡印刷機的出現，讓大家能以低成本的方式，有效率地快速量產書籍。

1450 年之後，上千本熱門書籍或報紙已可迅速且平價地印刷出版。來自全球各地、圖文並茂的豐富書報，也廣泛普及於大眾。古騰堡印刷機所帶來的影響，有時會被拿來和網路科技比較，因為兩者同樣能讓上百萬人接觸到新奇有趣的知識。由於知識是精進人類智慧的動力，因此人類過去五百年來在科技與科學領域方面的大躍進，都該歸功於了不起的古騰堡印刷機。

12. 奇妙的貓頭鷹　P.036

　　形容某人「像貓頭鷹一樣聰明」，是對其智慧的一種莫大讚賞。但你或許會覺得這是個奇怪的比喻，畢竟貓頭鷹沒有比其他鳥類靈巧多少，且烏鴉才是眾所皆知聰明絕頂的鳥類。那麼「貓頭鷹」與「智慧」經常相提並論的原因究竟為何？牠們絕佳的夜視能力以及精湛的狩獵技巧，或許是箇中因素，但是真正的概念可能得追溯至古希臘人。因為希臘智慧女神雅典娜的畫像中，經常可見貓頭鷹停在她手上。

　　的確，打從人類有歷史記錄以來，貓頭鷹一直都是民俗傳說的元素之一。貓頭鷹的夜行特性與尖厲的叫聲，甚至被某些文化聯想為厄運與不幸的表徵。舉例而言，古羅馬人認為，當貓頭鷹發出尖銳叫聲，表示死神近在咫尺。他們還相信女巫會化身貓頭鷹，飛到無辜嬰兒身旁吸血。

　　不過，你知道並非所有貓頭鷹都是夜行性動物嗎？一般來說，深色眼珠的貓頭鷹會在夜間捕捉獵物；而橘色眼珠的貓頭鷹則在天色微亮時活動，也就是在黃昏或破曉時覓食；黃色眼珠貓頭鷹的捕獵時間則為白天。

　　事實上，貓頭鷹的眼珠或許是牠最出色的特徵之一。與貓頭鷹的小頭顱相較下，其眼珠顯得相當碩大。此外，與人類眼球不同的是，貓頭鷹的眼珠呈長筒狀。雖然貓頭鷹的眼珠重量佔達體重的 5%，但因為其奇特的長筒狀，使得貓頭鷹無法像我們一樣轉動眼球。貓頭鷹為了能夠左右張望，必須轉動整個頭部，任意方向的最大轉動角度可達 135 度。如此驚人的視力，使貓頭鷹能在漆黑環境下，捕獵疾趨而過的昆蟲、奔跑中的老鼠，以及閃電般飛快的野兔。無論世人對貓頭鷹的智慧評價為何，牠們都是不同凡響的生物。

13. 愛迪生的發明　P.038

　　電燈泡是過去兩百年間的一項重要發明。它讓我們可以從事夜間活動，如果少了它，就辦不到了。你能夠想像在整條高速公路上點滿蠟燭的情景嗎？或是在油燈的暗淡光芒下開車？很多人都認為電燈泡是愛迪生發明的，但真的是如此嗎？

　　愛迪生在 1847 年出生於美國俄亥俄州的米蘭。在學校時，愛迪生常心不在焉，在老師的眼中，他不是個聰明的孩子。1854 年，他們全家搬到了密西根州的修倫港。在那裡，年少的愛迪生常在往來於底特律和修倫港的火車上兜售糖果和報紙。早年的銷售經驗讓愛迪生得以磨練自己在生意上的潛能。他最後創立了 14 家公司，其中還包括到現在仍生意興榮的通用電氣公司。

　　愛迪生在紐澤西的紐阿克開始他的發明事業。1878 年時，他成立了愛迪生電燈公司。1879 年 12 月 31 日首次公開展示明亮的電燈泡，他說：「我們會讓電便宜到只剩有錢人還在點蠟燭。」電燈泡不是愛迪生唯一發展的事業，他還在紐澤西的門洛花園設立了第一間工業研究室。在當地，愛迪生和他的助理威廉・漢默研究改良了電話、開發了電力火車，並申請到電影攝影機的專利權。

　　然而事實上，愛迪生並沒有像傳說中發明了那麼多東西，他只是將這些東西改良到可以販售給大眾。比如，他並沒有發明電燈泡，電燈泡早在 70 年前就已出現。但是愛迪生的確開發了長效且實用的電燈泡，並設立了第一家製造並販賣電燈泡的公司。而他唯一親手發明的主要產品是留聲機。他在 1877 年所發明的留聲機讓他一舉成名，而他也以紐澤西「門洛公園的魔術師」名號聞名於世。

14. 沙發衝浪，探索世界　P.040

　　「沙發衝浪」一詞的定義，近年來隨著時間更迭而演變。此名詞原指在親朋好友家擠沙發寄宿，沒有自己的定居地址。人們以往不會為了好玩而沙發衝浪，這麼做的緣故純粹是因為無處可去。但隨著網路時代崛起，歡迎他人寄宿的沙發量大增。現在，當人們說要去「沙發衝浪」，是指準備出發探索世界。

　　現代沙發衝浪運動的主流網站為 Couchsurfing.com。此網站的功能彷彿集臉書與 Airbnb 之大成。Couchsurfing.com 於 2003 年成立，可說是元老級的社群網站，目前已超過 1,500 萬名用戶。

網站的運作模式如下：只要家裡有沙發，就可以發文邀請即將前來當地觀光的網站用戶寄宿。如果你準備度假，即可搜尋目的地是否有可供沙發寄宿的用戶。提供沙發的人統稱為「當地主人」，根據網站規定不能收受沙發客任何費用。事實上，Couchsurfing.com 收取的唯一費用，是用於確認用戶身分的年費。

你也許會納悶，難道大家不會濫用此制度嗎？畢竟，誰不想免費旅行？Couchsurfing.com 將重心放在建立使用者評價以解決此問題。當地主人可自行挑選沙發客。他們可根據用戶簡介、照片與評價等各種因素做決定。但或許最重要的條件，是沙發客是否曾提供沙發借宿。Couchsurfing.com 為建立在雙向交流原則之上的緊密社群，有付出才有收穫。而當地主人和沙發客最在意的就是安全性。

沙發衝浪運動持續改變我們看待旅行的方式。對沙發客而言，不一定要花大錢才能旅行，也不見得要受到飯店客房的拘束；而是可以到當地人的家中，體驗在地生活與風俗習慣。最棒的是，沙發客還能在沙發衝浪的過程中，結交到畢生好友。

15. 關於爵士樂 P.042

有些人覺得爵士樂聽起來雜亂無章，有些人則認為爵士樂是最能表達情感、最生動的音樂類型。爵士樂結合了各種風格與音樂傳統，呼應其發源地所呈現的美國社會大熔爐特性。

爵士樂源自於 20 世紀初的美國，尤其深植於紐奧良與芝加哥。據說「爵士」（jazz）一詞原為美國西岸的俚語，意指「精神」或「活力」。第一次有此用字的記載，是在 1912 年的西岸報紙體育版，用以形容某棒球投手變化多端的曲球招式，這似乎與紐奧良音樂的領域相去甚遠。不過，大約 1915 年的時候，「爵士」首度被用來表達當時芝加哥所興起的一種活潑即興音樂。

爵士樂集結靈魂樂、藍調、散拍音樂，甚至是軍樂，其蓬勃發展的原因，絕大部分歸功於紐奧良非裔美國人社區所舉辦的厚葬隊伍。早期有

許多爵士樂手都在此類場合演奏，因此，大小鼓、小號和長號等葬儀樂隊使用的樂器，成為爵士樂的基本配備。

雖然爵士樂在初期影響力顯而易見，但其音樂性質卻難以定義。原因在於爵士樂的重要元素之一就是即興創作。在爵士樂曲裡，爵士樂手可隨意變化旋律、和絃或拍號。相對於歐洲古典樂常被視作曲家的音樂作品，演奏者只要照「譜」宣科即可，爵士樂則能由樂手自行掌控格局。爵士樂是一種臨機應變的產物，隨著台上樂手的互動而自然流露，未經事先套招，或受到任何嚴謹規則的限制。這樣的特性也讓爵士樂衍生出無數「類爵士」音樂，包括咆勃爵士樂（bebop）、搖擺樂（swing）、酷派爵士樂（cool jazz）、迷幻爵士樂（acid jazz）、自由爵士樂（free jazz）、爵士放克樂（jazz-funk）與爵士饒舌樂（jazz rap）等，族繁不及備載。

1-4 明瞭作者目的和語氣

作者寫作皆有目的。有時他們希望藉由趣聞或悲慘故事來娛樂讀者；有時則希望向讀者傳達重要的主題訊息。文章中一定藏有能讓我們洞悉作者目的的線索，那就是作者寫作的語氣。

16. 地表最強——國際動漫博覽會 P.044

對多數人而言，夏季的同義詞不外乎游泳、野餐、露營，或是到山區健行。但我不這麼認為。氣溫開始攀升時，我心心念念的只有一件事，那就是：國際動漫博覽會。

一年一度的聖地牙哥國際動漫博覽會為動漫暨流行文化盛事，每次展期為三天。對於像我這樣的蒐集同好而言，無疑是地表最強的展覽。展場設有攤位，販售動漫、桌遊、玩具和電影設備等任何你所能想到的相關商品。你可以排隊取得喜愛的藝人、作家或電影明星的親筆簽名。錢花光也不打緊（此情況時常發生），還可以參加眾星雲集的專訪座談會。還有，當年度最火紅的電影預告片，也會在國際動漫博覽會放映。

回溯到我剛參加國際動漫博覽會的情況，國際動漫博覽會仍名不見經傳。猶記 1978 年第八屆國際動漫博覽會人群稀落，觀展人不是門外漢、就是像我一樣的忠實粉絲。

如今，國際動漫博覽會不可同日而語！今年參展人數超過 13 萬 5 千人，堪稱世上規模最大的動漫暨流行文化慶典。博覽會每年幫當地經濟進帳 1 億 4 千萬美元。而且，觀展人已不再侷限於忠實粉絲。國際動漫博覽會現已成為主流盛事。排隊等候時，你很有可能撞見高中時的足球教練，甚或是你的祖母！

我的一些國際動漫博覽會老友卻不喜歡這樣的轉變。他們抱怨博覽會門票售罄是因為開放普羅大眾參加的緣故。他們碎念著博覽會過往的形態已不復見。我的想法是：「多多益善！」國際動漫博覽會的宗旨一向是凝聚大眾分享共同的嗜好。因此，希望能在明年的國際動漫博覽會見到大家！

17. 塔斯馬尼亞島　P. 046

塔斯馬尼亞是距離澳洲南端 240 公里的一座大島。

塔斯馬尼亞南北長約 364 公里，東西寬約 306 公里，隸屬澳洲的一州，範圍包括塔斯馬尼亞本島與周圍離島。

塔斯馬尼亞有何迷人之處？一時半刻也說不完！這座島嶼的獨特名稱取自荷蘭探險家阿布·塔斯曼，他於 1642 年 11 月 24 日率先發現這座島。關於塔斯馬尼亞的生活型態，可說是人煙稀少。2018 年塔斯馬尼亞居民僅 52 萬 6 千 7 百人左右，且將近 22 萬 5 千人居住於首都荷巴特。

塔斯馬尼亞人煙罕至的原因之一可能是氣候。當地十二月至二月為夏季，六月至八月是冬季，但溫差變化卻非常急劇。你可能今天還在 40 度高溫下啜飲芒果汁，幾天後的氣溫卻下降至足以讓杯中果汁結冰的溫度。

塔斯馬尼亞亦有「天然之州」的美稱，原因在於擁有杳無人跡的寬廣環境。島上共有 45% 的範圍列入自然保護區。此類保護區是各種獨特動

植物的家園，其中包括不少全世界絕無僅有的物種，袋獾即為一例。體型狀似犬隻的小型袋獾，以脾氣暴躁著稱。而澳洲土生土長的 211 種青蛙物種裡，有 11 種青蛙棲息於塔斯馬尼亞，其中三種為島上特有種，分別是塔斯馬尼亞樹蛙、塔斯馬尼亞小青蛙以及苔蛙。

觀光客們眼光獨到，因此近年來有不少遊客湧入塔斯馬尼亞。世上還有哪一個地方，能讓你早上觀賞雪梨到荷巴特帆船賽，下午體驗餵食小袋鼠呢？

18. 全世界最快的列車　P. 048

過去數十年來，列車速度不斷加快。現今有許多列車的速度可超越直升機，甚至是小飛機。各國紛紛運用此先進科技，建造高速鐵路來載運往返主要城市的乘客及貨物。

根據國際鐵路聯盟（UIC）的資料，高速列車的時速超過 200 公里。多數高速列車的時速範圍約 250 至 300 公里。引進高速列車的本意，在於挽回改搭飛機的乘客流量。如今，雖然高速列車網絡的營建成本不斐，但是竣工之後，就能為該國經濟發展帶來一大貢獻。事實上，與汽車和高速公路等交通運輸工具相比，高速列車更節能環保。

史上第一條現代化高速鐵路系統，於 1964 年首建於日本，剛好趕在東京奧運前夕通車。此列車路段稱為「東海道新幹線」，連接了東京與大阪，且時速可超越 256 公里。到了 1977 年，義大利建造了歐洲第一條高速鐵路，此路段可往返羅馬與佛羅倫斯之間。其後，高速鐵路網於歐洲和亞洲境內不斷擴增，但尚未風行北美地區。

高速鐵路的車速記錄似乎總是不斷被打破。1996 年，日本新幹線創下時速 443 公里的最高紀錄。2003 年，德國磁浮列車時速超越 500 公里，令新幹線望塵莫及。不過，德國磁浮列車享受第一榮耀的時間並不久。2007 年，法國高速列車 TGV 創下時速 574.8 公里的驚人紀錄，奪走最快高速列車的冠軍寶座。然而，世上最快列車的頭銜，還是落入日本 JR 磁浮列車手中。它運用磁原理讓列車懸浮於軌道上，時速可達 603 公里。

19. 第一次世界大戰　P. 050

　　第一次世界大戰於 1914 年爆發,是人類歷史上第一場全球性的戰爭。1918 年戰爭結束時,傷亡人數超過 4 千萬人(傷亡者比例幾乎各半),並有超過 6 千萬名歐洲軍人參戰。

　　一戰起因在於歐洲政權的牽制關係產生了變化。德國於 1871 年統一,逐漸擴大的勢力開始威脅到英國、法國與俄國等既有的歐洲巨頭。當波斯尼亞的暗殺事件迫使俄國不得不協助盟國的時候,同盟國(德國與奧匈帝國)進而向協約國(法國、英國與俄國)宣戰,就此引爆第一次世界大戰。

　　數週之內,多數歐洲國家紛紛參戰。義大利與美國分別於 1915 年和 1917 年加入協約國。鄂圖曼帝國和保加利亞則先後於 1914 年與 1915 年加入同盟國的行列。

　　「第一次世界大戰」、「一戰」、「歐戰」(World War I; The Great War; The War to End Wars),這場戰役無論有多少別稱,都是一場可怕的衝突。戰爭初始之際,軍事戰略尚未使用後期所引進的重砲與機關槍等新發明,導致後來演變為壕溝戰,也就是雙方交戰人馬各自開挖深長戰壕,且相距不過數百公尺遠。士兵花上數月時間待在壕溝中,飽受疾病、鼠害、頭蝨與食物腐敗之苦,等到指揮官下令開始攻擊敵軍戰壕,士兵會爬出壕溝,衝到兩軍交戰的「無人區」,隨時可能因為踩到地雷、被拒馬上的有刺鐵絲網纏住,或是被敵軍機關槍掃射而喪命。

　　坦克車與戰機等新發明問世後,即打破壕溝戰的僵局,讓第一次世界大戰於 1918 年落幕。協約國雖然贏得戰爭,卻失去了和平。而戰後短短 20 年的時間,第二次世界大戰再度爆發。

20. 科羅拉多大峽谷　P. 052

　　大峽谷是面積與深度皆堪稱世界之最的峽谷。遼闊的地理特性,加上對遊客來說交通非常方便,使它成為美國最受歡迎的觀光景點之一。

　　大峽谷以其雄偉多姿的地貌聞名,每天皆吸引將近 500 萬名遊客前來朝聖,其中有 17% 是外國遊客。科羅拉多河經過 600 萬年沖蝕巨石而切割出河道的結果,即為我們眼前的大峽谷,全長 446 公里,寬度約 6.4 至 29 公里,深度則將近 1.86 公里。

　　大峽谷的山壁記錄了上百萬年來,科羅拉多河緩慢沖蝕岩石的痕跡。對地理學家而言,山壁能透露出地球歷經許多不同年代的寶貴蛛絲馬跡。對於遊客來說,則是欣賞壯麗景緻與拍下難忘照片的大好機會。

　　西元 1540 年,第一位探勘大峽谷的歐洲人是西班牙人卡迪那斯。當時已有美洲原住民部落定居於此,並視大峽谷為聖地。如今,大峽谷已列入美國最具悠久歷史之一的「大峽谷國家公園」領域。此國家公園佔地 4,926 平方公里,多數範圍均於亞利桑納州內。大峽谷村設有國家公園總部,該處有許多廣為人知的熱門景點。

　　來到大峽谷的遊客有許多活動可選擇,包括湍流泛舟、直升機或小飛機觀景之旅。想要更加愜意欣賞大峽谷景色的遊客,還可搭乘大峽谷火車。國家公園亦於大峽谷邊緣拓建全新的玻璃步道——大峽谷天空步道,並於 2007 年完工。

　　不過,觀光客在大峽谷國家公園裡唯一被禁止的舉動,就是接近或餵食任何野生動物。這麼做不僅觸法,還十分危險,因為這有可能改變動物的習性,導致動物攻擊人類。

1-5　理解因果關係

　　事出必有因。你今天很累嗎?也許你昨晚不該熬夜。肚子餓了嗎?表示你還沒吃飽。確認文章內容的**因果關係**,能讓我們以符合邏輯的方式,整理文章透露的資訊,進而加深理解。

21. 貓與人類的淵源　P.054

　　一提到家貓，大家應該會想到「可愛」、「討喜」、「高傲」等字眼。不過，鮮少有人以「百依百順」來形容家貓。這不是有點奇怪嗎？因為人類養貓作為寵物已歷時超過九千年了呀！

　　在沒有任何可靠史實能幫助我們深究的情況下，我們僅能猜測當初人類和貓建立關係的方式。多數歷史學家認為，人類早期居住中東地區時，被馴服做為寵物的動物之一就是貓。牛、狗、豬與羊等有用的動物相繼受到馴服後，人類才開始馴養家貓。畢竟，家貓無法犁田、產乳或看家。

　　不過貓也有拿手功夫，例如捕殺老鼠和其他有害動物。根據某些研究學者推論，這或許是貓與人類開始互助的由來。人類早期開始以農耕維生時，糧倉經常被飢腸轆轆的老鼠攻佔。而野貓絕不會讓獵物逃脫，故尾隨老鼠進入人類村莊。時間久了，貓也習慣棲息在人煙附近。最後，九千年前的野貓，逐漸演變為我們現今認知中的家貓。

　　了解貓轉變為寵物的過程猶如發現新大陸，因為這說明了家貓仍然保有獨立性格的原因。與犬隻不同的是，貓似乎有辦法隨時拋下主人而重返野外。牠們絕佳的夜視能力、聽力、嗅覺與敏捷身手等本能天性仍尚未退化。

　　家貓還保有自行獵食的能力。某些「幸運」的飼主可能偶爾一早起來，發現自家寵物貓帶來的小禮物，例如已斷氣的鳥兒、老鼠或松鼠。不過這類情況似乎沒有對我們造成太大困擾，因為目前全球已有超過 6 億隻貓生活在人類家中。

22. 承接古今的尼羅河　P.056

　　全長近 6,853 公里的尼羅河，堪稱全世界最長的河流。

　　只要提及尼羅河，多數人就會聯想到埃及，殊不知僅有 22% 的尼羅河流域流經埃及而已。或許這樣的聯想來自於古埃及人。畢竟，全球最古老的文明之一起源於尼羅河河畔。古埃及人十分仰賴尼羅河來維持生計。每年六至九月，尼羅河就會開始泛濫。豐沛河水會產生一層厚實的黑色淤泥，成為適合耕種作物的肥沃土壤。每年洪水暴漲的情形維持了數千年，直到 1970 年，埃及政府建造的亞斯文水壩竣工為止。

　　尼羅河亦為貿易運輸的珍貴管道，能讓歐洲至西南亞地區的其他文明相互往來。也讓埃及轉變為集散所有古文明的貿易樞紐。

　　尼羅河有兩大支流，分別是白尼羅河與藍尼羅河。白尼羅河的名稱起於常有白泥流入河水。白尼羅河的源頭始於中非的維多利亞湖，藍尼羅河的源頭則始於衣索比亞的塔納湖，並於蘇丹首都喀土穆附近，與白尼羅河匯合。對埃及人而言，藍尼羅河舉足輕重，因為往北流經埃及與流入地中海的尼羅河流量中，藍尼羅河就佔了 56%。

　　尼羅河仍是埃及的民生基礎。埃及的飲用水幾乎全來自尼羅河，亦為灌溉作物的水源。但是不久的將來，埃及可能面臨水源短缺的問題。預計未來數十年，埃及的人口會不斷成長，屆時尼羅河的用水量亦將隨之增加。而衣索比亞與蒲隆地等尼羅河支流所在的國家，供水量的需求同樣會攀升。為了補救此問題，埃及政府預計整修亞斯文水壩以提高蓄水力。政府亦鼓勵民眾遷往遠離尼羅河的內陸地區，以改善人口稠密的情況。

23. 正面思考的力量　P.058

　　桌上放著半杯水，你會怎麼描述這杯水呢？是「只剩一半」，或「還有一半」？如果你的答案是「還有一半」，表示你以豁達的心情迎接充滿任何可能性的精彩人生。反之，倘若你的答案是「只剩一半」，等著你的可能是充滿挫敗與悲苦的人生。雖然聽起來很不可思議，但這就是正面思考的神祕力量！

　　專家認為，正面思考能帶來若干重要益處。首先，能讓我們對人生知足常樂。如果我們專注於現有的美好事物，就不太容易對自己的人生叫苦連天。和成天埋怨、發生任何事都緊抓負面想法不放的人相比，一般來說，正面思考的人會比較快樂。

正面思考也能改善我們的健康。許多研究結果顯示,人類的生理與心理狀態息息相關。一份研究結果尤其指出,工作壓力大的人,傷口較慢癒合。亦有研究證實,倍受壓力的人較容易傷風感冒。

有些人甚至相信,正面思考能影響周遭世界。2006 年,作家朗達・拜恩的著作《祕密》,闡述了「吸引力法則」。此法則的基本概念在於,正面思考能吸引正面事物,負面思考則促成負面事物的發生。所以,如果你考慮買部新跑車,願望可能就會實現。但不管你做什麼事,可千萬不要出現被挾持為銀行搶案人質的念頭!

既然正面思考能改善我們的身心靈狀態,甚至是周遭人事物,那麼應該如何開始?根據曾任魔術師的心理學教授李察・韋斯曼的説法,改變心境的最佳良方,就是改變自己的行為。如果每天笑口常開,就會產生較樂觀的想法。

24. 紅毛猩猩　P. 060

紅毛猩猩是一種原生於印尼和馬來西亞雨林的猿猴類動物。牠們具有碩大體型與高智商,且全身覆蓋著有助融入環境的獨特紅棕色毛髮。紅毛猩猩以修長上臂著稱,長度是腿部的兩倍。這樣的特徵來自於演化的結果。畢竟,紅毛猩猩有九成的時間擺盪於樹林之間。

野生紅毛猩猩的平均壽命約 35 歲,10 歲以前均依附在母親身邊。某些研究學者認為,紅毛猩猩之所以需要依靠母親這麼久的時間,是因為牠們必須先學會許多求生技能,才有辦法自力更生。母紅毛猩猩每八年才會生產一胎,是繁殖間隔最久的哺乳類動物。母猩猩的體重可高達 50 公斤,公猩猩則可超過 100 公斤。紅毛猩猩是類人猿動物中獨居特性最明顯的物種,只有在發情期的時候,公猩猩與母猩猩才會往來。公猩猩具有大型喉囊,能在發情期時大聲吼叫來吸引母猩猩。此類叫聲也有警告鄰近公紅毛猩猩不要靠近的用意。

同為靈長類動物的紅毛猩猩非常聰明,智商僅次於人類。成年的紅毛猩猩能教導幼小猩猩製作工具與覓食的技能。學習能力與解決問題技巧亦優於黑猩猩,而黑猩猩可説是現存的人類近親。

紅毛猩猩生活大多以覓食為重心。雖然水果佔飲食的 65%,牠們也會食用葉片、嫩芽、種籽、樹皮、昆蟲和鳥蛋。有時候,成年的紅毛猩猩甚至會在高處建造休息用的小型樹巢。

野生紅毛猩猩目前僅存 78,500 隻,某些人認為,紅毛猩猩可能會在未來十年內絕種。濫墾林地、開發礦坑、焚燒森林、盜獵行為、農地開墾,以及非法交易野生動物等問題,都危害到紅毛猩猩的棲息地。加上繁殖速度慢的緣故,使得紅毛猩猩的數量備受威脅。野生紅毛猩猩數量越少,我們就越難保育如此迷人的物種。

25. 慢跑能改變世界嗎?　P. 062

有一群慢跑人士下定決心恢復地球的樣貌。他們在路跑過程中,會停下腳步撿拾任何寶特瓶或包裝紙等垃圾。他們的目標在於淨化環境,同時健身。

這些人統稱「拾荒跑者」。原文「plogger」是由「jogger」(慢跑者)和瑞典文「plocka upp」(撿拾)組合而成。拾荒慢跑運動始於瑞典,發起人是艾瑞克・阿爾斯特朗。他關注環境議題,架設「Plogga」網站,初衷是邀請志工參加斯德哥爾摩的團體拾荒路跑活動,拾荒路跑就此聲名遠播。如今挪威、芬蘭、德國與美國均設有拾荒路跑俱樂部。而全球拾荒路跑效應,在社群媒體的推波助瀾下亦開始蓬勃發展。無論你來自何方,你的國家或許已有拾荒路跑的臉書社團。

拾荒路跑因各式各樣的因素廣受歡迎。最重要的一點,是讓群眾產生盡一己之力的成就感。在全球暖化此類大環境議題方面,我們常會覺得心有餘而力不足。然而,垃圾屬於區域性的問題,人人都能帶來明顯的貢獻。拾荒跑者對於自己從公共公園與空間撿拾的垃圾量感到自豪。在社群媒體搜尋「plogging(拾荒路跑)」關鍵字,就會發現世界各地的拾荒跑者,發布自己路跑撿拾而來大批垃圾的捷報照片。

拾荒路跑同樣具有健身效果。彎腰撿拾垃圾，可以運動到有別於慢跑的肌群。重複這樣的動作，能讓慢跑轉變為全身性的運動。拾荒路跑也是絕佳活動，激勵不常運動的人接觸戶外、動起來。畢竟，誰不想讓自己的居住環境變得乾淨整潔呢？

1-6 釐清寫作技巧

寫作技巧對作者而言十分重要。寫作的技巧包括文章整體結構，和運用特定語詞來導讀文章內容。寫作技巧的運用也常能為讀者解惑：例如此篇文章屬於年表、自傳或是敘述類型的故事。

26. 北歐神話　P.064

數百年前，高大金髮的斯堪地那維亞戰士，如野火燎原般橫掃北歐。雖然他們有諾斯曼人或諾曼人（Norsemen；Northmen；Normans）等別稱，但最家喻戶曉的稱呼是「維京人」。西元 9 世紀與 10 世紀期間，他們襲擊歐洲之後，最終定居於歐洲沿岸地區。他們的文化深植其引人入勝的豐富神話之中，藉由神話來為宇宙的運作與現象找到合理的解釋。

北歐神話包含九大世界，並以「亞斯」（Aesir）神族為中心。與維京人一樣，諸神均為傲氣十足、驍勇善戰的勇士。祂們居住於天堂般的「亞斯加德」（Asgard）國度。傳說中，眾神隨時養精蓄銳，過著為捍衛自己而戰的日子，等待「諸神黃昏」（Ragnarok）的到來。「諸神黃昏」的原文「Ragnarok」意指「神族的末日」。當「諸神黃昏」降臨時，眾神族將被迫與巨人族決鬥，多位主神將被殲滅。最後，這個世界將沉入海底，而新生命也將浴火重生。

北歐神話比其他古文化更令人著迷的原因即在於此神族傳說。雖然北歐諸神心知肚明他們最終必將滅亡，但他們坦然接受命運安排，試著活出精彩可敬的一生。以某種程度而言，諸神與人類極為相似。祂們也有其他人性特點，例如妒忌、憤怒、情慾以及貪婪。所有北歐神話的概念，都與現今許多重要議題息息相關。

北歐神話的另一件軼事，就是歷經上百年後，才真正留下文字紀錄。在此之前，北歐神話皆以口述的方式代代相傳。這讓神話故事不僅得以延續發展，更融入了斯堪地那維亞的文化，展現出嚴寒氣候和不斷遷徙而孕育出的民族性，刻畫了維京人的戰士精神。

如果你在閒暇時，想讀點充滿人性的諸神故事，可以參考一下《散文埃達》。這本書可謂了解斯堪地那維亞歷史的入門指南！

27. 拖鞋文化：切合實際的傳統　P.066

在家穿鞋走來走去，或許令人一想到就受不了。想像一下，鞋底從街上沾附的所有灰塵、垃圾和狗糞，就這樣隨著走動散播至每個房間！你同樣不會將鞋子穿進友人家中，因為將灰塵細菌帶進對方家裡，是不禮貌的行為。不過，令人吃驚的是，脫鞋進屋並非全球共通的習慣。

中國、台灣、韓國與日本等國家均遵循進屋前先脫鞋的禮節。在屋外脫鞋這項傳統已流傳千年之久！傳統形成的理由各異：日本住家的地板通常鋪有榻榻米蓆墊，可就地睡臥和進食。為了讓榻榻米保持乾淨，日本人會在屋內穿拖鞋，但踏上榻榻米之前就會脫掉拖鞋。韓國住家則以暖炕或地板下的熱水管線提高室內溫度。穿拖鞋而非外出鞋，能讓腳底感受熱度而保暖。現今的日本和韓國住家仍然沿用榻榻米和暖炕，脫鞋習俗因此得以延續。

脫鞋進屋的習俗，不僅有效保持屋內整潔，亦象徵尊重。韓國與日本師生藉由脫鞋換上拖鞋的方式，表達對學校的尊重。師生會在學校大門口脫鞋，換上拖鞋後，再提著自己的鞋子，放到教室外面的特製鞋櫃。

所以，拜訪他人時，該如何判斷進屋前是否需要脫鞋呢？可以尋找下列應脫鞋進屋的線索：也許屋外或屋內會有排列整齊的室外鞋，或是屋內設有鞋櫃。最後，主人迎接你入內時，可能已經幫你準備了一雙拖鞋。

28. 無畏無懼的蜜獾　P.068

當你必須打鬥的時候，會想選哪種動物幫忙？你或許會選獅子、老虎或犀牛，對吧？若真如此，你可能忽略了全世界最強悍的哺乳類動物：蜜獾。蜜獾的名稱雖然一點也不懾人，但是牠們生來只為兩件事而活：好鬥和覓食蜂蜜。

蜜獾的英文別稱又為「ratel」，分佈於非洲與南亞。說牠們是「全世界最無懼的動物」一點也不為過，蜜獾還是掠食佼佼者。常有消息傳出，蜜獾會攻擊比自己體型龐大許多的動物。甚至有報導描述蜜獾嚇退獅子使其放棄獵物，從「森林之王」面前偷走一頓大餐。

蜜獾的捕蛇技巧十分高明，牠們可以在不到15 分鐘的時間內，獵殺與啃食長度超過自己體長的蛇類。蜜獾也會捕食蚯蚓、蠍子、野兔、豪豬、陸龜，甚至是鱷魚。不過想當然爾，蜂蜜是牠們最愛的食物之一。蜜獾有辦法一邊從蜂巢挖出蜂蜜，一邊忍受上百隻蜜蜂的螫咬。然而，有時候牠們會付出極大代價，因為在蜂巢旁發現蜜獾被螫死的情況十分常見。

蜜獾身長約 67 至 107 公分，體重可達 16 公斤。雌蜜獾一次只生一胎，育兒時間將近 14 個月。小蜜獾需依賴母親餵食與保護。由於小蜜獾會妨礙媽媽的捕獵行動，因此媽媽通常會將小蜜獾留在巢穴裡，但是其他蜜獾卻會趁人之危，攻擊與捕食小蜜獾。雖然這樣的行為令人不齒，但這又是蜜獾名列世上最強悍兇狠動物的另一個原因。

而世人亦開始注意到蜜獾令人印象深刻的天賦。2011 年，一則名為「蜜獾才不在乎哩！」的 YouTube 影片在網路爆紅。現在，世界各地都可看到印有蜜獾圖樣的 T 恤、馬克杯與滑鼠墊。

29. 偉大的義大利歌劇作曲家——賈科莫・普契尼　P.070

約莫 150 多年前，阿碧娜・馬基在風光明媚的托斯卡尼生下了一名男嬰。孩子的爸爸米歇爾・普契尼第一次望見兒子時，驕傲之情油然而生。他一定沒想到，這個嬌小的新生寶寶，有朝一日竟會成為義大利歌劇史上最重要的劇作家。

賈科莫・普契尼出生於歌劇導演世家，家族為當地天主教教會服務的歷史已超過一百年。小時候的普契尼背負繼承衣缽的家族期望，但父親卻在他六歲時過世，使他幼小的心靈蒙上一層陰影。幸好，當地天主教教會肩負起養育他的責任，並為他保留了歌劇導演一職，等他年歲夠長後接任。

年輕時期的普契尼，對於自己是否接受長輩的安排猶豫不決。1876 年，他觀賞朱賽佩・威爾第的《阿依達》歌劇表演後，才確信譜寫歌劇是他的歸宿。普契尼於 1883 年畢業後，以首次完成的歌劇作品參加當地的獨幕歌劇比賽。雖然無法獲得評審的青睞，普契尼的朋友們仍堅持自籌經費，幫他籌辦一場公演。普契尼的《女妖》劇作初試啼聲後，幾乎所有觀眾都覺得此歌劇的優雅和戲劇張力令人驚艷。這個例子告訴我們，「專家」的看法不一定可靠。

普契尼於 1890 年時冒出一段醜聞，當時他與名為艾爾維菈・傑米納利的已婚婦女私奔。儘管兩人時常出現口角爭執，艾爾維菈的丈夫過世後，兩人仍於 1904 年結褵。

普契尼不斷創作，直到 1924 年逝於喉癌併發症為止。膾炙人口的鉅作《波西米亞人》、《托斯卡》以及《蝴蝶夫人》，奠定了普契尼義大利歌劇傳奇大師的地位。有些人甚至認為，普契尼是「繼威爾第之後，最偉大的義大利歌劇作曲家」。了解普契尼作品之美後，你會發現這樣的評價果然名符其實。

30. 數字的起源　P.072

數字是一種用於計算與測量的抽象概念。至於人類從何時開始運用此類抽象概念來算數，沒有人能確定。有可能是西元前 3 萬年左右，當時的古人開始懂得在穴壁上做記號，也許是為了幫助算數。這就是所謂的「計數符號」，最初發現的遺跡是在南非的岩洞裡。

但是計數符號的用途有限。畢竟，你很難以計數符號代表龐大的數字。如果早期的人類必須數到 1 萬，岩洞裡一定布滿了符號。如果要數到

10 萬，穴壁很快就會因為無數的符號而變得黑鴉鴉一片！

西元前 3400 年出現了解決之道。早期的美索不達米亞人發明了能夠應付龐大數字的第一套數字系統。美索不達米亞堪稱最古老的人類文明，常有「文明的搖籃」之美稱。其地點位於內陸，現為伊拉克領土的一部分。古美索不達米亞人於城鄉農耕維生。他們懂得利用銅金屬、黃金、木材、石塊和磚頭來製造器具與營造建築。美索不達米亞人必須找到方法來測量土地、運河、建築、城牆以及劃分節氣，因此他們發明了「60 進位」的精密計算制度。

率先出現計算概念的民族為古埃及人，採用的是「10 進位」計算法，例如我們現今採用的數字系統。古埃及人是偉大的建築工程師，他們在西元前 3100 年左右，開始使用 10 進位數字系統。

雖然古埃及人是所有古文明裡最進步的民族，但是他們只會使用正數，且沒有「零」的概念。一直到西元前 500 年，印度才開創「零」的用法。南美洲的馬雅人，同樣在其計算系統中納入數字「零」。到了西元 7 世紀，「零」的數學概念才傳到柬埔寨，而後陸續傳至中國與伊斯蘭世界。

1-7 進行推論

文句往往不只有單一意義。字裡行間所傳達的訊息，能透露出所隱含的各種可能性、看法以及結果。**作出推論**意指從閱讀內文的狀態抽離，判斷文字在整體文意中，可能代表的意義。

31. 傳奇領袖——凱撒大帝 P.074

在堅而不摧的羅馬帝國稱霸西方世界的年代，異軍崛起的凱撒大帝成了重要的領袖，和勢力強大的政治人物。凱撒大帝也是一位偉大的將軍，更是讓羅馬共和國變身為羅馬帝國的推手。

凱撒大帝在世時間約為西元前 100 年至西元前 44 年。他早年的人生充滿傳奇色彩。凱撒年僅 16 歲時父親過世，他開始肩負起一家之主的重任。17 歲時，凱撒擔任天神朱比特的大祭司（Flamen Dialis）。擔任大祭司的條件，不僅需要具貴族身分，也必須與貴族聯姻。因此，他解除了與平民女子訂下的婚約，轉而迎娶一位重要政治人物的女兒。凱撒 25 歲時遭海盜俘虜，但他設法與海盜談判而脫離險境，最後還追蹤到海盜的行跡，並將他們全部處死。

西元前 59 年，凱撒當選羅馬執政官，此官職近似總統。不過，古羅馬政府最重要的議會「元老院」，欲限制凱撒的權力。凱撒深知自己需要勢力龐大的政治盟友，因此他與富可敵國且勢力龐大的龐培將軍，以及人脈廣大的政治家克拉蘇，私下建立合作關係。在此二人的協助下，凱撒鞏固強權，卸任執政官後，又成為高盧（現為法國與比利時的範圍）總督。接下來的 15 年，凱撒拓展勢力，以入侵的方式為羅馬取得新領土，最後於一場戰役中，戰勝前任盟友龐培，繼而成為最高統治者。

不過，元老院對於凱撒不受其控制而統治羅馬的情況相當不滿。西元前 44 年，凱撒被引誘至神廟，遭一群元老亂刀刺殺 23 刀而亡。這些元老原本希冀共和國制度東山再起，但凱撒遇害一事卻導致羅馬內戰。羅馬也因此成為永久性的獨裁政權國家，並持續數世紀之久。

32. 餐桌禮儀須知 P.076

「餐巾放在大腿上，刀叉準備好。」

我父親曾在用餐前，對我和弟弟這麼說，提醒我們準備開動。意思是將餐巾放在大腿上，左手拿餐叉，右手拿餐刀。老爸並不曉得，他誤打誤撞教了我們「歐式」餐桌禮儀。而「美式」餐桌禮儀則是右手拿餐叉、左手拿餐刀。我們雖然是美國人，但規矩就是規矩。

雖然居家用餐較非正式，但許多餐桌禮儀的準則仍然適用家庭晚餐。例如暫時離開餐桌時，應將刀叉交叉置於餐盤上。結束用餐後，應該將刀叉平行置於餐盤上，餐具的握把處位於右側盤緣。此外,暫時離桌時,餐巾應放在椅子上。結束用餐後,則將餐巾放在餐具左側。

餐具擺設的方式是以「由外而內」為原則,也就是隨著餐點上菜順序,從最外側的餐具開始拿取,逐一往內側取用。以擺放於用餐器皿左側的餐叉來說,沙拉叉位於左邊最外側,往右是正餐用的大餐叉,再往右是甜點叉。只要每道菜一上桌,由左往右拿取餐叉即可。

那麼該何時開動呢?以非正式餐宴而言,只要等到每個人的餐點都到齊即可。不過,如果現場有宴客的主人,主人只要告知大家自便,即可開動。記得將各道菜往右傳遞,如果你有想吃的菜色卻拿不到,請務必開口請同桌的人遞給你。伸手橫越整個餐桌到另一端取菜,是非常無禮的行為。

多數人不見得完全遵循上述規矩,但令人感嘆的是許多人幾乎都不遵守。復興餐桌禮儀,就像老一輩的人的用餐情境,能讓用餐時刻成為更具社交性與特殊性的活動。所以,謝啦老爸,我仍然遵照你教導的習慣來開飯。

33. 飛上月球　P. 078

太空旅行曾是遙不可及的夢想,只有在政府鉅額計畫中受過高度訓練的太空人才得以參與。不過,從 2001 年 4 月 28 日起,這樣的印象從此顛覆。名為丹尼斯‧提多的美國商人在這天成為了第一位造訪太空的遊客。他的太空之旅開創了太空觀光業的商機。

接下來數年,共有六名遊客陸續追隨丹尼斯‧提多的腳步,前往太空。包括南非的馬克‧沙特沃斯與加拿大的蓋‧拉利伯特。這些遊客與提多一樣,搭乘俄羅斯的聯盟號火箭,參觀國際太空站。環繞在宇宙天體之間、為期一到兩週的太空之旅要價不斐,定價近 2 千萬至 4 千萬美元不等。但想必十分值得,因為名為查爾斯‧西蒙尼的遊客還意猶未盡,參加了兩次太空之旅。

不過早期的太空觀光熱潮並未延燒很久。2009 年,俄羅斯以席位不足為由,暫停了觀光之旅。因為美國太空總署停止發射太空梭後,俄羅斯的聯盟號火箭必須為美國太空人保留座位。

但 2009 年並非太空觀光業的終點,反而為各界醞釀更加浩大優質的太空之旅,開啟了新局。數家公司開始打造私人太空船,其中有伊隆‧馬斯克自有的「SpaceX」太空探險公司。2018 年,該公司的一艘「重型獵鷹號」火箭,在試飛時將一輛特斯拉電動汽車送上太空。亞馬遜網站創辦人傑夫‧貝佐斯亦創設名為「藍色起源」的太空觀光公司。該公司的「新牧羊犬號」太空船,計劃載送乘客至靠近太空邊界,體驗無重力的感覺。

不過,私人太空觀光業的進展並非一帆風順。「維珍銀河」公司原為太空觀光業的佼佼者,直到「太空船二號」試航機於 2014 年墜機導致副駕駛罹難後,聲勢重創。「太空船二號」墜機事件這場悲劇提醒了大家,太空之旅的風險極高。不過,人類如果不承擔風險,就不會進步。只要多下點苦功,加上運氣,也許有朝一日,人人都能登陸星球。

34. 婆媽經驗談　P. 080

「婆媽經驗談」意指本應用來解決常見健康問題或家務事的建議。通常是以口述的方式代代相傳,僅有少數例子以文字記載。雖然某些「婆媽經驗談」的解決之道屬實,但多數均經科學證實為無稽之談。

「婆媽經驗談」通常具有警示意味,或是用以勸阻小孩的不良行為。舉例來說,「睡前吃糖果會做惡夢」就是用來制止小孩吃太多有害零食,所杜撰出來的常見「婆媽經驗談」。同樣的,「指甲出現白斑表示你在說謊」完全是一種誘導調皮孩子講實話的手段,而虛構「看太多電視會讓眼睛變方型」說法的原因更不需多做解釋了。

某些「婆媽經驗談」則與抑止病症或治病有關。「頭髮濕濕的就出門,一定會感冒」,就是至今仍常聽聞的「婆媽經驗談」。不過,感冒的原因並非氣候寒冷、頭髮沒吹乾以及冷風,而是病毒所致。

「感冒要進食，發燒要禁食」意指感冒的時候要吃得好，但發燒的時候別吃太多。之所以會有這句「金玉良言」，可能是因為發燒的人本來就不太有胃口。醫學研究結果顯示，發燒的時候，人體會自行抑制食慾，以便促進免疫系統抵禦細菌感染的問題；感冒多攝取食物的話，則能促進免疫系統戰勝病毒。

「婆媽經驗談」的例子實在不勝枚舉。某些很荒謬，某些則很有道理。無論如何，這些經驗談均為迷信與民俗習慣充斥且未受質疑的時代產物。儘管有少許說法屬實，但當你聽到這類諺語時，最好不要太信以為真。

35. 神秘的 51 區 　P. 082

在內華達沙漠的中部，介於前核武測試場與空軍基地之間的偏遠地區，就是知名的「51區」。美國政府從未正式承認 51 區的存在，直到近期之前，51 區都未出現於此範圍地圖上。你根本不可能步行或開車進入該區，數十年來，飛機均禁止飛越 51 區的領空。51 區如此神祕，也難怪謠言與傳說四起。這麼多年來，51 區不斷傳出最為精彩怪誕的外星人與飛碟故事。

51 區著名的背景資料顯示該基地是於 1950 年代中期所建，內有各種建物、軍機起降跑道與停機坪。冷戰期間，美國政府在此建造與測試概念機，包括 U2 偵察機和 F-117 戰鬥機。軍機和武器試驗至今從未間斷，此基地「最高機密」的稱號亦流傳到現在。

51 區之所以會有外星訪客與飛碟事件的傳聞，其實可想而知。受測的某些新型戰機擁有非比尋常的外型、照明燈和飛航模式。大型地下基地藏有冷凍外星人遺體的故事，源自於 1947 年某架太空船墜落於新墨西哥州羅斯威爾的謠言。況且經過證實，51 區的確設有地下基地。最怪誕且難以解釋的傳言，就是美國政府與外星人之間簽訂的保密條約。據說美國政府允許外星人綁架當地居民並研磨為食用粉末。

大家對 51 區產生的好奇心恐怕沒那麼快退燒。眾多電影、書籍、電視節目和網站都以此基地為主題。雖然前任員工近期獲得許可，能公開談論他們過去在 51 區測試的部分軍機，陰謀論者仍堅信他們在研究外星人飛碟，只不過至今仍無確鑿的飛碟證據。同時，來自世界各地的遊客紛紛湧入內華達沙漠，為的就是希望能一睹可能與「外太空」有關的任何事物。

1-8 問題與解決之道

對讀者而言，文章常以提出一項**問題**為開頭，再以**解決方法**做出結論。介於兩者之間所透露的內文資訊十分重要，因為通常會述說解決問題的過程。所以，閱讀時請記得在心裡提問：現在閱讀的內容是一項問題抑或解決之道？

36. 極限運動：定點跳傘 　P. 084

「定點跳傘」（BASE jumping）是一項極限運動，玩法就是穿上降落傘，再從高處定點一躍而下。這項運動在喜歡追求新奇刺激的同好圈子裡蔚為風潮。由於定點跳傘十分危險，因此常被稱為「特技跳傘」或「冒險活動」而非運動。

定點跳傘原文中的 BASE，代表摩天大樓（Building）、天線高塔（Antenna）、大橋水壩（Span/Bridge）和懸崖溶洞（Earth/Cliff）此四種定點的首字母縮寫。定點跳傘玩家會以這四種地形做為跳傘起點。如果定點跳傘玩家跳過這四種地形，即可申請「定點跳傘編號」。擁有定點跳傘編號，表示自己是經認可的定點跳傘玩家。

卡爾·波尼西是定點跳傘運動的最初推動者，源起於他在 1978 年拍攝了四個朋友從加州「艾爾船長巨石」（El Capitan）縱身跳下的影片。1984 年，卡爾從挪威著名的巨牆山（Troll Wall）一躍而下。但是兩天後，當他想從同一定點再次試跳時，卻不幸身亡。

此極限運動發明者意外死亡一事，證明了這項運動有多麼危險。雖然裝備不斷改良，提高了定點跳傘運動的安全性，但是每年仍有許多資深狂人與菜鳥玩家受傷或喪命。雖然並無可靠的定點跳傘受傷人數統計數據，但是人們通常認為這種極限運動比高空跳傘危險許多。

由於喪命人數太多，大眾對於定點跳傘的接受度仍未普及。事實上，多數國家甚至明令禁止此項運動。如果有人想玩定點跳傘，必須取得許可證，才能合法使用跳傘起點以及降落地點。而挪威巨牆山等景點，也因為此項運動過於危險而禁止玩家在此進行定點跳傘運動。

定點跳傘是一項極度危險的運動，輕則受傷，重則送命。所以，當你想尋求刺激快感的時候，縱身一躍前，絕對要三思而後行！

37. 大將軍漢尼拔　P. 086

漢尼拔是一位迦太基將軍和軍師，生於西元前 247 年，卒於西元前 183 年。世人封他為史上最偉大的軍事將領之一。

漢尼拔在世時，正逢羅馬共和國統治大部分地中海地區。雖然他想進攻羅馬，但因船艦數量不足，故無法從南邊跨海接近羅馬人已做好防備的沿海城市。因此，漢尼拔反其道而行，帶領大批軍隊與戰象，從西班牙出發，翻越庇里牛斯山脈，再穿越阿爾卑斯山，最後南下前往羅馬警戒最鬆懈的義大利北部。

漢尼拔在義大利北部征服了當地部落，並於多次戰役中擊敗赫赫有名的羅馬軍團。由於軍備不足而無法圍困羅馬城，他發動小規模的戰役來累積自己的軍力資源。他設法以這樣的狀態，在義大利北部立足整整十年，直到羅馬人襲擊祖國迫使他撤軍返鄉。

雖然漢尼拔於西元前 202 年返回迦太基，並於扎馬戰役迎戰羅馬軍隊，但他的兵力卻無法招架這樣的交戰局勢。羅馬於此次戰役獲勝，進而結束了為期 17 年的第二次普尼克戰爭，而迦太基卻再也無法重建過往的強大帝國榮景。漢尼拔則是轉戰政治與推動改革。但是他的改革舉動觸怒了迦太基貴族與羅馬，只好流亡在外。流亡期間，他擔任敘利亞國王安條克三世的軍師，當時的敘利亞正處對抗羅馬的戰亂時期。但是，羅馬再次贏得勝利，漢尼拔二度被迫逃亡。

儘管漢尼拔身亡已久，光是提及他的名號，還是會讓羅馬共和國不寒而慄。拿破崙與威靈頓公爵等偉大領袖，均為漢尼拔兵法的忠實追隨者。至今人們仍會以「漢尼拔兵臨城下」這句著名諺語，來形容某國家可能會一敗塗地的窘境。

38.「深海巨怪」大王酸漿魷魚　P. 088

數世紀以來，斯堪地那維亞水手間皆口耳相傳某種狀似烏賊的巨型海怪「克拉肯」（Kraken）。有人說克拉肯會拍擊船邊，運氣不好的水手就會因而落水。有人則說克拉肯會以巨型觸手包圍整艘船隻後，將其捲入驚濤駭浪之中。

雖然聽起來有點像恐怖片裡的情節，但如果克拉肯是真實存在的生物呢？或許基於極為罕見的緣故，我們很難證實有此生物。畢竟，克拉肯有比鯨魚或其他龐大海洋生物還要奇特嗎？

此傳奇性的海怪很有可能是「大王酸漿魷魚」。牠還有「南極魷魚」的別稱，是目前體型最大的已知烏賊物種。大家以為大王酸漿魷魚分佈於南極洋，但是眼尖的觀察人士亦於南美洲、南非，以及紐西蘭發現牠們的蹤影。

我們很難深入了解大王酸漿魷魚的原因，在於牠們棲息於深海。不過，我們可藉由研究其他較容易捉摸的動物，來略知大王酸漿魷魚的習性。例如，我們可從抹香鯨身上出現割傷和瘀血的情況，得知抹香鯨喜歡捕食大王酸漿魷魚。此類傷勢是由大王酸漿魷魚觸手上的尖鉤所致。有些科學家甚至認為，大王酸漿魷魚可以戰勝抹香鯨。

科學家亦思考出幾種辦法，在大王酸漿魷魚的自然棲息環境中進行研究。2004 年，日本的研究人員將死烏賊掛於巨鉤做餌，沉降至太平洋海面下 900 公尺處。有一隻大王酸漿魷魚上鉤，讓研究人員得以拍下牠的身影。可惜這隻大王酸漿魷魚終究逃脫，並且在掙扎過程中失去了一隻觸手。科學家以此觸手的長度判斷，成年的大王酸漿魷魚身長大約 14 公尺。可說是公車的兩倍長，巨大的體型可能足以摧毀一艘木船。

39. 聯合王國，分裂歐洲　P. 090

　　2016 年 6 月 23 日，51.9% 的英國投票人選擇退出歐盟。此事件別稱「英國脫歐」（Brexit），有國家決定脫離以布魯塞爾為總部的歐盟，可說是史上頭一遭。雖然脫離歐洲尚未拍板定案，但是雙方均已見識到此舉並非易事。

　　脫歐運動獲得支持的主因之一在於移民。英國對於歐洲的門戶開放政策十分不滿，等於罔顧英國意願被迫接納移民。其他問題包括歐盟公民可自由進出歐盟會員國，以及歐盟的拓展計劃。最後一點，是英國每週均需支付 3.5 億英鎊（約 140 億台幣）的歐盟會員費。脫歐派則認為自己贏得了英國獨立的勝利。

　　很多人不同意脫歐。蘇格蘭和倫敦的留歐票數勝出，反映了英國國內與城鄉之間的差異。主張留歐的英國首相大衛・卡麥隆，於公投開票後立即辭職。英鎊幣值跌至 1985 年以來的新低。就連前美國總統歐巴馬也呼籲，投票人若選擇脫歐，貿易方面恐怕將困難重重。不過多說無益，因為「英國脫歐」已成事實。

　　但是，脫歐這樣的事情到底該如何發生？經過兩年多以來無數次的會議後，似乎無人確定該怎麼做。卡麥隆的繼任者德雷莎・梅伊認為，當前挑戰在於脫歐之餘，還得讓大家都滿意。多數英國政客偏好「硬脫歐」，拒絕歐盟插手英國的法律或貿易決策。其他派系則認同歐盟提出的「軟脫歐」政策，也就是雙方仍維持較多的互相配合模式。「英國脫歐」期限為 2019 年 3 月，協議時間已所剩無幾。有些人擔心這將導致「崩潰式脫歐」，也就是沒有達成任何協議便立即脫歐。

　　近來新聞事件透露，英國和歐盟的領導人在協議英國脫歐的條件方面，均互不退讓。因此，我們現在唯一能做的就是靜觀其變。

40. 非暴力民權鬥士——自由乘客　P. 092

　　1955 年至 1968 年，美國黑人民權運動崛起，目的在於爭取黑人在美國生活的平等權利。全國上下許多人努力推行，每個人追求的唯一目標，就是「人人平等」。

　　「自由乘客」就是為此運動奮鬥的一群人。來自各年齡層與不同背景的人士齊聚一堂，希望挑戰美國南方既有的種族隔離政策。當時南方的所有巴士、火車以及飛機航班，均設置白人區與黑人區。不過，美國最高法院裁決，跨州巴士如有黑白之分的座區配置即違法。因此，充斥各種族的「自由乘客」會在北部某州搭車，坐到南部之後下車，藉此挑釁南部當地的法律。

　　雖然以現今環境而言，似乎是小規模的抗議行動，但在當時可是天大的創舉。發起自由乘客運動的 13 名元老，第一次搭乘巴士進入南部時，遭人圍毆數次。無論傷勢多重，他們從未反擊。因為他們堅信「非暴力抵制」的哲學。

　　1961 年 5 月 14 日，情勢越演越烈。當巴士逐漸停靠阿拉巴馬州安尼斯敦站點時，已有一群暴徒在車站守候，因此司機決定不靠站。然而，還是有人設法刺穿巴士輪胎，使得巴士於不遠處拋錨。巴士停駛後，有暴徒打破車窗，往裡頭丟入一顆汽油彈。「自由乘客」只好匆忙下車，一著地就被亂棍毆打。根據目擊者的說法，當時有一名臥底警探往空中開槍驅散暴徒，解救「自由乘客」免於私刑致死的危險。

　　「自由乘客」前往南部的情形與日俱增，甘迺迪總統終於意識到暴行的嚴重性。他與南方政府談好條件，只有在確保「自由乘客」人身安全的情況下，南方政府才能逮捕他們。但是，「自由乘客」仍不斷湧入南部，最後終於促使南方政府修改種族隔離法律。

1-9 分辨事實與意見

　　每個人都有自己的意見，這是無法避免的。我們所能避免的，就是不經思考就接受他人的意見。當你閱讀一個句子時，應該問自己：「每個人都會同意這點嗎？」如果答案為「是」，那麼這個句子可能是一件**事實**。

41. 玻璃簡介 P. 094

玻璃可用於製成窗戶、瓶罐、太空船玻璃磚、防輻射玻璃、光纖通訊電纜,甚至是特定布料。由於生活中的玻璃製品無所不在,因此大家常會忘了好好珍惜此必需品。

玻璃既不是固體,也不是液體,而是介於兩者之間的物質。這樣的特性讓玻璃獨一無二。玻璃是由石英砂所製。必須先以極高溫熔化石英砂,再將火紅燙熱的石英砂倒入任何形狀的模具塑型,隨後冷卻定型。在玻璃仍為燙熱狀態的時候加入特定化學物質,就能改變玻璃的基本屬性。舉例來說,用來打造智慧型手機與筆記型電腦的「Gorilla 強化玻璃」擁有高硬度的特性,即因經過攝氏 400 度高溫的鉀鹽浴處理。

視玻璃的種類而定,熔點範圍可達攝氏 500 度至 1,650 度。不同種類的玻璃比重,可達水的兩倍至八倍。此彈性特質讓玻璃成為世上最為實用的材料。

人類使用天然形成玻璃的歷史,可追溯自數萬年前。不過,一直到西元前 3500 年,埃及人和美索不達米亞人才開始自製玻璃珠。大約經過 3,250 年後,羅馬人發明了製造平價玻璃的新方法,以便製成玻璃窗和其他家用品。玻璃製造技術後來流傳至斯堪地那維亞與中國。

玻璃既實用又美觀。事實上,人類文明史上有許多精緻藝術品,均以玻璃製成。20 世紀末,大家開始懂得欣賞玻璃古文物和現代玻璃藝術品。紐約康寧市的「康寧玻璃博物館」,擁有全球最大宗的玻璃藝術品館藏,共有超過 20 萬件玻璃展品。有時玻璃藝術品的規模甚至是一棟建物,例如洛杉磯的水晶大教堂。該教堂善用玻璃,絕美設計令人留下深刻印象。

42. 貝都因人 P. 096

居住在全世界最大、最熱的沙漠有點瘋狂。但貝都因人已在撒哈拉沙漠居住了數世紀,且有些人仍遵循好幾世紀前老祖先的生活方式。

「貝都因人」(bedouin)這個字起源於阿拉伯文 bedu,指的是「居住在沙漠的人」,它是眾多游牧民族的總稱,這些遊牧民族生活在沙漠,照顧羊群、駱駝群、帶領駱駝商隊穿越廣大沙丘,並且和途中的鄉鎮及村莊進行貿易。他們經常旅行,紮營一段時間後,再與他們的畜群一同遷移,這種生活方式是多麼的有趣!

貝都因人鮮少注意國家的法律,但他們有自己強悍的道義法規。他們的司法系統是根據這些行為準則設定的。根據這些規範,犯罪的懲罰通常即時且嚴屬。舉例來說,火刑就是一種用來偵測謊言的著名方式。火刑是一種自願性的懲戒方法,被控犯罪者須以舌舔燒得滾燙的鐵器,如果在三次舌舔後舌頭被燒傷,即表示有説謊行為。火刑是一種被認為該被禁止的殘酷刑罰。

貝都因人並不遵守國與國的邊界,他們任意在各國之間游移。這些國家政府容忍貝都因人的流浪行為,但是他們這種游移的習俗並未得到正式的認可。

近幾百年來,許多貝都因人開始將其生活模式改為半游牧型態。他們開始在中東地區幾個城市定居。對於更好生活的期望,加上埃及、以色列與其他國家的政府政策,使得一些貝都因人被勸服成為正式的國民,而非居無定所的游牧人。許多國家也藉著提供房屋、學校、醫院、健保來幫助貝都因人定居。

43. 區塊鏈:革命性的科技 P. 098

如果你長時間使用科技,應該會有一長串的密碼清單。在這個科技世代,要記住眾多使用者名稱和繁複密碼實屬麻煩。而駭客竊取密碼與金融資訊的報導亦時有所聞。許多公司斥資上百萬元維護資訊安全並遏止駭客。而化名「中本聰」的某位人士,則在 2008 年發明了一項解套技術。

區塊鏈技術透過創意的解決方案,讓網路交易更加安全。此技術不將重要資料放在同一個資料庫,而是散布在眾多電腦組成的網絡。由於所有電腦均同時記錄該筆資料,因此即使某部電腦被駭客入侵也無妨。因為該筆資料已儲存於一個「區塊」中,此區塊又與前後區塊相連,形成一連串的資訊區塊,「區塊鏈」一稱由此產生。

由於區塊鏈可用於不同交易類別,因此勢必成為日常生活不可或缺的元素。區塊鏈可用於記錄金融交易、協議與合約內容,並可儲存數據資料和加密貨幣。中本聰設計區塊鏈的目的,在於保存以虛擬加密貨幣「比特幣」買賣的記錄。科技公司已經開始運用區塊鏈。微軟和 IBM 均採用區塊鏈來幫助各公司記錄供應鏈的來龍去脈。例如食品公司能迅速追蹤導致食物中毒的食品,亦可運用區塊鏈的數據資料預防食物浪費,進而節省開支。區塊鏈可設為公開狀態,例如兩人之間的交易;亦可設為隱私狀態,例如兩家公司之間的交易。

《哈佛商業評論》雜誌稱區塊鏈為「寧靜革命」。越來越多公司採用區塊鏈,進而增加買賣效率。各類資料與記錄亦免於駭客盜取。銀行類的事業體可能不再那麼重要,因為大家可直接透過區塊鏈交易並加以記錄。由於區塊鏈的用途如此廣泛,這項技術有朝一日或許會像網路一樣,成為日常生活不可或缺的一部分。

44. 神秘金星　P. 100

「Venus」一字本指代表愛情與美麗的羅馬女神維納斯,而運行軌道介於水星和地球之間的明亮星球,即以「Venus」命名(譯註:中文名為「金星」)。金星看似美麗寧靜,但是登陸星球表面就會發現,金星其實是一片死寂的荒原。

除了月球之外,金星是夜空中最耀眼的天體,有點像是米膚色的大理石。古時候又稱金星為「晨星」或「暮星」,因為只有破曉或黃昏時才看得見。數世紀以來,籠罩一層厚實雲霧而無法令人窺探究竟的金星,一直讓天文學家嚮往不已。金星有時又稱地球的「姊妹星」,因其大小、質量、體積和重力均與地球相仿。

以地球時間計算的話,金星繞太陽公轉一圈需要 225 天。但是金星自轉一圈,卻需要 243 天。也就是說,在金星上度過一天的時間,比度過一年的時間還要久。

金星地表的環境條件十分嚴峻。乾燥的大氣層主要以二氧化碳構成,地表氣壓是地球的 90 倍以上。金星的氣溫可高達攝氏 471 度。造成高溫環境的原因始於高濃度的二氧化碳大氣層,地表的氣體與溫度無法退散,因此形成威力強大的全球暖化效應。

俄羅斯曾派遣多艘探測船登陸金星,以深入了解此星球的特性。但是沒有一艘探測船能撐得過 50 分鐘。金星的高溫與氣壓實在過於極端。美國也曾嘗試窺探金星面貌。他們派出「先鋒金星 1 號」與「麥哲倫號」進入環繞金星公轉的軌道。這些無人探測船能以雷達繪製地表圖,將無數高原、大型火山、綿延的熔岩流、深谷,以及流星撞擊金星所產生的隕石坑等詳細照片回傳地球。這些金星圖片絕對堪稱人類太空探測史上最壯麗的行星圖片。

45. 雷克斯暴龍　P. 102

超過 6,500 萬年前,在恐龍支配地球、哺乳類動物小如嚙齒類動物的年代,無庸置疑地,「恐龍之王」就是雷克斯暴龍(Tyrannosaurus rex;T. rex)。雷克斯暴龍的原文取自希臘文,意指「暴君般的蜥蜴之王」。此名稱果然名不虛傳,因為多數證據顯示,雷克斯暴龍是食物鏈頂端的王者。

美國出土的化石顯示,雷克斯暴龍居住於叢林中,擁有與生俱來的狩獵體型,比如說可追殺獵物的兩隻強壯後腿,還有一口銳利尖齒,足以咬穿皮肉、骨骼以及堅硬無比的鱗片。由於具備強而有力的短頸和演化良好的下顎肌肉,無論是在任何現存或絕種的已知生物中,雷克斯暴龍的咬力均無人能出其右。牠可以狼吞虎嚥地一口吞下 230 公斤的帶骨肉塊。

雷克斯暴龍身長約 12 公尺,身高約 4.6 至 6 公尺,可重達 7.5 噸。碩大的頭顱長達 1.5 公尺,連眼球的直徑都有 7.6 公分。雷克斯暴龍絕對是世上最冷血的掠食者。奇怪的是，牠卻不是體型最大的肉食性恐龍，而是棘龍。棘龍的體型確實超越雷克斯暴龍許多。

雷克斯暴龍的移動速動有多快呢？某些專家指出可達時速 24 公里，也有專家說雷克斯暴龍僅能達到時速 17 公里。無論如何，雷克斯暴龍的速度，足以令其他恐龍聞風喪膽。光是想到一邊逃命、一邊聽見背後傳來的怒吼，以及地面重震的情景，就會讓人嚇到惡夢連連！

有些專家認為雷克斯暴龍既是獵食動物，也是食腐動物，另有些專家表示牠只有食腐動物的特性。不過，單以雷克斯暴龍的外表判斷，不難想像牠應該是世上最危險的獵食者。

1-10 實力檢測

46. 蘇俄女大公爵安娜塔西亞　P. 104

蘇俄皇室的小女兒安娜塔西亞，年幼時期十分淘氣、聰慧又討人喜歡。她生於 1901 年 6 月 18 日，還有四名手足，並且獲得與三位姐姐一樣的「女大公爵」封號。

她心地善良且悲天憫人，第一次世界大戰期間，還跟隨母親探望與關懷受傷的士兵。然而在那個年代，身為蘇俄皇室一員卻是件不幸的事。1917 年 2 月，蘇俄發生大革命。安娜塔西亞的父親尼古拉二世放棄皇位，與家人遭軟禁於皇宮。但是厄運尚未結束。共產黨於十月掀起第二次革命，目的在於推翻取代尼古拉二世的臨時政府。雖然臨時政府將安娜塔西亞與其家人遷至安全之地，但共產黨最終全面掌控蘇俄，所有皇室被送往葉卡捷琳堡的一棟「特殊待遇別墅」，留下他們的最後身影。

1918 年 7 月 17 日清晨，尼古拉二世、妻子與四女一子遭到蘇俄秘密警察處決。

在俄共統治的數十載期間，安娜塔西亞墓地一直下落不明，因此她很有可能逃過一劫，此說法成了 20 世紀最著名的謎團之一。有些人認為，或許有警衛偷偷協助脫困，讓安娜塔西亞逃過鬼門關。

不少女性現身自稱安娜塔西亞，目的在於繼承安娜塔西亞本尊能享有的可觀遺產。其中最知名的分身就是安娜‧安德森，她宣稱自己倒臥在皇室家人的遺體之間裝死，並透過警衛幫助而順利逃離。安娜‧安德森逝於 1984 年，她的遺體經過 DNA 檢驗後，證實與皇室沒有血緣關係。2008 年，法醫調查結果終於揭露安娜塔西亞確實與家人共赴黃泉的事實，而她生死未卜之謎也終於落幕。

47. 珍貴白金　P. 106

你可能聽過某張專輯銷售超過一百萬張，而打出「破白金銷量」的名號，或是富商以「白金卡」刷卡付費等説法。白金是一種象徵財富與豐饒的金屬，常被誤認為是銀，不過其實白金更為罕見。事實上，白金是地殼中最稀有的金屬之一，也因此價值連城。

白金可是不同凡響的金屬。不僅能抵擋氣候的摧殘，許多酸性物質亦腐蝕不了白金，而且幾乎能在任何情況下，保持銀亮的美觀狀態。白金的獨特屬性，因此成為生產實驗室設備的重要材質，當然也用於製造珠寶。多數限量錶款均以白金製成，因為不會像金錶一樣容易失去光澤或沾附髒汙。

擁有白金珠寶，堪稱世上金字塔頂端的地位象徵。黃金的普及度為白金的 30 倍，因此在經濟穩定與景氣的時候，白金價格幾乎維持黃金價格的兩倍。白金的罕見特性，甚至讓法國國王路易十五宣告白金是國王唯一御用的金屬，而英國女皇伊莉莎白二世的母親所戴的皇冠，飾框即以白金製成。

雖然白金擁有奢華外觀，應用於華麗配件方面的比例卻不多。約 45% 的白金礦不是用在製造昂貴珠寶，而是在汽車產業裡製成排氣系統的必需零件。白金能將汽車引擎所排放出的有害廢氣轉換為較安全的氣體，進而減低空氣汙染。

過去，白金主要來自南美的礦藏，當地的原住民部落使用白金的歷史已有數世紀之久。如今，全球約有 80% 的白金來自南非。然而，我們若想維持穩定供應白金的狀態，就要做好長途跋涉的心理準備，因為盛產白金之處並非地球，而是月球。

48. 節能綠屋　P. 108

拯救環境是現代的熱門話題，而許多公司都在思考著如何「綠化」，也就是降低汙染與節省電能。在建築產業上，這個潮流也愈來愈普及，不只是運用在大型建築物中，同時也運用在一般住家房舍上。人們想要知道如何使住屋更為永續，並希望過程中能節省水電費。

在家裡怎麼降低能源的使用呢？如何讓住家做到利於生態環境？答案可能就是建造一座「節能綠屋」。「節能綠屋」和現今所居住的房屋差不多，只有幾個顯著的差異。節能綠屋在屋頂設有太陽能板或風力發電裝置，以供給家中用電。白天無人在家時產生電能，儲存於電池中以供天黑後使用。這些電力完全免費，而過剩電力也能回頭儲存於電板中以獲益。想像一下從電力公司獲利，而不是付錢給它們！最重要的是，太陽能或風力發電是種純淨的電能，不會危害環境。

節能綠屋對環境友善的另一方式，是盡量節省能源用量。在家中使用這麼多電的主因之一，就是用來加溫或降溫。「節能綠屋」特別設計可以不使用任何電能，就能保持室內溫度的穩定，因此能冬天蓄熱、夏天散熱。

最後，節能綠屋多以回收材質建造，其中包含回收塑膠、紙類與橡膠。如此一來，便能降低原料對於環境的負擔。你可以為下一座房子漆上任何喜歡的顏色，但如果想省錢並幫助環境，就要確定它是徹底「綠能」的。

49. 學會相信自己　P. 110

想要成為外向又自信的人宛如登山。如果培養良好習慣，你就會覺得自己變得更好，峰頂彷彿近在咫尺。不過，小挫折很容易令人陷入更多困境。你可能一眨眼間又回到山腳下，峰頂已不復見。

那麼該如何繼續攻頂？先從培養正面行為與習慣開始。最重要的是，不要時時刻刻與他人比較。這個道理確實知易行難，因為總是有可拿來與自己比較的對象。也許是你所喜愛的電視影集主角，或是社群媒體上的朋友動態。但就像時下流行的格言：「做自己就好」。別擔心他人在做什麼，你只需要做自己即可。

第二重要的，是為自己設定目標。也許你想學習新語言、開始慢跑、抑或在班上拿到優異成績。目標本身並不重要，重點在於這是「你的」目標。達標後，就會產生成就感。先從小目標做起，再慢慢擴大實踐目標的野心。

接下來，就是與正能量的人來往。正能量可讓生活產生許多美好的變化。如果周遭的人生性刻薄或負面，你就會感到焦慮與挫敗。想想你的朋友、同學或是生活圈所認識的人，捫心自問：這個人是否能帶來正面影響力？如果答案為否，你也許應該與他們保持距離。

瞭解建立自信所需培養的基本習慣之後，仍需謹記以下寶貴建議：別太苛求自己。成功達標後，一定要肯定自己。更重要的是，失敗之後可別苛責自己。畢竟人非聖賢，接受這個觀念，才是真正接受自己的關鍵。

50. 惡夢的起因　P. 112

很多人常會半夜驚醒，全身冒冷汗又恐懼不已。一邊回想剛才經歷過的恐怖情境，腦海中一邊閃過慷人的畫面。但是過了一下子，就會如釋重負，因為全都是一場惡夢罷了。

「惡夢」意指讓你從熟睡之中驚醒，且伴隨強烈負面情緒的生動夢境。古人以為惡夢是由稱為「夢魘」（Mare）的邪靈所造成，以可怕的夢境折磨入睡的人，所以原文「nightmare」成了「惡夢」的同義詞。不過，我們現已清楚，心理和化學反應等因素都會讓人做惡夢。

壓力與煩憂是讓人做惡夢的兩種常見因素。成人可能常有無法逃離險境、或從高處墜落的夢境。此類惡夢通常與工作或私生活中，所面臨的強烈懷疑或恐懼有關。不斷重複的惡夢，則可能與現實生活中所害怕或煩惱的經歷有關，例如遭受攻擊或目睹暴力事件。日復一日不斷重現惡夢情景的人，有時可能需要專業人士的協助來擺脫惡夢。

另一個較容易避免的做惡夢原因，就是吃宵夜。吃宵夜會讓大腦在睡眠的時候呈現較為活躍的狀態，所以很有可能產生非常真實的生動夢境，而且是惡夢居多。此外，服用特定藥物，尤其是抗憂鬱等會影響大腦化學反應的藥物，都很容易讓人做惡夢。

如果你常被相同的惡夢干擾睡眠，可以運用一個簡單的解決辦法。請試在清醒的時候，對你的惡夢情境想像全然不同的美滿結局，並且在腦海裡排演畫面。睡前再回想一次，那麼你的大腦應該會以你自己想像的快樂結局取代惡夢。祝你做個好夢！

Unit 2 字彙學習

如果句子裡有任何單字你不知道，就很難培養優越的閱讀技巧。這對英文來說難度尤高，因為英文一共有超過 40 萬個單字要背。還好有一些單字技巧可以幫助我們判斷生字意義。本單元將教你這些單字技巧，讀完本單元之後，遇到不熟悉的單字也不會那麼害怕了。說真的，你可能還會開始期待遇到生字呢！

2-1 同義字

英文的字彙量冠於任何語言，其中有許多意義相近的單字。閱讀時若是遇到生難字詞，盡可能想一個簡單的替代字。能夠想出同義的各種單字，是提升閱讀理解力的一大技巧。

51. 備受寵愛的家庭成員　P. 116

瀏覽社群媒體時，我們常會看到人們自豪地分享寵物照片。漫步街上，推車裡坐的往往是汪星人或喵星人，而不是嬰兒。雖然在許多亞洲文化中，飼養寵物曾經象徵「豪奢」行為，但隨著中產階級擴增，越來越多人養得起寵物。而寵物風潮開始崛起的國家包括日本、南韓、台灣、印度、新加坡與印尼。

對於在職年輕人以及子女已成年的長輩而言，寵物就像自己的家人。這類飼主心甘情願花錢呵護寵物。寵物愛好者與寵物產品製造商，造就了「寵物經濟學」。中國的寵物產品銷售額，預計每年成長 21%。以亞洲地區整體而論，預計每年成長 8%。

如今，寵物產業囊括各種寵物產品，從實用又奢華的狗狗服飾到華麗的貓跳台，應有盡有。你可以幫狗狗購入靴子和雨衣來抵禦惡劣氣候；當然，可別忘了昂貴的牽繩和項圈。寵物 SPA 店提供修剪毛髮、洗澡與剪指甲的服務，甚至還提供舒緩肌肉痠痛的按摩服務。

寵物愛好人士希望毛小孩都能健康平安。他們偏好高品質寵物食品，食材必須符合與人類食品相同的標準。事實上，每個月採買優質寵物食品的費用，和人類食品的花費相當！除了營養的餐點之外，所有寵物當然需要定期接受獸醫檢查，以保持健康狀態。

飼主出門度假時，他們的喵星人或汪星人可留置於寵物旅館。更棒的是，有些飯店本身就歡迎寵物入住。遍布全亞洲的五星級四季飯店，甚至供應專為寵物設計的菜單。

寵物經濟學的蓬勃發展，顯示許多飼主十分樂於花錢保持寵物乾乾淨淨與身心健康。畢竟毛小孩是家庭的一份子。

52. 安地斯山脈　P. 118

在南美洲的地圖上，你可以看到一條漫長蜿蜒的山脊，綿延大陸的整個西岸。這座由火山峰和崇山峻嶺所構成的巨大山脈，由北而南橫亙七個國家，延伸超過 7,000 公里，跨越赤道，直到接近冰冷的南大洋為止。

安地斯山脈的平均高度為海拔 4,000 公尺，其最高峰阿空加瓜山可達 6,962 公尺，也使得安地斯山脈成為亞洲之外最高的山脈。毫無疑問，喜馬拉雅山脈是世界最高的山脈，然而安地斯山脈橫跨赤道，因此位於赤道上的欽博拉索山的峰頂，才是地球表面距離地心最遠的一點。

安地斯山脈無論在景觀、氣候，還是野生動植物的多樣性都十分驚人。山脈的北段氣候濕熱多雨，是最適合雨林生長的環境。的確，亞馬遜雨林涵蓋了安地斯山脈北段的一大部分，而壯觀的亞馬遜河，竟源於山脈高處崖面湧出的一條涓涓細流。山脈的中段較為暖和，而南段的氣候嚴寒，大部分地區杳無人煙。安地斯山脈的氣候詭譎多變，當地居民表示他們經常「一日如過四季」。

雖然氣候變化無常，過去千年來最重要的文明之一——印加文明，卻是在安地斯山脈發展出來的。印加人在山脈的陡坡上開鑿梯田，種植馬鈴薯和玉米等作物。1532 年時，西班牙人征服了印加人，有人便認為安地斯這個名稱來自於西班牙文「andén」，意即「平台」。

西班牙人在基多建立了殖民城市，現在每年吸引許多遊客前往參觀。遊客可以從基多出發，從事健行、登山、泛舟、探險的一日遊，同時將安地斯山脈的巍峨美景盡收眼底。

53. 香奈兒傳奇　P. 120

1909 年，嘉布麗葉兒·波納·「可可」·香奈兒設立了 House of Chanel 這間巴黎時尚小店。香奈兒生於 1883 年 8 月 19 日，她是 20 世紀最受推崇的設計師，對時尚界產生了深遠的影響。她用嶄新的優雅休閒設計，取代傳統既不舒服又拘束的服裝，重新詮釋了高格調時尚，讓女性在保有時尚品味之餘也能穿得舒適。

可可·香奈兒原本替重視時尚的法國女士製作帽飾，但是到了 1913 年，她推出了一系列舒適的女性運動服，讓身體活動更方便，她的優雅服飾也以樸素風格風靡法國。數年之後，她的傳奇

香水「香奈兒 5 號」問世，自此成為有史以來最負盛名的香水之一。過去 60 年來，幾乎每一位大牌女明星都會噴這款香水。瑪麗蓮·夢露甚至曾說，她只擦香奈兒 5 號睡覺。

香奈兒的時尚傳奇地位，在她發表了「黑色小洋裝」這款黑色薄絹製的性感洋裝後，更加屹立不搖，並在時尚圈刮起一陣旋風，至今仍被爭相模仿。

第二次世界大戰爆發之後，香奈兒退休並結束製裝事業，她的公司只繼續賣配件和珠寶。她在戰時與一名納粹黨員過從甚密，致使她流亡瑞士，聲望也逐日下降。1954 年，她回到法國，重新開始販售衣服，沒多久又重返時尚行銷和設計的崇高地位。

可可·香奈兒於 1971 年 1 月 10 日辭世，享年 87 歲。她一生引領的時尚改革，至今仍啟發了許多頂尖的時尚設計師。德國設計師卡爾·拉格斐在 1983 年被指派為香奈兒（House of Chanel）的藝術總監，帶來新穎、現代，同時更大膽的設計風格，而香奈兒則再度成為時尚界的龍頭。

54. 歷史悠久的倫敦地鐵　P. 122

倫敦地鐵於 1863 年 1 月 10 日啟用，是全世界最早的地下鐵路系統，至今仍是全球規模最大的地下鐵路網之一。它又被稱為 the Underground（地下的）或 the Tube（管子），一共設有 270 個車站，鐵軌長約 402 公里，就路線長度而言，是全世界第四長的地鐵系統。

倫敦地鐵一年載運約 13 億 5 千萬名通勤者，每個上班日有高達 5 百萬名乘客搭乘地鐵系統。倫敦地鐵之所以如此方便，原因之一就是其簡潔明瞭的路線圖。倫敦地鐵路線圖於 1931 年設計，設計手法獨具一格，此後幾乎所有的都會鐵路路線圖都採用這種方式。路線圖所標示的車站，和它們在都市地圖上的實際地理位置無關，因為那樣標示會太混亂而不易閱讀。設計重點反而在於各車站的順序要正確，轉接站的排列不能有誤。除此之外，地鐵系統的 11 條支線分別用顏色標示，讓乘客更容易看懂。

不過，如同許多洩氣的倫敦人紛紛證實的一樣，倫敦地鐵是出了名的常誤點。據估計，一般通勤者每年因為列車誤點所浪費掉的時間大約有三天。另外一個嚴重的問題是人潮擁擠，尤其是早晚的尖峰時刻。即便很多車站都已經重建來克服這個問題，還是不時被擠爆，列車經常無法停靠某座車站，必須直接開往下一座乘客較少的車站。有些車廂沒有空調系統，也使得夏天搭乘時炎熱難耐，有些深層隧道的溫度高達攝氏 34.5 度，甚至更高。

不過瑕不掩瑜，倫敦地鐵是世界上最安全、最便利的交通方式之一，意外發生率極低，每行駛 3 億趟才有一次致命的意外發生。再者，每位到過倫敦的人一定會告訴你，如果沒有地鐵，還真不知道該如何探索這座偉大的城市呢。

55. 應急者運動 `P. 124`

你是否曾想過，災難來襲時該如何應對？從何處尋覓食物？又該如何在斷水斷電的情況下生存？如果你曾思慮上述問題，你也許具備成為「應急者」的條件。

所謂的「應急者」或「求生者」，意指為生存環境做最壞打算的人。有些應急者或許過度恐慌而狀似瘋癲，因為他們深信世界末日即將到來，但這些是少數極端份子。多數應急者不過是為可能發生的事件，例如森林大火、地震或經濟崩盤等事件做好準備。有些人單純憂心萬一摯愛的親友離世，會對家庭經濟來源造成問題。

應急者通常有五大生活原則：備妥一年份的基本必需品，例如食物和水；性格獨立、可自給自足、認真工作、不浪費。這幾項原則對於擔憂未來的人而言，多為良好的建議。目前受到公眾譴責的族群主要是較為極端的末日求生者，因為他們持有槍械，並且訓練自己的孩子使用致命武器，好比在敵我不明的情況下備戰。

從起源觀之，生存主義的意識形態會衍生出如此極端的行為，其實情有可原。應急者運動是從冷戰時期開始萌芽，當時的人民每天活在恐懼中，深怕核子彈會夷平家園。政府廣播節目提供人民如何在核子武器攻擊下求生的建議，導致上百萬人開始瘋狂成為生存論者。冷戰之後，千禧年危機、911 恐怖攻擊以及 H1N1 流感大爆發等事件，致使生存主義之狂熱更是有增無減。這種現象顯示，人類的求生欲望永不衰減。

2-2 反義字

有一「好」（good）必有一「壞」（bad），每個「黑夜」（night）也終究要「破曉」（day）。英文充滿了意義相反的字彙，作者經常運用這些相反的概念，讓寫作更有趣。所以當你學一個生字的時候，花點時間想想它的反義字吧。

56. 智慧新視界 `P. 126`

智慧型隱形眼鏡？你沒聽錯！科技的發展已經將算盤打到人類的眼球上。看似科幻小說的產物，目前已在實驗室研發完成。

2014 年，谷歌宣布為糖尿病患者研發特殊的隱形眼鏡。此款「智慧型」隱形眼鏡能持續測量患者淚液的糖分來監控血糖值，並將數據傳送至佩戴者的智慧型手機，亦可同時傳給主治醫師。結果是：糖尿病患者不需驗血，即可隨時追蹤自己的血糖。

可惜的是，淚液所含的糖分並不足以作為準確測量血糖值的標準。專家駁斥谷歌的隱形眼鏡根本不可行。研發程序仍默默進行，卻尚無下文。

不過，其他公司倒是成功駕馭了這項科技。Colormax 公司的隱形眼鏡可治療色盲，且已上市販售。研究人員亦研發可立即對焦眼球的隱形眼鏡，幫助具有視力問題的患者。

到底是怎麼辦到的呢？原來是在隱形眼鏡的中間夾層置放超薄迷你微晶片。夾心的作法讓微晶片不會直接觸及眼球表面，因此不會造成危險──但願如此！晶片所儲存的資訊，可外傳至其他裝置，抑或直接儲存在隱形眼鏡裡，可說是相當前衛的研發技術。

雖然智慧型隱形眼鏡最有可能廣泛應用於醫療方面，但還是有其他用途。夜視隱形眼鏡就是一例。索尼公司以專利技術，製造可記錄佩戴者所見影像的隱形眼鏡。信不信由你，只要眨眼就能啟動與執行錄影程序。三星公司亦不惶多讓，研發專為電玩設計的隱形眼鏡。顯然，智慧型眼鏡未來將持續發展，且更易取得。

57. 尼斯湖水怪傳說　P. 128

在蘇格蘭中部遠離城鎮之處，座落著神秘的尼斯湖。雖然尼斯湖不是蘇格蘭境內最大的湖泊，卻是英國最深的湖泊。它的淡水比英格蘭和威爾斯兩地所有湖裡的水體都來得多，且在湖裡某些地方可深達 230 公尺。然而，尼斯湖並非以其驚人的深度聞名於世，它最有名的還是傳說中的棲息者「尼斯湖水怪」（the Loch Ness monster，簡稱 Nessie）。

幾百年以來，人們不斷宣稱見過湖中奇怪生物的身影。它第一次出現是在 1933 年時，當時一名英國人和妻子看到了一隻怪獸般的動物，正緩慢地橫越馬路往湖邊走去。從那時起，出現了一連串的目擊事件。人們形容尼斯湖水怪是隻有著長脖子、小頭顱的奇怪動物，近似活在侏儸紀早期的恐龍「蛇頸龍」。好幾年來，大家都稱此奇怪的生物「巨魚」、「水蛇」或「龍」，最後，人們決定稱牠為「尼斯湖水怪」。大部分人聲稱曾在漆黑一片的湖中捕捉到這個怪物的身影，不過也有少數人堅持是在靠近湖岸的陸地上看到。有些人甚至還拍到了這隻生物的照片，但這些照片都非常模糊粗糙，事後更證明其中許多照片根本只是惡作劇。

儘管有些人用盡方法想證明尼斯湖水怪的存在，但結果仍令人存疑。多數科學家認為，這樣的生物不可能存在於湖中。他們也認為，人們所看到的景象只是一些惡作劇和一廂情願的想法。然而，這樣的說法並未阻擋人們親身前往一睹奇景。每年有數千名觀光客來到尼斯湖，只為親眼一瞥怪物的身影。不論真假，尼斯湖皆因此成為英國最著名的觀光景點之一。

58. 諾貝爾和平獎　P. 130

諾貝爾的六大獎項當中，和平獎無疑是最為人知的一項。諾貝爾獎最早在 1901 年由瑞典科學家阿弗列德・諾貝爾的遺產中頒出，一共有和平、物理、化學、文學、醫學五個獎項。1969 年增加了經濟學獎。阿弗列德 ・ 諾貝爾在遺囑中表示，和平獎必須頒發給「為國際間的友好、廢除或削減常備軍、促進和平會議貢獻最深」的人。每一年，諾貝爾和平獎的得主必須前往挪威的奧斯陸領獎，其他五個獎項的頒獎儀式則在瑞典的斯德哥爾摩舉行。在挪威國王親自出席觀禮之下，諾貝爾和平獎得主受頒包括獎狀、勳章以及確認獎金的文件。

諾貝爾和平獎的得主是由一個五人的評委會，在審閱過數千名申請者的資料之後所選出。對於申請人的嚴格篩選，是和平獎之所以被大眾視為無上榮耀的一個原因。

過去的一些和平獎得主有：艾伯特・史懷哲、馬丁・路德・金恩、德蕾莎修女、米哈伊爾・戈巴契夫、納爾遜・曼德拉、達賴喇嘛、德斯蒙德・杜圖主教和前美國總統吉米・卡特。過去這些諾貝爾和平獎的得主，通常是因為勇氣可嘉和致力倡導和平，或堅持不懈地為人道議題努力而獲殊榮。還有許多得主是自己國家的民主鬥士。

諾貝爾和平獎過去在提名和遺珠兩方面都備受爭議，其中一例就是 2009 年把獎項頒給美國總統歐巴馬，當時他才剛上任沒多久，許多人質疑他在短短一年內能夠為世界和平貢獻多少。

儘管有一些得主具爭議性，諾貝爾和平獎仍然是全球共同從事正面貢獻人士的強力象徵。

59. 王權珠寶　P. 132

「王權珠寶」是指國家王室所擁有的珠寶，這些價值連城的寶物通常會代代相傳，強烈象徵著王室的治國權。世界各地的王室都有王權珠寶，最有名的當屬英國王室的收藏。

英國王權珠寶自 1303 年起就被收藏在倫敦塔內，包含皇冠、權杖、寶球、佩劍，和其他貴重的手工藝品。英國王權珠寶被認為是全世界最貴重的珠寶收藏品，也是品項最多的珠寶收藏之一，其中最古老的一件品，是一支可以追溯至 13 世紀的金湯匙。

對許多人來說，英國王權珠寶裡最迷人的就是皇冠。帝國皇冠造於 1838 年，上面有許多歷史悠久的寶石。它一共使用了 2,800 多顆鑽石（其中一顆是 317 克拉的「庫里南二號（或譯小非洲之星）」鑽石）、270 多顆珍珠、17 顆藍寶石、11 顆綠寶石、5 顆紅寶石。自維多利亞女王時代起，每一屆的英國國王都會在加冕典禮上戴此皇冠，不過維多利亞女王自己則是配戴一款較輕的帝國皇冠。

1661 所造的十字權杖，也是這套收藏裡的重要手工藝品。它的特色是正中間所鑲的庫里南鑽石，又稱為「大非洲之星」，是全世界最大的寶石級鑽石。同樣造於 1661 年的鴿子權杖是聖靈的象徵。國王在加冕典禮上，右手持十字權杖，左手持鴿子權杖。

國王寶球也造於 1661 年，它是一個宗教象徵，代表國王具有英國國教會最高領袖的身分。

湯馬士‧布洛德曾於 1671 年竊取王權珠寶，但他隨即被捕，王權珠寶完好歸位。之後也不時有人企圖竊取珠寶，不過都沒有成功。

60. 洞穴探險 P.134

「探洞」（spelunking，探洞；洞穴探險）是一項刺激又危險的休閒運動，內容是探勘世界各地的洞穴。聽起來好像是個有趣的探險活動，但是可別忘了，探勘者要在泥濘上匍匐前進、攀爬陡峭的岩壁、擠過狹窄的石頭縫隙，甚至游過滿是黑水的隧道。這一點也不像是休閒運動！事實上，在外人看來，探洞算一項小有危險的「極限」運動。

有許多洞穴系統尚未有人去過，探洞愛好者總想爭先拔得頭籌。不過正因為這些地區從未有人探勘過，因此會有難度。洞穴地形可能會突然出現落差；如果洞穴靠近水邊，更有可能瞬間湧入大水。探洞者萬一受傷、迷路或與地面失聯，都會有生命危險。

是否攜帶適當的配備，可能是探險成功或悲劇發生的一線之差。充足的光源非常重要，如果探洞者看不清楚周遭環境，就可能會受傷。探洞者一定要全程佩戴加裝頭燈的硬式安全帽，手邊也必須要有備用電池。厚實的衣服鞋子、繩索、急救箱、糧食、梯子，還有其他緊急設備也都非常重要。

探洞時還有可能面臨空氣品質的問題。有的洞穴密不透風，二氧化碳含量極高，沒有昂貴的偵測設備很難知道洞穴內的空氣品質是否不佳。通常，洞穴空氣污濁的先兆，是探洞者開始感到疲倦、焦慮、燥熱或行動遲緩。為了避免這種情況或其他危險發生，探洞者最好都團體行動。

探洞在 20 世紀初開始成為一項休閒運動。spelunking 這個用語是克雷‧裴瑞在 1940 年代所創，之後就在世界各地逐漸盛行。許多國家都有管理和監督洞穴探勘活動的探洞組織，成立最久的當屬 1895 年的法國國家洞穴協會。

2-3 依上下文猜測字義

當你遇到一個不熟的單字，不確定它的意思時，記得仔細看看它前後的文字，同一句裡的其他單字會是寶貴的線索。以 Jim was cold, wet, and miserable.（吉姆又冷又濕又悲慘。）這個句子來說，miserable 這個字有可能是好的意思嗎？恐怕不可能。

61. 奧妙的昆蟲世界 P.136

我們每天都會遇到昆蟲，大部分人討厭昆蟲。但是這些討人厭的小生物，卻是我們的生態系統中不可或缺的重要角色。

所有的昆蟲都有六隻腳，和我們不一樣的是牠們沒有骨骼。昆蟲的身體可以分為三個明顯不同卻又相連的軀段。牠們的身體外面裹著一層甲殼，尤如盔甲一樣可以提供身體硬度。雖然有許多種類的昆蟲會飛，但不會飛的也很多。

我們能獲得這些關於昆蟲的知識，要歸功於昆蟲學家的努力。所謂的昆蟲學家是指專門研究昆蟲的人。昆蟲學家之所以把他們的研究獨立出來，是因為地球上的昆蟲品種，比其他現存動物的品種加起來還要多。根據一些來源指出，已知的昆蟲品種大約有 1 百萬種，可能還有 3 千萬種尚未被發現。昆蟲學家估計昆蟲大約佔了地球動物種類的 95%。

昆蟲的體型可以從小約 0.139 公釐的纓小蜂，到可以超過 55 公分長的竹節蟲。雖然沒有人能確定世界上最重的昆蟲是什麼，但是重約 70 公克的巨沙螽絕對有實力角逐這個頭銜。

有些昆蟲屬於害蟲，像是蚊子、蝨子、床蝨、蒼蠅、白蟻、蝗蟲和象鼻蟲，牠們會傳播疾病、損害建築物或破壞農作物。然而還是有很多有益環境的昆蟲，牠們會翻鬆土壤、替花卉和其他植物授粉，或生產有用的物質像是蜜、蠟和絲。有些昆蟲以動物屍體和掉落的樹枝為食，其他動物也會吃昆蟲為生。因此，使用殺蟲劑來控制害蟲有時是危險之舉。這些化學製品不僅會破壞環境，也會殺死許多無害的昆蟲。

62. 埃內斯托 ·「切」· 格瓦拉　P. 138

埃內斯托·格瓦拉於 1928 年出生於阿根廷，童年時期好讀詩書，也是西洋棋高手和傑出運動員。1948 年，他進入布宜諾斯艾利斯大學修讀醫學，完成學業之後周遊南美洲的貧窮國家行醫。這趟旅行讓他體會了日復一日的窮苦日子，於是發誓要改變這一切。

他成為革命人士的第一步跨向了瓜地馬拉。為了協助瓜地馬拉總統哈科沃·阿本斯完成其土地改革的雄心，埃內斯托於 1953 年前往該國。由於埃內斯托常在演說時使用「切」（Che）這個感嘆詞，使他得到了「切」這個綽號，意思是「嗨」。切在瓜地馬拉待沒多久，阿本斯總統就在 1954 年被美國政府推翻。切旋即展開抗爭，不久仍被迫逃往墨西哥。

1956 年，切加入了菲德爾·卡斯楚指揮的反抗軍，目標是推翻古巴政府，並以共產體制取而代之。此時，切放棄了醫師的專業，成為一名游擊隊長。他們在 1959 年擊敗古巴政府，奪下政權。

切並未因共產主義在古巴的勝利而滿足，他認為還有更多事要做，他視自己為鬥士，而非政治家。1965 年，切·格瓦拉離開古巴，到其他地方宣揚共產革命。兩年後，他在玻利維亞被捕，遭到玻利維亞軍方處決。

切被處決的 40 多年後，依然是個謎樣的人物。他一生中寫過一些詩書，發表多次令人難忘的演說。有些人視他為浪漫英雄，為了救助窮人勇於犧牲一切。有人說他是叛徒，協助毀滅性的共產專政掌權。無論你相信何為事實，印有切的 T 恤、帽子、海報、刺青，甚至是汽車保險桿貼紙，總會讓我們不時地想起他的一生。

63. 發起運動的推文　P. 140

你走進教室才發現自己忘了寫作業，朋友應和道：「我也是！」，發現自己並不孤單的當下，你大概會鬆一口氣。「我也是」這一用詞令人知曉對方也感同身受。2017 年，一則推文希望大家分享自己曾遭遇不堪的性侵害或性騷擾經驗，也就是受到不當的性評論或舉止迫害。這則推文就此帶動了「＃我也是」運動。

「＃我也是」主題標籤雖然始於美國，卻迅速傳播全球。2017 年 10 月，《紐約時報》發表一篇文章，講述眾多女性被某位知名好萊塢製片人性騷擾或性侵害的親身故事。這些女性表示，如果拒絕該製片人進一步的索求，事業就會受到影響。數日後，女星艾莉莎·米蘭諾發表第一則「＃我也是」推文。而「我也是」此用詞，最早發跡於塔拉娜·柏克為支持性犯罪受害者所創立的組織。短短九天，「＃我也是」推文已於 85 個國家轉載 230 萬次。

「＃我也是」運動蔓延全球之際，範圍亦跨出了娛樂界。一年後，《時代》雜誌公布曾遭控職場性騷擾或性侵害的 140 位知名男士名單，其中包括政治人物、公司主管、記者、作家、醫師、藝人與教授。某些國家則以自己的語言響應「#MeToo（我也是）」運動，例如法文的 #BalanceTonPorc（意指「讓好色沙豬現形」）以及義大利文的 #quellavoltache（意指「事發當下」）。即使在一些國家，文化上習慣將矛頭指向性侵與性騷擾受害者，受害女性仍挺身分享故事。「# 我也是」運動讓世人知道，譴責受害者的心態並不可取。

讓社會大眾傾聽女性的受害經驗並非易事。有些人認為「# 我也是」運動矯枉過正，在沒有證據的情況下輕易提出指控。但顯而易見的是，「# 我也是」運動讓曾在職場或校園受到騷擾或侵害的受害者，不再保持緘默。

64. 希臘神話怪物：米諾陶爾　P. 142

在古希臘傳說中，米諾陶爾是人身牛頭的野獸。他被囚禁在克諾索斯市地底，一座盤纏曲折的拉比林斯迷宮內。克諾索斯當時是克里特島上米諾斯文明的中心。

但是這頭生物又是哪裡來的？故事要從米諾斯國王和兄弟爭奪克里特的統治權說起。米諾斯國王為了取得優勢，請求海神波塞頓賜給他獲得統治權的天意。他要求給他一頭白牛，讓他獻祭給海神波塞頓。但是當這頭牛被送來的時候，米諾斯國王發現牠太美了，捨不得獻祭，反而將牠佔為己有。海神波塞頓得知後，計劃報復。既然米諾斯國王這麼愛這頭牛，海神波塞頓就讓國王的妻子也深深愛上這頭牛，於是她與白牛交媾生下了米諾陶爾這頭怪獸。

一年又一年地過去，米諾陶爾變得越來越殘暴，他屠殺許多人民並四處為害，在克里特造成恐慌。米諾斯國王終於命令建築師戴達羅斯建造一座巨大的迷宮，或稱做「拉比林斯迷宮」，來囚禁這頭生物。米諾陶爾繞不出曲折的迷宮，發現自己無法逃脫。

每隔九年，雅典會進貢七對童男童女，丟進迷宮供米諾陶爾食用，作為獻給天神的祭品。有一天，英雄忒修斯自願佯裝成祭品前往克里特，要殺死米諾陶爾。忒修斯在米諾斯國王之女阿里阿德涅的協助之下，帶著一個線團以避免在迷宮內迷路。他一遇到米諾陶爾便揮劍將他刺死，救出其他獻祭給米諾陶爾的人。忒修斯的英勇多謀也讓他成為希臘神話中最偉大的英雄之一。

65. 鉛筆的沿革　P. 144

我們大多數人想到科技，總是會想到電腦、智慧型手機，或 3D 立體電視。但是科技可以有許多種形式，有時我們容易將過去的科技發展視為理所當然。以鉛筆為例，鉛筆也曾經被視為一項革命性的工具，讓人類可以快速簡潔地把想法記錄下來。到底有多革命性？這個嘛，距離石墨鉛筆最初被發明已經快要 460 年了，但至今仍能在全世界的教室裡看到它呢。

最早的鉛筆是由羅馬人所發明，他們用鉛管在早期的紙張「紙莎草紙」上做記號。而「pencil」這個字也是從拉丁文「penicillus」演變而來，意思是「小尾巴」。雖然今日的鉛筆並不含鉛這個化學元素，許多人還是把現代鉛筆所使用的石墨稱為「鉛」。

現代鉛筆可以回溯至 1564 年，當時在英格蘭發現了一大片的純石墨礦床。大家發現石墨非常適合用在羊身上做記號，之後也開始於紙上書寫。一開始是用繩子或羊皮包裹石墨，迅速受到全歐洲藝術家的青睞。義大利人進一步改良用木頭包覆石墨，他們把兩片木頭夾住石墨條之後黏住，到現在鉛筆都還是採用這個妙法製作。

今日的鉛筆種類繁多，全部依照硬度分級，從極硬的 9H 到極軟的 9B。有的鉛筆不用黑色石墨改用彩色石墨。人們愛用鉛筆是無庸置疑的，它們到底有多普遍呢？每年全球的鉛筆產量超過 140 億枝，至於製造這些鉛筆所消耗的木頭，一棵大樹大約可以製造 30 萬枝鉛筆。

至於那個永遠都會被問到的問題：「一枝鉛筆可以畫多長的線？」到底有沒有答案？專家甚至都算出來了，答案就是「113 公里」。

2-4 實力檢測 ————————

66.「王牌飛行員」道格拉斯 · 貝德 P. 146

　　道格拉斯 · 貝德是第二次世界大戰中最負盛名的英國戰機飛行員之一，不僅因為他是傑出的飛行員，更因為他沒有雙腿。

　　1928 年，18 歲的貝德加入了英國皇家空軍（RAF）。他是天生的飛行好手，也是戰力十足的領袖，因此名氣很快傳開，兩年後就被任命為軍官。貝德向來不是乖乖牌，也無視空軍中隊指揮官「在 2000 英尺的高度之下不准表演特技」的命令，1931 年時，他在極低的飛行高度表演了「低速翻滾」，導致左翼擊地而墜機。他奇蹟似地保住性命，卻必須接受雙腿截肢，一腿膝蓋以上，另一腿膝蓋以下。

　　即便傷勢很重，貝德仍不願意自英國皇家空軍退役。手術恢復之後，他又展開飛行訓練，並且通過所有的飛行考試。但是英國皇家空軍拒絕讓他歸隊，並以醫療因素為由讓他退役。而後在 1939 年，第二次世界大戰爆發，貝德再次聯繫英國皇家空軍，請求歸隊效命。當時的作戰需求十分缺乏飛行老手，英國皇家空軍便讓他再次披掛上陣。

　　他成了二次大戰期間的王牌飛行員，一共擊落了 22 架德國戰機，最後在法國遭擊落。他被德國士兵俘虜，並囚禁到戰爭結束為止。不過高超的飛行技巧卻讓他備受敵方尊重，甚至允許英國轟炸機空投一隻新的義肢，讓他替換被擊落時受損的義肢。貝德用他的義肢不斷嘗試逃脫，他認為不計一切反抗敵人逃回祖國是他的責任。

　　貝德在戰後為殘障人士的權利奔走，奉獻餘生為他們謀福利，也因此於 1976 年受封爵位，而後於 1982 年 9 月 5 日心臟病發辭世。

67. 雪怪傳說 P. 148

　　很少有神秘傳說能像雪怪這樣抓住我們的想像。雪怪是一種人形生物，一般認為居住在尼泊爾和中國邊境的喜馬拉雅山脈。喜馬拉雅山傳說有雪怪已有數百年之久，自 19 世紀西方人涉足探索該區的崇山峻嶺開始，在雪中看到奇怪腳印和孤單黑影就時有所聞。但是這些生物真的存在嗎？抑或是登山者太累、天候不佳、想像力太豐富之下的產物？

　　Yeti 在藏語中指「岩石區的熊」，當地人如此自然而然地將雪怪和熊相提並論，雪怪的真實身分似乎也有了端倪。許多專家表示，大熊的足跡在風雪中暴露一段時間之後，常會變得像人的腳印。此外，我們一般聽到雪怪的描述是長了黑色長毛的高大生物，同樣也有可能是在描述一隻熊。

　　1986 年，一名登山客設法拍下了雪怪的照片。他目擊雪怪不動聲色地佇立在約 500 英尺遠的雪中，不只如此，經過鑑定發現他的照片真實性很高，許多人相信這是雪怪真實存在的證據。但是隔年人們回到照片中的拍攝地點，發現所謂的「雪怪」，只不過是在風雪中被誤認為生物的一塊黑色大石頭而已。

　　雖然大多數雪怪存在的「證據」都被科學一一駁回，2003 年的一項發現卻顯示，雪怪這個概念可能並非過去所認為的無稽之談。在印尼的弗洛勒斯島，存活至距今僅一萬兩千年前的早期人種出土了，證明早期人種和現代人類曾經並存。因此，或許真的有早期人種生存於喜馬拉雅高山上，只是尚未被現代人所發現。

68. 摩斯密碼 P. 150

　　摩斯密碼是運用點和劃這兩種長短元素來傳送訊息的通訊方式，一連串的點和劃代表了訊息裡的字母、數字和標點符號。只要能發出長短波動的器材，舉凡無線電波、手電筒、鼓，都可以收發訊息，因此即使在通訊困難的情況下，也能高度靈活運用這套系統。

　　這套密碼原先是山謬 · 芬利 · 布里斯 · 摩斯所創造，要用在他新發明的電報上面。摩斯原本是位畫家，有一次在華盛頓作畫時，驛差送來一封信，信上寫著他的妻子命危。他趕回紐哈芬的家卻為時已晚，妻子早已下葬。摩斯明白，若是早點收到那封信，他就能在妻子過世前陪伴她，於是他開始致力於研究快速長途通訊的方法。

1836 年，摩斯製造出第一台電報機。這套系統可以透過電線傳遞電子脈衝到接收端的電磁體上面。電磁體每收到一道電流就會啟動機械作用，把金屬筆推向紙條，畫出一系列的點和劃。

原先由專員負責讀取紙條訊息，再翻譯成文字。慢慢地，電報專員學會直接聽機器推金屬筆畫線又歸位的滴嗒聲，就翻譯出文字，也不一定要使用紙條。現在有經驗的摩斯密碼專員每分鐘可以輕鬆翻譯出 30 字之多。

雖然電報已經式微，但是專業和業餘無線電使用者仍將摩斯密碼視為一種重要通訊方式。其中最出名、到現在都還被使用的一組字母是 SOS，這是國際公認的求救信號，用法是三點（S）、三劃（O）、三點（S），或者寫為「...- -...」。

69. 十四行詩 P. 152

十四行詩於 13 世紀開始出現於義大利，而後被義大利詩人佩脫拉克發揚光大，經常被視為情詩的一種經典韻體。莎士比亞曾創作一系列共 154 首以美、愛與死亡為主題的十四行詩，建立其十四行詩人的翹楚地位。莎士比亞的詩作所帶來的衝擊，使他與佩脫拉克齊名，成為十四行詩的兩派主流。

不管是佩脫拉克式還是莎士比亞式，十四行詩一定是 14 行，並且一定要有「轉折」。詩人通常用一首十四行詩來探討兩個截然不同的主題，而「轉折」就是兩個主題轉換的地方。以佩脫拉克的十四行詩為例，轉折都是出現在第九行，其他形式的詩，轉折處則較多變化。

由於義大利文的押韻字非常多，因此佩脫拉克式的十四行詩，韻式較密集，需要用到很多押韻字。不過，一首佩脫拉克式的十四行詩不會以兩行押韻句作結，也就是說，兩個鮮明的主題不會有結論，而是互相抗衡，強調彼此的緊張或對立關係。

莎士比亞用英文寫詩（英文的押韻字比義大利文少很多），他喜歡用另一種韻式，並且會以兩行押韻句來總結一首詩。這種結尾寫法讓詩人可以為兩個對比的見解下結論，甚至語出驚人來個最後一刻的大逆轉，將兩種想法雙雙推翻，這也讓莎士比亞式的十四行詩比佩脫拉克式更具戲劇效果。

在一些現代詩人眼裡，十四行詩已經退流行了，嚴格的韻式讓喜歡即興發揮的詩人卻步。雖然如此，許多現代詩人也曾嘗試將這種詩體運用在現代詩的創作上。其中有一首特別有趣的《單字十四行詩》，同樣是十四行，但是每一行只有一個字。十四行詩問世七百年後，還能持續啟發新生代詩人的創作靈感，著實令人驚奇。

70. 你的碳足跡是多少？ P. 154

「碳足跡」常被定義為一個國家、機構或個人，每年因消耗能源和排放廢棄物所產生的二氧化碳量。二氧化碳和其他溫室氣體會暖化地球，導致兩極冰帽完全融化，因此減少碳足跡絕對是一項重要目標。

全球三大二氧化碳排放國家為中國、美國和印度。然而，不論你住在哪個國家，只要過著典型的現代化生活，你的碳足跡可能也很大。大部分已開發國家的最大污染源來自汽車。美國家庭的碳足跡是一年 48 噸二氧化碳，是全球平均值的五倍。其中大部分的碳足跡來自於間接排放（遠端廠商為了製造商品所燃燒的燃料），不過美國家庭倒是可藉由更換車種，讓直接碳足跡減少許多倍。居家排放僅以些微差距排名第二，暖氣設備、照明、家用廢棄物，都貢獻了不少家庭碳足跡。

那麼，你可以做些什麼來縮減碳足跡呢？小小地改變生活型態就可以大大減少你的碳排放量。空調只要調個兩度：夏天高兩度、冬天低兩度，一年就可以減少約 1 噸的碳足跡。冷暖空調的確是碳足跡的主要來源，所以只要適度的調節室內氣溫，你所造成的污染就會降低，電費開銷也會減少 24%。

如果還想進一步徹底消滅碳足跡的話，可能要多下點功夫，安裝太陽能板、貫徹資源回收，並徹底改變交通方式。說不定未來所有人的環保意識抬頭，足以達成個人零碳足跡的目標。

Unit 3 學習策略

本單元將為英語學習者介紹兩種重要的工具，第一種是各類型的**影像圖表**，包含照片和圖解資料，可將內容視覺化以輔助閱讀。視覺化的資料能強化學生的閱讀感受，幫助他們在考試時記起重要資訊。

第二種工具是**參考資料**，是我們需要更具體的資訊時可以查閱的各種資源。讀完本單元，你將學會查詢資料並且有效地整合這些資訊。

3-1 影像圖表

有些資訊適合用圖解，不適合用文字表達。你會想用文字來描述一張地圖嗎？會想用長條圖來寫論文嗎？當然不會！所以我們要有影像圖表，和原始參考資料相輔相成。

71. 地圖：飛行的夢想 P.158

數千年來人類一直夢想飛翔，早在 15 世紀義大利的文藝復興時期，李奧納多·達文西就曾起草繪製直昇機和滑翔翼的設計圖，不過他所設計出的模型都宣告失敗。直到數百年後，美國的萊特兄弟才造出一系列成功的飛行器。他們隨後發明了第一架可操控的固定翼飛機，成為現代最重要的發明之一。

飛行博物館是下列地圖上的一個地標。地圖是用以呈現實際地點的圖表，每張地圖標示景點和地標的圖示都不同。地圖的種類繁多，有氣候圖，也有顯示標高的地形圖，觀光地圖和街道圖也很普遍。請用下頁地圖來回答以下問題。

72. 行事曆：琳達出差 P.160

琳達這三個月都在擔心要去荷蘭出差的事，這次出差是她公司目前為止面臨的最大考驗，因為她將與許多進出口業的重要人士會面。如果會面進展順利，她就有機會在荷蘭設立分公司，反之她必須重新思考公司的未來。不論結果如何，擔心了這麼久，她只希望早點解脫。

琳達出差是下頁行事曆的重要記事之一。把日曆想成地圖，只不過標示地點改成標示時間。西式的行事曆多半是一年分，分成 12 個月，用方格代表每一天，大家會把筆記或約會記在格子裡。請用下頁的行事曆來回答下列問題。

73. 表格：英里賽 P.162

「英里賽」是英格蘭盛行數百年的一英里賽跑，距離相當於 1,600 公尺，目前的世界紀錄保持人是摩洛哥的希查姆·艾爾·奎羅伊，跑出 3 分 43.13 秒的成績。事實上，英里賽行之有年，在歷史上頗負盛名，因此英國國會早在 1593 年就制訂了正式的比賽距離。即便我們多已改用公制，世界各地還是有人參加英里賽。

下頁表格是古早的英里賽記錄。表格可以清楚羅列大量的資料，是非常實用的工具。表格也可以用來集結各種統計資料、進行資料間的換算，或比較兩組不同的資料。請用下頁的表格來回答以下問題。

74. 長條圖：全世界的摩天大樓 P.164

「世界貿易中心一號大樓」（1WTC）原稱為「自由塔」，是紐約市新建的世界貿易中心的主建物。這座高樓是建造來取代在 2001 年 9 月 11 日的恐怖攻擊事件中被摧毀的世貿雙塔，2014 年落成之後，成為世界最高的摩天大樓之一。

下頁有一張世界最高樓的長條圖，世界貿易中心一號大樓是圖中列出的其中一座摩天大樓。「長條圖」是一種圖表，將以統計數據為主的資訊，用直條或橫條來表示。它可以提供基本的統計資料，方便我們估算一系列數值、進行簡易對照。既然條柱代表數值，那麼最長的即代表數字最大，最短的代表數字最小。請用下頁的長條圖來回答以下問題。

75. 試算表：追蹤存貨清單 P. 166

要隨時保持更新的存貨清單，可能是小公司老闆最頭痛的事情。大家每天忙得不可開交，經常忘了更新紀錄。但是正確的庫存記錄才能提高訂單效率，創造更高的利潤。畢竟，沒有老闆想看到一堆無謂的商品在架上放到爛吧。

存貨清單經常被做成試算表，下頁的圖是一間唱片行的存貨清單。試算表可以有效將資料製成欄列交錯的表格形式，但是有別於表格可能只佔一兩頁，試算表好像可以無止境地列下去。試算表是可以容納大批資料的資料庫，尤其是統計數字。請用下頁這個範例來回答以下問題。

3-2 參考資料

一篇真正有趣或參考價值高的文章，一定含有一些資訊，我們可以參考原始資料找到非常有用的資訊。不管是字典、百科全書或網際網路，每一種參考資料都有其優缺點，必須要善加了解。

76. 目錄：鈴木一朗 P. 168

鈴木一朗是有史以來知名度最高的日本棒球選手之一，他於 2001 年加入美國職棒大聯盟西雅圖水手隊，迅速躋身聯盟球星之列。雖然他到美國的時候已經 27 歲，但憑著一身非凡的球技，被認為退休後應該入選名人堂。

在下頁的目錄裡面，鈴木一朗是其中一章的主題。目錄一定位於書刊雜誌的開頭，裡面涵括有助於讀者的資訊，例如該出版物包含哪些部分、類別或章名。目錄也會標示每一章的頁碼，便於讀者翻閱。請用下頁的目錄來回答下列問題。

77. 索引：煉獄 P. 170

「煉獄」是天主教的信仰之一，介於天堂和地獄之間某處。根據天主教義，好人上天堂，壞人下地獄，不好不壞的人則先去煉獄，洗滌他們的靈魂。

煉獄是以下索引裡出現的一個字。索引通常位於書末，內容依照字母排列。索引就好比是目錄，只是包含更多明確的主題。同時，索引裡的主題通常會列出好幾個出現該條目的頁碼。以下頁索引來說，如果你想多了解煉獄這個主題，就要翻到第 330 頁。請用下一頁的索引來回答下列問題。

78. 百科全書：農業演進 P. 172

農業是個相當複雜又重要的題材，因為人類務農已經有數千年之久。早期的農業改革如今看來都是非常簡單的概念，例如土地必須輪作以維護土壤品質。這是因為農業已經成為龐大的國際事業，我們所吃的穀物、肉類和乳製品，都由經營大規模複合式工廠化農場的跨國大企業來管控。

農業是下頁百科全書中的一個主題。百科全書是收錄龐大事實和資料的書。裡面的資訊依照字母排列，主題涵蓋人物、地點、歷史事件、發明——幾乎你想得到的都應有盡有！百科全書之所以是非常好用的參考資料，和內容的編排有關。它的條目不會太複雜，讀者花一點點時間就可以學很多。請用下頁的百科全書圖片來回答下列問題。

79. 字典：伯達尼的拉撒路 P. 174

拉撒路，或是「伯達尼的拉撒路」，是著名的基督教聖經人物。他是耶穌的信徒，有一天他生病了，他的姊姊派人請耶穌來救他，但是當耶穌抵達時，拉撒路早已死亡四天。耶穌到他的墓前禱告，拉撒路竟完好的從墳墓走出。此事被許多基督徒視為奇蹟，證明耶穌確實是聖人。

拉撒路是下頁字典出現的單字。字典是條列單字和字義的書，通常依字母順序排列。除了單字意義之外，字典也常補充其他資訊，像是詞性和字源，有的字典還會提供例句。請用下頁的字典摘錄圖片來回答下列問題。

80. 網際網路：愛美不怕荷包失血　P.176

如果被問及「你想變美嗎？」，應該沒有多少人會回答：「不想」。事實上，多數人都想讓自己容光煥發，而大公司深諳此道。2018 年的一項研究顯示，美國女性每年在美妝用品上的開銷平均是 3,756 美元。換算下來，美國女性一生會花費將近 225,360 美元。難怪如同下一頁照片中所示的此類保健與美容網站，在網路上如此繁多。

網路是買賣產品的強大工具。但是該如何善用網路？以搜尋引擎找到網路商店後，請先看一下網頁最上方。通常可看見數種不同類別，點選各類別後，就會看見分門別類的產品清單。若想搜尋特定品項，先找到網頁上的放大鏡圖標——這就是可輸入特定品名的搜尋列，有時還可直接發問「運費多少？」等問題。

請運用下一頁的彩妝網站圖片，來回答以下問題。

Unit 4　綜合練習

在研讀本書時，你會密集地學到各種閱讀和單字技巧，同時也會練習一些重要的學習策略，現在就來演練你所學到的技巧吧。在前面的單元中，每篇文章之後只評量一種閱讀或單字技巧，現在，你必須嘗試在同一篇文章中綜合運用各種技巧。藉此機會，你可以強化學習效果、測驗你所學的新技巧，並且找出你的強弱項。如果你一直卡在某一項學習策略上，就回頭複習相關的課程，然後再試一次。勤練才是成功的不二法門！

4-1 綜合練習（I）

81. 緬甸的人道危機　P.180

「種族滅絕」是各界對政府最沈重的控訴。原文「genocide」（種族滅絕）意指蓄意屠殺某種族、政治或文化族群。這個名詞創於 1944 年的納粹反猶太大屠殺事件。當某政府或團體針對特定種族或宗教族群而濫殺無辜，便視為「種族滅絕」行為。

聯合國與國際刑事法院均認為，緬甸政府針對羅興亞人展開種族滅絕行動。羅興亞是一個擁有自己語言和文化的種族。將近 88% 的緬甸人為佛教徒，而羅興亞人卻是穆斯林。雖然羅興亞人自 19 世紀以來即於緬甸生根，但政府卻既未承認他們的公民身分，也未認可其為官方名列的種族。緬甸有 100–130 萬名羅興亞人，多數居住於若開邦。政府限制羅興亞人的居住與行動範圍、上學或工作地區，以及可生育的子女人數。

驚人的是，羅興亞人種族滅絕事件，竟發生在翁山蘇姬領導的民選政府執政期間。翁山蘇姬曾因政治犯身分遭到軟禁 20 年，其民主鬥士精神，使她在此期間榮獲諾貝爾和平獎。

翁山蘇姬成為國家顧問（首相）後的一年，即發生種族滅絕事件。逃離至鄰國孟加拉的羅興亞人表示村莊遭到襲擊。緬甸官兵和鄰村的佛教徒民兵挨家挨戶屠殺無辜、燒毀屋舍以及強暴婦人和女童。自 2016 年的第一起攻擊事件發生後，已有近 90 萬名羅興亞人逃離家園。超過四萬三千人失蹤，極可能已喪生。

記者與人權團體紛紛呼籲國際重視此危機。他們要求翁山蘇姬盡快針對此暴力事件表態。雖然翁山蘇姬並非緬甸軍方的領導人，她仍有一定的影響力。沒想到，她竟然反控羅興亞人為恐怖分子，指涉他們自導自演、縱火燒屋以博取同情。儘管她的反應令各界驚愕，國際社群仍持續設法保護羅興亞人的安危。

82. 鯊魚真有那麼危險嗎？ P.182

很多人都把鯊魚看做會追殺吞食無辜泳客的邪惡食人魔。然而這種印象其實是大錯特錯，而且多半要怪好萊塢的電影製片，為了電影恐怖又危險的元素需要，才替鯊魚塑造了這種錯誤的形象。

事實上，很多鯊魚品種根本不是肉食性動物，而是專吃動物死屍的腐食性動物。有的鯊魚沒有牙齒，除了浮游生物這種微小生物之外，他們傷不了任何其他動物，龐大的鯨鯊就屬於此類。470多個鯊魚品種當中，只有四種曾發生過多次殺人攻擊行為：大白鯊、長鰭真鯊、虎鯊和公牛白眼鮫，這四種體型龐大、強而有力的品種才有能力重創他們的獵物。不過這幾種鯊魚通常不會接近人類，因為我們並不是他們的主食。大部分的鯊魚攻擊事件是因為鯊魚把人類誤認為其他海洋哺乳動物，咬一口之後，他們通常會發現咬錯了而把人放掉。平均每年發生六起鯊魚攻擊致死事件，跟每年被人類補殺的鯊魚超過 1 億隻比起來，反而是鯊魚應該怕我們才對。

看看這些數字：光是斯里蘭卡每年就有大約 400 人被蛇咬死，每年有 4 萬名左右的美國人死於車禍。專家甚至表示，你被蜜蜂螫死的機率都比被鯊魚咬死要高。

這代表什麼呢？和所有危險動物一樣，我們對鯊魚一定要敬而遠之。只是事實上，他們並非電影演的那種「殺人機器」，而是一種奇妙的生物。鯊魚在地球上已經存在將近 4 億 5 千萬年，不但練就一身解決問題的好本領，甚至還能感應生物的磁場。我們應該放下成見，別再把鯊魚當成海怪，開始懂得欣賞他們，這才是他們應得的。

83. 迷信 P.184

你知道嗎？打破鏡子會倒楣七年，星期天剪指甲也會惹禍上身，更別想在室內撐傘──衰事肯定會發生！

所謂的迷信，是我們非常相信一些事，通常到了不理性的地步，導致我們的行為舉止也受影響。別以為迷信是老太太或過度天真的人的專利，難道你不曾穿幸運褲去考試嗎？或者體育競賽時在口袋裡放一枚幸運幣以祈求獲勝？你可能比你想的還要迷信。迷信本身或許教人匪夷所思，但是人之所以會迷信，道理也很簡單。

有一次你穿了一雙粉紅點點襪去學校，剛好考試又考得不錯──或許只是巧合，那麼第二次、第三次呢？肯定不是純粹運氣吧。其實也未必，人類喜歡把完全不相干的事情聯想在一起。有時湊巧穿那雙襪子加上考試考得好又再度同時發生，更難讓人不去聯想。而你同樣穿那雙可笑的襪子，卻什麼也沒發生的時候，你卻可能沒注意到。我們往往選擇性地記住能支持我們想法的蛛絲馬跡，反之則忘得一乾二淨。

以心理學家斯金納的實驗為例：斯金納先把幾隻鴿子放進籠子裡，然後在籠子旁邊放一個定時餵食機，鴿子開始把機器餵食和他們在餵食時所做的動作連結在一起。斯金納觀察到，鴿子會轉圈圈、搖頭晃腦，或者反覆走到籠子某個角落，期待食物會因此出現。他們以為這麼做就得吃，但是事實上，不管他們做什麼動作，食物都會掉下來。你是不是也有似曾相識的感覺呢？人類或許是最聰明的動物，但是一提到迷信，我們跟期待被餵食的鴿子沒兩樣。

84. 一點一滴淨化海洋 P.186

太平洋垃圾帶是一個聚集驚人塑料垃圾量的海洋區域，位於夏威夷和加州之間，大小為 160 萬平方公里，超過法國面積的兩倍。7 萬 9 千噸的塑料在降解過程中被吞食，而威脅到海洋生物的性命。再者，塑料一旦進入食物鏈，也可能影響人體健康。幸好這個問題已有潛在的解決之道。此解決方案的發想過程以及年輕有為的發明人，均令人佩服不已。

2018 年 9 月 8 日，名為「海洋吸塵器」的系統正式前往太平洋垃圾帶。海面上，該系統看起來像是巨型「U」型浮動管線。此 600 公尺長的類管線結構維持整體裝置漂浮狀態，底下則是 3 公尺深的偌大擋板。堅固的擋板能在「海洋吸塵器」

隨波逐流時收集塑料。除了洋流之外，海風與海浪亦為系統的推動力。裝置的移動速度緩慢，因此不會危害海洋生物。由於此系統不以網狀設計攔截塑料，因此不會困住魚隻，魚群可從裝置下方或旁邊游過。

「海洋吸塵器」是荷蘭人柏楊・史萊特想出的點子。現年 24 歲的史萊特，是在希臘潛水後得到啟發。當時年僅 16 歲的他，對於海裡的塑料量感到吃驚。他想不通為何沒有人正視如此嚴重的問題。史萊特發現，以傳統方法處理此問題工程浩大，既耗時又需龐大經費。經過一年的腦力激盪，他於 18 歲提出「海洋吸塵器」的構想。多虧他出類拔萃的發明，五年內，太平洋垃圾帶的半數垃圾將可清空。史萊特的雄心壯志不只於此，他期望在 2040 年以前，淨空 90% 的全球海洋塑料量。

85. 托斯卡尼之美　P. 188

托斯卡尼位於義大利的西岸，這個美麗的地區素以壯麗的美景和卓越超群的藝術史名聞遐邇。

托斯卡尼最大的產業是觀光業。每年有數百萬名觀光客來到這些名符其實的「藝術之都」：佛羅倫斯、盧卡、比薩（著名的「斜塔」所在地）、西耶納和聖吉米納諾。歷史上一些偉大的藝術家如李奧納多・達文西和米開朗基羅，都在這些城市裡出生或創作出非凡作品。其中景色最壯觀的佛羅倫斯，擁有美侖美奐的建築物和豐富的藝術收藏，每年吸引超過 1 千萬名觀光客前來參觀。來到托斯卡尼絕對不能錯過佛羅倫斯，不過要盡量避開炎熱的夏日旺季，此時觀光客與當地居民的比例竟高達 14:1。事實上，許多佛羅倫斯人一到夏天就離開城市，寧可跑到美麗的托斯卡尼鄉間，找幾間靜謐別墅去避暑。

很多人說，造訪托斯卡尼鄉間彷彿來到天堂。一片片葡萄園和橄欖園交織而成的起伏山丘，沐浴在托斯卡尼夕陽的溫和橘色光輝下。主人家豪邁地喝著葡萄美酒，桌上堆滿了舉世聞名的美饌佳餚。

就算你不特別愛喝紅酒，來到托斯卡尼也破例一次吧，這裡的美酒一定會讓你改觀。托斯卡尼是著名的優質葡萄酒產區，專業釀酒商遵循幾世紀代代相傳的古法釀造葡萄酒。康堤、蒙塔奇諾布內洛和蒙特普恰諾貴族酒都是世界頂級紅酒，其中一些好酒更是所費不貲，蒙塔奇諾布內洛就是眾所皆知世界最貴的酒之一。所以品嚐這些美酒和了解釀造過程的最好方法，可能是參加當地許多葡萄園所開的釀酒課。

不論你是想認識這裡的美食、讚嘆這裡的藝術或暢遊獨特的鄉間，托斯卡尼絕對不會讓你失望。

86. 捕鯨文化　P. 190

捕鯨議題在全球分成兩派，有些國家認為捕殺鯨魚這種高等海洋哺乳動物，是既殘忍又非必要的行為，有些國家則不顧國際強烈譴責，堅持這是他們必須捍衛的文化權。

人類捕鯨取用其肉和油脂已有數千年之久，可是一直是相當小規模地獵捕。然而到了 19 世紀，油被廣泛應用在油燈、美容用品等重要商品上，導致需求量增加。捕鯨業在 1930 年代發展到顛峰，當時每年遭到捕殺的鯨魚超過 5 萬隻。

鯨魚的數量急遽下降，許多大型的鯨魚品種也瀕臨絕跡。1980 年代中葉時，國際捕鯨委員會（簡稱 IWC）下令禁止商業捕鯨行為，以期恢復鯨魚數量。

如今只有少數國家依然熱衷捕鯨，辯稱鯨魚已經恢復到允許有限度捕捉的數量。儘管國家捕鯨委員會已經下達禁令，幾個贊成捕鯨的國家仍然尋求突破限制。以日本政府為例，他們堅稱國內的捕鯨業者僅為科學研究目的而捕鯨，不過許多人對此抱持強烈懷疑。

鯨魚體型巨大、力大無窮，獵殺一頭鯨魚要耗費多時，導致鯨魚必須承受莫大的痛苦和掙扎，反捕鯨人士認為這樣的行徑太殘忍，令人無法接受。但是這個理由非常棘手，因為許多贊成捕鯨的國家如挪威和冰島，幾世紀的捕鯨傳統由來已久。對他們而言，捕鯨是民族認同的一部分，也是許多人民的重要收入和食物來源。

2010 年時，一項折衷方案被提出，讓捕鯨國得以在嚴格監督之下，限量獵捕鯨魚，唯獨南大

255

洋全面禁止捕鯨。然而這項方案遭到兩百多名科學家和專家反對,於是,目前捕鯨業的未來仍然懸而未決。

87.「沐浴」於大自然之美 P. 192

哪一種「沐浴」並非傳統認知的沐浴方式?這個特別問題的答案是「森林浴」。森林浴無關寬衣或碰水,而是精神上的沐浴——讓感官「沐浴」大自然中。森林浴亦非指艱辛的林中健行活動,弄得汗流浹背,而是屬於偏向冥想的祥和運動,據說對健康好處多多。

也許你從未聽聞這般有趣的保健方式,但此法已行之有年。自 1980 年代,日本人即深知森林浴的優點且施行已久。當時日本政府的研究結果顯示,森林浴和良好健康息息相關。森林浴有益特定身體機能健康的功效著實令人印象深刻,包括增強免疫系統、減低心臟病風險以及降低血糖值。不只如此,沐浴在林間,也能降低血壓以及減少引發壓力的化學物質。就連政府都推崇森林浴,甚至納入國民健康計畫。日本農林水產省稱此活動為「shinrin-yoku」,譯為「森林浴」。

森林浴有益健康的真正原因仍廣受討論。主要因素有可能只是與友人在汙染少、較能放鬆心情的環境裡共度時光。另一方面,某些研究人員推測保健效果可能來自樹林所釋放的化學物質。這類物質或許有增強免疫系統的功效。

不論森林浴是以何種方式達到保健效果,這股風潮已從日本席捲到國外,近年在英國和美國蔚為流行就是一例。由於正面的研究結果佐證森林浴的功效,這股養生潮流很有可能繼續延燒。

88. 拜倫勳爵的傳奇人生 P. 194

曾被一位戀人形容為「瘋狂、惡劣又危險」的拜倫,是英國最偉大的詩人之一,他的人格造成的轟動完全不亞於他的詩作。

一系列震驚社會的緋聞和鉅額負債,使他在 1816 年離開英國,終其餘生自願流放歐洲。後來在希臘獨立戰爭時,拜倫加入了對抗土耳其人的軍隊,途中染上熱病,於 36 歲英年早逝,奠定他浪漫悲劇英雄的傳奇人生。

多年來,人們為拜倫寫過無數傳記,如果想要快速找到拜倫一生中某個時期的資料,可以查找下頁的索引。索引依照字母排列,人名則會依照姓氏排列,每一個條目後面都有該主題出現的頁碼。以威廉·史考特為例,出現在第 376 頁。請用下頁的索引圖片來回答以下問題。

89. 折線圖:廣告大戰:傳統 vs. 新式 P. 196

廣告界近期掀起新舊大戰。一方是電視、廣播、報章雜誌等傳統媒介;另一方則是網站、APP 應用程式與社群媒體等新一代的數位媒介。過去五年以來,許多公司在傳統廣告媒介的花費已縮減許多,反觀數位廣告的銷量卻一飛沖天。

以下折線圖顯示美國從 2013 年到 2018 年,傳統與數位廣告的花費成長率。左側的 Y 軸顯示廣告花費成長率的百分比,底部 X 軸則代表時間。此類折線圖非常適合用於比較一段時間的相對表現差異。例如我們可從此圖看出,數位廣告花費的成長率遠高於傳統廣告花費,顯示傳統廣告支出逐年下降。

90. 耶魯大學最熱門的課程:快樂法則 P. 198

現在的你,或許正努力爭取進入心目中的理想大學或工作。但如果夢寐以求的大學或職位錄取你,你卻意識到自己並不開心呢?對許多人而言,想在職場或學業上飛黃騰達的這種壓力,經常主導他們的生活。即使游刃有餘,卻不見得樂在其中。美國最高學府耶魯大學的學生便面臨這種情況。

頂尖大學的耶魯學生均深諳學業優異之道。但耶魯大學的心理學教授蘿莉·桑托斯博士,希望學生能將心理健康狀態列為優先,而非分數。她發現學生常因壓力喘不過氣,完全無法享受校園生活。2013 年耶魯報告顯示,半數學生接受過心理諮商，這與桑托斯博士的觀察結果不謀而合。桑托斯教授開設一門「心理學與美好人生」的課程，有 25% 的耶魯大學生選修，成為耶魯史上人數最龐大的一門課。

桑托斯博士透過「心理學與美好人生」課程，教導學生改變自己看待「快樂」的方式與習慣。桑托斯博士在課堂上運用正向心理學和行為心理學授課。學生了解到有意義的快樂人生真諦後，桑托斯博士就會指派作業，希望學生面對改變行為的挑戰。作業內容包括一週至少三天睡飽七小時、寫感謝信、運動，及以貼心舉止對待朋友或陌生人。

由於上課人數實在過多，耶魯大學難以再開課。不過，耶魯決定開設線上課程「幸福的科學」。短短兩個月內，全球報名人數將近九萬一千人。線上課程學生的評價與耶魯學生雷同：桑托斯博士確實幫助他們著眼於人生的重要面向，並改善了他們的心理健康。

4-2 綜合練習（II）

91. 奇妙的含羞草　P. 200

我們都聽過害羞的人，但是有聽過害羞的植物嗎？聽起來可能很誇張，但誇張的是真的有這樣的植物！它就叫做「含羞草」，是從拉丁文「敏感的植物」衍生而來，英文又稱之為「touch-me-not」（勿碰我）。

含羞草原產於中南美洲，是一年生或多年生的攀緣草本植物，也就是說，含羞草會沿著它所攀附的物體表面往外生長。不過，真正讓含羞草成名的原因，在於它被碰觸之後的奇特反應。如果有人碰一下含羞草的葉子，這些葉子就會立刻闔起來，所以才會讓人感覺含羞草比較像動物而不像植物。

含羞草的反應來自於被碰觸當下所釋放的一種化學物質，這種化學物質會將植物內部的水分導向莖部，造成葉子往中間收合。部分科學家認為，這種特殊的反應其實是為了抵禦草食性動物。

含羞草之所以是世界上最奇妙的植物，原因不只是它的反應，它的葉子可以磨碎治療多種疾病。印度傳統醫學用含羞草來治療腺體腫脹；在剛果則用它來舒緩疼痛和腎疾。事實上，有含羞草生長的地方，通常都有用含羞草治病的文化。

如果你覺得會動的植物很有意思，你倒也不用替含羞草擔心，因為它可不是好惹的品種，事實上恰好相反。含羞草名列全球的入侵種之一，所謂入侵種，是被移至新棲地之後會消滅在地品種的物種。雖然含羞草原產於美洲，但是現在已經擴散到非洲、南亞、太平洋島群和澳洲，讓其中許多國家非常頭痛。

92. 為兒童文學發聲——美國紐伯瑞獎　P. 202

閱讀一本好書可以開啟通往美妙新世界的大門，這個新世界充滿了神奇事物和發現，這也是為什麼全世界的人都愛閱讀。每本書的背後都有一位創意十足的作者，為了獎勵他們而設立的重要獎項非常多。其中頒給最佳童書新作的美國紐伯瑞獎，有著悠久而耐人尋味的歷史。

該獎項始於 1921 年，弗雷德瑞克·梅爾契爾建議美國圖書館學會，頒發一個年度獎項以表彰新書類的最佳童書。這個想法受到眾人支持，最後決定以 18 世紀的英國書商約翰·紐伯瑞來命名，他在當時不遺餘力推廣兒童文學。紐伯瑞獎的初衷是為了獎勵創意，並建立兒童文學成為與詩歌、小說和戲劇同等地位的藝術形式。

既然紐伯瑞獎是屬於美國圖書館學會的獎項，得獎者自然必須是美國公民或永久居民。得獎書每年由不同的評委會選出，通常包含大約 15 名評審委員。遴選得獎作品耗時一整年。首先會有一輪提名，由評委選出合格的書籍，接著評委利用一整年的時間，將這些書籍一讀再讀，最後投票選出得獎者。有時候評委會也會指定「榮譽獎」，頒給未能得獎但令人驚艷的書籍。

所以下次你去逛書店，經過本年度諾貝爾獎得獎作品區的時候，或許會想再往前走一點點到童書區。因為紐伯瑞獎給我們的啟示是：請認真看待兒童文學這門藝術。

93. 反式脂肪知多少　P.204

反式脂肪的故事很有趣，因為它最初被視為奇蹟，最後卻發現會致人於死。

反式脂肪是稠化植物油使之變硬的工業過程產物，又名「部分氫化油」。許多肉類都含有少量的天然反式脂肪，但是一些加工食品，例如罐裝湯、速食、冷凍晚餐，也常添加反式脂肪。

1980 年代時，保羅‧薩巴堤耶發現了氫化油的製法，開始運用來生產乳瑪琳，至今乳瑪琳仍被大量用作奶油的替代品。早期還有一種反式脂肪產品叫作白油，於 1920 年首度上市。白油常取代豬油用來烘焙麵包、餡餅、餅乾和蛋糕。一直到 1950 年代，反式脂肪都還被視為一項神奇的發明，因為它比動物性的同質商品便宜，民眾也多半認為它比較美味。直到 1960 年代，情況開始有了轉變。

1960 年之後，開始有一些科學研究發表指出，反式脂肪會危害健康。一開始並沒有引起太大的注意，尤其靠著反式脂肪商品大發利市的食品商，更是忽略這些研究。一直到 1990 年代，民眾才正視與反式脂肪相關的健康風險。研究指出，反式脂肪會使壞的膽固醇上升、好的膽固醇下降，造成罹患心臟病、中風和糖尿病的風險升高。大多數研究都認定，每年有大約 63 萬名美國人是受反式脂肪影響死於心臟疾病。

鑑於這些風險，留意你愛吃的食物是否含反式脂肪，或許才是聰明之舉。美國心臟協會建議，反式脂肪攝取量必須限制在每日卡路里的 1% 以下。令人慶幸的是，大多數國家現在都已經通過法令，要求食品公司在商品上標明反式脂肪的含量。

94. 慘烈的愛爾蘭歷史悲劇：「大饑荒」　P.206

愛爾蘭的大饑荒可說是最慘重的饑荒事件，更是政府的作為幫倒忙導致情況雪上加霜的真實故事。愛爾蘭馬鈴薯饑荒始於 1845 年，直到 1852 年才落幕。當時的愛爾蘭以馬鈴薯為主食。

由於民眾過度依賴馬鈴薯，饑荒才會如此嚴重。將近 100 萬人因挨餓與其他相關因素而死亡。

饑荒的起因來自造成馬鈴薯大量歉收的黴菌。第一年就有半數馬鈴薯腐壞。起初，大家並不以為意，因為作物問題時有所聞。然而，此黴菌卻接連幾年重創馬鈴薯作物。

歷史學家常指出，英國政府的作為，或可謂毫無作為，是導致大饑荒的元凶。雖然政府確實有採取行動，但許多觀察學者卻認為領導人並未盡力。政府減稅來讓其他食物的價格降低；此外，推動鋪路工程等勞動專案，讓男性可賺取工資。但是，這樣的政策卻遭受撻伐。耗費體力的工作，反而令已經因為飢餓而虛弱的男性損害健康。此事實很有可能是加劇不幸工人過勞死的主因。

歷史學家認為，英國政府當時最大的錯誤，就是在饑荒時期仍出口愛爾蘭的食物，事實上，甚至增加部分食物的出口量，例如豆類作物、兔子等家畜和水產，均不斷輸出愛爾蘭，罔顧成千上萬名愛爾蘭人民餓死的慘況。

「大饑荒」的衝擊在愛爾蘭與世界各地留下深刻烙印。這是史上最慘不忍睹的饑荒事件，亦促使愛爾蘭人湧入當時所謂的「新世界」──也就是北美地區。如果不清楚英國這段慘痛的歷史，就不算真正了解愛爾蘭與其人民。

95. 希利爾湖：澳洲的粉紅色湖泊　P.208

西澳大利亞州的一個島上有座湖泊，長約 600 公尺，寬 250 公尺，叫做「希利爾湖」，它和一般湖泊沒兩樣，唯獨湖水呈現粉紅色。

希利爾湖以明亮的粉紅色湖水聞名於世，最早關於希利爾湖的記載是在 1802 年，當時英國的探險家馬修‧弗林德斯在前往雪梨的路上，意外發現了這座湖泊。你能想像當他發現一大片泡泡糖顏色的湖水時，有多麼震驚嗎？

泡在希利爾湖水裡並不會對人體有害，只是水的味道可能有點噁。如果你在水裡張開眼睛，也只能看到厚厚一片粉紅色，那種感覺就好像泡在一大缸胃藥裡面一樣。希利爾湖的湖水還有一樣奇妙之處，就是不管到哪裡都能維持粉紅色，如果你裝一點湖水回家，它還是一樣的粉紅色。

科學家對於什麼原因造成希利爾湖的招牌粉紅色未有定論，有的認為它是綜合了微量的某種養分、細菌和水藻的結果；有的認為這是海鹽和岸邊的紅色嗜鹽菌作用後所造成的。或許我們永遠不得而知希利爾湖特殊呈色的原因，也或許不知道最好，讓希利爾湖繼續蒙著神秘面紗，留待後世去解密。

如果你不想飛去澳洲，又想一睹希利爾湖的廬山真面目，可以試著用谷歌地圖或其他衛星繪圖軟體查詢，要找不到很難！

96. 有趣的猢猻樹　P. 210

有一種樹生長於馬達加斯加，名稱林林總總，有人叫它猢猻樹，有人叫它瓶子樹或「猴麵包」樹。科學家們稱它為「Adansonia」。

先不管你怎麼稱呼它，猢猻樹是非常有趣的樹種。它用來儲水的樹幹非常粗，上方樹葉組成的林冠卻非常小。事實上，它的林冠小到看起來像一般的樹根，所以最後又有了「倒栽」樹的別名。一些的當地傳說也與猢猻樹有關，有人說，因為猢猻樹一直逃跑，所以被上帝翻成倒栽蔥，也有人說猢猻樹就是撒旦的化身。

令人印象深刻的不只是猢猻樹的外型，還有它的大小。猢猻樹可以長到 30 公尺高，樹幹直徑可達 10 公尺，果實富含維他命和營養成分。

九種猢猻樹品種中，有六種是非洲離島的馬達加斯加特有種。馬達加斯加素以豐富的奇特動植物聞名，但是如今它們在島上的天然棲地卻飽受威脅。許多當地居民一天只以低於 2 元美金度日，他們強烈仰賴砍伐樹木為生，使得島上 80–90% 的雨林已遭破壞。政府為因應此危機已成立國家公園，歡迎生態觀光客前往參觀。唯有時間才能證明此舉是否足以拯救壯觀的猢猻樹。

97. 目錄：建立公司品牌　P. 212

「建立品牌」已經成為國際貿易的重要一環，幸運的是，商業人士若想知道如何成功建立品牌，有非常多書籍和資料可以參考。

下頁圖片是其中一本書的目錄，它顯示出此書的內容和商業品牌操作的各個面向有關。舉例來說，如果你想知道品牌如何影響價格彈性，可以翻到第 51 頁閱讀第 9 章。另外一方面，如果你想知道品牌如何影響顧客忠誠度，可以翻到第 71 頁閱讀第 12 章。請用下頁的目錄來回答以下問題。

98. 社群媒體成癮：尋求存在感的負面影響　P. 214

在社群媒體發文獲得「按讚數」與留言，確實讓人感覺良好。得知有朋友喜歡閱讀自己的發文或瀏覽照片，是社群媒體人氣居高不下的原因。但萬一你開始覺得社群媒體會對心情造成負面影響，又佔用太多時間呢？有些社群媒體使用者的生活被按讚數和留言左右。心理學專家表示，大眾已經對社群媒體上癮，走火入魔的程度已經不健康。

多數社群媒體使用者會發布生活趣事或令人雀躍的事件。他們投入大量時間呈現完美照片，目的就是讓追蹤者印象深刻。他們不好好經營現實世界的友情，卻依賴留言和按讚數來自我感覺良好。此現象與社群媒體的另一個負面效應有關，也就是「每個人都過得比自己好」的假象。人們也許會分享在咖啡廳的照片，卻不一定會分享在家讀書的照片。瀏覽社群媒體可能會讓你覺得，自己是唯一無法時常享樂的人。但社群媒體其實不會顯露一個人的真實生活。

社群媒體還可能鼓吹危險行為。目前出現令人擔憂的潮流，是大家竟然流行在危險地點拍照，或接受危險的社群媒體挑戰，好讓朋友驚艷。近年來已有不少人因為自拍而從瀑布和橋邊跌落。還有人潛入摩天大廈頂樓，站在牆緣拍照。社群媒體挑戰還包括甘冒嗆到的危險，吃下一湯匙的肉桂粉，以及可能凍傷皮膚的冰塊挑戰。

社群媒體使用過當極可能有損自尊與人際關係，甚至鼓勵危險行為。避免上癮最簡單的辦法，就是限制自己使用社群媒體的時間。與親朋好友聚會時，請把手機放一旁。著眼於按讚數與留言以外的世界，就能好好保護你的人際關係與心理健康。

99. 行事曆：忙碌的社交生活 P. 216

我有很多朋友是工作狂，他們每天從早忙到晚，一整個禮拜連週末都不休息。他們從來沒有時間出去玩或享受他們的嗜好。更討厭的是，他們都沒有時間跟我出去！我跟你說，瘋狂工作的生活實在不適合我。當然我也很努力工作，人總是要吃飯的嘛，對吧？不過我是那種主張為生活而工作，而不是為工作而活的人。你應該有聽過吧：只工作沒有休閒會把人悶傻的！所以我才努力經營社交生活，包括常常和朋友出去、參加一些活動、加入社團、上上課，你說得出來的我都會嘗試。但是社交活動這麼多，需要好好規劃，所以我才寫行事曆。來看看我未來兩週充實好玩的行程表吧。

100. 為日本而戰：
遭人遺忘的台籍日本兵歷史 P. 218

論及第二次世界大戰，在牽連眾多國家的此衝突事件中，大家通常會先想到德國、日本、美國與大英帝國等主角。但是台灣在此時期扮演的角色卻鮮為人知，尤其在日本與中華民國以外的世界更不甚清楚。不過，從歷史與文化角度來看，相當耐人尋味。其中最有趣的團體莫過於「台籍日本兵」。

台籍日本兵的成員包括軍人以及工作非關戰役的人民。確切來說，各種行業人士皆有之，包括廚師、勞工、譯者與機師。總共約有 20 萬 7 千名台灣人服役於日本軍隊。剛開始，日本軍方採自願、非強制性的募兵制，招募台灣人入伍。讓台灣人自願成為日本兵的強大動力，就是希望能夠享有更好的生活。一般而言，自願成為皇民的台灣人，會比一般台灣人得到更好的待遇，為自己和家人爭取到額外的糧食。越來越多日本人戰死後，所需的替代人數與日俱增。最後，台灣於 1945 年被迫接受徵兵制，加入日本陸軍與海軍。

台籍日本兵各有不同身家背景。上千人為台灣原住民，當時日本人稱為「Takasago（高砂族）」。1988 年第一位台灣民選總統李登輝，同為台籍日本兵的一員。李登輝的哥哥李登欽亦為台籍日本兵，服役日本海軍時戰歿於菲律賓。第二次世界大戰期間，包括李登欽在內，日本軍隊中的台籍死亡人數達 30,304 人。台籍日本兵的年代雖然現已被眾人遺忘，卻仍是值得令人回顧的一段台灣歷史。

Unit 1 Reading Skills

1-1 Subject Matter

1	1. a	2. c	3. b	4. b	5. d
2	1. b	2. c	3. b	4. b	5. a
3	1. a	2. d	3. a	4. b	5. c
4	1. a	2. a	3. d	4. c	5. b
5	1. c	2. a	3. b	4. b	5. d

1-2 Main Idea

6	1. d	2. d	3. c	4. a	5. b
7	1. a	2. d	3. b	4. a	5. d
8	1. a	2. d	3. a	4. b	5. b
9	1. c	2. b	3. a	4. b	5. d
10	1. a	2. c	3. d	4. c	5. a

1-3 Supporting Details

11	1. b	2. a	3. c	4. d	5. a
12	1. a	2. c	3. d	4. b	5. a
13	1. c	2. d	3. d	4. a	5. b
14	1. b	2. d	3. c	4. a	5. b
15	1. b	2. c	3. a	4. d	5. d

1-4 Author's Purpose and Tone

16	1. a	2. d	3. b	4. a	5. b
17	1. c	2. d	3. a	4. b	5. a
18	1. a	2. d	3. c	4. a	5. d
19	1. d	2. a	3. b	4. c	5. a
20	1. b	2. d	3. a	4. d	5. b

1-5 Cause and Effect

21	1. d	2. a	3. b	4. a	5. d
22	1. c	2. b	3. a	4. a	5. b
23	1. b	2. c	3. a	4. b	5. a
24	1. b	2. a	3. b	4. d	5. b
25	1. b	2. c	3. a	4. c	5. b

1-6 Clarifying Devices

26	1. c	2. a	3. b	4. d	5. c
27	1. c	2. a	3. d	4. b	5. d
28	1. a	2. b	3. a	4. c	5. a
29	1. b	2. d	3. b	4. a	5. b
30	1. a	2. d	3. b	4. c	5. c

1-7 Making Inferences

31	1. a	2. c	3. d	4. b	5. a
32	1. c	2. a	3. d	4. c	5. b
33	1. b	2. a	3. a	4. c	5. b
34	1. d	2. a	3. c	4. b	5. c
35	1. c	2. b	3. a	4. d	5. a

1-8 Problems and Solutions

36	1. c	2. c	3. a	4. c	5. d
37	1. b	2. a	3. d	4. b	5. c
38	1. c	2. a	3. b	4. c	5. c
39	1. b	2. b	3. d	4. a	5. c
40	1. c	2. b	3. c	4. b	5. b

1-9 Fact or Opinion

41	1. a	2. c	3. a	4. c	5. a
42	1. b	2. d	3. b	4. a	5. b
43	1. d	2. b	3. a	4. b	5. c
44	1. b	2. b	3. a	4. b	5. c
45	1. b	2. b	3. d	4. a	5. a

1-10 Review Test

46	1. c	2. a	3. c	4. c	5. d
47	1. b	2. a	3. d	4. b	5. c
48	1. c	2. d	3. a	4. d	5. b
49	1. b	2. a	3. d	4. b	5. c
50	1. c	2. a	3. d	4. d	5. b

Unit 2 Word Study

2-1 Synonyms

51	1. d	2. b	3. c	4. a	5. a
52	1. a	2. c	3. b	4. b	5. d
53	1. c	2. b	3. d	4. b	5. a
54	1. c	2. d	3. a	4. c	5. b
55	1. d	2. a	3. b	4. c	5. d

2-2 Antonyms

56	1. b	2. c	3. a	4. a	5. d
57	1. a	2. c	3. c	4. b	5. d
58	1. b	2. c	3. a	4. d	5. b
59	1. c	2. d	3. a	4. a	5. c
60	1. a	2. b	3. c	4. b	5. a

2-3 Words in Context

61	1. d	2. a	3. b	4. c	5. b
62	1. a	2. c	3. b	4. b	5. c
63	1. b	2. a	3. a	4. d	5. c
64	1. b	2. a	3. d	4. d	5. c
65	1. c	2. a	3. d	4. c	5. a

2-4 Review Test

66	1. c	2. a	3. b	4. c	5. d
67	1. d	2. a	3. c	4. b	5. b
68	1. b	2. a	3. d	4. c	5. c
69	1. c	2. a	3. d	4. b	5. b
70	1. a	2. c	3. d	4. b	5. a

Unit 3 Study Strategies

3-1 Visual Material

71	1. c	2. a	3. b	4. d	5. c
72	1. b	2. d	3. c	4. d	5. c
73	1. b	2. b	3. a	4. d	5. d
74	1. d	2. a	3. d	4. c	5. c
75	1. c	2. d	3. a	4. d	5. a

3-2 Reference Sources

76	1. c	2. b	3. d	4. d	5. a
77	1. d	2. b	3. c	4. a	5. b
78	1. c	2. c	3. d	4. a	5. b
79	1. a	2. b	3. a	4. d	5. c
80	1. b	2. a	3. d	4. c	5. b

Unit 4 Final Reviews

4-1 Final Review (I)

81	1. c	2. b	3. a	4. a	5. c
82	1. b	2. a	3. d	4. c	5. b
83	1. d	2. a	3. c	4. b	5. c
84	1. b	2. c	3. a	4. c	5. d
85	1. a	2. c	3. b	4. b	5. d
86	1. b	2. c	3. b	4. d	5. a
87	1. c	2. b	3. c	4. a	5. b
88	1. c	2. a	3. d	4. b	5. a
89	1. b	2. a	3. d	4. b	5. c
90	1. a	2. d	3. b	4. c	5. b

4-2 Final Review (II)

91	1. c	2. c	3. d	4. b	5. d
92	1. b	2. c	3. a	4. b	5. a
93	1. a	2. d	3. c	4. a	5. c
94	1. d	2. c	3. d	4. a	5. c
95	1. b	2. a	3. a	4. d	5. c
96	1. b	2. d	3. a	4. a	5. c
97	1. c	2. d	3. b	4. a	5. c
98	1. b	2. c	3. d	4. b	5. c
99	1. c	2. d	3. a	4. b	5. c
100	1. a	2. d	3. b	4. d	5. c

英語閱讀技巧

Success With Reading 完全攻略 2

二版

作　　者	Zachary Fillingham / Owain Mckimm / Judy Majewski
協力作者	Anna Kasprick (27, 43, 51, 63, 81, 90, 98) / Gregory John Bahlmann (13, 42, 48, 57) / Brian Foden (84, 87, 94, 100) / Richard Luhrs (32, 39, 56)
譯　　者	劉嘉珮／丁宥榆／林育珊 (13, 42, 48, 57)
審　　訂	Treva Adams / Helen Yeh
企畫編輯	葉俞均
編　　輯	呂敏如／丁宥暄
主　　編	丁宥暄
校　　對	申文怡
內頁設計	鄭秀芳
封面設計	林書玉
圖　　片	shutterstock
製程管理	洪巧玲
發 行 人	黃朝萍
出 版 者	寂天文化事業股份有限公司
電　　話	+886-(0)2-2365-9739
傳　　真	+886-(0)2-2365-9835
網　　址	www.icosmos.com.tw
讀者服務	onlineservice@icosmos.com.tw
出版日期	2024 年 7 月二版三刷　（寂天雲 Mebook 互動學習 APP 版）

郵撥帳號　1998620-0 寂天文化事業股份有限公司
訂書金額未滿 1000 元，請外加運費 100 元。

國家圖書館出版品預行編目 (CIP) 資料

英語閱讀技巧完全攻略 (寂天雲 Mebook 互動學習 APP 版)/
Zachary Fillingham, Owain Mckimm, Judy Majewski 著 ; 劉嘉珮,
丁宥榆譯 . -- 二版 . -- 臺北市 : 寂天文化事業股份有限公司,
2024.07 印刷
　面；　公分

ISBN 978-626-300-265-4 (16K 平裝)

1.CST: 英語 2.CST: 讀本

805.18　　　　　　　　　　　　　　　113009327